Time's Echo

After a varied career including stints as a foreign-news desk secretary, cook on an outback cattle station, production assistant and expedition interpreter, Pamela stumbled into writing as a way of funding a PhD in Medieval Studies. For the past twenty years she has been able to combine her historical research with an award-winning career as a romance writer, and is now also a writing tutor and freelance project editor. She lives in York.

Follow Pamela on Twitter @PamHartshorne

PAMELA HARTSHORNE

Time's
Echo

PAN BOOKS

First published 2012 by Pan Books
an imprint of Pan Macmillan, a division of Macmillan Publishers Limited
Pan Macmillan, 20 New Wharf Road, London N1 9RR
Basingstoke and Oxford
Associated companies throughout the world
www.panmacmillan.com

ISBN 978-0-330-54425-2

1 3 5 7 9 8 6 4 2

A CIP catalogue record for this book is available from
the British Library.

Typeset by Ellipsis Digital Limited, Glasgow
Printed and bound by CPI Group (UK) Ltd, Croydon, CR0 4YY

For my parents, with love,
and for the people of York, past and present.

A. Micklegate Bar
B. Holy Trinity Church
C. Walgate Bar
D. Monk Bar
E. The Minster
F. St. George's Close
G. York Castle
H. Clifford's Tower
I. St. Leonard's Landing
J. Common Hall
K. St. Martin
L. King's Staith

N
W E
S

I

Micklegate

A

To London

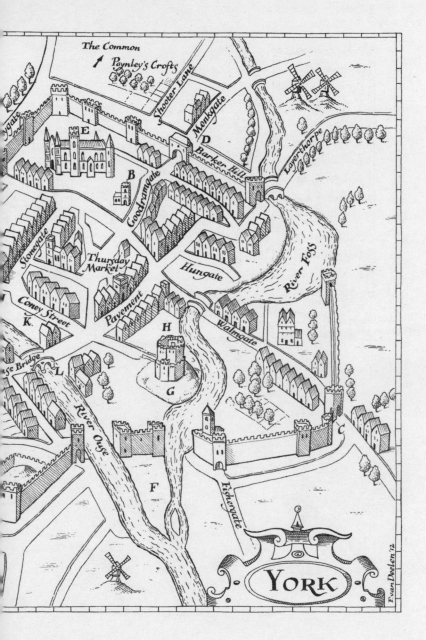

YORK

F. van Deelen '12

Chapter One

I feel no fear, not yet. I am just astounded to find myself in the air, looking down at the murky rush of the river. It is as if time itself has paused, and I am somehow suspended between the sky and the water, between the past and the present, between then and now. Between disbelief and horror.

It is All Hallows' Eve, and I am going to die.

Part of me knows that quite well. But another part refuses to comprehend that it is really happening. Refuses to believe that this is not a dream, that I won't wake up. That this morning was the last time I would ever feel the floorboards cool and smooth beneath my feet, the last time I would hear the creak of the stairs or the rain pattering on the roof.

The last time I would smooth my daughter's hair under her cap.

'I won't be long,' I promised her.

In the distance, a bell is striking. The city is going about its business, the way it always does. The market on Pavement is open. The stallholders will be poking at their sagging awnings to get rid of the rain that has pooled in the morning downpour. They will be grumbling at the mud and the lost business when everyone was huddled indoors.

I should be there. I have things to do. We need fish, we need salt. Bess is growing fast. I want to buy her some new shoes. I will go this afternoon.

Except that I won't. I will die instead.

It seems odd that it should be the thought of something as ordinary as shoes that bumps time onwards, out of that strange moment when everything stopped, but so it is. It is *now* after all, and suddenly everything is happening too fast. I plunge into the water and it closes, brown and bitter, over my face. I can feel it rushing into my petticoat, filling my sleeves, dragging me down with the weight of the cloth.

And I remember him, bending over me, whispering that he is going to take Bess now, he will raise her as his own, and no one will say him nay.

'I will do what I like with her, Hawise,' he said.

Now I am afraid, remembering that.

Now I struggle, as horror clogs my mind, but my thumb is tied to my toe and I can't swim, even if I knew how. My skirts are too heavy, the water is too cold, and when I open my mouth to scream, to curse him again, the river gushes in through the stocking tied around my face to keep me quiet. It is cold and rank and thick in my throat. It is too late. The river is fast and furious, sweeping me away like a barrel, down towards the sea

I have never seen, and never will. I am jetsam, tossed overboard to save the city.

I sink and rise, then sink deeper, and the more I choke, the more water invades me. There is a terrible pain in my ears, behind my eyes, and my lungs are on fire.

I am flailing, thrashing in the water, but I sink deeper and deeper. I don't know which way is up and which is down any more. There is nothing but panic and pain and the water blocking my throat, and the bright, terrifying image of Bess looking up at him trustingly, taking his hand.

I need to go back. I need to do things differently, so that I can keep my daughter safe.

'*Bess*,' I try to say, as if I could reach her, as if she could hear me, as if she could understand my fear and my anguish.

But I can't speak and I can't breathe, I can't *breathe*. My lungs are full of water, my throat is clamped shut. The pressure behind my eyes is agonizing, and there is a screaming in my ears, but how can I be screaming when I can't draw a breath? Sweet Jesù, I have to have air – I have to, or I will die – but I don't know where the surface is and I flail desperately, uselessly, against the terror as the river, uncaring, sucks me down, down, down and away into the dazzling dark.

I lurched awake on a desperate, rasping gasp. My eyes snapped open and I stared into the darkness, gripped by anguish for a daughter I had never had, while fear clicked frantically in my throat and my pulse roared with the memory. I could feel the weight of the strange dress I had been wearing, and the stiffness of the linen cap binding my hair. The foul taste of the river was so vivid still that I gagged.

I'm used to drowning. I've drowned so many times in my dreams that you would think my subconscious would learn to stop fighting the terror and the choking and the screaming of my lungs and the pain, the *pain* of it. You'd think that at some level it would know that eventually I will pop up out of sleep, the way I popped up in the middle of the sea, where the wave spat me out of its maw at last; but it never does.

My usual nightmares are so tangled up with memories of the tsunami that it's hard sometimes to distinguish one from the other, but that night in York the dream was different. That night, there were no palm trees stirring languidly above my head, the way there usually were in my nightmare. I wasn't standing on the hot sand, and Lucas wasn't digging on the beach, his thin little back bent over his spade. There was no decision: to turn back or go on. No mistake. That night, the sea didn't rush out of nowhere and gobble me up.

Instead, I dreamt of a river, brown and sullen. I dreamt of wearing heavy skirts instead of a sarong over my bikini. I dreamt of a daughter, not a little Swedish boy I barely knew.

Only the drowning was the same.

Slowly, slowly, the agonizing pain in my lungs eased and I could breathe properly. As my heart stopped jerking, my eyes adjusted to the darkness and I blinked, puzzled by the strange light and the muffled quality of the night.

I strained my ears for the slow slap of the overhead fan, the mournful cry of the satay-seller pushing his cart along the *gang*, even the rasp of insects in the tropical night, but instead all I heard was the swish of tyres on wet tarmac and the faint clunk of a car changing gear.

That odd, orange light through the curtains was from a street lamp. I struggled towards full consciousness. I wasn't drowning in a cold river. I was in my dead godmother's bed in York.

It was the smell I'd noticed first. Sweet, putrid, faintly disquieting. I wrinkled my nose as I pushed the door open into a pile of accumulated junk mail and unpaid bills. Grunting, I lugged in my suitcase and swung my backpack off my shoulder and onto the tiled floor, before shoving the door shut with my foot. The click of the Yale lock was loud in the silence.

The house was dark, the air thick and unfriendly, but that was only to be expected. It had been closed up since Lucy's death, more than a month earlier. I felt around for a switch and stood, blinking in the sudden light, taking stock of my surroundings. I was in a narrow hallway with two doors on the left. Straight ahead was a steep staircase rising into shadows. It was a small, unpretentious Victorian terraced house, and the only thing that surprised me about that first evening was how very ordinary it was. Lucy had always prided herself on being unconventional.

'*Bess.*'

The voice sounded so close that I jumped. 'Hello?' I said uncertainly.

Silence.

'Hello?' I said again, feeling a bit silly. 'Is there anybody there?'

But of course there wasn't anybody there. The house had been locked up. On either side people were watching television, curtains drawn against the wet April night. All I'd heard was someone talking in the street outside.

Embarrassed by the way my heart was thudding, I switched on the overhead light in the front room. This was more like the Lucy I remembered, I thought. The walls were painted a stifling red and decorated with strange, symbolic pictures. A dream-catcher hung in the window, and everywhere there were crystals and dusty bowls of herbs.

I wandered over to the fireplace and poked through the jumble of candles and figurines on the mantelpiece. There, lurking amongst all the knick-knacks, I identified the source of the smell that had been nagging at me: a rotting apple. It was brown and puckered with mould, and something in me jerked at the sight of it.

'*Bess.*'

The name rippled in the air, like a breath against my cheek, and I looked up, startled, to catch a glimpse of myself in the dusty mirror above the mantelpiece. For a moment it was as if another woman was looking back at me, a stranger with dark hair and pale-grey eyes like mine, but such an expression of horror on her face that I gasped and recoiled.

But it was only me. A pulse was hammering in my throat, and I put a hand up to still it.

God, I looked awful, I realized. It wasn't surprising I hadn't recognized myself for a moment. I'd spent the past thirty-six hours on the move, from check-in desk to departure gate, from baggage carousels to station platforms, shuffling along in endless queues and through interminable security checks. Trapped in planes and trains and artificial lighting, my body clock was so confused that I'd lost track of time completely.

I stuck out my tongue at my reflection and turned away.

The second door led to a parlour, similarly decorated in oppressive reds and purples, and beyond it a galley kitchen, where I found another apple on the worktop. No wonder the house smelt of rotting fruit. Lucy must have had a thing about apples, I decided. This one was yellowish-brown with sagging skin. Repelled, I threw it in the bin and let the lid clang shut.

I was buzzing with exhaustion, but too wired to sleep. I put the kettle on and decided to take my bags upstairs while it boiled, but when I picked up my backpack and put a foot on the bottom step, I found myself hesitating. It did look dark up there.

'Don't go,' Mel had said when I rang her. 'York'll be boring and cold. Come to Mexico, Grace. I can get you a job at the school. You'd love it here,' she said. 'Think jugs of margaritas.' She lowered her voice enticingly. 'Think hot beaches and hot chilli and hot Mexican men. What more could you want?'

I laughed. 'Nothing,' I said. 'I'd love to come. I just need to sort out my godmother's stuff first.'

'Get the solicitor to do it all,' Mel advised. 'You should be out here having a good time, not poking around in an old person's house.'

'Lucy wasn't that old,' I protested, 'and the solicitor did say he'd arrange everything for me.'

'Well, then.'

'It's just . . . I feel I owe it to Lucy to do it myself,' I tried to explain. 'It's a question of trust.'

I'd been shocked when John Burnand rang me in Jakarta to tell me that my godmother had died. 'Preliminary enquiries suggest that she drowned,' he said.

Drowned. The word closed around my throat like a fist, and I was back in the water, eardrums screaming, lungs on fire, while the wave tumbled me round and round and round. It was a moment before I could speak.

'What happened?'

'There'll be an inquest, of course,' he said, 'but there's no evidence to suggest that it was anything other than an accident.'

Then he astounded me by saying that she had made me joint executor with him. I hadn't seen Lucy for years, and was sure it had to be a mistake, but John Burnand was very precise.

'Miss Cartmell made a number of pecuniary legacies, and it's likely that her house will need to be sold in order to fulfil them, but the residue of the estate will come to you.'

For a fee, he said, he would deal with everything for me. 'Or would you prefer to make arrangements to come to York and sort things out yourself?'

I could have said no, but I didn't. I'd been in Indonesia two years, and I was restless and ready to move on. Mel was in Mexico. We'd taught English together in Japan, and had a wild time, and she'd been lobbying for me to join her for months. I gathered from John Burnand that by the time the house was sold and the legacies paid, I wouldn't come into a fortune, but when he mentioned a possible sum, I nearly dropped the phone. It sounded an awful lot of money to me. It would certainly buy me a ticket to Mexico City and mean that I could travel for a while before finding a job.

So I said yes without really thinking about it. The smallest of choices have consequences. It's easy to forget that.

But standing there at the bottom of the stairs, I wished for a moment I'd taken Mel's advice. Then I told myself not to be so wet. I was just tired. If it was dark up on the landing, all I needed to do was switch on a light.

Putting down my backpack, I searched around, found a likely-looking switch and pressed it. All the lights promptly went out with a huge crack that sent my heart lurching into my throat.

'Shit!'

There was a horrible banging in my chest and my ears rang. I made myself take a deep breath. A fuse had gone, that was all. I had to find a torch, find the fuse box. No need to panic.

Turning to grope my way back to the kitchen, I fell over the backpack.

'Shit,' I said again as I knocked over the suitcase in my struggle to get up. 'Shit, shit, shit!'

No sooner was I up than I tripped over the backpack again, and I spent the next few minutes blundering around in the dark, getting more and more disorientated. The last time I fell, I cracked my knee on the tiled floor, which was painful, but at least did the job of making me stop and pull myself together.

Rubbing my knee furiously, I scowled into the dark. Now I'd stopped crashing around, I could hear the faint sound of classical music through the dividing wall. One of my neighbours at least was awake. And then I saw that it wasn't completely dark after all. Dim orange light from the street outside filtered through the stained glass above the front door and I could orientate myself. I used the case to haul myself to my feet and limped towards the light. Stubborn independence was my normal mode, as more than one ex-boyfriend had complained, but on that dark evening I was prepared to make an exception.

His name was Drew Dyer. He opened the door looking distracted, a middle-aged man with glasses and hair that was beginning to recede. Feature by feature, he wasn't attractive, but he had a good-humoured expression that meant that somehow he was, and something in me jumped oddly at the sight of him.

'You must be a relative of Lucy's,' he said when I apologized for interrupting and explained that I had just arrived next door.

'Her god-daughter. I'm Grace Trewe.'

We shook hands. His palm was warm, and I felt a little jolt of recognition as my flesh touched his. Probably just because I was so cold. The night was spitting an unfriendly mixture of sleet and rain at me, and I was shivering in a T-shirt and a thin hooded cardigan. I hadn't been in England for seven years and I was ill-equipped for the vagaries of a northern spring.

'I really just came to ask if I could borrow a torch,' I said, tucking my hands back in my armpits and trying not to look too longingly at the bright warmth of the hall behind Drew. 'A fuse has blown, and I can't see what I'm doing.'

I'm not sure if he picked up on the shivering or the yearning looks, but he stood back and held the door open. 'Come in,' he said, and I limped gratefully inside.

'Thanks.'

He showed me into the front room and waved me to a faded armchair. It was a much more inviting room than Lucy's. The walls were lined from ceiling to floor with bookshelves, and on the desk opposite the mantelpiece a computer glowed blue. Bending my knee hurt, and I winced as I sat down.

'You've hurt yourself.' Drew looked at me rubbing my knee, and I took my hand away self-consciously.

'It's nothing. I fell over my case, that's all. I hope I didn't disturb you with all the shouting and swearing,' I added. 'I'm afraid I had a bit of a lapse on the stiff-upper-lip front.'

'I didn't hear you,' Drew assured me. 'I've been in sixteenth-century York.'

I gaped at him. '*What?*'

'I'm a historian.' He had one of those smiles that aren't really smiles at all, hardly more than a deepening of the crease in one cheek and a crinkling of the eyes. 'I've been absorbed in my records,' he explained. 'I'm writing a paper for a conference, or trying to.'

'Oh, I'm sorry. I've interrupted you,' I said a little stiffly, embarrassed at having made it so obvious that for a second there I'd actually thought he was talking about time-travelling. I was usually quicker on the uptake.

'To be honest, I'm glad of the distraction,' he said, taking pity on me. 'It's not going very well. It's not going at all, in fact.'

I sat back and made myself more comfortable, not sorry to put off the moment of going back to Lucy's dark, empty house. 'What's it about?' I asked, noting regretfully that Drew Dyer had chosen to lean against the edge of his desk rather than take the other armchair. He might say that he welcomed the distraction, but it didn't look to me as if he was settling down for a chat. He answered readily enough, though.

'I'm looking at neighbourliness in Elizabethan York.'

'Did they disturb each other by knocking on the door and asking to borrow torches in the middle of the night?'

Behind his glasses his eyes were starred with laughter lines. 'They were more likely to eavesdrop on each other's dirty secrets at night.'

'Sounds like fun.'

'Actually, they spent most of their time fretting about the state of the roads and rubbish disposal. Not so different from today, as you'll discover if you ever meet Ann Parsons in number four. She runs a one-woman campaign about the communal bins, and will try and get you roped in to writing to the council, so make sure you're always in a hurry when you go past that gate.'

'Thanks for the warning,' I said. I'd never given waste disposal much thought before. I rented accommodation six months at a time, so I was never tied to a place for too long, and although I wasn't normally short of opinions, rubbish collection wasn't something I could talk about for very long. I wouldn't have minded being able to prolong the conversation, though.

'I was sorry to hear about Lucy,' said Drew. 'It must have been a shock for you.'

'Well, yes,' I said doubtfully, 'but to be honest, the bigger shock was finding out that she'd made me an executor. I hadn't seen her for years. You probably knew her better than I did.'

'I wouldn't say that.' I could see him choosing his words. 'We'd exchange good mornings and a comment about the weather if we met in the street, but that was about it. Sophie always liked Lucy, though,' he went on.

'Sophie?'

'My daughter. She's very into all of Lucy's weird ideas,' he said, and I gathered from a certain rigidity in his expression that his daughter's friendship with Lucy had been the source of some conflict. 'Sophie spent quite a lot of time with Lucy,' Drew went on. 'She was very upset when she heard what had happened.'

'It's nice to think that someone was,' I said carefully. 'I know Lucy was a bit eccentric, but she had a good heart, or so my mother always used to say, anyway. I certainly never expected her to entrust me with her affairs, though. I feel a bit bad I didn't make more of an effort to keep in touch now,' I confessed. 'I sent her the occasional postcard, but that was about it.'

An enormous yawn caught me unawares in the middle of the sentence, and I wished it hadn't, when Drew clearly took it as a signal that I wanted to go. He levered himself upright.

'Let me find that torch for you.'

He came back a few minutes later with a serviceable-looking torch. By that time I was nearly asleep in the comfortable armchair and the house felt warm and safe.

Safe? Where had that thought come from?

'Thanks.' I mustered a smile as I got reluctantly to my feet and took the torch. 'I'll bring it back straight away.'

'I'll come and give you a hand,' he said, dragging on a sweat-shirt.

Of course I protested, but not too hard. I would go back to being independent the next day, I vowed. Until then, it was dark and cold and I was very tired and my knee hurt, so I let Drew Dyer be a good neighbour.

He fixed the fuse with a minimum of fuss and the lights sprang back on, revealing my heavy suitcase tipped over on the tiles, and the backpack, which lay abandoned where I had last tripped over it.

'Like me to carry that upstairs?' he said, eyeing the case.

I followed him up to the bedroom. Lucy had decorated in a deep, dark blue and there were stars on the ceiling. Just right for an adolescent. For a woman in her fifties it felt a little odd, but that was Lucy for you.

'Thank you so much,' I said gratefully to Drew and then broke off as a name drifted through the air.

'*Bess . . .* '

I frowned. 'Who's Bess?' I asked Drew.

'Who?'

'Didn't you hear that?'

'Hear what?'

'I keep thinking I hear someone calling for Bess.'

He shook his head. 'I didn't hear anything.'

'Oh. Well, I must be imagining it,' I said after a moment.

'You must be tired,' said Drew.

It was true, I was. Too tired to think clearly, that was for sure.

I thanked Drew at the door and, when he asked if I would be all right, I didn't even hesitate. 'Of course,' I said. 'I'll be fine.'

But now it was the middle of the night, and the nightmare was still roaring in my memory and I didn't feel so confident any more. Shakily I threw my legs over the side of the bed and sat up, dragging my hands down my face, as if I could pull the horror of the dream from my mind.

It had seemed so real: the churning river, the chime of the bell, the downward drag of my sodden woollen skirt. The desperation and the grief. My throat felt raw where I had tried to scream and, as I rubbed it, my fingers found the pendant I always wore, and I twisted the braided silver chain until it dug into my flesh. It reminded me of what was real.

'*Bess . . . Bess . . .*'

There was desperation in the whisper that trickled through the air, and my heart stuttered in alarm before I remembered that Bess was the child in my nightmare. I let go of the chain before I choked myself. The words were just a hangover from the dream, and the dream tied up with the voice I had heard calling earlier.

'*Bess . . .*'

There it was again. I rubbed my palms over my ears as if I could rub out the sound, and then pressed the heels of my hands into my eyes. It was a nightmare – that was all, I reminded myself. I wasn't properly awake. I was exhausted and jet-lagged and in an unfamiliar house. Small wonder my mind was playing tricks on me.

But my hand was shaking as I reached out for the light and clicked it on. It was only a small lamp, but I shrank back from the glare as the room leapt at me.

'It was a nightmare,' I said out loud, and I cringed to hear the quaver in my voice. 'It's over.'

It's hard to fix the moment when a story begins. I used to think that you could lay time out in a straight line, see one event following another in a steady forward march. But it doesn't work like that. There is nothing orderly about time. Sometimes the past loops forward, or turns back on itself, weaving present and future together, until the threads of time tangle into an impenetrable knot of countless choices and coincidences and consequences.

At first, I thought the nightmare was when it began, but it's impossible to disentangle the stories that went back and back and back, endless turning points and decisions that led to me being wrenched awake in Lucy's bed that night.

I wasn't like Lucy. I liked fact, not fantasy. Given the choice, I would always go for the rational explanation. Lucy always revelled in the mysterious, but it made me uncomfortable. So when I woke from that nightmare I tried straight away to make sense of it. And it *did* make a certain kind of sense. I'd never been to York before, so I was in a strange place, sleeping in a strange bed. Even in my befuddled state it seemed obvious that my usual drowning dream was muddled up with thoughts of poor Lucy drowning in the Ouse, while the niggling disquiet of hearing someone calling for Bess had been transformed into the small girl (*my daughter*) I had imagined with her apron and her stiff skirts, her face bright beneath the linen cap.

As for the clothes in my dream – well, my brief conversation with Drew Dyer about Elizabethan York had clearly lodged in my subconscious. True, he had talked about rubbish collection rather than clothes, but dreams weren't always logical, I reasoned. There was no reason to think it was anything but a nightmare.

Still, I'll admit I was spooked enough to get up and find a glass of water. I was very thirsty and my throat was as sore as if I really had been screaming. I squinted at my phone. It was twelve minutes past three in the morning, the loneliest time of the night, and beyond the pool of light from the bedside lamp the world was dark and muffled in silence.

Wrapping my sarong around me, I made my way down to the kitchen, switching on lights as I went, and so fuzzy with exhaustion that I kept bumping off the walls.

The kitchen tiles were cold beneath my bare feet. I filled a glass at the sink and drank the water as I stood there in the glare of the ceiling spotlights. One of the lights was angled directly at a plate that hung on the wall between the two windows. It was decorated with a childish impression of breakfast: a splodge of yellow for an egg, a red, vaguely sausage-shaped smudge, some green blobs. *To Lucy* was printed around the top edge in a wobbly hand and, below, *Love Grace*.

It's odd how moments we think we've forgotten can slam back as perfectly detailed memories. I was five, and breathing heavily through my mouth. We were in some kind of sunny workshop. I remembered the smell of the paint, the clumsy feel of the brush between my fingers, the pots of bright colours.

'What are the green things?' my mother asked.

'Peas.'

'Peas for breakfast?'

I shrugged. It didn't seem strange to me. Lucy, I knew, wouldn't think it was strange, either.

Now I felt a twist of regret that I hadn't known that Lucy had liked the plate enough to keep it for more than twenty-five years. I'd sent the odd postcard over the years, but otherwise had assumed that I had faded out of Lucy's life, just as she had faded out of mine.

Thinking about the past, I gazed absently out of the window in front of the sink. I had been too tired earlier to bother pulling the blind down. Now the window was black and blank and smeary with rain, and I could see my own reflection superimposed on the darkness outside. My hair was pushed behind my ears, and my shoulders were bare above the sarong. The reflection was so clear that I could even make out the darker patch of the port-wine stain on the slope of my breast, a small purple splodge, like a baby's hand-print. When I was younger I was very self-conscious about wearing bikinis, but later I was quite proud of it. I told myself it was distinctive.

I looked younger in the glass, I remember thinking that. Younger and wide-eyed.

I'd almost forgotten the nightmare, in fact, when my eyes focused on my reflection in the glass, which had doubled oddly, almost as if my shadow had stepped slightly to one side.

An icy finger dragged down my spine. That wasn't a shadow. There was someone standing right behind me. Someone who had dark hair and pale eyes like me, but who wasn't me at all.

The glass slipped from my fingers and smashed into the sink as I whipped round, my heart jamming in my throat, blocking my breath. My hand went instinctively to my neck as if to push it back into place.

There was no one there. My pulse roared in my ears, and for a moment I thought I would faint. My knees were so weak I had to lean back against the sink and make myself take some deep breaths.

Enough, I thought. I was overwrought and overtired. All I needed was some sleep.

I left the broken glass in the sink and found another one. My hands were still shaking slightly as I filled it with water, but when I turned to take it back to bed with me, my eye snagged on an apple sitting on the worktop. Its skin was yellow and wrinkling, just like the one I'd thrown away earlier.

Puzzled, I put down my glass and picked up the apple instead, grimacing a little at the saggy feel of it between my fingers. I couldn't understand how I had missed seeing it before, but I was half-asleep still and, frankly, spooked by the apparition in the window, so I tossed it in the bin with the other apple and thought no more about it.

*

'I don't know *where* I'm going to be, all right? Somewhere you aren't!'

I was standing on the doorstep, fumbling with the unfamiliar key, when Drew Dyer's front door was wrenched open and a girl stomped out. She was fourteen or so, perhaps a bit older, and ungainly, with intense, sullen features half-hidden by a tangle of chestnut hair.

Hoisting a heavy bag onto her shoulder, she slammed the door behind her with such force that Lucy's door trembled too. It was only when she turned for the gate that she saw me.

'Oh.' She stopped dead and eyed me warily from beneath her fringe.

'Hi.' My head was pounding after my broken night, and tiredness throbbed behind my eyes, but I was feeling much more myself. In the daylight I was embarrassed to remember how rattled I had been by my nightmare.

I'd found the broken glass in the sink, but when I wrapped it in newspaper and threw it in the bin, there had been no trace of the apple I thought I'd seen the night before. I must have imagined it, I decided, along with that ghostly figure in the glass.

I smiled at Drew's daughter. 'I'm Grace, Lucy's god-daughter,' I said. 'You must be Sophie.'

Sophie nodded. 'She talked about you.'

'Really?' I was surprised. 'I haven't seen her for years. I wouldn't have blamed her if she'd forgotten all about me.'

'No, she liked you. She showed me the cards you sent her from all round the world. She said you were a free spirit,' said Sophie with a touch of envy.

I was touched, and also rather ashamed. A postcard every now and then hadn't required much effort. 'If I'd known she liked them so much, I'd have sent her a card more often.'

I finally managed to lock the door and dropped the key into the battered leather bag I'd slung over my shoulder. I'd bought it in a market in Jaipur years before and it went everywhere with me. It was the perfect size, just big enough for a passport, a purse and a pair of sunglasses – everything I needed to jump on a plane.

'I didn't think Lucy was particularly interested in travel,' I excused myself.

'She used to say that she was a spiritual traveller,' said Sophie. That sounded like Lucy.

'You were so lucky to have Lucy as a godmother,' she added wistfully.

In truth, Lucy had always been an odd choice – Christianity being one of the very few spiritual paths that my godmother hadn't tried. But she and my mother had been old school friends, and Mum apparently thought Lucy would be more 'interesting' than more conventional friends and family. 'It's only a symbolic role anyway,' Mum had argued when my father pointed out that Lucy wasn't exactly a churchgoer. 'Lucy can broaden Grace's horizons.'

I pulled open the gate and joined Sophie on the pavement. 'You had her as a friend,' I reminded her. 'You knew her much better than I did.'

'She was great.' Sophie shifted her bag of books from one shoulder to another and looked sad. 'I'm really going to miss her,' she said. 'She was the only person I've ever met who actually *talked* to you and listened to what you had to say.'

I made a non-committal noise. I remembered Lucy as someone who talked *at* you rather than to you, but perhaps she had been different with Sophie.

'Everyone thought she was weird, but she wasn't,' said Sophie. 'She was a witch, you know.'

'A witch?' I fought to keep the scepticism from my voice. 'Really?'

'Didn't you see her tools?'

'I haven't really had a chance to look round much yet,' I said. 'What did she have? A broomstick?'

Sophie didn't approve of my flippancy, that was clear. 'It wasn't like that!' she said, eyeing me with contempt. 'Wicca is a serious belief,' she told me fiercely. 'Witches revere the Earth. Lucy said we have to stop fighting nature and learn to live in harmony with it. What's wrong with that?'

'Nothing, I suppose,' I backtracked, but my heart was sinking. Dealing with Lucy's estate was going to be complicated enough, without adding witchcraft into the equation.

Chapter Two

'Lucy was teaching me wisecraft,' Sophie went on. 'I was going to join her coven as soon as I was old enough, but I don't know if I will now. I've found a new spiritual path,' she said.

'Oh?' I zipped up my hooded cardigan against the chill. It was early April, but it felt more like winter than spring. I would have to buy myself a proper coat.

'I'm a pagan,' said Sophie proudly, and I suppressed a sigh. No wonder she had got on so well with Lucy. 'I'm one of the Children of the Waters,' she continued, 'or I will be, when I'm properly initiated. I'm not ready yet.'

'Right,' I said, running out of non-committal responses.

It was partly because I was distracted by the strangeness of my surroundings. The tarmac gleamed wetly after the rain, and a breeze was tearing the clouds apart to reveal straggly glimpses of blue sky. It was going to brighten up. Perhaps that explained the jagged quality to the light, which made the street look so odd.

I dragged my attention back to Sophie. 'What do your parents think about that?'

'They don't understand.' Sophie scuffed her boots against the wrought-iron gate in a reassuringly adolescent gesture. 'Mum only thinks about the latest status symbol, and Dad's only interested in dead people.'

'*Dead people*?' Then I remembered that he was a historian.

'And books.' She made it sound like a perversion, and I had to smother a smile. Drew Dyer seemed an unlikely pervert.

I was surprised, in fact, by how vividly I could picture Drew and the amusement gleaming in his quiet face. I remembered how inexplicably familiar he had seemed. My palm had tingled where it had touched his.

To my dismay I felt my cheeks redden at the memory, and I pushed it hastily aside before Sophie could notice and wonder at my blush.

I looked up the street instead. It was a narrow road, with cars parked on either side. At the end I could see a row of trees in front of the city walls, and behind them the great bulk of York Minster. I hadn't noticed it in the dark the night before, but now my whole body seemed to jolt with recognition, although I knew I'd never seen it before.

Sophie was watching me curiously. 'Are you going into town?'

I pulled myself together. 'Yes. I've got an appointment with Lucy's solicitor.' I half-pulled the piece of paper with the address out of my bag and squinted at it. 'Coney Street.'

Coney Street. I'd read the address before, but now the name seemed to pluck at some deep chord of memory.

Frowning, I stuffed the paper back into my bag. 'I was planning on walking there. Is it far?'

'Nothing's far in York. I can show you a shortcut through the car park, if you like,' she offered.

Sophie pointed me in the right direction before slouching off to school. I watched her go, troubled in a way that I didn't understand, before heading for the car park.

The light was peculiarly intense, and I wished I'd brought my sunglasses after all. I walked past cars with fat yellow number plates, past street lamps, past houses, and the sense of wrongness persisted. It was almost as if I had never seen bricks before, never walked along a pavement.

It was a long time since I'd been in England, I tried to reason with myself. Of course everything was going to look strange. I was used to the *gang* where I lived in Jakarta, to the deep gutters on either side of a walkway too narrow for anything but the satay-seller's cart, and to houses half-hidden behind high walls and lush banana trees.

A broken night hadn't helped, either. Shreds of the nightmare lingered disturbingly in my mind, and I felt light-headed with lack of sleep.

I'd never suffered badly from jet lag before, but now the feeling of dislocation was overpowering. I found I was walking carefully along a path beside the car park, but I kept starting at the sight of the high brick wall on my left and I slowed.

Ahead, children were being hustled into school by harassed parents. Two girls overtook me. One of them was talking on a mobile phone. The jagged light was intensifying, making the whole scene waver, like a painted backdrop stirring in a draught. Behind it, I glimpsed a rough track between hedgerows lush with cow parsley and forget-me-not.

I stumbled, blinked, and it was gone, but the smell of long grass and summer sunshine remained.

My heart was beating hard and I put out a hand to steady myself against the wall, the brick rough beneath my fingers. I stared ahead, fixing my attention almost desperately on the two girls. The one on the phone switched it off and said something to her friend, and they both laughed, and then the colour was leaching from the world around me, and laughter rang in my ears.

My laughter.

I am breathless with it. Elizabeth and I are running along Shooter Lane, with Hap lopsided at our heels, his ears flying. Our skirts are fisted in our hands, our sides aching with suppressed giggles. We're not supposed to run. We're supposed to be modest and demure, to walk quietly with our eyes downcast, but it is a bright May day and the breeze that is stirring the trees seems to be stirring something inside me too. I want to run and dance, and spin round and round and round until I am dizzy.

All day long we have both been giggly and skittish as horses with the wind up their tails. Exasperated, our mistress sent us off after dinner to gather salad herbs from our master's garth in Paynley's Crofts, and my apron is stained and grubby. Elizabeth's, of course, still looks as if it is fresh back from the laundresses in St George's Field.

Our baskets were full and we were just closing the gate to the garth when we met Lancelot Sawthell. I tease Elizabeth about poor Lancelot, who turns red whenever he sees her, and coming face-to-face with him unexpectedly was almost too much for us. We had to press our lips together to stop giggling while he stammered a greeting, his Adam's apple working frantically up and down, but oh, it was hard! We are cruel maids, I know, but not so cruel that we would laugh in his face, and we had to run as fast as we could so that we could explode with laughter out of his earshot.

'Oh, Elizabeth, I told you so!' I cry as we stop for breath at last. We drop our baskets into the long, sweet grass and collapse beside them, tugging at our bodices to ease our aching ribs. Hap flops beside me. He looks as if he is smiling too. His pink tongue lolls on one side of his mouth and his panting is loud in my ears. He can run fast, though he only has three good legs.

'Lancelot is *sweet* on you!' I insist to Elizabeth. 'And now that he has seen how rosily you smile at him, he will be on his way to speak to your father, right now!'

'Please, no!' Elizabeth is almost weeping with laughter.

We are laughing at nothing, the way silly girls do. We are laughing because we can.

'I will miss you when you are married, Mistress Sawthell!'

I will miss you. There is an odd moment when the words seem to hang in the air. The back of my neck prickles – someone is watching – but when I turn my head no one is there. The next moment I am toppling over as Elizabeth shoves me into the grass, and I am laughing again, the strangeness forgotten.

My laughter fades as I sit up, and I pluck a sprig of rosemary from the basket. One day Elizabeth *will* marry, I realize for the first time, drawing the rosemary under my nose so that I can breathe in its fragrance. I love the smell of it, so clean, so true.

Rosemary for remembrance. Strange to think that one day all this will be past, no more than a memory. No longer will we share the feather bed in the tiny chamber at the top of the Beckwith house in Goodramgate. There will be no more whispering and giggling until Dick, our master's apprentice, bangs on the wall and begs us in God's name to be quiet so that he can get some sleep.

Of course Elizabeth will marry. She is a year older than me and she has a dowry. She is pretty, too, with bright-blue eyes and a sweet expression. Any young man would be glad to have her for a wife.

I twiddle the rosemary round and round between my fingers. 'I will miss you,' I say again.

Elizabeth sits up and hugs her knees. 'I don't even have a sweetheart yet,' she reminds me. 'Nor am I likely to have one, when the Beckwiths keep us so close.'

We brood for a moment on the strictness of the household.

'Perhaps you will have to settle for Lancelot Sawthell after all,' I say.

'I think I'd rather stay with the Beckwiths.' Elizabeth flops back into the grass. 'You can have Lancelot.'

'I thank you for your kindness, but I cannot look so high for a husband, I fear.'

I am smiling, but it is true. It is common knowledge that my dowry has gone to dice and I do not even have any beauty to tempt a husband. I am dark and scrawny and sallow-skinned, and my eyes are a strange, pale grey. Sometimes Elizabeth tries to comfort me by telling me they are beautiful, like silver, but I've seen how folk cross themselves surreptitiously sometimes when I pass. Even Lancelot Sawthell could do better than me.

I cannot see anyone wanting to marry me. But I don't want to think about the future. I want to stay in this moment, with my friend beside me and the sun in my eyes, and the smell of rosemary on my fingers and my ribs aching with laughter.

Hap is still panting. 'I shouldn't have made you run so far,' I say to him. 'It must be hard with only three legs.' He rolls over so that he is lying against my leg, and when I rub his chest in apology, he closes his eyes with a little sigh of pleasure.

I smile at the sight of him. Hap is not a handsome creature, even I can see that, but his expression is alert and he is clever, much cleverer than Mistress Beckwith's pretty spaniel or our master's blundering hounds. I hardly notice any longer the withered paw he holds tucked into him.

My hand resting on Hap's warm body, I lie back and look up at the sky. It is blue and bright and the air is soft with summer. In the thorn tree behind us I can hear two blackbirds chittering at each other.

Above us, a flock of pigeons are swooping through the air. They turn as one, their wings flashing in the sunlight. I watch them enviously.

'Don't you wish you could fly?'

'No,' Elizabeth says lazily.

'I do. Imagine what it would be like, to be up in the sky looking down on everyone!'

A billowy cloud drifts past. It blocks out the sun for a moment, and for some reason the shadow passing over my face makes me shiver. But then it is gone and the sudden chill with it.

'I'd be terrified,' Elizabeth says without opening her eyes.

'I think it would be wonderful.' My fingers are still absently caressing Hap's sleek coat, and he huffs out a sigh and wriggles into a more comfortable position against me. 'You could see everything that's going on, but there would be no one to see you, or tell you to walk slowly or speak quietly, or fetch more wine or . . . or do *anything*.'

'And nowhere warm to sleep and nothing to eat but worms.' Elizabeth is nothing if not practical. 'You'd hate it.'

I make a face at the idea of worms. 'But if I could fly, I could go wherever I wanted,' I say. 'I could fly far, far away. I could go to London!'

I have never been further than the white stone cross on Heworth Moor. Mr Beckwith went to London once, but even though I teased him to tell us all about it, he just said it was a godless place. I suspect they made fun of his northern ways.

'You'd like to see London, wouldn't you, Elizabeth?' I poke her and she bats my hand away.

'Not if I have to eat worms,' she says. 'Why can't you just be happy to stay in York?'

'It's just . . . don't you ever want more, Elizabeth?'

'More what?'

I pluck discontentedly at the grass. 'I don't know . . . more something.'

'Oh, more *something*!' she mocks. 'Now all is clear!'

'You know what I mean.'

'Hawise, you want too much.' She sits up properly, serious now. 'Why can't you want what everyone else wants?'

'I do!'

'You don't. You don't *think* like everyone else. You want to fly like a bird and see the Queen and go on a ship and travel to Cathay . . . ' Elizabeth rolls her eyes at the impossibility of my dreams. 'You know what our mistress says. You must be careful.'

I do know. Careful, careful, careful. The word has been dinned into me for years. I have no looks, no dowry, few kin. And I am different. My father brought me back from his adventuring when I was but a babe. All anybody knows about my mother is that she was French, and my father is close-mouthed on the subject. For years I told myself it was because he was broken-hearted, but now I think that too much ale has addled his memory and he doesn't remember. For all anyone in York knows, I'm not even baptized.

It was fortunate for me that Mistress Beckwith had a fondness for my father when he was young and charming, in a way he still can be when he tries. When he wants something. The Beckwiths took me on as a servant when I was twelve and I have been learning how to run a household ever since, although unless I marry I will never be able to put all I now know to good use.

There is no use wishing that I could fly or stand by the ocean or see where peppers grow. My life is here, in York, and little comfort it will be unless I have a husband. I know that. I want to be like everyone else, I do, but it isn't that easy to stop thinking thoughts. But I need to. I need to have a care for my reputation, just as Mistress Beckwith says, just as Elizabeth says.

'You're right,' I tell Elizabeth. 'I will try harder.'

Over the city walls the Minster bell is ringing the hour. Elizabeth gets reluctantly to her feet and brushes down her skirts. 'We'd better go. Hawise, your cap is all crooked. Mistress Beckwith will skelp you if you go back looking like that!'

She will too. Our mistress has a kind heart, but a firm hand. I scramble up. My hair is dark and fine, and no matter how carefully I bind it, my cap is always slipping and sliding. I straighten it on my head. 'Better?'

She studies me critically. 'Better,' she agrees and hands me my basket. The lettuce and parsley have already wilted in the afternoon sun, but the rosemary is stronger and its smell is a shimmer in the air. 'Come on, we'll be late.'

Hap follows with his skewed gait as we hurry along the lane, but as we turn the corner at Mr Frankland's orchard, he stops with a whimper.

'Hap?' I look back at him in surprise.

Elizabeth grips my arm. 'Hawise, look!' She points round the corner to where an old woman, bent and buckled as a bow, is standing in the middle of the path, muttering to herself.

I suck in a breath of consternation and exchange a glance with Elizabeth. Mother Dent is a poor widow, a cunning woman

by some accounts, but my sister Agnes told us once that she
has heard Sybil Dent is a witch. She had a familiar, Agnes said,
a cat she called after the Devil himself, and then she lowered
her voice so that we shivered. 'It sucks the blood from her cheek.'

Mistress Beckwith says that such stories are nonsense, but
still, I falter, and instinctively I reach for Elizabeth's hand.

'Let's go back,' she whispers.

'It will take too long. We're late. Besides,' I add valiantly,
'she won't hurt us. She is just an old woman.'

I call urgently to Hap, but he won't come any closer to the
widow and in the end I have to pick him up. He whines as we
edge past Sybil, mumbling, 'Good day to you.'

We are almost past when Sybil swings round and fixes us
both with a fathomless gaze.

'Take heed,' she says, her voice old and cracked, and we
hesitate. I can feel Hap trembling in the crook of my arm.

'Take heed of what?' I ask, more boldly than I feel.

Sybil's eyes seem to look into us and through us. It is as if
she sees something we cannot, and the hairs on the back of my
neck lift. 'Ware the iron,' she says. 'Ware the water.'

'What does that mean?' Elizabeth's voice is high and thin,
but the Widow Dent just turns away, hunching her shoulders.

'Take heed,' is all she will say.

I tug Elizabeth away. 'Leave her,' I say. 'She knows not what
she says.'

When we are past her, I put Hap down. We walk quickly
away, and then faster and faster until we are running, running
back to Monk Bar and the city, giggling with relief, and the

breeze against our cheeks blows the widow's warning from our minds.

The touch on my arm jarred me back to reality so abruptly that I gasped with fright. I felt sick and faint, as if I had fallen down a step in the dark.

'Grace? Are you all right?' Drew Dyer took his hand away, eyeing me warily. 'Sorry, I didn't mean to startle you.'

'I'm . . . It's . . . '

Desperately I tried to pull myself together. I clutched at the chain around my neck, feeling its silver warm from my skin. Its braiding was reassuringly familiar beneath my fingertips. I was Grace Trewe, I remembered that straight away, but I had been that girl – Hawise, her friend had called her – too. She was still there, in my head. I could feel her frustration as she faded, unwilling to let me go.

I looked down, half-expecting to see a little black dog under my arm. I was sure I could feel the warm weight of him, his shiver as we passed Widow Dent. But Hap had gone. I was wearing jeans and a long-sleeved top under my cardigan, not an apron over my kirtle, but I could still feel the linen frill at my neck, the tightness of the bodice laced over my red petticoat.

Cautiously I looked around. This path was Shooter Lane. The patchwork of small enclosed fields and orchards was sealed now with tarmac, and houses and cars stood where once the wildflowers frothed in the hedgerows. When I reached out to touch the wall beside me again, the brick was rough and real beneath my fingertips.

'Grace?' said Drew again. He was watching me in concern. 'You were just standing there as I came up behind you. Are you sure you're okay?'

I shook my head to clear it. I'd had a peculiarly vivid hallucination – that was all. It had to have been. Clearly only moments had passed while I lay in the long grass with Hap pressed into my leg and my friend by my side.

'Yes . . . Yes, I'm fine,' I managed. I couldn't tell Drew that in my mind I'd been another girl, in another time. He would think I was mad. *I* would think I was mad. 'I just didn't sleep very well, that's all. And I'm still jet-lagged.' I even mustered a smile of sorts. 'It's not a good combination. I blanked out completely there for a moment.'

'You're very white. Perhaps you should go back and lie down?'

'No!' My recoil was instinctive. I didn't want to go back there. 'I mean . . . no, I'm okay, honestly,' I said, even while a part of my mind was asking: *Back where?*

To prove the point I started walking again, but very gingerly. I found myself watching the pavement, afraid that it might disappear again. My mind was still jerking with the immediacy of the scene, and I could feel Hawise clamouring to be let back in, a weird dragging sensation at the edges of my consciousness that made me think of the wave, and the inexorable swirl and suck of the water pulling me back, back, back . . .

'Where have you come from?' asked Drew after a moment.
'What?'
'You said you were jet-lagged.'
'Oh . . . yes – Indonesia.' All at once I longed to be back in

Jakarta, where I knew where I was and what I was doing. Where I never doubted the pavement beneath my feet. 'I've been teaching English there.'

'Must be a bit of a change arriving in York.'

A bubble of hysterical laughter lodged in my throat and I had to bite down on the inside of my cheeks to stop it erupting. I thought of my nightmare, of the strange, rotting apples that disappeared overnight, of that extraordinarily vivid scene I had just imagined.

'You could say that.'

Drew was wearing a shabby tweed jacket and carrying a briefcase bulging with papers and books. He was blessedly ordinary. He was solid, real, and I noticed that, as I fixed my attention on him, the tugging sensation in my head faded.

I cleared my throat. 'Are you going into town too?' That was it, I congratulated myself. Make conversation, be normal.

'To the city archives,' he said. 'I'm working on local court records there at the moment.'

'Did you finish your paper?'

'I wish. No, I'm taking a break from it. There are only so many dung heaps and clogged gutters that I can write about at one time.'

'It must have smelt a bit like the canals in Jakarta,' I said. Odd that, right then, Indonesia seemed more knowable and familiar than York, with its jarring light and its wavering air. I felt giddy again, remembering how reality had slipped sideways.

I must have imagined it. I must have.

'Maybe,' Drew was saying. 'I expect we'd have found the

streets of Tudor York pretty whiffy, but they had their own notions of cleanliness and they were pretty good at enforcing them.'

'So what are you going to be looking at in the archives?' I asked, anxious not to let the conversation lapse. I wished I could hold Drew's hand, but the poor man would have a fit if I grabbed him. I would have to hang on to his words instead. 'More nosy neighbours?'

'Yes, as a matter of fact. I'm on research leave at the moment and I've a book to finish. I'm working on social identity, in a nutshell, but the chapter I'm writing now is about misbehaviour.'

I nodded along as he talked, interested, but increasingly frustrated by that insistent itch of familiarity. I studied him under my lashes. He had one of those quiet, restrained faces that are almost impossible to describe, but I couldn't imagine where I would have come across Drew Dyer in the past.

'We haven't met before, have we?' I asked at last.

'No,' said Drew. His eyes rested on my mouth for a moment and then he lifted them to meet mine. 'I'd remember,' he said, and there was a moment – just a tiny moment – when there was an unmistakable zing between us. Which was ridiculous, because he was much older than me, and definitely not my type.

I looked away, unaccountably flustered.

'Must have been in another life,' I said, and I laughed, not very successfully.

And then I shivered.

'Cold?'

'I'm fine,' I said. 'Just getting used to the change of climate.'

Drew Dyer was clearly comfortable with silence, while my fingers were wound tensely around my pendant and my shoulders hunched against the intrusive tug in my head. She was there – Hawise. I could feel her, wanting me to remember how I had lain in the grass with my friend and my dog, and I set my jaw stubbornly. I wasn't going to give in to it.

Deliberately I untangled my fingers from the chain and let it fall back against my neck as I thought about the clothes Elizabeth and I had been wearing. I'd never had any interest in history, but they seemed vaguely Tudory to me, and Drew Dyer was a historian of Elizabethan York.

I glanced at him as he walked beside me, his stride easy and unconcerned. It couldn't be a coincidence. My subconscious had obviously stirred together a mish-mash of impressions from the night before and seasoned it with jet lag and a touch of culture shock.

Because it couldn't be true . . . could it?

I bit my lip. 'This area,' I said, gesturing vaguely at the car park. 'Have there always been buildings here?'

If Drew was surprised at the abruptness of my question, he gave no sign of it. He shifted his briefcase to tuck it under the other arm, and I had a sudden, shocking flashback to lifting Hap, holding him wedged under my arm. My subconscious again, I told myself firmly.

'It was mostly market gardens around here until the nine-teenth century,' Drew said. 'Further out was the common land,

but this close to the city there would have been small allot-
ments, orchards, that kind of thing.'

Orchards.

An inexplicable dread prickled over my skin, catching me
unawares. I pulled the sleeves of my cardigan down over my
fingers as I shivered.

Drew was still talking. 'This path we're walking on is an
ancient right of way. In Roman times it was a road leading to
the praetorium, where the Minster is now.' He pointed ahead
to the city walls with the cathedral behind. 'Later in the Middle
Ages they moved the gate to where Monk Bar is now, and they
called this—'

'Shooter Lane,' I murmured, and he stopped and looked at
me, astonished.

'How on earth did you know that?'

'I don't know,' I said honestly, and I shivered again.

I really had to get myself a warm jacket.

York is a very old city, and it shows. There are crooked,
cobbled streets and buildings misshapen with age. There are
narrow alleyways with quaint names and an ancient church every
time you turn a corner. There are handsome Georgian houses
jostling with half-timbered shops and modern office blocks, and
dominating them all is the bulk of the Minster, looming above
the city like a great limestone liner. It's not quite as pretty as
you think it will be, but there is a sturdiness to the city that has
seen off the centuries. Swept up within the circle of city walls,
indented like a child's drawing, this is a practical place where
people live and work and play, the way they have always done.

But that first day I knew none of that. I knew only that disquiet was beginning to claw at my spine once more, as we walked under a great stone gateway through the city walls. A taxi ride from the station in the dark with a taciturn driver was my only experience of York at that point, but I didn't need Drew to tell me where we were. I *knew* the gate was called Monk Bar. I felt as if I had walked beneath it countless times before, and as we headed down Goodramgate, recognition began to clang like a bell inside me.

Déjà vu, I tried to tell myself, but the uncanny sense of familiarity and wrongness persisted. The streets weren't quite right. The houses weren't quite right. Nothing was quite right. Only the Minster towers, soaring above it all, looked as they should . . . but that couldn't be right, either.

I caught the unmistakable whiff of open drains and sniffed at the air. Drew saw me wrinkling my nose. 'Chocolate,' he said.

'What?'

'The smell. It comes from the Nestlé factory.' He pointed behind us. 'When the wind is in the right direction you can practically taste it.'

I sniffed again. It didn't smell like chocolate to me. I detected a much more pungent combination: wet straw and wood smoke, perhaps. Mud and freshly cut timber. Shit, lots of it. Stagnant water. Something earthy and raw that caught at the back of my throat.

Not a hint of chocolate.

A monstrous headache was building behind my eyes. The sense that I ought to recognize the street had grown oppressive, and I found myself staring from side to side, searching for something that would trigger a memory of when I might have been there before, and why.

Delivery vehicles were parked half-on, half-off the pavement in Goodramgate, holding up the traffic that was trying to make its way along the narrow city streets. I was frowning, which Drew evidently took for disapproval.

'They've got to unload before eleven,' he told me. 'After that, vehicles are banned and the streets revert to pedestrians.'

He stood back and gestured for me to go ahead of him, past a lorry laden with scaffolding. There was only room for single file on the pavement, and even then I had to flatten myself against a shop window to squeeze past the wing mirror. As I turned my shoulder, the pavement tipped beneath my feet without warning and my heart jumped into my throat as I felt myself falling.

It's still beating hard as I edge past the end of the cart and step over the gutter into the street, but I don't understand why I am suddenly afraid. The feeling only lasts a moment, and then I shake it aside. The world is not out of kilter. Nothing is wrong.

The cart taking up most of the street is laden with tar barrels. A shaggy horse waits patiently between the shafts. Hap, scavenging in the gutter, gives its hooves a wide berth, but I stop to stroke its nose while the carter and his apprentice hoist barrels off the cart and roll them towards Mr Maltby's door, ignoring the bad-tempered cursing of the countryman on his wagon who is trying to pass.

I like horses. I like the feel of the velvet lips feathering my palm, the warm, grumbly breath, the patient eyes. I wish I could ride. Even country girls get to perch on the rump of a pony sometimes, but I am a mercer's maidservant and I must walk everywhere. Once I told Mr Beckwith that I would like a horse of my own one day, and he threw back his head and laughed so that I could see the gaping hole where the barber drew his tooth. 'Where would you go on your horse, Hawise? You don't need a horse to get to market.'

That is true. It doesn't take long to walk from one side of the city to another. I have no need of a horse, and nowhere to go.

Scratching the horse between its ears, I catch myself feeling restless and make myself stop. I have tried so hard not to think that way. I must be quiet, I must be ordinary. I mustn't think or wish or dream.

I am giving a final pat and turning to go on, when there is a loud scraping sound and a thud behind me. Too impatient to wait, the countryman has pushed on. His wagon has scraped against Henry Lander's stall, and now it is stuck and Henry is shouting and swearing at the countryman in his turn. Edward Braithwaite's apprentice is offering pointless suggestions from across the street, until Henry and the countryman turn on *him*. They are having a fine old row.

Between their cursing and the loud quarrelling coming from the alehouse, the air is rent with vexation, but beneath their noise and fury, the sounds of the street make a music of their own: a burst of laughter through a window, the snip of shears, banging and clanking from the spurrier's workshop. An apprentice is whistling. Somewhere a baby is crying. And, weaving through it all, the thrum of conversation. Isabel Ellis has her head together with two of her gossips. They are clustered in her doorway, leaning eagerly in to discuss what she has seen in the fields, or heard under a window. I can't hear what they are saying but it will be something scandalous. Their faces are bright, their hands clapped to their mouths to hide their delighted shock.

They stop talking as I pass and watch me in silence. I know what they are thinking: there she goes, the odd servant of the Beckwiths with that strange dog of hers. I bite my lip and pretend not to notice. The consensus in the street is that Hap should have been drowned after the accident that cost him his paw. He is too black, too different. They don't understand how clever he is. They don't understand that now he is my only friend.

For Elizabeth is dead.

As always, the thought of her grabs me by the throat, and for a moment I cannot breathe for grief. Mr Beckwith had the old stable pulled down last September and built a fine new one, but the carpenters left an old nail in the yard, and Elizabeth stepped on it one day. It went through the sole of her shoe. Later, I remembered that day in Paynley's Crofts when we lay in the grass and laughed – the day we met Widow Dent. 'Beware the iron,' she had said. We didn't think she meant a little nail.

At first we thought it would be all right, but that puncture in her sole grew red and angry, and then the whole foot puffed up. We watched helplessly as the poison spread up her leg until it consumed all of her. Elizabeth died one day when the mist hung heavy over the city and spangled the spiders' webs with tears. I held her hand until she had gone and felt pain close around my heart like a fist.

It was God's will, I know, but oh, I miss her so.

Two small boys are chasing another, even smaller, one down the street. Their quarry dodges through the crowd. He bumps into William Paycock's stall, swerves around Margery Dickson, and narrowly avoids falling over one of Percival Geldart's pigs, but his luck runs out when he gets to me. He crashes into me and I stagger back.

I sucked in a breath at the impact as someone jostled past me on the narrow pavement and I fell back against a window, unable to tell at that point where I was, *who* I was.

'Grace!' Drew came up, frowning, and took hold of my arm. 'That guy nearly knocked you off your feet!'

His grip was extraordinarily reassuring. 'Really,' I said, through the roaring in my ears, 'I'm—'

'Fine, I know,' he interrupted me. 'Where are you going?'

Back to the Mr Beckwith's house, of course. I've been to the market. My mistress will be waiting.

I struggled to focus. 'Solicitor,' I managed. 'I've got an appointment.'

'What time?'

It took a few seconds to remember what he was talking about. 'Ten-thirty,' I said at last, a hand to my pounding head.

'Then you've got time for a coffee.'

Chapter Three

Drew took charge, steering me into a coffee shop and pushing me into a leather chair. The roaring had moved from my ears to my brain by then, and darkness was rushing in. Without thinking, I leant forward and dropped my head between my knees.

He put a steadying hand at the nape of my neck. I could feel it resting there, warm, safe. 'You're not going to throw up on me, are you?'

I managed to shake my head.

'When was the last time you ate?'

I tried to think. They had served breakfast on the plane, but I'd been too tired to eat after I landed. 'Somewhere over Turkey, I think.'

'No wonder you're ready to pass out.' He took his hand away. 'Stay there.'

I didn't have much choice. My mind was reeling still, and my legs felt boneless, while my heart galloped with disbelief, but I managed to sit up at last and close my eyes.

'Here.' I opened them as Drew set down a cup of frothy coffee in front of me. 'I didn't know what you would like, but I got you a cappuccino. Eat the brownie too. You need the sugar.'

I hadn't realized until then how hungry I was. 'Thank you,' I said. 'You're very kind.' Shakily I reached out and broke off a piece of the brownie.

I love food. I hoard memories of wonderful meals I've eaten: duck liver with fried apple on a little square of toast in France; prawn curry by the beach in Goa; a bacon-and-egg sandwich, warm and fatty and oozing yolk on the train to Brighton; *nasi goreng* served on a chipped plate at a *warung* in Sumatra.

But none of them tasted as good as that brownie did. When I put it in my mouth, the sugar burst on my tongue in an explosion of sweetness and chocolate, and I chewed slowly, astounded by the lightness of texture, the density and complexity of taste.

'God, what's in this?' I mumbled. 'It's *fantastic*!'

Drew raised his brows. 'Well, you're a cheap date,' he said, and the creases around his eyes deepened in amusement. 'I don't think I've ever seen anyone enjoy a plastic-wrapped brownie quite so much before.'

'It's just . . . it's as if I've never tasted chocolate before,' I tried to explain. 'It's incredible.' I took a sip of the cappuccino. It was rich and smooth and creamy, and the froth left a moustache on my upper lip. 'This is too.'

I was licking it off when my eye caught Drew's, and I saw myself as he must have seen me, running my tongue round my mouth as if I were auditioning for a porn flick. I snapped my tongue back in my mouth and my colour rose. 'Sorry! I get a bit carried away.'

'Don't apologize. My ex-wife spends her whole time counting calories, so it's a nice change to see someone really enjoying her food. Are you like this with everything, or is it just chocolate and coffee?'

'Do you know, I'd have said it was everything *except* chocolate,' I said. 'I don't normally have much of a sweet tooth.'

I took another piece of the brownie. The second bite was just as miraculous as the first. I tried to look cool, but judging by the smile tugging at the corner of Drew's mouth, I didn't do very well.

'Feeling better?' he asked when I had finished.

'Much.'

It was true. I could feel the sugar rushing along my bloodstream, steadying me. I picked up my cappuccino again and cradled the cup between my hands. Was it possible? Could those two vivid experiences, as Hawise, simply be the result of forgetting to eat?

Drew had been stirring his own coffee. He tapped the spoon against his cup and set it carefully in the saucer before looking up at me. Behind his glasses, I saw that his eyes were the bluish-grey of the English Channel and very astute. He might have enjoyed the play of sensation across my face, but he hadn't forgotten that I had almost passed out as I reeled between one reality and another.

'Why don't you tell me what happened?' he said.

Not many people look at you with that kind of attention,

as if they are really seeing you. I shifted under his unwavering focus, aware all at once of the tiny spot on the side of my nose, of my hair escaping from its clip. My eyes slid away from his.

'I don't really know, to tell you the truth. I think you're right. I was tired and hungry and my blood-sugar levels must have been very low. I just had this overwhelming sense of déjà vu . . . ' I laughed nervously, embarrassed. 'I was ready to swear I'd been here before, although I'm certain I haven't.'

'York's a popular place for tourists,' Drew said. 'Most visitors have seen so many photos of Stonegate and the Shambles, or whatever, before they arrive that it all looks familiar when they actually get here.'

'Maybe.' I wanted to believe it, but I couldn't. I'd seen iconic sights before. I'd been to the Pyramids and the Taj Mahal and Sydney Harbour Bridge, and not once had I felt like this. Besides, I was sure that no tourist brochure, no website about York would have pictures of two maids with a three-legged dog or the gutter choked with filth outside Mr Maltby's door.

Pressing chocolate crumbs from the plate with my finger, I eyed Drew Dyer under my lashes and wondered if I should tell him exactly what had happened to me on the way into the city.

He was leaning forward, contemplating his coffee, a tiny furrow between his brows and his fingers splayed around his cup. He had nice hands. Strong and square with clean nails. There was something solid and reassuring about him. I remembered that from the night before, when I had followed him up the stairs.

I tried to imagine telling him about Hawise, about how I thought she was in my head, and how in a blink of time I had seemed to slip back to the past. And then I remembered how my jaw had dropped when I had misunderstood Drew's absorption in his old records. Drew hadn't said anything, but I knew he'd thought I was ridiculous for even thinking he might have meant time-travelling.

Just as he would think I was ridiculous now. I didn't blame him. If anyone had told me that story, I thought, I would be rolling my eyes and twirling my finger against my temple while I looked for the quickest way to end the conversation.

And I didn't want to end it. I wanted to sit there, safe – that word again! – in the coffee shop with Drew Dyer, calm and sensible, beside me. Fiddling with the chain around my neck, I searched for a topic that would keep us sitting there a while longer.

'Do you teach at the university here when you're not on research leave?'

'I used to,' said Drew. 'That's why we came to York in the first place. I got my first lectureship here.' He looked up at me and I was struck again by how acute his eyes were. 'I got a job in London a couple of years ago, but I only teach three days a week and it was worth keeping the house here, so that I could see Sophie more regularly after the divorce. She took the separation badly.

'Maybe there isn't a good way to take it, when your parents decide they can't live together any more,' he went on, hunching forward over his coffee once more. 'Karen lives in a village outside York with her new husband now. I thought it would be good for Sophie if she and I could spend more time together. I had this idea that she would be happy if she had a bit more continuity.' His mouth twisted as he put his cup back in its saucer. 'It hasn't really worked out like that. Sophie has never settled at a school, and "happy" seems to be the last thing she's feeling at the moment.'

'I don't think many teenagers do happy,' I said, but I was remembering the two girls laughing in the grass outside Monk Bar, and a pang twisted like a cord deep inside me.

'You don't have any children?'

I shook my head. 'Nope. No kids.' For a moment my mind flickered to Lucas on the beach, and then away. Lucas wasn't anything to do with me. 'I don't do commitment,' I said to Drew, making my voice cheerful. 'I like to keep moving. Never look back: that's my motto.'

'We'll never make an historian of you then,' he said lightly.

'I'm afraid not.' I chased the last brownie crumbs around the plate. 'I've never seen the point of thinking about the past. I mean, you can't change it, can you?'

'No, but you can try and understand it. How can you make sense of the present unless you understand what has made it the way it is?'

'I'm not sure I want to understand it,' I said. 'I just want to live it.'

'You're not planning on staying in York then?'

'No. As soon as I've sorted out Lucy's estate, I'm off—' I broke off as my neck prickled, but when I swung round to look behind me, there was no one there, just a couple of women in an exhaustive discussion about some work crisis.

Drew didn't seem to have noticed. 'Back to Indonesia – oh, no – you never go back, do you?'

'I'm thinking Mexico next. I've never been there.' I pushed aside the conviction that someone was eavesdropping. 'But I've got to sell Lucy's house before I can pay the various legacies, and I'm not sure how long that will take. I'll have to get myself a job to see me through, but York looks like the kind of place that would have some language schools, so I should be okay. I suppose I'll have to sort out something about a funeral for Lucy too. I've no idea what she would have wanted.'

I hesitated, fingering the top of my pendant. 'Sophie said that Lucy was a witch. Is it true?'

Drew blew out a long breath. 'I don't know what she was. All I know is that she filled Sophie's head with a lot of nonsense, and I wish to God she hadn't. Sophie's always been . . . ' He searched for the right word. ' . . . intense,' he decided at last. 'And she's struggled to fit in. Lucy encouraged her to "explore her spiritual side",' he said, hooking his fingers in the air for emphasis, 'and now she's joined some cult set up by one of my ex-students. I didn't trust the little toerag when I taught him, but he's clever. He'll make sure he always stays on the right side of the law.'

Drew sighed. 'Karen and I have both tried telling Sophie how dangerous it is, but the more we try and discourage her, the more committed she is.'

'She'll grow out of it,' I said. 'If it's any comfort, I did everything that would most make my father's life a misery when I was Sophie's age, but I got over it. Poor Dad,' I remembered, shaking my head. 'I gave him a really hard time.'

'At least you weren't messing around with the occult,' said Drew gloomily.

'Sophie's just picked what will wind you up most. If you'd been a druid, she'd probably have joined the Young Conservatives.'

He smiled reluctantly at that. 'Maybe you're right,' he said. I saw him look at his watch. 'I'd better get on. Are you sure you're going to be okay?'

'Absolutely.' Doing my best to disguise my disappointment, I got to my feet too and thanked him again for the coffee and the brownie. 'I feel like a new woman,' I said as I left.

It was true. By the time I came out of John Burnand's office, tucking the envelope with Lucy's few effects into my bag, I was back to my old self, and able to scoff at my earlier conviction that someone called Hawise (*Hawise*! Where had my subconscious come up with a name like that?) was in my head. Clearly the brownie had done the trick. Now all I needed was a square meal and a good night's sleep, I decided.

I set off back to Lucy's house, mentally compiling a list of everything that needed to be done before I could sell it, not really noticing where I was going until I found myself on the edge of a square.

I looked around, puzzled. I saw a hot-dog stall, a cycle rack jammed with bikes. It was still cool, but people were enjoying coffee at the tables and chairs set out in the spring sunshine.

The shop on the corner was selling televisions, their brightly coloured pictures flickering at the edge of my vision.

I frowned. Where was the market cross? Where was the toll-booth? Where were the stalls and the peddlers, and the good-wives tutting over the vegetables and the countrywomen squatting by their baskets of eggs and butter? Thursday Market should be packed with traders and beggars and servants, and all the folk who come to gossip and to bargain and to buy.

'Hawise!' The hand on my arm makes me jump and I swing round, my hand at the ruff of my linen smock.

'Oh, it's you, Alice!'

'I've been calling your name for an age,' Alice complains. She is plump and pretty – *and knows it*, Elizabeth would have said – and beneath her cap she has very blue, slightly protu-berant eyes, with long, fair lashes that she flutters against her milk-and-roses complexion. 'Didn't you hear me?'

'No, I—' I glance back at the market, but everything is as it should be. I can't remember why I thought it wasn't, and I shiver suddenly.

A goose walking over my grave.

'Daydreaming again, I suppose,' says Alice dismissively. She isn't the kind of girl who wastes time on things that aren't real.

She is distracted by Hap, sniffing at her gown, and she draws her skirts away with a shudder, pursing her rosebud mouth in disgust. 'Get it away from me!' she says and crosses herself furtively.

'He's not doing any harm,' I say, but I click my fingers and

Hap returns reluctantly to my side and sits, his withered paw tucked into his chest. I can't understand why everyone can't see how clever he is, but if they could, they would probably be even more afraid of him. Being black and only having three legs is bad enough. If they thought he was clever, too . . . well, I have noticed that cleverness is not much admired.

'You shouldn't take it around with you, Hawise,' Alice says, eyeing Hap with dislike. 'People talk.'

People don't like it. I remember Elizabeth saying that. She said I had to be careful of my reputation, and I have been trying. I keep my eyes downcast and I walk slowly, and I don't think about what it would be like to fly any more. I don't wonder about the lands where cloves and peppers grow any longer – or not out loud. Instead I talk about the neighbours and wonder where I will find a husband. I have changed. I am just like everyone else, the way Elizabeth said I should be. But I cannot change how I feel about Hap. I don't care what folk say; he is a good dog.

'Did you want something?' I ask Alice coolly.

'I've got something to tell you.' Ignoring my tone, she tucks a hand into my arm, taking care to stay on the other side of me from Hap, and we head into the market together.

'Oh?' It's not like Alice to be so friendly. I know she thinks I'm odd. Dick overheard her saying so once, but she would never say it to my face. In spite of their peculiar choice of a servant like me, the Beckwiths have a good reputation in the city. My master, William Beckwith, is an alderman, and warden of the ward. He is a prosperous draper, a warm man, as they say, and owns tenements all over York, as well as a fine house in Goodramgate. Alice is servant to a hatter. The Swinbanks are well enough, but they can't compare with the Beckwiths. Alice may not envy me my looks or my dog or my father, but she envies me my place in the Beckwith household, and she is always careful to be polite to my face.

'I am betrothed to John Wightman. Look!' She flaps the pair of gloves she is carrying. 'My betrothal gift,' she says proudly.

'That is good news indeed, Alice,' I say.

Alice leans closer. 'And we've done it,' she whispers.

I am half-shocked, half-envious. I have never even kissed a boy. Mistress Beckwith keeps her servants close, but I am afraid that the real reason I have never been courted is because I am dark and thin and sallow-skinned, and my eyes are odd. What man is ever going to want me, with my fierce brows and my flat bosom and my strange eyes? It's not even as if I have a dowry.

Still, I would like to know what it is like to be courted, to be wanted. I would like someone to make me smile the cat-that's-got-the-cream smile that Alice is wearing. Too often these days I can feel my blood pumping, and something restless and dark quivering deep in my belly. The thought of kissing, of *doing it*, kicks my pulse up a notch. I don't like to admit it, even to myself, but the truth is that I am envious of Alice.

We are pushing our way through the crowded market, dodging the puddles as best we may. The chamberlains still haven't mended the paving, in spite of the pains laid on them in the wardmote court, and there are deep ruts where the countrymen's carts have stuck, while the cobbles are covered in mud and vegetable scraps and fish scales and sodden straw and dung.

The stallholders are shouting enticements over the sounds of the peddlers crying their trinkets and the clucking of chickens in their wicker cages. Beggars skulk on the edges of the market, plucking at gowns and calling for charity. A boy weaves past us, balancing a tray on top of his head, and the smell that drifts from it makes me sniff appreciatively. 'Hot pies! Hot pies!' he cries, but you can hardly hear him in the hubbub of conversation. It is always like this on market days.

There is so much noise that no one is going to overhear us, but I lower my voice anyway. 'What is it like?' I ask Alice, because I want to know and there is no one else I can ask. Elizabeth would have told me, if she had known. 'You know . . . doing it?'

'It's all right,' she says carelessly. 'Hurts a bit at first, but it gets better.' Her lips curve as she thinks about it. 'A lot better. And it keeps John happy.'

I would like to ask more, but don't want Alice to know how ignorant I am. 'And when will you be wed?' I ask instead.

'Soon. My family have given their consent, so now it's just a dowry to be agreed. It is time you had a sweetheart too, Hawise,' Alice says, her smile sharp as pins. 'You must be, what, twenty?'

'I am nineteen,' I say stiffly, turning my basket out of the way of a wheezing goodwife.

'I hear that you have an admirer,' she says with a sly look.

'I? No!'

She arches her brows at me. 'Don't tell me that you haven't noticed?'

Infuriatingly, she stops then to admire some ribbons on a peddler's tray. I know she is just doing it to tease and I am tempted to ignore her, but I am intrigued, I admit it.

'Noticed what, Alice?'

'Mistress Rogers has new lodgers. They say Mr Phillips is a notary from London. He has business with my Lord President, no less.'

I gape at her. My Lord Mayor and his brethren are pleased to think they rule this city, but we all know that they have to do whatever the Council of the North tells them. The Lord President is here in place of the Queen herself, and there is no one in York who dare say him nay.

A notary who has dealings with the Council of the North, let alone my Lord President . . .

'And he has noticed *me*?'

'Not Mr Phillips!' Alice rolls her eyes. 'His assistant!'

'But I don't know any assistant.'

'Well, it seems he knows *you*. He asked Anthony Pusker who you were, after church. I can't believe you didn't see him, Hawise. It's not as if there are that many new faces in the congregation!'

She is fingering the ribbons, pretending to consider buying a blue one. 'A farthing to you, pretty lady,' cajoles the peddler, but Alice is more interested in my reaction, which is clearly exactly what she wanted.

'Anthony told him you were in service with the Beckwiths. I'm surprised he hasn't found an excuse to meet you. He is a

clean and sober man by all accounts, and he will be a notary.'
She purses her lips, totting up his prospective worth in her head.
'You could do worse.'

I am dumbfounded. 'But why would he be interested in *me*?'

Alice surveys me critically. 'You're dark,' she agrees, 'but
there's something about you, all the same. Haven't you seen the
way men watch you?'

'What men? How?' I stutter. 'How do they look?'

'You know . . . with heat in their eyes. No, not today,' she
adds to the peddler, dropping the ribbon back on the tray and
turning away.

'Two for a farthing!' he calls after her desperately, but Alice
just waves a dismissive hand. 'I'll let John buy me a ribbon at
the fair. Come on, Hawise.'

With Hap still at my heels, I trail after her. I'm not sure why.
I think I am too astounded by the vision of myself as someone men notice. Is it possible? I think of Mr Beckwith's guests.
Sometimes, when I serve at table, I catch their eyes and they
always look quickly away. Their cheeks grow ruddy and my
master snaps at me to leave them. I have never seen any heat
in their eyes. Alice is mistaken, I am sure of it.

But I long to believe that she is right.

We are skirting the edge of the market, past the countrywomen who squat by their baskets filled with lumpy beans and
onions, with carrots and fresh green peapods. It has been a poor
summer so far, but at last there are fresh salad herbs and spinach
and cucumbers to buy again. My mistress has sent me to buy
eggs, but she has a fondness for strawberries, and I hesitate

when I see some. The countrywoman sees me looking and immediately holds out a strawberry for me to try.

'Fresh and very sweet, Mistress,' she promises. Her fingers are stained red with the juice, and there are splatters like blood on her apron, but when she catches sight of Hap by my side, she curls her lip back with a hiss and crosses herself.

I am not going to buy her strawberries now. I am about to tell her how ignorant she is, when a furious shouting and snarling erupts over the cacophony of the market place and, not sorry to have the excuse to leave her, I turn.

'What is it?' says Alice.

'Let's find out.'

I take a step, but then hesitate. I have the same feeling I had when Alice startled me at the entrance to the market. It is almost as if I'm not properly here, as if I am looking at myself from afar and there is a voice in my head shouting, 'No!'

I shake the feeling aside. Too much cheese when I broke my fast this morning. 'Hap, stay close,' I say, snapping my fingers.

'You're one as would push to see a hole in the calsey,' my mistress always says, and adds darkly, 'one of these days you'll fall down it, if you're not careful.'

But I'm not alone. A dense crowd has already gathered, and Alice and I have to hold our baskets in front of us as we squeeze our way through. Hap is pressed into my skirts. He doesn't like it when folk stand too close. There are too many opportunities for kicking, and I bend to pick him up. He's a small dog, and it's easy to tuck him under my arm.

When we duck at last under the jostling arms, we find

ourselves on the edge of a circle that has formed around two men. I see Miles Fell holding back his snarling mastiff, while Nicholas Ellis, a tailor, is hopping up and down, one hand to his bloody leg and the other clenched into a furious fist.

'You whoreson!' Ellis is shouting. 'You lumpish, Hell-hated knave! I will have you arrested, yes – and that toad-spotted dog of yours too. Do you know how much I paid for this hose? I'll see you whipped out of the city at the cart's arse!'

Opinion in the crowd is divided. Nobody likes Fell. He is a miller, and surly as they come, with dark, heavy features and slovenly habits. Mr Beckwith is always trying to get him to repair the calsey at Castle Mills, but the road is as bad as ever, and all my master gets in return is a mouthful of abuse. That bitch of his is as bad-tempered as her master too. Even I cross to the other side of the causeway to avoid walking past her.

She is big even for a mastiff, and when she snarls she looks remarkably like her master. Her bite must have been painful, but Nick Ellis seems more concerned about his hose.

'Peacock!' my master snorts contemptuously whenever Ellis's name is mentioned, but I think he is more like a cat, picking his way carefully along the street and shuddering at dung heaps. He is always complaining about the blocked gutters that ooze onto the footway and spoil his shoes.

Beside me, two apprentices are jeering, calling out insults and encouragement indiscriminately to both men. The miller has such a savage hold on his dog that she is like to choke, but he is spewing curses back at Nicholas Ellis and doesn't notice.

'That dog should be muzzled,' Nick shouts over him, trying

to get the crowd on his side now. 'The city passed an ordinance. You all know that. Where are the constables? Those mangy louts are never around when you need them!'

We have formed a big circle around them as if watching a show, but I'm losing interest. 'I'm going,' I say to Alice, but that's when my gaze snags on the young man across from me. He is so neat in comparison to his neighbours that I am surprised I haven't noticed him before. He has glossy, chestnut-coloured hair, a tidy beard and eyes so intense that, when they meet mine, my heart seems to stumble.

'That's him!' Alice pinches my arm. 'Mr Phillips's assistant!'

I look back at him, and he smiles as if he knows we are talking about him. Still I can't help glancing over my shoulder to see if it is really me he is smiling at, but everyone else is watching Miles Fell, who is running out of curses and turning away like a sulky bear. When I look back, I suppose *Me?* must be written across my face, because his smile broadens and he nods.

Alice nudges me. 'See?'

A young man has smiled at me. It is nothing. For most girls – girls like Alice – it would mean nothing at all, but I feel flushed and elated and apprehensive all at the same time.

Miles Fell lumbers towards us, still cursing, followed by his shambling dog, and we all fall back hastily to clear a path for them both. Few folk are brave enough to make him walk round them, even when he is in the best of moods.

There is a sense of anticlimax. The fight many were hoping for hasn't materialized, and the crowd disperses as quickly as it gathered, back to buying and selling and trading gossip and insults. Nicholas Ellis is left to limp off alone, muttering about speaking to my Lord Mayor.

The notary's assistant has drifted off with the others, it seems, and I turn, disappointed, only to find that Alice has vanished and he is standing right there. He smiles at my expression and sweeps off his hat to bow, as if I were the Queen's Majesty herself.

'Francis Bewley, at your service, Mistress . . . ?' He darts a beseeching look up at me. Close to, he is less handsome than he seemed at first, but there is a sleekness to him that fits with his southern accent. He has a very red mouth, small, plump hands and those strange, intense eyes are like the Ouse on a bright day, reflecting back the light so that it is impossible to tell what colour they are.

I know I should lower my gaze and walk away. I know how important my reputation is. I know that however much people seem busy about their own affairs, there will be someone watching me. There will be a woman who will tell her gossip, who will tell *her* gossip, who will tell Mistress Beckwith that I stood in the middle of Thursday Market and was bold with a stranger.

But I cannot help myself. How can I walk away when a handsome young man is bowing before me, when his eyes are fixed on mine and he doesn't seem to have noticed that I am dark and plain? How can I not smile back at him? I forget that if Alice is right, he is dissembling and already knows my name.

'Hawise Aske,' I admit. I follow his gaze as it drops to the dog in my arms. 'And this is Hap.'

To my surprise, Hap's ears are flattened and I can feel his entire body vibrating with a low growl. It's not like him. Normally he is the most sweet-tempered of dogs.

I set my basket on the ground and lay my free hand reassuringly on his head. 'Quiet, Hap,' I say. 'Friend.'

Sensing someone at my shoulder, I turned to see two women, strangely dressed, watching me with a concerned expression.

'Are you lost, dear?'

'Lost?' I said blankly. Why should I be lost in Thursday Market?

'You've just been standing in the middle of the pavement, staring.'

I looked slowly around me. The stalls had vanished. There were no carts laden with cabbages, no women crouching by their baskets of fruit, no jabbering throng of people, laughing and gossiping and bargaining. My eyes dropped to my hand. No small dog, growling softly.

And no Francis Bewley. In his place stood two elderly women pulling shopping trolleys behind them.

I was blocking their way. The realization was a slap, jarring me into the present, and I drew an unsteady breath as I remembered where I was. *Who* I was.

'Sorry. I . . . I was just . . . ' I couldn't think of an excuse to explain my odd behaviour until I remembered Alice and her accusing expression. '. . . just daydreaming,' I said as I stepped aside and they trundled their trolleys past me.

My mind scrabbled with the shock of the abrupt return to

reality, and my heart was banging painfully under my ribs. I felt sick and very frightened as I crossed the square and cut through the narrow alleyways that riddled the city centre, too preoccupied by what had happened to think about how I knew the way.

I wasn't mad. I *wasn't*. I held onto the thought of Drew Dyer, who had treated me as if I were perfectly normal. He had said that I should eat, I remembered, but all I could find near Monk Bar were charity shops. I didn't want to go back to the market—

My thoughts broke off. What was I thinking? There had been no market. I had imagined it.

I made myself stop and take a deep breath. I needed to eat, that was all. I asked a newsagent where I could buy food, and eventually found a Sainsbury's, where I bought some basics. The ordinariness of the task was calming, and I was feeling steadier as I let myself back into the house.

There had to be an explanation for this. I couldn't be slipping back in time and reliving another life. The whole idea was absurd.

But I kept thinking about that nightmare, about being Hawise and drowning, and I thought about the voice I'd heard whispering for Bess, when I hadn't been dreaming at all.

The house was very quiet. I shut the door behind me and braced myself for that creepy whisper – *Bess* – but heard nothing. A faint suggestion of putrid apples lurked in the air. I told myself I was imagining it. There had been no apples in the bin that morning, so I must have dreamt them.

Still, the smell lingered unpleasantly as I carried my bags through to the kitchen and made myself a sandwich. Cheese and chutney, sliced brown bread. The rush of sugar from the brownie had long since evaporated and I'd been too tired to think about cooking a proper meal as I wandered around Sainsbury's. Too tired, and overwhelmed by the choice and the amount of packaging on the shelves.

And afraid to wonder whether it was remembering the *pasars* in Jakarta or the markets in sixteenth-century York that made the supermarket feel so alien.

I ate my sandwich standing up, looking out at Lucy's back yard. I didn't want to think about what had happened that morning. The earlier promise of the day had clouded over and the garden looked huddled down, as if reluctant to believe that it really was spring. Lucy had clearly made an effort with it. I'm not very good with plants, but I could identify clumps of woody lavender and rosemary, and in spite of myself I found myself thinking about Hawise. Found myself remembering the smell of the rosemary that she – I? – plucked from the basket, and how its pungency filled her – my? – nostrils.

Rosemary for remembrance. I could have heard that anywhere, I reasoned to myself. It was the kind of thing Lucy used to say all the time.

I looked away from the rosemary to where a stiff breeze bullied some cheery daffodils in a tub by the back gate. I'd never thought of Lucy as a gardener, but then I'd never thought of her as a witch, either.

I'd never thought she would die and leave me her house.

I hadn't known her at all.

I sighed, brushing crumbs from my fingers, and was turning back to the kitchen when something caught my eye. For a moment I could have sworn I saw a gnarled apple tree in the corner of the yard, but when I swung back to stare, it was just a straggly rose being buffeted by the wind.

I made a mug of coffee and took it through to the sitting room along with my laptop and the envelope of Lucy's effects that John Burnand had given me. It was cold in the house and I put on the gas fire, huddling in front of it while I drank the coffee and tried to get warm.

The air felt spongy and sour. Lucy had painted the walls a dark, disturbing red, and they seemed to be leaning in, crushing the light from the room. I wriggled my shoulders uneasily. My imagination had been working overtime since I arrived in York.

In one corner Lucy had laid a cloth over a round table, and set it with two tall candles. A pewter goblet was placed carefully between them, with a carved wooden wand and a ritual knife on either side. Crystals were laid in a circle around the edge.

It was an altar, I realized with distaste, and I remembered what Sophie had told me about Lucy being a witch. I studied the table while I nibbled at my thumbnail. It's a bad habit of mine when I'm unsure of myself. Outside, in the bright morning air, the notion of witchcraft had seemed just one more of Lucy's mad ideas, but here in this oppressive room it was harder to roll my eyes at the image of her dabbling in the occult. It felt more real, more dangerous, and I found myself thinking about the apple that I had found on the mantelpiece the night before and thrown away. The apple there was no sign of in the bin.

All at once my pulse was thudding in my ears, and I realized that I was crouched in front of the fire, holding myself tense and still like an animal deciding whether or not to flee. My eyes were bulging with exhaustion.

Jet lag catching up on me, I told myself firmly. All I needed was a nap.

Chapter Four

I lay down on the sofa and closed my eyes, but I couldn't relax. My mind careened between Lucy and the nightmare that had wrenched me out of sleep in the early hours of the morning.

I could pass that off as a dream, but what about those other experiences? I didn't even know what to call them. Hallucinations? They weren't dreams, that was for sure. They had been too consistent for that. Besides, who fell asleep walking along a street?

I abandoned my efforts to ignore what had happened and deliberately opened my mind to the memories. Surely I could look at them rationally? In each, I had been Hawise, and I could see some parallels with myself. I was small-boned and dark-haired, and I had the same silvery-grey eyes.

There were other similarities too. I was curious and restless, just like Hawise. That feeling of not belonging, of always being an outsider, was familiar to me, but unlike Hawise, I welcomed it. It meant I never had to get too close to anyone, and that suited me fine. It was easier that way.

Hawise had to be some kind of projection, I decided, although why I had chosen to project myself as a servant in Elizabethan York was a mystery to me.

The alternative was too bizarre to contemplate.

I didn't believe in reincarnation or ghosts or past lives, I reminded myself. I wasn't like Lucy. I didn't look for another world. I'd told Drew Dyer that I wasn't interested in the past, and I'd meant it. I liked the here and the now. I liked the surface of things, tastes and textures. I entwined my fingers in the chain of my pendant. Things like that – things I could touch, things that were real. I wanted to make sense of things, not marvel at the mystery of them.

So there had to be an explanation. There was nothing wrong with this house, nothing wrong with Lucy's death. Nothing wrong with *me*.

The explanation was simple: I was overtired and getting things out of proportion, and that meant it was time to get a grip. No more letting my imagination run away with me. No more freaking myself out.

I still couldn't relax enough to fall asleep, though, and in the end I gave up. Remembering the envelope with Lucy's things, I sat back by the fire and shook the contents into my palm. Two rings fell out, along with a silver pentacle pendant on a leather cord. I held it up, half-mesmerized as it swung gently, the reflected flames from the fire shifting over its shiny surface. It wasn't really my kind of thing, and besides I already had the jade pendant that I wore all the time. I wondered if Sophie would like it. She had known Lucy better than I had.

I tried on the rings instead. One was a narrow silver band engraved with some kind of writing – runes? – while the other was engraved with Celtic knots. They looked pretty together, and I left them on my finger. I would wear them in memory of Lucy.

For a while I sat by the fire, listening to the guttering hiss of the gas flames and turning my hand idly to admire the rings, but it wasn't long before Hawise was back. I could feel her knocking on my mind, wanting to come in, wanting me to remember, and I found myself looking at Lucy's altar. I found myself wondering what she had stirred up there.

Hawise was persistent, but I was stubborn too. I didn't want to remember.

I settled myself back on the sofa, opened my laptop and logged onto Facebook. My friends had been on, leaving each other jokey messages, grinning in photos, the way I usually did, but that day I felt detached from it all. They seemed to belong to another world, one that had nothing to do with me any more. Right then, sixteenth-century York seemed more real to me than the cyberworld where we could all keep in touch, no matter how far-flung we were.

For a while I sat with my fingers on the keyboard, wondering what to write, but in the end I just posted a short note saying that I was in York and that it was cold. I couldn't think of anything else to say.

Staring at the screen, I thought about my message hurtling

through space, bouncing off some satellite and then zooming back down to my friends' computers around the world. At least, I assumed it went via a satellite. The truth was that I had no idea how the Internet worked. How was it that the words I had just typed could appear in Jakarta or Sydney or Mexico City at the same time as they popped up here in York? And when messages went astray, as they sometimes did, where did they go?

I toyed with my pendant. When it came down to it, was slipping through time any more mysterious than the Internet? Could Hawise's experiences be messages that had been lost in time, rather than cyberspace? I played with the idea, my lips pursed as my eyes rested unseeingly on my Facebook page. I imagined her memories circling endlessly like some strange video or jpeg, waiting for a mind that could download it.

I could think of those experiences as mere blips on some weird circuit. I was on my own in a strange place. Perhaps that made me more susceptible than usual? I sat up straighter. Why not treat Hawise just as I would a computer virus that struck equally mysteriously, but which was ultimately controllable?

I've always had a straightforward approach to computers. If it doesn't work, I turn it off and hope the problem will go away by itself. It's amazing how often ignoring it works. I would do the same now, I decided. All I had to do was keep busy, keep focused on the present, and I would be fine. I would sort out this creepy house, sell it to the first bidder and leave.

Mel had a whole album of her Mexican photos on Facebook.

I clicked through every one, needing the distraction. She was obviously having a great time.

She'd left me a message. *R u ok?* Mel knew perfectly well that I had an old-fashioned loathing of abbreviations, and deliberately peppered any message to me with as many as possible. In return, mine were always perfectly punctuated. *What r u up to?*

How could I tell Mel what it was like here? She couldn't possibly understand about York, with its strange, shifting streets and the unnerving feeling that if you turned a corner or slipped down a little alley you'd find yourself in a different world. Mel wouldn't understand if I tried to tell her about the dizzying sense that time was warped and buckling, about the feeling that was part-horror, part-fascination as the present tipped into the past and back again. She wouldn't know what I meant if I told her how it felt when the present was siphoned away by a force stronger than reason. It made me think of standing on a beach in my bare feet, feeling the tide suck the sand from beneath my toes.

Off to Yucatan @ weekend, Mel's message continued. *Check out pics! U should be here.*

She was right. I should be there, I thought wistfully. I should be dancing in bars until the small hours, then nursing a hangover in the shade with my friend, not teetering on the edges of time in this old, cold northern city. I clicked on the link Mel had sent and found myself looking at a screen full of beautiful white sand beaches, complete with the obligatory leaning palm tree.

I'd been to beaches since Khao Lak. I'd got over the fear

that the sea would rise up again. There was a tiny moment when I first saw the photos when my throat closed in panic, but it only lasted a second or two, and then I was fine again.

I tried to concentrate on the images, but I kept looking up. The air had grown padded. It settled around me like a sigh, squeezing the energy out of me with every breath I took, while the silence thickened, broken only by the putter of the gas fire, the muffled click of the mouse.

I was about to close the page when I saw it, and the breath stopped in my lungs. A beach like all the others, but this one showed a child. Barely more than a speck on the screen, he was digging alone on a beach.

It wasn't Lucas. I knew that, but my heart was beating high and hard. I swallowed, blinked and looked again.

The child had gone. It was just a photo of a pristine beach fringed with palms.

My palms were damp. I rubbed them on my jeans. I had seen it – I knew I had. Not Lucas, no, but there had been a child in one of the pictures. I was sure of it.

Methodically I went through every single photo, but none of them showed a small boy with a spade.

So I'd imagined it.

I squeezed my eyes shut, wanting to squeeze the image from my mind, but I couldn't. Lucas was there, so clear that I could see every bump in his knobbly spine, every one of the fine, fair hairs at the nape of his neck. When I think of him, I think of his back, because that was mostly what I saw. Lucas didn't like to make eye contact.

He never played with the other children on the beach. He didn't play at all. He spent Christmas Day digging a complex network of channels in the sand, and I was fascinated by his single-minded approach. When the channel he had planned cut across the bit of beach where Matt and I were lying, his parents tried to call him away. That's how I knew he was called Lucas. They were Swedish and lifted their hands in helpless apology when he simply ignored them.

'It's okay,' I said, digging Matt in the ribs. 'We'll move.'

Lucas didn't say thank you. His face was set and he carried on digging. Matt sighed and grumbled, but I picked up the spare spade and set it in the sand.

'Here?' I said to Lucas.

He did look then – one quick, fierce look – then he nodded. We dug for hours, side by side, Lucas directing occasionally with a pointing finger. We didn't say another word to each other.

Just that once, that's all it was, but whenever I thought about that afternoon, my chest grew so tight that I could hardly breathe. I sat in Lucy's sitting room and I kept my eyes closed so that I wouldn't have to look at the photos of all those beaches where Lucas wasn't digging any more.

'Hawise!' My eyes snap open as my mistress bustles out into the yard and catches me with my face turned up to the sun, the tablecloth clutched to my chest. 'What is the *matter* with you today?' She looks at me narrowly. 'You've been like a great gawby gawping at the moon all day!'

'I was just thinking what a beautiful day it is,' I say, hastily

74

shaking the crumbs from the cloth. I don't understand the sadness that welled up inside me when I closed my eyes. It *is* a beautiful day, and I should be excited, not sad.

For today I am going to meet Francis Bewley in my father's orchard.

He insisted on walking me back to the house after I'd made my purchases that day in the market, even though Hap went for his boot the moment I put him down. I thought I saw a flash of something ugly in Francis's face as he shook Hap off, but the next moment he was smiling again and congratulating me on my fierce guard dog, so I must have been mistaken. I hope I was.

Francis even carried my basket for me, although it wasn't heavy: a dozen eggs, brown and shit-spattered, some green peas, a large pat of butter, that was all. I pleated my fingers in my skirts because I didn't know what to do with my hands.

He told me about his master, Mr Phillips, about how the Lord President had sent for him especially, and how much his master valued him. There was something pompous about the way Francis spoke. I told myself it was just his southern accent. I wanted to like him, but I couldn't help noticing how pleased with himself he seemed, and then I chided myself for being critical. Who was I to expect perfection, after all? And Francis was a Londoner, I reminded myself as we walked back that day. There was a sheen to him that the young men of York lacked. It made it all the stranger that he would want to be with me.

'Tell me about London,' I said when the conversation flagged.

'York is but a village in comparison,' he told me. 'London

is bigger and noisier and crueller. Folk walk more quickly there. There is a hastiness to everything they do. You would not want to go there, Mistress Hawise.'

I opened my mouth to contradict him, to tell him how many times I had dreamt of going to London, but remembered just in time that I mustn't be different. I must be quiet and agree and forget my strange ideas.

Truth to tell, I was shy of him. Something about him made me uneasy, but at the same time I was intrigued. Francis Bewley was so different from anyone I had met before, and when he suggested that we meet again, of course I was tempted.

I felt restless and reckless that day, I remember that. I wanted to know what everyone but me seemed to know. I wanted to be like Alice and have a sweetheart of my own. Perhaps if I hadn't been envious of her, I wouldn't have agreed to meet Francis outside the bar walls today. I would have remembered everything Mistress Beckwith had to say about modesty, and my master's distrust of southerners. I would have thought about Hap baring his teeth, and the shiny reflection of Francis's eyes, and I would have shaken my head and stayed at home.

But I was jealous and I was curious, and I agreed.

I fold up the cloth. The best damask today, because Mr Hilliard is here. He is a wealthy merchant, and no doubt has fine cloths of his own, but he is a widower, and perhaps is lonely in that big house of his in Coney Street, for he comes to dine with us often. His wife died in childbirth, I heard, and after that he came to York from somewhere in the east. It seems he is in no hurry to marry again, although his friends are no doubt in search of a suitable bride for him. It shouldn't be too hard. He is a stranger still, with no kin in the city, and his neighbours think him outlandish, I've heard, but what does that matter when he is rich? A man as wealthy as Ned Hilliard will need a wife to give him a son, else what good is all his gold?

I like Mr Hilliard. He does not seem odd to me. He is a quiet man, and not well favoured with his pox-pitted cheeks, but he has good teeth and he looks at you when he talks to you. There is a stillness to him that is surprising when you think how far he has travelled. He has stood on the quaysides of Rouen and Lübeck and Venice, bargaining for bags of pepper and saffron, filling his ships with ginger and nutmeg and sugar, with oils and almonds and exotic dyes. Sometimes when we have finished our chores, Meg and I sit on stools and listen to him talking with Mr Beckwith and our mistress, and it is the next best thing to going myself.

Why am I thinking about Mr Hilliard? I catch myself up. I should be thinking about Francis. But the truth is that I am nervous. My mistress is right. I have been clumsy and fidgety all day.

I, Hawise Aske, am going to meet a young man, and the idea is both thrilling and unsettling. I know my mistress wouldn't approve, and I know why. I shouldn't be risking my reputation with a stranger, but how can I give up my very first chance to be like everyone else? So I feel guilty, but excited too.

I wish I could remember better what Francis looks like. He won't really be my sweetheart, of course, and he'll be going back to London soon, so what harm will it do to pretend, for today? If not today, when? There may never be another young man who will ask me to meet him in the crofts. Perhaps I will like him better this time.

I take the cloth back inside. My mistress has said that once my chores are done I can have the rest of the afternoon to visit my sister, Agnes. I just need to tidy the hall after the meal, and then I can go.

The afternoon sunlight slants through the high window into the hall, and I watch the dust drifting lazily across each beam as I put the pewter dishes in the buttery and straighten the carpet on the chest. Maybe it's because I'm anxious to leave before I lose my nerve, but time seems suddenly languid, as if it is gathering itself for a leap into the unknown.

Or perhaps it is I – not time – that is poised on the edge of change. The thought makes me shiver with excitement. I am longing for change, for something to happen. Perhaps, I think, I will look back on this moment, on this last hour before I met Francis, and realize that nothing was ever quite the same again.

I stand in the hall, the crimson velvet cushion embroidered with flowers of green clutched to my chest, and all at once I am conscious of how familiar everything is. Meg and I put down fresh rushes the day before yesterday, and their sweetness mingles with the scent of the onions and garlic stacked in the corner, and the smell of the last bacon hanging from the ceiling. The windows are open, and I can hear wood pigeons burbling on the roof. Dick is whistling in the yard, my mistress is scolding Meg in the kitchen. Brushing crumbs from his doublet with a napkin, my master has taken Mr Hilliard into his closet and they are talking business over a cup of wine.

And I am going to meet Francis.

I set the cushion back on the turned chair by the fireside and draw a breath. I am stepping away, growing up, becoming a woman at last.

My hands shake a little as I untie my apron up in the chamber that I now share with Meg. I don't dare change into my best gown – my mistress would be bound to notice – but I brush down my kirtle, shake out my gown and straighten my cap. I am hoping to slip out quietly through the back gate, but Mistress Beckwith is in the yard, and she raises her brows when she sees me.

'I am going to visit my sister, Mistress. You said that I might,' I remind her, and when she nods I bob a curtsey and sidle towards the gate. I have my hand on the latch when she calls me.

'Hawise?'

I turn. 'Yes, Mistress?'

'Be careful.'

I bite my lip. My mistress has a nasty habit of seeing more than I want her to, but I do indeed visit Agnes. That much is true.

As usual my sister is abed, and the air in the chamber at the top of the steep staircase is tired and stale.

'It's a lovely day,' I say. 'Shall I open the shutters?'

'No! I can't bear the noise, and the light makes my head ache so.' Agnes leans back and lays her arm over her eyes. She is peevish and out-of-sorts today.

I sit on the edge of the bed, guilty as always for being the lucky one. I am scrawny, but I am strong, unlike Agnes, who has been sickly since she was a child. We are almost exactly the same age. Her mother was a widow when my father married her after he came back to York. I think I have a memory of him throwing me up into the air and laughing at my squeals of delight, but perhaps I have made it up. After he married Agnes's mother, there was little laughter, that is for certain. My father began to spend more time in the alehouse than his workshop, and her mother's temper – never sweet to begin with – soured even further, so I was glad to get away when the Beckwiths offered me a place in service.

I was twelve then, and it was Elizabeth I grew up with, Elizabeth I giggled and whispered with, Elizabeth whose loss I mourn still as if she were in truth my sister.

Since her death I have tried to get to know Agnes better. The sickness carried her mother off two years since, and now she is alone with my father and Jennet, the sour old widow who cooks and cleans. It is too much for Agnes to keep house, she says.

It is not much of a house, either.

Mr Beckwith's house has twelve rooms as well as a shop, and it is richly decorated. My father's has only six, and there is a slatternly air to everything. I look around the room. In the dim light coming through the shutters, it is dreary. The curtains around Agnes's bed are silk, but they are tatty and worn. There is no silver on my father's table, no cushions in his hall. Once he was a merchant and adventured across the seas, but his fortunes have dwindled to naught, squandered on dice and cards in the alehouses of York. He is a member still of the mystery of mercers, but he is no merchant, no mercer. He is barely a chapman, eking out a living from his friends and his former reputation.

I feel sorry for Agnes, stuck here with little chance of marriage, either. Like me, she has no dowry, and like me, she is plain, but otherwise we are the contrary of each other. Where I am dark, everything about my sister is pale. She has pallid skin and hair so fine it seems almost colourless. Discontent tugs at the corners of her pale mouth. Agnes is very devout, while I attend divine service and let my mind wander outside the walls, where I used to run when I was a girl. She is sickly and I am sturdier than I look. I want to be friends with her, but she is not like Elizabeth.

Still, I try.

I tuck my feet beneath me. 'Agnes,' I say, lowering my voice so that Jennet won't hear. 'I think I may be in love.'

I can't remember exactly what Francis looks like, but I like the idea of being in love. I want to be.

Agnes drops her arm and pulls herself up on her pillow, her eyes sharpening. 'In *love*? Who with?'

'His name is Francis. He is from London.'

'London! Who vouches for him?'

When my gaze slides away from hers, she purses her lips in disapproval. 'Hawise, you cannot be so foolish! Where did you meet this man?'

'In the market.' I know where this is going. Who are his friends? Who are his kin? Do the Beckwiths know? 'I just want to meet someone who's been further than Fulford Cross. I want to *talk* about something different. Is that so bad?'

'Not if talking is really all you'll be doing.'

For someone so pious, Agnes's mind can dip surprisingly close to the gutter at times. I flush.

'I just want to talk to him,' I say, sulkily pleating my skirts. Elizabeth would have been excited for me. She would have understood.

'Consider your reputation, Sister,' says Agnes. 'Do not go. Stay and pray with me instead.'

The room is stifling. I cannot breathe in here. Jumping up, I go over to the window and open the shutters in spite of Agnes's protests, so that I can lean out. The street below is potholed and flies swarm around the midden outside the door, but if I lift my eyes the sky is a beckoning blue, while a soft breeze stirs the leaves of the overgrown trees in the old friary garden.

'Oh, Agnes, it's such a beautiful day,' I cry, swinging round. 'Don't you ever want to escape? I know!' Seized by the idea, I run over to the bed and grab her hands, though she shrinks back into the pillow. 'Why don't you come with me? How long is it since you went out of the house? It will be cool out in the crofts and the air will be fresher. It wouldn't be improper for me to meet Francis if you were with me, would it?'

'Hawise, please, you're giving me the headache!' Agnes sags back into the pillows.

'I'm sure you'd feel better if you got up,' I try and coax her. 'You never have any fun, Agnes. I'm sure you'd enjoy it if you came with me. Please come!'

'I'm too tired.' She turns her face away. 'If you have so little care for your reputation, you go. I will pray for you.'

So I leave her there, guilty at how relieved I feel to be out of that chamber with its stale, sluggish air. Hap scampers ahead of me along the street. Agnes doesn't approve of him, and he knows now to lurk outside the house and wait for me. He is a clever dog.

I push my way out of Monk Bar and through the crowd of vagrants who hang around by the cluster of carts and wagons and ramshackle booths. A woman hardly older than I sticks close beside me, her hand held out. Her other arm holds a baby whose head lolls listlessly, and I dig a coin from my purse while the Minster bell strikes six o'clock.

'God bless you, Mistress!' she cries as she catches the penny and bites it, then slips back into the crowd.

I said I would meet Francis at the stile by the ash tree in Shooter Lane. My father has a garth there, an orchard really, but he never goes there. The last time I saw it, the old apple tree was bent under the weight of apples that were never gathered, and the grass grew thick and rank with nettles where there could have been a crop. No one will see us there. For all my bravado at agreeing to meet Francis, I am nervous. I don't want my mistress to find out, so I am sticking to the back paths that criss-cross Paynley's Crofts as far as I can, with Hap snuffling ahead of me.

The long grass almost covers the path in parts. It is tangled with daisies and lady's bedstraw, with willowherb and wild carrot and the soft blue of meadow cranesbill. My skirts brush against the feathery tops of the grass and pick up the cuckoo spit that clings to their stems, but I have no time to stop and brush it off. I am late.

What if Francis has given up waiting for me already? Or what if he has forgotten? It is three days since we arranged to meet. He might have met any number of maids far prettier than I since then.

At the crossroads by a cluster of thorn bushes I hesitate. I can hear boys shouting and jeering, and when I look along the path that crosses mine, I see them standing around a dark shape at the ground and pelting it with stones. It is a dog, I think, a dog like Hap, and anger propels me forward before I have a chance to think.

'Stop it!' I cry. 'Stop! How can you be so cruel? Shame on you!'

They are not very big boys and they jerk back at my cry, their faces pinched and defensive.

'She's a witch,' the bravest of them flings back at me.

The others nod vigorously. 'Mildewed Mr Bolt's corn, she did.'

'Aye, and turned me mam's milk.'

And now I see it is not a dog at all. It is an old woman crumpled on the ground, an arm flung over her head to protect herself. It is Sybil Dent. In spite of myself I recoil, but then I am ashamed. What harm has Widow Dent ever done me?

I whistle for Hap. These boys will turn their ignorance on him if I am not careful. But Hap is cowering against the hedge and won't come any closer.

'She's allus forspeaking the cattle on the common.' The boys are eyeing me warily, and I wonder if they know who I am, if they have heard about my strange eyes and my crippled dog.

'That's nonsense,' I say as firmly as I can.

'It's true. Mr Weddell's man saw the Devil fly out of her eye!'

On the ground Sybil Dent groans and stirs, as if at the word 'Devil', and we all take a hasty step back.

I swallow. 'He was blethering – probably drunk,' I say. 'She's just an old beldam. Leave her alone now. Be off with you!' I make shooing motions with my hands.

For an instant they hold their ground. Hap chooses that moment to come slinking to my heel, and their eyes go round at the sight of his blackness and his poor withered paw.

'It's the Devil's dog,' the biggest boy whispers, backing away, looking from Hap to me in horror. I have a sudden urge to bare my teeth and jump at them, to shout 'Boo!' and watch them run away, but their nerve has already broken and they are taking to their heels, running down the path as if the Devil himself is behind them.

I am left alone with Widow Dent. I crouch down to her. 'Are you hurt? Can you walk?'

I have forgotten how old she is. Her mouth is sunken into a seamed face, but her eyes, when she opens them, are fathomless pools that dry the breath on my tongue.

'I can, if you will help me up,' she says.

I put a hand under her arm and lift her to her feet. She weighs no more than a bundle of twigs, and her bones feel as thin and as fragile. Bent as she is, she barely reaches my shoulder as she stands and looks around her.

Her gaze falls on Hap, who whines and cowers into the hedge. 'Oh, don't bother yourself,' she says to the dog, 'I'm only looking for my stick.'

A smooth piece of ash is lying a yard or so away, and I bend to pick it up. 'Here,' I say, handing it back to the widow.

'I thank you.'

With the stick to steady her, she seems stronger, even powerful. My heart is beating fast, and all at once I understand why folk are so afeared of her. Then she lifts a shaky hand to touch the blood trickling from her temple, where a stone caught her, and I feel ashamed again.

'I'm sorry,' I say helplessly.

Sybil's eyes rest on my face and I find myself shifting from foot to foot, convinced that she can look deep inside me. Does she see my vanity, my deceit? Does she know that I am churning with nervousness and excitement, with anticipation and fear for my reputation? With pity for her, and a deep unease?

''Tisn't your fault,' she says. 'You didn't throw stones.'

I glance up the path. I am thinking about Francis, waiting for me by the stile. 'Can you get home from here?'

'Aye, it's not far.'

'Good. Well, then . . . ' I draw a breath. 'I should go,' I say.

I begin to turn away, but Widow Dent lays a hand on my sleeve. It is gnarled and knotted and mottled with age, but there is strength to it too, which stops me in my tracks, and Hap whimpers.

'Go back,' says the widow.

Her eyes have taken on an eerie blankness, just as they did that day Elizabeth and I met her. 'Go back,' she says tonelessly. 'Go back while you still can.'

I look down at her in confusion. 'I don't understand. Go back where?'

'Back the way you came,' she says. 'Or take a different path.'

I bite my lip. I am late as it is. What is the point of taking a different path?

'*Go back!*' The urgency in the widow's voice makes the fine hairs at the back of my neck stand up.

Frightened, I step back from her and click my fingers for Hap. 'I'm sorry,' I say. 'I have to go.'

Picking up my skirts, I run along the path, to the ash tree and to Francis, with Hap at my heels.

I choose not to go back. I go on.

I am nearly there when I stumble over a twisted root and pitch forwards.

I jerked awake, heart slamming from the fall, and found myself staring blankly at my computer where the screensaver circled remorselessly. How long had I been asleep? Dry-mouthed, I pressed the heels of my hands to my eyes.

I wanted to tell myself that it had been no more than a dream, but how could it have been? I might have been sleeping, but a story was unfolding that was too vivid and too coherent for a dream.

Hawise's story, not mine.

I lowered my hands, not quite steadily, and stared at them. I could remember the roughness of the Widow's cloak under my fingers, how fragile she had felt as I helped her up. I remembered the smell of the midden by the door, the dull gleam of the pewter in the Beckwiths' hall. I churned still with a jumble of guilt and fear and anticipation.

And frustration.

I wanted to know if Francis had waited, whether the assignation had been as sweet and thrilling as I had longed for it to be.

As *I* had longed for it to be? I caught myself up. *I* hadn't been running through the crofts. I was Grace Trewe, fixed firmly in the twenty-first century. There was no way I had been in sixteenth-century York. But if I accepted that it had been more than a dream, that meant that Hawise was in my head . . . and what did *that* mean?

Possession. The thought of someone else in my head, someone else controlling me, was terrifying. My mind veered away from the idea, and I clutched at my theory about Hawise's story circling in some cybertime instead. It allowed me to be fascinated and intrigued by what was happening while keeping the experience firmly at arm's length. I couldn't believe in ghosts and clamorous spirits, but a pseudo-scientific explanation suited me fine.

I was going to stick with that.

Putting the computer off my lap, I swung my legs to the floor and stood up.

'*Bess . . .* '

I jerked round at the whisper, and the room skittered back in alarm.

I had forgotten Bess. She didn't fit into my nice, safe theory. Her name made the air clench with grief and fear and I didn't like it.

'Stop it,' I said out loud, and I didn't let myself think about whether I was talking to myself or the room.

Or to Hawise.

Unable to move, I stared at myself in the dim mirror over the mantelpiece. My face was white and strained, my expression stark.

'It's in my head,' I said out loud. 'It isn't real.'

'*Bess* . . . ' The whisper came again, but it was fainter now and I drew an unsteady breath. It was all in my mind. As long as I remembered that, I would be fine.

But when I turned round to pick up my laptop, there was an apple half-hidden under a cushion, rotting beside it. Its skin was browning and beginning to pucker with mould.

I looked at that apple for a long time. I didn't want to pick it up. I knew I was being ridiculous. I knew, logically, that it couldn't be the apple I thought I'd thrown away the night before, because that had been a figment of my imagination. There had been no trace of it that morning, which meant that I'd dreamt it.

I wasn't dreaming now.

And that meant it was just an apple, I told myself. Lucy must have put it there (*under a cushion?*) and forgotten about it. Of course it would start to rot. My skin crawled at the thought that I had been sitting right next to it. I would only have had to move a little and I would have squashed it like a slug. I felt my gorge rise and I clutched my arms together, fighting down the revulsion.

I had to get a carrier bag and use a knife to manoeuvre the apple into it. Irrational or not, I couldn't bear to touch it. I took it outside and threw it in the wheelie bin, and when I went back inside it seemed to me that the air was lighter. The misery had dissipated, the room was empty, and in my head Hawise had gone.

Chapter Five

'Interesting ceremony,' said Drew with a sidelong glance at me as I joined him by the window.

'Wasn't it?' I tipped my head from side to side, stretching out the kinks.

It had been a busy few days. I was feeling a lot more in control by then. My imagination finally seemed to have settled down, and there had been no more dreams of Tudor York.

I'd convinced myself that Hawise was no more than a bizarre crossed line, a blip in time. I chose not to examine why I was being so careful to keep my mind firmly fixed in the present, or why I was so afraid of succumbing to the twitch at the back of my brain. I did what I always do when I don't want to face something. I just shut down part of my mind and pretended it wasn't happening. I'd always been good at compartmentalizing.

I kept myself occupied. I found myself a part-time job at a language school and began to tackle the worst of the clutter in Lucy's house. I folded up her clothes and carried bags of them along to the charity shops in Goodramgate. According to John Burnand, the house was 'eminently sellable', but I planned to have a good clear-out and slap on a coat of fresh paint before I put it on the market. There was a lot to do, but I didn't mind. As long as I was busy I wasn't thinking about Hawise.

'I might have known Lucy wouldn't go for a straightforward funeral,' I said to Drew, breaking off a tiny piece of cake from the plate he had put down beside him. 'I suppose I should think myself lucky I didn't have to sacrifice a chicken, or collect up newts' eyes and toads' toes.'

At least Lucy had left detailed instructions, so I hadn't had to do anything but get in touch with Vivien Price, the priestess who had performed the ceremony, and invite everyone back for poppy-seed cake and nettle tea afterwards. The menu had been decided after consultation with Sophie. I could have done with something stronger than tea myself, but Sophie seemed glad to be involved and even offered to make the cake.

'It was nice of you to come too,' I said to Drew. As non-believers, he and I had been relegated to observers at the back, and I had been glad of his company. 'I know you don't have much time for all that alternative stuff.'

'Lucy was a neighbour,' he said. 'I wouldn't have missed it for the world. Where else would I get to hear such wonderful chanting?'

I laughed. I liked Drew's dryness, and the way his eyes crinkled when he was amused. He was a bit older than most of my fellow teachers, but I always felt very comfortable with him. I wasn't planning on staying in York any longer than I had to, but if I had been, I thought he could have been a friend.

'The chanting was pretty dire, wasn't it? But Lucy would have loved it, and it's what she wanted, so I guess that's what's important. To be honest, there were bits of the ceremony that I found sort of moving too,' I confessed. 'You've got to admit that Vivien has presence.'

'The priestess?' Drew looked across the room to where Vivien was talking to Sophie, and his expression was unfriendly. 'She's got a certain charisma, I grant you, but I don't trust people like that, whatever beliefs they're peddling. They're experts at manipulating weaker minds.'

'I don't think there's anything sinister about it,' I said doubtfully, pushing my hair behind my ears. 'It's just all a bit silly.'

'It starts out silly, but it can turn nasty. My mother was like Sophie,' said Drew. 'She started off dancing around trees and ended up joining a cult.'

Drew's mother had been in a *cult*? I almost choked on my nettle tea.

'*Really*? How old were you?'

'Six,' he said briefly.

Six. Lucas had been about six. I wondered what Drew had been like as a small boy. 'Did she take you with her?'

'No, the whole business of looking after a child wasn't mystical enough for my mother.' Drew's expression didn't change, but there was an undercurrent of bitterness to his voice. 'I stayed with my father, who remarried a sensible woman a couple of years later. My stepmother brought me up, and she's still the person I think of as my mother.'

I was still trying to get used to the idea of Drew having a mother who was into alternative living. 'What happened to your real mother?'

'She got herself to the States – God knows how – and joined some community in the middle of nowhere. She died when they all took a suicide pact.'

'That's . . . terrible,' I said inadequately.

I was shocked, but Drew simply shrugged. 'It was a stupid waste, but that was my mother for you. You can see why it worries me to watch Sophie drifting down the same path. Everyone says she'll grow out of it, but my mother didn't.'

I bit my lip. I'd said that too. 'Well, I won't tell you not to worry, but I don't think Sophie is that otherworldly. We had a laugh when we were making the cake yesterday, and she was telling me about people at school. She's a pretty good mimic, isn't she?'

'Yes, she can be good company when she tries, or when she forgets that she's supposed to be a surly teenager.'

'I think she feels like she doesn't fit in anywhere,' I said. 'I remember feeling like an odd duck too. I'm not saying Sophie doesn't believe in all this stuff, but maybe she's just trying to find somewhere she can be one of the crowd, and not the odd one out for a change.'

'Let's hope so.'

There was a strangely companionable silence as we stood in the window. I was thinking about Drew and the mother who had abandoned him, but Drew, it appeared, had more prosaic matters on his mind.

'Do you fancy coming to supper tonight?' he asked after a while. 'I'm not much of a cook, so I can't promise anything exciting, but I'll open a bottle of red. I think we'll both need it after this.'

I brightened. 'I'd love to,' I said. I'd been missing my friends in Jakarta, and the thought of an evening away from Lucy's house was very inviting. An evening not letting myself remember hurrying through the crofts. Not letting myself wonder if Francis had waited. Not letting myself listen for the anguished whisper, or sniff for the reek of rotten apples.

'Can I bring anything?' I asked. 'Some poppy-seed cake perhaps? I can tell how much you've enjoyed it,' I added, nodding down at his plate. Apart from the tiny piece I'd broken off, it was untouched.

Drew smiled. Really smiled this time, not that tantalizing almost-smile, and just for a moment my breathing got all tangled up. 'Delicious as it was, I couldn't possibly deprive you of the leftovers,' he said smoothly.

'I'm going to be eating it for weeks,' I grumbled, to disguise the fact that my lungs had momentarily forgotten how to function.

'You could always try burying it under a full moon and see what comes up.'

'Don't joke. It might well come to that.' I paused. I was reluctant to move on, but I still had to speak to a number of Lucy's friends. 'I'd better circulate. I'll see you later then?'

'About seven?'

'Great,' I said.

It wasn't exactly a date. It was just dinner with a friend. Still, anticipation fizzed along my veins and I had that fluttery feeling beneath my skin that makes it impossible to settle to anything. That was how I had felt the day I went to meet Francis in the orchard, I remembered involuntarily, and I stumbled mentally at the thought, cursing myself.

I'd been doing so well not thinking about Hawise, not thinking about the way the air in Lucy's house seemed to pulse with frustration sometimes. That day the atmosphere was fractious, fretful, although none of the so-called witches seemed to notice anything amiss.

I'd been on my own too long, I decided. I hadn't been aware of the atmosphere when I was talking to Drew, but now it seemed to press in on me again. I looked across the room to where he stood, head bent towards a wheezing woman in a flowing blue robe. I recognized her from Lucy's funeral rites. Her expression was intense as she talked, while Drew listened courteously, only a twitching muscle in his cheek betraying the impatience that I knew he felt.

He was a nice man, I thought. It was good to feel such a sense of connection that wasn't muddled up with physical attraction. I could just enjoy Drew as a friend without complicating things with sex. Absently I touched the pendant at my throat. Perfect.

'That's a beautiful necklace.' I swung round to find Vivien Price watching me watching Drew, and to my annoyance I felt colour creeping up my throat. Vivien had penetrating blue eyes that reminded me uneasily of the Widow Dent. But there the similarity ended. I guessed Vivien to be in her forties, with smooth skin and dark, thick hair that fell almost to her waist. Although she was dressed no differently from any of the others in the room, she wore her simple robe with an air of authority.

I forced a smile. 'Thank you. Yes, it's lovely, isn't it? It was a Christmas present from a boyfriend a few years ago.'

'May I see?'

Obligingly I held the pendant out from my neck. The jade was cut in a simple oblong and was the clear translucent green of a tropical lagoon. It hung from a braided silver chain and sat just below the hollow of my throat, as it had done since Khao Lak. I hadn't taken it off once.

'What a wonderfully intense colour.' Vivien's eyes lifted to mine. 'He must have been a nice boyfriend to choose something so beautiful for you.'

'Yes, he was,' I said evenly.

'Jade is of the heart chakra, did you know that? It's worn to attract love.'

I laughed. 'That's not why I wear it. I'm not looking for love.'

'Your pendant says that you are.'

'In that case, it's lying,' I said pleasantly. 'I like to be able to move on whenever I need to. That doesn't go too well with intense love affairs.'

'You're afraid to get too close to people,' said Vivien. 'You yearn for it and fear it at the same time.'

'The only thing I'm afraid of is that I'll be left with all that seed cake,' I said lightly enough, but my jaw was tense, and when I caught a glimpse of myself in the mirror, the tendons in my throat were standing out. 'Do have some more.'

'You're afraid of this house too,' said Vivien as if I hadn't spoken. 'You're right to be.' She looked around the sitting room. I'd got rid of the altar, much to Sophie's horror, taken down the weird pictures and rubbed out the pentagrams Lucy had chalked at the windows and doors, but the room was still disturbing in a way that I couldn't put my finger on. 'I see what you have tried to do, but there is still violence here,' she said. 'Violence and hate and fear.'

Violence. Hate. Fear. The words jangled in the air. I swallowed.

'And here was me thinking everyone was getting on so well,' I said flippantly to cover my unease.

'You can feel it,' Vivien continued, unperturbed. 'You're a sensitive.'

'No,' I said, taking an instinctive step back. 'No, I'm not.'

'Yes,' she said. 'You must take care. And you must be careful of Sophie.'

'Sophie?' I had been about to make an excuse and move away, but I stopped and looked at her sharply. 'Why? What's wrong with Sophie?'

'She's floundering around, looking for somewhere she can be accepted. That makes her . . . vulnerable.'

'Vulnerable to what?'

'She's open to the spirits, she yearns for them in fact, but not all spirits are good spirits or safe spirits.'

'I don't know what you're talking about,' I said uneasily.

'Just look out for her,' said Vivien.

'Vivien, I hardly know Sophie,' I protested and she fixed me with those far-seeing blue eyes.

'You know her father.'

Heat stung my cheeks. 'Not really.'

'Still, watch out for her. You'll be better for her than Lucy. Your godmother was a fool,' said Vivien calmly. 'She dabbled in things she didn't understand and strayed too far into the darker paths. Don't let Sophie go the same way.'

Drew was still cooking when I went round at seven. 'It's supposed to be a vegetable lasagne,' he said, surveying the crowded worktop in dismay. 'I always forget how long it takes to chop everything up. It's not nearly ready.'

'Let me do those.' I nudged him aside with my hip and took over slicing aubergines, without thinking about how familiar I was being. Inappropriately familiar, I worried afterwards, but at the time it just seemed the natural thing to do. I hadn't been cooking much for myself, and it felt good to be in a warm, light kitchen. Sophie had opened the door to me and was slouching on a stool at the tiny breakfast bar. I tossed her a couple of peppers. 'You could chop those up, Sophie.'

She fumbled the peppers, looking surprised, but got up to get a knife without objection. Drew looked at her and then at me. 'I can't invite you round for supper and let you make own meal.'

'Pour me a glass of wine and we'll be quits.'

'That I can do.' He had wrenched off the tie he had worn

to the funeral, and with his shirt sleeves rolled above his wrists he looked relaxed and much younger than he had seemed that first night. There was a luxurious pop as the cork came out, and Drew lifted the bottle to his nose, grunting in satisfaction. 'Opening a screwtop just isn't the same,' he said.

He poured the wine into two glasses, and my hands stilled as I watched him. Time slowed and I braced myself against the tug of the past, but it turned into one of those intense, inexplicable moments when all your senses are heightened and everything seems to be happening in slow motion.

I heard the unhurried glugging from the bottle, saw the leisurely swirl of the wine in the glasses, the rich ruby colour of it. I could smell the wine and garlic and feel the weight of the knife in my hand. When I looked down, I was dazzled by the purple shininess of the aubergines, the redness of the tomatoes, the greenness of the courgettes, piled like jewels on the chopping board. It was as if I'd never seen vegetables before, and I stared at them, feeling time begin to spiral.

'Here.' Drew's voice startled me back to the present. He was holding out one of the glasses, and my hand was unsteady as I put my smile back in place and accepted it.

'Thanks.'

Drew didn't let go immediately. 'You okay?' He looked at me searchingly and I automatically brightened my smile.

'Yes, sure. Why?'

'You looked a bit strange there for a moment.'

'Did I? I'm just spaced out, I guess, with the funeral and everything.'

I picked up the knife once more. The strangeness of the aubergines had evaporated and they were once more ordinary vegetables that I'd cooked with a thousand times.

'At least it's over now,' I said, 'and I feel as if I've done right by Lucy, which is the main thing. She would have approved, don't you think, Sophie?'

Sophie nodded. Her head was bent over the peppers, which she was cutting up very slowly and precisely. 'I still miss her,' she said, and her voice cracked. Hers had been the only tears at the ceremony. 'I still don't understand why Lucy went to the river,' she burst out. 'If she hadn't done that, she wouldn't have died. What was she doing down there?'

'I don't know,' I said, feeling helpless. Feeling as if I ought to know. 'Lucy's solicitor told me there'd been an inquest and that it had returned an open verdict.' Knife in one hand, I lifted my glass with the other and took a sip as I looked at Drew. 'What does that mean?'

'That the police found no evidence to suggest either that it was suicide or that foul play was involved.'

'Basically, nobody knows?'

'There isn't always an answer, Grace. You both have to accept that you're never going to know exactly what happened to Lucy.'

I frowned down into my glass. 'That feels wrong.'

'You were the one who said the other day that the past is past,' Drew said. 'You can't change it.'

'And *you* said that we should try and understand it,' I countered, and his expression relaxed into one of those tantalizing almost-smiles.

'Touché. I was thinking about history generally. Look, it's not as if Lucy's death was brushed under the carpet. The police investigated. They will have talked to her friends. They talked to *us*.'

'I *told* them Lucy would never have gone near the river on her own,' said Sophie, 'but they didn't listen to me.'

'Because there's no evidence that her death was anything but a tragic accident,' said Drew firmly. 'Lucy's dead, and nothing's going to change that.'

'She's not really dead, anyway,' said Sophie.

My mind twitched so violently that I actually flinched. I put down my glass.

'What do you mean, she's not really dead?'

'She'll be reborn sometime, somewhere. It's part of the cycle. Lucy had lived before.' Sophie sounded absolutely certain. 'She told me about it. That's why I know she wouldn't have committed suicide. She was afraid of water,' she said. 'She said she had drowned in her past life. She wasn't afraid of dying, but she didn't want to drown. She said it's a horrible way to die.'

I pulled a tomato towards me. 'Yes,' I said, thinking of the tsunami. Of the agonizing pain in the lungs, the pressure in the ears. Of not being able to breathe, and of the horror clogging the mind. 'Yes, it is.'

Quickly I chopped up the tomatoes and scraped all the vegetables into a roasting tray. Slugging olive oil over it all, I stirred them around and thought about what Sophie had told me. Lucy, she said, had drowned in a past life. Was it possible that Lucy had dreamt of Hawise too? My mind tiptoed up to the idea, only to veer away at the last minute like a horse spooked at the edge of an abyss.

'I don't suppose historians have much time for the idea of past lives?' I said to Drew. 'It would be interesting if accounts of regression were true, though, don't you think? You'd think historians, of all people, would want to know what life was really like in the past.'

'Historians are only interested in evidence,' said Drew, bringing the bottle over to top up my glass. 'There's no evidence that any of the cases of people supposedly remembering past lives actually took place.'

'Then how do you explain the detail they recall?' Sophie hunched a truculent shoulder. 'They know things they couldn't possibly have known otherwise.'

'If you look at documented cases of so-called regression, you can nearly always make an argument for recovered memory,' said Drew, and I looked up from the roasting tray.

'Recovered memory? What's that?'

'The brain is an extraordinary thing. It takes in a huge amount of information every day. The mind can't cope with it all at once, so it files it away. Those details you talk about, Sophie, usually turn out to have been in a play heard on the radio, or read in a book, that the person has long forgotten. Or they remember a place they think they've been to before, but in fact were taken as a small child.'

Was that why York was so familiar? I wondered. Was it possible that my parents had brought me here, before Lucy ever thought about moving to York? My father had remarried and was living in New Zealand. I could email and ask him. He might remember.

'If you think about it,' said Drew, 'the mind's capacity to recall details it learnt years ago is just as incredible as the idea of reliving a past life.'

I could see that Sophie wasn't impressed by that argument, but I was ready to be convinced. It did make sense. A lot more sense than messages circulating through time. I could easily have seen a film or a television programme set in Elizabethan York featuring a maidservant called Hawise and a missing child called Bess. I'd obviously just forgotten about it.

What about the apples? Doubt niggled in my mind, but I brushed it aside. Lucy had had a fondness for apples and had left them in odd places around the house – that was all.

'That was a lot better than anything I could ever cook,' said Drew later. He tipped the dregs of the bottle into my glass. 'Are you sure you don't want to give up teaching English and come and cook for us instead?'

'Oh, yes, *please*,' said Sophie with such a heartfelt look that I couldn't help laughing. 'Dad's so crap at cooking. He even makes a mess of ready-made meals.'

'Hey!' Drew hooked an arm around her neck and rubbed her hair until she squealed. 'I'm not that bad.'

I liked seeing Sophie lose her sullenness. 'I love cooking,' I said, resting my arms on the table, while she made a big to-do about straightening her hair. She was smiling, though. 'In my next life I'll be a chef, I think.'

'Why not in this one?'

'Oh . . . because having a restaurant of your own means settling down, and I don't do that. My feet are too itchy.'

Drew tipped back in his chair and regarded me thoughtfully. 'Don't you ever get tired of travelling?'

'Honestly? Sometimes,' I said, 'but when I think about stopping, about making a home and acquiring more stuff than I can carry, I get all panicky.'

'So you won't be staying in York?' Sophie looked disappointed.

'No,' I said after a tiny pause. 'Just until I've sold Lucy's house.'

Sophie looked at me, then at her father. 'Pity,' she said.

I didn't want to leave, but we'd drunk the wine and cleared up. Sophie went upstairs to do her homework. 'Fancy some coffee?' Drew asked.

I really wanted to say yes. I wanted to sit on at his table, listening to him talk about his research and watching his face, but because I wanted it so badly, I said no.

There was no point in getting involved. Getting involved meant getting close and talking about your emotions and sharing how you felt. The very idea of it seemed like standing on the edge of a crumbling cliff. The moment I felt the urge to look over the top and see what it would be like, I would scuttle backwards.

I said an abrupt goodbye and told myself I'd made the right decision, but when I got back to Lucy's house I couldn't settle. At Drew's I had been relaxed, but the moment I walked through the door of Lucy's house my nerves started jangling.

I kept thinking about Vivien Price and the look in her eyes. *There is violence here, and hate and fear.*

Irritably I pushed the memory away. Vivien was just playing up to her priestess role. Drew was right – those hallucinations were simply recovered memory, a private rerunning of some film I had once seen and had forgotten. Nothing else made sense.

I drew the curtains against the dreary night. It was cold, but not cold enough to put the heating on, so I lit the candles on the mantelpiece to make the room look cosy. I wanted company, but when I opened the laptop and tried to Skype Mel, the screen kept going blank and the connection would cut. I tried switching it on and off a couple of times, but it didn't make any difference, and in the end I gave up and threw myself back on the sofa. Holding onto my pendant, I stared morosely at the candle flames as they dipped and swayed in a perfect synchronized dance with their reflections.

The spell of fine weather has broken at last. It is warm still, but it has been raining for three days and the hall is dark and gloomy as I carry a jug of spiced wine through to the parlour. This is my favourite room, especially like it is now, when it is ablaze with the best wax candles, and I pause in the doorway, my eye caught by their flickering light. I love the rich colours of the carpets on the cupboards, of the embroidered silk cushions and the painted cloths hanging against the wainscot. They make the room cheerful even on an evening like this. There is a flowerpot full of daisies on the cupboard under the window, and the silver plate on the other chest gleams in the candlelight.

It's not nearly cold enough for a fire, but Mr Beckwith and his guests are clustered in front of the empty fireplace, as if wishing they could lift their robes and warm their backsides as they do in the winter.

The jug in my hand jerks in surprise when I see my father standing there with Mr Hilliard, and the warm wine slops over the rim onto the rushes. My mistress is sitting on the turned chair and she sucks in her teeth at my carelessness. Biting my lip, I carry the jug over to the table where the goblets are waiting.

Mr Beckwith, a choleric man, is holding forth about his favourite topic of the moment, the worrying increase in the number of carriages trying to enter the city.

'The world runs on wheels these days,' he grumbles as I pour the wine. 'I saw it in London and now it's the same here. Any upstart, it seems, can set himself up as a gentleman and ride in a carriage, though his parents were glad to go on foot. And what is the result?' he demands, taking the goblet that I hand him with a grunt of acknowledgement. 'The pavement ruined by carriage wheels, and we have to knock down our stalls and posts so they can pass!'

I have heard all this before. I suspect Ned Hilliard has too, but he is listening courteously and saying little, as is his wont. Standing next to my father, the contrast between the two men is startling. Mr Hilliard is serious and quiet-faced, while my father is swaying slightly and has a bibulous nose and resentful eyes. Mr Hilliard looks sober and discreet in his velvet gown, while my father's padded doublet is stained and the band at his neck is distinctly grubby. He is making no attempt to hide his boredom at my master's discourse, but he manages a smile for me as I bob a curtsey and hand him his wine.

Mr Beckwith has a red, meaty face like the slabs of beef that hang in the Shambles. 'Where will it end?' he asks. 'They'll be asking us to knock down the bar walls next! Change with the times, they say . . . ' He snorts. 'In my day, I thought myself lucky to have a horse!'

I would never have thought my mistress had anything at all in common with my father, but like him she is doing a poor job of containing her impatience.

'Indeed, Husband, but perhaps we can get back to the matter in hand?' she says, tight-voiced.

The jug is almost empty. I will go and warm some more wine, but as I turn for the door, Mistress Beckwith gets to her feet and beckons to me.

'Leave that, Hawise, and come here. We have been talking about you.'

'Me?' I gape at her until she frowns at me. Recollecting myself, I set the jug on the table and fold my hands at my waist.

'Yes, Mistress,' I try again, eyes demurely downcast.

'We have been discussing your marriage, Daughter,' my father says.

'*Marriage?*' I can't help it. Certain that I must have misheard him, my eyes fly back up to meet his. I wonder if he is mocking me, but he has his thumbs stuck in his belt and is regarding me with a mixture of complacency and speculation as he rocks back on his heels. 'Marriage?' I say again in disbelief. There is no money, I know that, and who would take me without a dowry?

There is only one person I can imagine who would want me, and the sudden sinking of my heart tells me everything I need to know about what I feel for Francis Bewley.

My mind works feverishly. Surely Francis hasn't taken matters into his own hands and sought out my father?

I was flushed and breathless by the time I met Francis that first day, and shy once I had finished apologizing.

He wasn't as handsome or as charming as I had let myself remember. He was stouter, and shorter, but the sleekness was the same. There is something strange about his eyes too. They are shiny like a mirror, so that you can't see anything when you look into them.

After an awkward pause we agreed to go into the orchard and sat together under the apple tree. Hap didn't like it. He kept snarling at Francis. In the end I made him sit on my other side, and I put my hand on him to keep him still, but I could feel him vibrating with tension. Every now and then he let out a low, warning growl, which didn't help the atmosphere.

I was disappointed, I admit it. I didn't think it would be like that. There was an intensity about Francis that made me uneasy.

'I'd better go,' I said at last, and got to my feet, brushing down my skirts. 'My mistress will wonder where I am.'

Francis was on his feet too. 'Say you'll come again.' He tried to take my hand, and Hap leapt for his arm with a snarl. Francis snatched it out of the way just in time, but I saw something shift in his eyes at last.

'I'm sorry,' I stammered. 'He's not usually this protective.'

'Leave him behind next time, hmm?' Francis recovered his composure quickly and was smiling once more.

I hesitated. Our meeting hadn't been as exciting as I had imagined, but how much of that was Hap's fault? Perhaps, I thought hopefully, it would be better next time, when we would be more comfortable together.

'All right,' I said. 'Next time I'll come alone.'

I did, but it wasn't much better, although Francis kissed me when I was leaving.

That wasn't what I was hoping for, either. His lips were moist and very red, and it was over so soon that I scarcely had time to think that I was being kissed at last, before Francis had lifted his head and was begging my pardon. It wasn't awful, it just didn't make me want to smile, the way Alice had smiled when told me she and John Wightman were betrothed and had *done it*.

But what do I know? Perhaps Francis was disappointed in *me*. I have so little experience, I don't know what I am supposed to do. I assumed that it was my fault. If I had a bit more experience, I would know how to make him kiss me again, perhaps.

The trouble is that I don't really want him to kiss me. I realize that now. I don't want him as my sweetheart. I wanted him to tell me about London, I wanted him to make me laugh and gasp with stories of the places he had seen and the things he had done, but he just talked about himself instead. I wanted a friend.

I was reluctant to go back for a third meeting, but Francis was so insistent, and I didn't know how to refuse. I told myself that he would be going back to London, and that would save me from saying anything. Sick or not, surely his master must return soon?

I have to face it: I was a fool. I wanted a sweetheart, and when Francis showed an interest in me, I thought it could be him. I made him up, and it turned out that he is not the way I invented him at all. My mistake.

He is full of bombast, as puffed up as his doublet, and his stories make me uneasy. They don't quite match up. Once he said that his master was cruel, the next time that he was sick and like to die, and had promised to bequeath Francis all his goods.

'Then I will be able to marry,' he said the last time we met, and he looked at me meaningfully.

What if he has spoken to my father, to my master, already? And what if they have said yes?

My throat is dry. 'Marriage?' I say again now, and my voice is thin and scratchy. 'Who with?'

There is an awkward pause. I see my father look to his right. My mistress smiles and inclines her head in the same direction. Still uncomprehending, I follow their gazes to where Edward Hilliard is standing next to my master. He meets my eyes gravely as my jaw sags.

'If you are willing,' he says.

Chapter Six

'Say I wanted to find out if someone existed in the past,' I said to Drew, carefully casual. 'How would I go about it?'

My bare feet were tucked up beneath me as I balanced a glass of Pinot Grigio on the arm of a chair in his study. We had met at our front gates. I was laden with books, he with Sainsbury's bags.

'You look tired,' Drew said.

'I teach until seven on Tuesdays. It's always a long day.'

I didn't tell him how badly I was sleeping. I was tense when I went to bed, afraid that if I gave up consciousness, Hawise would be back. I kept dropping off, then jerking myself awake, heart pounding with relief to find myself still in the twenty-first century.

I hadn't . . . what was the word? slipped? tipped? . . . plunged back into Hawise's life since I stood there gaping at Ned Hilliard's marriage proposal, but I could feel her tugging at my mind, desperate to draw me back. I didn't want to go. I might be intrigued by her story, and fascinated by seeing Elizabethan life through her eyes, but I was frightened too by the sheer intensity of the experience.

I clung still to Drew's idea of recovered memory, but it was wearing thin. It was increasingly hard to accept that a random memory could account for the frightening intensity of my experiences as Hawise. When I thought about films I had seen or books I had read, I remembered atmosphere. I remembered the story, the *feel* of it. I didn't know how thin and sour the wine tasted. I didn't smell the freshly woven rush mats on the floor, the way their sweetness drifted on the air as I crushed them beneath my feet and mingled with the scent of camomile and fleabane strewn among them. I didn't feel the slight bump in the glaze of the jug's handle. I might have remembered the clang of the church bells that punctuated the day, and I could easily have remembered what a gown looked like on the screen, but taste and smell and feel . . . how could I remember those in such startling detail from having watched a film?

But I was resisting the alternative. I didn't want to be possessed. The very word made me sweat. Possession meant control, and the thought of anyone playing around with the mind I kept so carefully guarded was horrific. I couldn't bear it when boyfriends tried to get too close, let alone a girl who had been dead for a good four hundred years – if she had ever existed at all.

'Come and have a drink,' Drew had said, shifting all his bags into one hand so that he could manoeuvre the key into the lock. 'I could do with one.'

It was the opportunity I had been waiting for. I was tired of Hawise probing relentlessly at my mind the moment I let my guard down. It was fine when I was teaching, but sometimes when I walked along the streets the air would waver and the thin veil between this time and that would billow seductively. I learnt to steel myself, to fix my attention on the present: something plastic, something electronic.

It was time to take back control, I'd decided. I would approach the problem rationally, and the first thing was to establish whether or not Hawise was real. If there was no evidence that any of the story unfolding in my head was true, then I would have to accept that she was a figment of my imagination. I wasn't sure which I wanted her to be: a ghost, or a symptom that I was losing my grip on reality. Either way, I would know what I was dealing with.

I'd googled what I could about Elizabethan York, but that didn't get me very far. The library was my next step, but it seemed ridiculous not to make use of a specialist on my doorstep before that, especially when I didn't understand enough to know what I was looking for. I'd broached the subject carefully, knowing already that Drew wouldn't have any time for wild tales of ghosts or time-travelling.

'It depends on the period, for a start.' Drew pushed up his glasses and pinched the bridge of his nose as he considered my question. He looked tired too. 'It depends on where you are, and it depends on what kind of someone you're talking about.'

'A girl,' I said. I kept my eyes on my wine, running a finger round and round the rim of the glass. 'A servant.' I thought about the clothes Hawise wore, about Francis Bewley sweeping a bow as if to the Queen's Majesty herself. I couldn't remember if there had been anything to indicate a specific date. 'Say in Elizabethan York.' It felt right. Beyond that, I couldn't say.

'It wouldn't be easy,' said Drew. 'Not all the records for that period survive. You'd have to be very lucky to be able to trace an individual, especially a girl.'

'Why? Because servants weren't important?'

It was what he would expect me to say, but Drew didn't rise to the bait. 'Actually, at that period service was a part of almost everyone's life. Even noble families sent their children to be servants in other households. Servants were part of the family,' he said. 'That was the way young people learnt how to behave, how they learnt a trade, how they made connections that would stand them in good stead later in life. A girl in service in a well-to-do urban household would learn how to run a household, how to cook, how to sew, how to treat everyday ailments. She worked *with* her mistress, rather than *for* her.'

I nodded, remembering Mistress Beckwith, and the firmness with which she had run her household. My mistress – *Hawise's* mistress – had worked just as hard as anyone else. She would have been agog at the notion that she might sit and eat sweetmeats while her servants waited on her hand and foot. So at least my sense of Hawise's role in the Beckwiths' house was consistent with historical fact, but it didn't get me any closer to proving whether or not Hawise herself had really existed.

'Why do you want to know all this anyway?' asked Drew, eyes narrowed, and I looked away.

'Oh . . . ' I said vaguely. 'I was just wondering what you would do if you wanted to find out about someone who wasn't famous, that's all.'

I could tell he was still puzzled. 'It would help to know the parish where she died, whether or not she married, that kind of thing. You might be lucky and find a will in which she's mentioned. Members of the civic elite are more likely to be in the council records – those do survive – but you usually only come across other individuals if they break the law in some way. The records I'm working on at the moment are an exception to that.'

I made one of those noises that mean 'Go on, I'm listening'. I taught a range of noises like that to my students. If you can use your ums and ers correctly, you sound much more fluent.

'The wardmote courts were local courts that enforced environmental regulation,' he said, unconsciously slipping into lecture mode. 'They were held twice a year, around Easter and Michaelmas, and they dealt with ordinary people and ordinary concerns: who's mending the streets, who's not disposing of their waste correctly, who's a noisy neighbour, and so on. Householders are listed, along with an order to, say, pave the street in front of their doors, or clean the gutter; and they would have to pay a fine if they hadn't complied by the following court – although most of them did.'

'So what are you saying?' I leant forward, frowning with concentration. 'Do you think I might be able to find . . . my servant girl . . . in your records?'

'Very doubtful,' said Drew. 'For a start, only a decade or so of these records survive, so unless you've got a very specific date in mind, you'd have to be very lucky to find one individual. The vast majority of those mentioned are men too. There were some female householders – usually widows – but the few women mentioned are either presented for antisocial behaviour of some kind or for breaking petty market regulations. Even then, they're usually referred to as someone's wife. If your servant girl is respectable, you won't find her in these records.'

I was disappointed. It didn't sound as if Drew could help me after all. I sat, chewing the edge of my thumb, wondering if I could at least ask him to search his records for Mr Beckwith or Ned Hilliard, but I didn't know how to do that without telling him about Hawise, and I had no idea how to do *that* without sounding completely mad.

Drew's unnervingly keen eyes were still fixed on my face. 'What's all this about, Grace?'

'Nothing,' I said. 'At least . . . No, nothing.' Of course I couldn't tell him. Drew was a *historian*. He was sane, he was rational. He didn't believe in ghosts or reincarnation or regression.

And neither did I. Not really.

'Where's Sophie?' I decided it was time to change the subject before Drew started asking too many searching questions that I wasn't ready to answer. That I *couldn't* answer.

'God knows,' said Drew with a sigh. 'She stomped off earlier. Apparently I am selfish, controlling, completely extra – whatever that means, but it's not good – stupid, uncaring and . . . I forget the other thing. Basically, I'm a bad father.'

'Oh, dear,' I said. 'What did you do?'

'Asked her where she was going. More fool me.'

He sounded so defeated, I had to fight an absurd urge to put a comforting hand on his shoulder.

'Is she still with that group she talked about?'

'The Temple of the Waters.' Taking off his glasses, Drew nodded and rubbed his hand wearily over his face. 'She spends all her spare time with them now – at least when she's supposed to be with me. It's harder when she's staying with her mother out in the village, but Karen says she's always down by the river, performing little ceremonies. She's worried about Sophie too, but what can we do? Sophie's fifteen. We can't lock her in her room.'

I thought about Vivien's warning. *Not all spirits are good spirits or safe spirits*, she had said. There was no point in telling Drew that. He was worried enough as it was.

'It's difficult,' I said sympathetically. 'I can see why you're concerned. I don't suppose there's much I can do, but if I can help . . . ' I trailed off, feeling useless. What could *I* do, after all? When was I ever a help when it really mattered? Lucas's face flashed into my mind, and I closed my eyes against it.

'Actually, there *is* something,' said Drew and my eyes snapped open. 'I know it's a lot to ask,' he said, unusually hesitant, 'but would you go out with her sometime? Have coffee or go to a film or something?'

'Me?'

'Sophie likes you. She thinks you're cool.'

I was fascinated by the way he could smile without curving

his lips. I couldn't decide whether his eyes were blue-grey or grey-blue, but they gleamed in a way that set a little tingle tingling inside me, while the warmth spread outwards, deepening the creases in his face and hovering tantalizingly around his mouth.

I shifted self-consciously, aware all at once of the Toda earrings dangling against my neck and the jade pendant at my throat. I'd pulled back my hair and clipped it up with a beaded comb before I went out to teach, but as always by that time of the day most of it was falling messily around my face.

I pushed it behind my ears as I glanced down at the crinkled silk tunic I'd bought from a charity shop for a couple of pounds. With it I wore a vintage waistcoat that had been an even better bargain, at fifty pence, perhaps because it had two buttons missing. As an outfit, it was cheap and comfortable, but . . . cool?

'I don't feel very cool,' I said.

'To someone like Sophie, you're exotic,' Drew said.

I couldn't help laughing. 'You make me sound exciting!'

'You *are* exciting,' he said.

His voice was quite level, but when his eyes met mine, there was a sudden, perilous silence. I was the first to look away, uncomfortably aware that my cheeks were hot.

'You've got a confidence that she can't imagine having in a million years, right now,' Drew said as if the moment had never happened. Had he even noticed? I wondered. Or had I imagined it, like I was imagining so much else right now?

'I just think that if you told her about your travels, about working in Indonesia, she'd be interested and flattered by your attention.'

'I can hardly invite her in and then bore her to death by telling her about where I've been!' I protested.

'I can't imagine you being boring,' he said. He leant forward, fixing that acute gaze on my face. 'Please, Grace,' he said. 'I'm at my wits' end with Sophie. Her mother and I are too conventional, and too close to her to have any influence at the moment. She's lonely and she's looking for a role model. I'd rather it was you than Ash.'

'Ash?'

'Ash Vaughan.' Drew sat back. 'He was a student of mine once – one of those who are a little too clever for their own good. He dropped out in the end, and I for one wasn't sorry to see him go. But the next thing I heard of him, he was leading this cult that Sophie's got herself tangled up in. The "Temple of the Waters".' Drew practically spat out the name. 'It's a load of bollocks, but try telling Sophie that.'

I chewed my thumb. I'd offered to help, and I meant it, but I didn't want Drew thinking that he could rely on me. I didn't want to let him down, the way I had let Lucas down. Guilt rolled through me as the memory spun in its familiar cracked groove.

Practical things – those I could do, but be a role model? Drew could hardly have picked on anyone less suited to the task!

Look out for Sophie. Vivien's words stopped the record that played so relentlessly in my head, and I thought again about what she had said about Drew's daughter. I didn't like the idea of Sophie being led astray. She reminded me too much of myself at fifteen.

And Drew was sitting there, watching me with quiet desperation in his eyes. He wasn't asking me to save Sophie, I realized, just spend a bit of time with her. A coffee, a film, that was all. Neither was a great commitment, and I had offered to help.

'I don't think I'd be much of a role model,' I said, 'but I'll try.'

Clouds brooded in the distance as I sat down to write my lesson plans for the following week. It was unseasonably warm for that early in May, and I had all the windows wide open to air the house while I could. No matter how often I cleaned it, I couldn't get rid of that faint whiff of rotting fruit.

I cleared a space for my laptop on Lucy's desk. I'd avoided her study up to that point, unable to face making sense of her paperwork. God only knows how she ever found anything. As far as I could see, her filing system amounted to little more than throwing everything on the desk, which was covered with papers and books and bills. I had to push them into a tottering pile to make room for my computer.

While I waited for it to boot up, I looked down at the back yards below. Sophie had gone back to her mother's, I knew, and Drew was out. I'd knocked on his door as I passed on my way home, to suggest a Friday-night drink, but there had been no answer. I wondered where he was.

Not that I cared. I was leaving soon anyway.

Drew's garden was hidden by the extension, but I could see into the yard that matched Lucy's on the other side. The neighbours there had evidently decided to make the most of the unexpected warmth and were celebrating the weekend with a barbecue with friends. Someone was telling a funny story, but I couldn't catch any details. There would be a great whoop of laughter and, just when it was tailing off, the storyteller would say something else and they'd be off again, until they were breathless and gasping with it.

I smiled, but maybe I was feeling a little wistful. It felt like a long time since I had laughed like that, laughed until my stomach hurt. Nobody likes to admit that they're lonely. There seems to be something shameful about it, although I know that's stupid. I'd always prided myself on my independence, but that evening, yes, I was lonely, and I thought about Hawise and how much she had missed her friend Elizabeth.

The computer screen was glowing expectantly. Pushing Hawise from my head, I clicked to bring up a new document and typed *Past Continuous*. Then I stopped to twist up my hair and fasten it with a clip. Down below, the laughter was getting more hysterical. It was starting to get on my nerves.

Setting my fingers back on the keyboard, I wrote: *Uses of the past continuous. 1: An ongoing action interrupted by a single event. E.g. What were you doing when you heard about . . . ?* Disasters were good to practise that exercise: 9/11, earthquakes, Princess Di's sudden death – any number of terrible events burnt into the collective memory.

I was walking back to the room when the tsunami struck.

I typed instead: *I was watching television when the telephone rang.*

I couldn't concentrate. There were no apples in sight, but the odour of a wet autumn orchard clung to the inside of my nostrils. In spite of the heat, the air was taut. I kept thinking of a bow being drawn back, of gut and muscle quivering with strain. I looked over my shoulder. The room was empty.

Of course it was.

I forced my eyes to focus on the screen. *2: Action interrupted by specific time. E.g. This time last year I was working in Jakarta.*

On Christmas Day I was digging on the beach with Lucas.

It was very close. I wiped the sweat from the back of my neck.

3: Parallel actions, I typed. *Two actions in the past happening at the same time. E.g.*

I stopped. I couldn't think of a sensible example.

While I was holding onto the rail, Lucas was drowning.

I could feel the room crowding in behind me. I didn't want to look round again. I knew there was nothing there, but still I found myself holding my breath.

Music thumped from an open window further along the street, and in the distance a siren whooped and wailed a warning.

'*Bess* . . .'

The name rippled out of nowhere, brushing against my cheek like a breath, and I sucked in a scream as I swung round, dislodging a file and sending a whole sheaf of papers cascading to the floor.

Of course there was no one there.

My heart was knocking painfully against my ribs as I turned back to the table, and I nearly screamed again when I saw what had been lurking under the file I knocked aside.

An apple squatted there like a malign slug, fat and soggy and suppurating with mould. It was the kind of apple you find in the long grass under a tree, its crisp outline sagging as its skin puckers and browns and it rots from within. I stared at it, my breath coming in staccato puffs, my mouth open to avoid breathing in its putrid stench. There was something malevolent about it, a wrongness that made the air around it thicken and waver.

The apples I'd found around the house had been creepy, but this . . . this was something else. I couldn't bear to pick it up. I had to find a dustpan and brush in order to carry it down to the wheelie bin in the front garden. I didn't know what else to do, and at least then it would be out of the house. Gagging with revulsion, I threw it in and let the lid smack back into place.

My hands were shaking as I made my way back to Lucy's desk. In the garden below the funny story had finally come to an end, but the party was still going strong. Glasses were being refilled, jokes told. I watched them for a while, longing to be able to join them. I could tell them how frightened I'd been by an apple, and we would all laugh together.

Beyond the back yards and rooftops the clouds were massing ominously, but the air was still warm with the scents of summer. They must have finished the barbecue, because all I could smell was long grass, dusty tracks and the drowsy sweetness of newly mown hay.

Which was odd, because it was only May.

The computer was thrumming quietly on the edge of the desk. Its screensaver turned endlessly, serenely, mocking my jitters, but the air was still snapping and trembling about me, and when I turned back to clear the papers, I saw the stain where the apple had sat on a sheet of scrawled notes and I shuddered.

Snatching up the paper, I scrumpled it up and was about to throw it in the wastepaper basket when something made me stop and unfold it slowly. I stared down at Lucy's writing, black and loopy and almost illegible. Between all the heavy under-linings and arrows and question marks, I made out a couple of dates – 1577 and 1583 – and a scribble that looked as if it might be 'Bess'. But there was no mistaking one word. There, circled in the middle of the page, Lucy had printed in capitals: HAWISE.

Gnawing my thumb, I sat and stared at the name until it shimmered in front of my eyes.

I am waiting for Francis and nibbling at my thumb. I do this when I am nervous, even though Mistress Beckwith scolds me for it. Thinking of my mistress, I drop my hand. For years she has been telling me not to fidget or laugh too loudly or ask too many questions. I must be quiet and modest and discreet, she tells me. I wish now that I had heeded her advice. Then I wouldn't be standing in this orchard, wondering what I am going to say to Francis.

Well, it is too late for that. I straighten my shoulders. I wasn't modest and I wasn't discreet, and now I must deal with the consequences. At least, I think, my betrothal is an excuse not to meet Francis any more, but I need to tell him myself. I owe him that. He will hear about it in the street otherwise, and that would be unfair to him.

I don't want to see him again, but I don't want to hurt him. All he has done is not be the man I wanted him to be. That is not his fault – it is mine.

The long grass is wet after all the rain, and the guards on my skirt are already sodden. It is not actually raining now, but I am standing in the meagre shelter of the apple tree and the air is so damp that moisture clings to my face.

'Good day, my lady,' Francis says when he arrives, and he bows with the flourish that so delighted me the first time I saw it. Now I can't help thinking that it looks faintly ridiculous. I am not a queen, after all. I am not even a lady. I am just a foolish maid who forgot everything her mistress taught her.

'Good day to you, Francis.' I smile nervously. He is so intense that he smothers what little lightness there is in the air, and when he seizes my hands I pull them away instinctively.

He barely seems to notice. 'I have bought you a gift, Hawise. Look!' From his pocket he pulls a pair of silk gloves, embroidered with tiny flowers and bees. A lover's gift.

I moisten my lips. 'They are very fine, Francis, but I cannot accept them.'

'Oh, why so shy?' He smiles, pressing the gloves into my hand even as I push them back at him. 'They are a token of my love for you.'

'No, Francis. Stop!'

He doesn't like that. His brow darkens. 'I want you to have them,' he says, sounding like a petulant child.

'I can't,' I say, and something in his face makes me take a step back. 'I only came today because there is something I must tell you.' I draw a breath. 'I am betrothed.'

He laughs at that. 'Impossible!'

'It's true. I'm sorry, Francis, I didn't know . . . ' I trail off at the expression in his eyes. 'Last night was the first I'd heard of it.'

'Why didn't you say that you were promised to me?' He is standing there, staring at me, while he twists the gloves tighter and tighter and tighter in his hands.

He had never even mentioned love. Two brief kisses . . . How could he even think of it? 'I'm not. I never made you a promise, Francis. You know that.'

Francis tosses the poor mangled gloves aside and grabs my hands again. 'Promise me now,' he says, his voice throbbing with urgency.

'Francis, I can't.' I thought it would be a courtesy to tell him about my betrothal, but now I am wishing I hadn't come. With some difficulty I tug my fingers from his. 'I would lose the good-will of my family and friends.'

'Do they mean more to you than I do?'

He asks it almost jovially, as if confident that I will say no. I stare at him uneasily. It is as if he has been in a different orchard, a different world, those times we met. Doesn't he re-member the stiffness of the conversation, the awkwardness of our kisses? There were no promises, no words of love.

His green eyes glitter with delusion and I am afraid. He is not rational.

'My master and mistress have been good to me,' I say carefully.

Francis brushes that aside. 'They love you. They would forgive you.'

'It would shame them.' I pause, wondering how to make him understand. 'Mr Hilliard is a wealthy merchant, a member of the guild. The match reflects well on the Beckwiths. I would not have such an opportunity if it were not for them. They are well pleased, as is my father.'

As well he might be, I reflect with some bitterness. It seems that Ned Hilliard is prepared to take me even without a portion, and my father is rubbing his hands in the expectation of having all his debts paid so that he can gamble some more. Everyone is delighted at the betrothal.

Everyone except me. But nobody asks me what I want. Nobody thinks what it is like for me to find myself betrothed to a man almost twice my age.

It seems I have explained too well. Francis's expression has turned ugly. 'A wealthy merchant!' He spits out the words. 'I see. So I am not good enough for you in fact?'

'Francis . . . ' I feel helpless. 'This is the way of the world. You, of all people, must know how things are.'

He pounces on that. 'I, of all people? What do you mean by that?'

'You told me that you have to make your own way in the

world. You are dependent on pleasing your master. You said that you have little money.'

'Now I have none, but it won't always be that way, Hawise. My master is sick.' Francis's face lights up with an eagerness that makes me recoil. 'I have completed my apprenticeship. He has promised me his house and his goods when he dies, and it cannot be long. I will see to it. Will I be good enough for you then?'

I will see to it.

I am horrified. More than ever I think there is something wrong about Francis's eyes. 'It wouldn't make any difference,' I manage through numb lips.

'It would be enough. And the Beckwiths are kind to you.' Francis is pacing through the long grass. 'Everyone says you are their pet. You will inherit everything from them. We will have plenty of money then.'

'I, inherit?' My horror turns to astonishment. 'Who told you that? The Beckwiths have married daughters of their own. They have grandchildren. There will be no money for me, and nor should there be. Already I owe them more than I can say. No, Francis,' I say, shaking my head. 'I have nothing save a father burdened with debts. I cannot whistle a wealthy merchant down the wind,' I add bitterly. 'I had no choice, Francis. I had to agree.'

It was done. I had made my promise in front of witnesses, and when Ned Hilliard touched his mouth to mine, his lips were cool and firm. It cannot be undone now.

'But you love *me*!' Francis swings round aggressively, and

his words beat at me like staves, but I stand firm. I am shaking inside, but I lift my chin and look him straight in the eyes.

'No, Francis, I don't.'

'You kissed me,' he reminds me, advancing on me, and I back away until I am pressed right up against the apple tree. I can feel the roughness of the bark, the dampness of the green-grey lichen, the squelchiness of the rotting apple I stepped in. The smell of it fills my nostrils, mingling with the odour of wet grass and the high, rank nettles that clog the orchard. I remember how eagerly I once hurried to this place, and I marvel at myself.

'I . . . I'm sorry,' I stutter.

'You kissed me,' Francis says again, his eyes blank and green. 'You led me on. You little whore!'

'Francis!' I am so shocked I don't know what to say.

He keeps on coming, and I can see the spittle at the corners of his red mouth. 'You thought to make a fool of me, did you?'

'No!'

'You were just amusing yourself with me before you got married to your fat merchant, hmm?'

'I didn't know about Ned until yesterday,' I protest, but that only inflames Francis further.

'Oh, it's Ned now, is it? It was Mr Hilliard before, but perhaps you have remembered now that he has rutted with you? What did it cost him? More than the price of a pair of gloves, I warrant!'

I recoil from his crudeness. 'Francis, please . . . '

'Please what?' he practically spits. 'Please crawl back under the stone you came from? Please go away and leave me to my rich husband? Tell me, did you tease his cock the way you teased mine? Did you give him the same smiles that you gave me, leading him on until he was panting like a dog at your knees? I should have seen the Devil in your eyes. I should have known you for what you were – nothing but a hot little harlot!'

'Stop it!' I bring up my hands to push him away, but he grabs my wrists and shoves me back against the tree, so hard that my head thumps against the rough bark and I cry out.

'Betrothed, are you? He has had you, I can tell. You're like a bitch in heat.'

I'm struggling, really frightened now. 'Francis, no!'

'Francis, yes!' he mocks. 'I don't see why I shouldn't have you too. I'm due some recompense for all this time wasted on gentle wooing.'

I twist my face away from his lips as he tries to kiss me roughly. 'Please, Francis, let me go,' I beg. 'I am a maid still, I swear it!'

But that is the wrong thing to say. 'All the better. If I am the first to have you, it is as good as a betrothal, is it not? You can go back to your merchant and tell him that you're mine after all.'

With one part of my mind I am marvelling that there could ever have been a time when the thought that Francis might want to kiss me would have thrilled me. Now the very idea fills me with horror. With the other, I am twisting and turning frantically, disgusted at his attempts to press his spittle-flecked lips to mine.

He has turned into a beast, a monster, and I am desperate to get away from him, but he is so much stronger than me. He manages to pin both my wrists together in one hand and scrapes them viciously against the trunk of the tree while he drags my skirt up with the other and tries to smother my screams with his mouth. His tongue is like a fat, wet slug, shoving between my lips, and I gag at the feel of it. I buck my body against his as I try to push him off me, and at last manage to wrench my mouth from his and spit out the taste of him.

'Before God, leave me alone,' I shout at him and kick frantically at his legs.

'You little bitch!' Francis drags me from the tree and throws me down into the long grass, and I cry out as I fall hard, jarring my bones.

'Stop it. Stop it!' I am flailing at him with my hands, frantic to get him off me, but he only laughs.

'Scream all you want. There's no one to hear you out here. Isn't that why you chose it? Somewhere quiet we could be together, wasn't that right? Somewhere no one would *see*.'

He's lying across my chest, pinning me to the ground as he yanks up my skirts, rips at my shift, his hands cruel. He likes hurting me. I think he likes it that I am fighting him too, but I won't give up. I am twisting like a cat in a sack, cursing and spitting.

'I will tell my master. He will have you strung up from the nearest gibbet!'

'You won't tell him. Then you'd have to tell him that you'd been sneaking off to meet me, and then what would be left of your reputation, hmm? Will your fat merchant want you then? I don't think so.'

His voice is gleeful, but his eyes are terrifyingly blank. He doesn't care, I realize. I can almost hear the rushing in his head, the need to crush me, to hurt me, to destroy me.

'Sweet Jesù, help me!' I cry, but I know there is no one to help as he tears at my sleeves, pulling them from their laces and baring my shoulders while he slobbers at my neck like a hound in heat.

I am so crazed with disgust that I barely notice at first when he pauses and lifts his head to stare down my breast to where it swells above my bodice and a birthmark, shaped like a small, blurry hand, shows red against my white skin.

'What is this?' His voice sharpens.

'Get off me!' I'm beating at him with my fists, but Francis doesn't even register my blows.

'It is the mark of a witch, is it not? The mark of a harlot. By God, I know you for what you are!'

The sight of it prods him into a new frenzy. Now he is fumbling with his hose, throwing his legs over mine to pin them down, grunting obscenities, and I can feel him, horrifyingly stiff and smooth, pushing at my privy parts. The rotten apples squelch beneath me as I squirm desperately to free myself. Their stench is suffocating.

'For God's sake, be still,' he mutters, swiping a blow at my head, and then he is jabbing at me with his fingers.

'No!' I am screaming. 'No, no, no! Jesus, save me!'

But it is not Jesus who saves me. There is a thwack, a thud, and it is Francis's turn to cry out. He rears back from me and I see Widow Dent standing over him with a stout stick.

'She said no.'

Chapter Seven

Widow Dent is only a sparrow of a woman, but her eyes are deep and uncanny, and as she stands over Francis she looks strangely powerful.

Sobbing with relief, I start to scramble away from him, but he grabs my ankle. 'Where are you going?'

'Let go of her.' Widow Dent barely raises her voice, but she lifts her stick.

'Get out of here, you old hag,' he snarls at her. 'This is nothing to do with you.'

I am panting, kicking desperately to rid myself of his hand. 'For God's sake, let *go*, Francis!'

'No,' he says, tightening his fingers and pulling me back towards him. His yard still juts out of his hose, twitching like a grotesque faceless creature, and I shudder at the sight of it.

'Take your hands off her,' Widow Dent tells him, still quiet. 'Or I will curse you. All I need to do is touch you with this stick and I can unman you for the rest of your days. Is that what you want?'

I feel Francis pause. Does he know that Widow Dent is reputed a witch? Is that filtering through his red haze?

'Let her go,' she says again.

His lips curl back exactly the way Hap's do, and I see fear mixed with malevolence in the look he gives her. 'You would not dare!' he says, but he releases my ankle all the same.

'Would I not?' She lifts the stick and points it towards him. 'I can shrivel your balls with one touch, if I choose. Shall we see?'

Under my astonished gaze I see Francis's thing deflating, and Widow Dent laughs as he shoves it hurriedly back in his hose. The expression in his eyes is murderous.

'Witch!' he hisses, making the sign to ward off evil. 'I'll get you.'

'Begone,' she tells him, 'or it won't be just that cock that shrivels!' She shakes the stick at him again and Francis backs away, his eyes darting between me and the widow.

Quite suddenly she lunges for him, and he stumbles back with a yelp of fear. 'Shall I send my familiar to suck your blood? He'll melt your eyeballs and eat your brains. He'll creep in the night and make you itch until you scratch out your own eyes. He'll make you shit blood out your arse.'

But Francis is already running. 'I'll see you in Hell!' he shouts over his shoulder, but the widow only laughs contemptuously as she lowers her stick at last.

'More than likely,' she says.

Overhead there is a rumble of thunder. I am retching and shivering in the grass as a gust of wind lifts my hair and splatters rain against my face.

I blinked at it, and abruptly I was back at Lucy's desk with the rain pounding on the windowsill and the screensaver on my computer twisting and circling silently.

Lightning crackled across the sky and I flinched. The window was still wide open and the rain was splattering over Lucy's papers, half of which had been blown onto the floor, where they lay damp and reproachful. The temperature had dropped dramatically, and I was shivering as I stood to pull the sash window down. I was very cold, and not just because of the rain.

It was a long time since I had had a bath. I was used to sluicing cold water over myself from a *mandi*, and it felt very strange lowering myself into hot water, but my teeth were clacking together so hard that my jaw ached, and I knew I had to get warm.

Lying back in the water, I listened to the rain splattering against the windows, and willed myself to relax, but the harder I tried to empty my mind, the more I churned with memories of that brutal assault in the orchard. The stench of rotting apples clung in my nostrils and I ached all over. I couldn't get the feel of Francis out of my mind – his vicious hands and slobbery tongue, and the violence as he tried to push himself into me.

The memory of it made me gag. Perhaps he hadn't succeeded in raping me completely, but I still felt sick and soiled. I found some soap and a flannel and scrubbed my body vigorously, trying to obliterate the disgust, the fear, the powerlessness, but no matter how hard I rubbed, I couldn't get clean.

Eventually the water grew cold, but I couldn't face getting out, so I leant forward and turned on the hot tap, and let it run while I soaped my arms and shoulders mindlessly. Encountering the familiar texture of my birthmark, I paused and my fingers traced the outline of it unsteadily. Hawise had the same mark, in the same place. *The mark of a witch*. Francis's words echoed around the bathroom and I shuddered.

Why couldn't I stop *thinking*? After the tsunami I'd been able to shut down any thoughts I didn't want. I put them in a box and didn't look at them. I didn't want to rehash the experience endlessly. What was the point in that? It was over. Sometimes, it was true, a memory would prod at the edge of my consciousness and my throat would close with apprehension, but I learnt to deal with the fear. The moment I felt myself start to remember, I would stop. I made myself breathe through it, deliberately blanking my mind until the memory subsided back into the darkness. I was good at it.

But lying there in Lucy's bath, the thought of Francis felt too raw and too vicious to be pushed away easily. Still, I tried. I gritted my teeth and closed my eyes and told myself to breathe.

Don't think, I said to myself. *Just breathe.*

'Breathe,' says the widow as I gasp and retch in the grass. 'Don't think about what happened. Don't think about anything. Just breathe.'

Her voice is strong and I do as I am told, closing my eyes and closing my mind to Francis, and concentrating instead on breathing laboriously – in and out, in and out – until the panic recedes and the awful tightness in my chest begins to relax. I have the strangest feeling that I have done this before, but how could I have done? I have never felt this fear and disgust before, this realization that, for Francis Bewley, I am not a person. I am not Hawise. I am just a thing.

I look up at Sybil Dent with a mixture of fear and gratitude. She must be a witch. I saw with my own eyes what she did to Francis, but if she hadn't been there I would have been lost.

Trembling, I wipe my mouth with the back of my hand. 'Thank you.'

'Are you hurt?'

I realize that my wrists are bleeding and that I'm scratched and bruised. My cheek is aching, and when I touch my throbbing mouth, my fingers come away bloody. Francis's ring must have cut me.

'Less than I would have been if you hadn't come along,' I say.

She nods. 'You can't go back like that. Can you get up?'

My legs are shaking so much I can barely stand, but I haul myself up using the tree for support. Shaking off the pieces of crushed apple staining my skirt, I pull my sleeves back into place as well as I can.

The widow studies me with those strange eyes that seem to know everything about me without me saying a word.

'Come,' she says in her odd, abrupt manner, and turns to shuffle off.

I am afraid to follow her, but afraid not to, and after a moment I follow her to her cottage. It's a lonely place, tucked amongst some trees beyond the crofts, and I can't help remembering all the stories I've heard about witches. Will she make me serve the Devil? I am trembling all over, but right now I think I would prefer Satan himself to Francis Bewley. I can hardly believe how quickly he changed, and when I think about the viciousness in his expression, I could almost believe he *was* the Devil.

I hesitate in the doorway of the cottage. It's a single room, dark and smoky, with just a rough plank table, a couple of stools and a pallet of straw, but the mud floor is swept and tidy.

At a gesture from the widow, I sink down on one of the stools and she fetches a bowl of water with some herbs floating in it: lady's mantle, mint, pennyroyal and rosemary. It smells good, it smells clean, the way rosemary always does, and it comforts me.

The widow's gnarled hands are gentle, a strange contrast to her manner, as she sponges the blood from my hands and face. Afterwards she helps me retie my sleeves and brings me some spiced ale. I drink it under the unblinking yellow gaze of a cat with dark, striking markings.

She is a beautiful creature, and I rub my fingers to beckon her, the way I do to Hap sometimes. After a moment's consideration she comes and inclines her head to let me scratch her chin.

The widow watches me as the cat strops herself against my skirts and I stroke her soft fur. 'What is her name?' I ask.

'Mog.'

'She is very fine.'

'So she thinks.' The widow's unnerving gaze rests on my face. 'You're not frightened of her.'

I shake my head. 'I like cats.' Then I pause, wondering if she is trying to tell me that Mog is her familiar. 'She's not . . . '

Widow Dent smiles mirthlessly. 'She's just a cat,' she says, reading my mind without difficulty. 'Though there's many as would say different.'

I bite my lip. 'I am afraid Francis might try and do you some mischief, if he can.'

'He won't be the first to try. What were you doing with a man like that, girl?'

'I didn't know he was like that.' I keep my eyes on the cat, which is purring now as I run my hand rhythmically along her spine and up to the end of her tail. 'I was a fool.'

'You're not the first, and you won't be the last.'

The widow is shuffling around the little room, poking the fire and stirring a set of little pots that are lined up on the table. I watch her curiously. This isn't how I expected a witch's house to look. I expected demonic figures lurking in the shadows, toads and birds, and piles of terrible entrails. Only the cat, vibrating throatily at every stroke, is as it should be. Widow Dent moves around her home just like my mistress in her dairy.

'Are you really a witch?' I blurt out before I realize what I am saying, and she turns a beady look on me.

'What do you think, girl?'

'I think,' I say slowly, 'that you would be wise not to say.' I hesitate. 'But if you *were* a witch, would you . . . could you make me a spell?'

'*If* I was, that would depend, wouldn't it?'

'I am frightened of what Francis will do now,' I tell her. 'I thought perhaps you could cast a spell to make him forget.'

She shook her head. 'Nothing I could do would work on one such as him.'

'But you made his . . . his thing disappear. I saw it!'

'That wasn't me. That was his fear, and his body. You want to change what's in his head.' She tapped her hood. 'There are some as aren't put together in the head the same as the rest of us, and he's one. He can only see one thing, and if that one thing is you, you'll have to be careful. I can give you a potion to help heal those cuts,' she said, nodding at my wrists, 'but a man like that – no, there's a wrongness to him. I'm not powerful enough to change that. Ask your priest and see if God can change him. The Devil wouldn't want to.'

The cut on my face throbs as I make my way unsteadily along the paths to Monk Bar. I will have to find some way to explain it, but I can't think about anything but the shame roiling in my belly.

It hurts to walk, but somehow I keep my shoulders back and my spine straight. My thighs are bruised where he forced them apart with his knees, and the privy place between my legs is sore, but worse is the way I can still feel his tongue pushing into my mouth, still feel his hands on me and the scrape of bark against my back as he pushed me against the tree. My gown is stained with grass, and the stench of rotten apples that clings to it is making me feel sick. I want to tear the dress off and scour my skin until my hands are as red and as rough as the laundresses in St George's Field. I want to beat and bleach every-where he touched me – the way they beat and bleach the linen until it is clean.

I am not sure I will ever feel clean again.

The clang of the Minster bell rings out over the crofts and garths. I lift my skirts higher and try to hurry. I am late, and Mistress Beckwith will frown and want to know where I have been, why my bodice is stained and split. I cannot tell her the truth: that I am shamed.

And it is all my own fault.

The bell clangs insistently on, louder and louder, until the ringing fills my head and presses against the back of my eyes. Wincing at the pain, I lift my hands to my temples, only to see my fingers turning white and grotesquely wrinkled in front of my eyes, and horror sends my heart lurching into my throat and pushes out a scream.

Screaming, I jerked upright, sending water sloshing over the edge of the bath. The hot-water tap was still running, straight into the overflow. Shakily I leant forward to turn it off and reached for the plug.

Somehow I managed to get out of the bath and wrap myself in a towel. I pressed the back of my hand against my mouth as I slid to the floor and dropped my head between my knees. My hair dripped down my neck and I was shaking. The Minster bells were still ringing in my head, on and on. Why wouldn't they stop?

I don't remember at what point I realized that the ringing came from the doorbell. I tried to ignore it, burying my head under my arms, but whoever was there had their finger on the bell and clearly had no intention of going away, and in the end I struggled to my feet. I was aching all over, and it was all I could do to make it to the front door. Clutching the towel around me, I put it on the safety chain and opened it a crack.

'Who is it?' I croaked.

'It's me, Drew. Open your door! I've been knocking and knocking. There's water pouring down my kitchen wall and you've been screaming . . . What's going on in there?'

I didn't understand what he was talking about. 'Water?' I repeated blankly.

'For Christ's sake, Grace, hurry up!'

Still dazed, I managed to get the door open. Drew stepped inside and I shrank back, remembering Francis, remembering what an angry man could do to me.

'Is that tap still running?' He was about to push past me to the bathroom when he caught sight of my face and stopped in shock. 'Jesus, what happened to you?'

Disorientated, I could do little more than stare at him. 'What . . . ?'

'Your face . . . '

My mouth was sore, I realized, and I lifted a hand to it.

'Grace, what's happened?' said Drew in concern, but I didn't answer him. I turned to look into the mirror above the narrow hall stand. My cheek was bruised and swollen, my lip bleeding where Francis's ring had split it.

There was a great roaring in my head then. My eyes rolled up, and for the first time in my life I fainted dead away.

'Drink that.' Drew thrust a glass into my hand, and it rattled against my teeth as I lifted it obediently to my mouth. I was wrapped in Sophie's bathrobe, a silky purple affair emblazoned with moons and stars, and sitting on Drew's sofa, doing my best to stop shaking.

Drew sat down opposite me. I noticed he had poured himself a stiff brandy too. He probably needed it, after dealing with a flooded kitchen and a naked, bleeding neighbour who had passed out at the sight of her own face. He hadn't been quick enough to catch me as I fell, and I had a nasty graze on my forehead where I had smashed into the radiator on my way down. My head was thumping, my body battered and bruised, and my mind was swirling frantically between that terrible scene in the orchard, the disgusting stench of apples in the bath and the sick realization that I had lost control.

The brandy burnt my throat and settled steadyingly in my stomach.

'Can you talk about it yet?' Drew was watching me, a furrow of anxiety between his brows. 'Did someone attack you?'

In spite of myself, I flinched at the memory of Francis's jabbing fingers. Of the brutal flat of his hand, the smothering weight of his body, the revolting thrust of his tongue. If Widow

Dent hadn't come, he would have raped me there amongst the rotting apples.

My horror must have shown in my expression. 'I think we should call the police,' said Drew gently.

I shook my head as he made to reach for his phone. 'No,' I said. 'There's no point.'

'But you're hurt. They can stop whoever it is doing this to someone else.'

I almost laughed. 'They won't be able to stop Francis, that's for sure.'

'Francis?' His brows snapped together. 'Is this someone you know?'

How did I answer that? I took another slug of brandy. 'In a way.'

'There'll be evidence.' Drew was still convinced that we should call the police.

I didn't know what to do. I couldn't even begin to imagine trying to explain Hawise to a stolid policeman, but I couldn't cope by myself any more, either.

'I'm frightened.' The words were out before I could stop them. I leant forward and put my glass very carefully on the coffee table in front of me. 'Something's happening to me.'

'I can see that, Grace. Who is it? Who's doing this to you?'

'You won't believe me.'

'Tell me anyway.'

So I did. I told him everything, right up until the overflow pipe had leaked into his kitchen, sending him storming out to bang on Lucy's door. My appearance had shocked him out of his anger, but I could tell that he had been pretty pissed off and, when I saw the state of his kitchen wall later, I didn't blame him.

The more I talked, the more unlikely it all sounded. Drew's expression was unreadable, but by the time I reached that desperate scene in the orchard, I was stumbling over my words.

'You don't believe me,' I said flatly at last. I had known that he wouldn't.

'I don't believe you've been reliving the experience of someone who died hundreds of years ago, no,' he said. 'The past is over, Grace. We can't recover it, we can't change it. It's the same for five minutes ago as for five hundred years ago. The past is past.'

'Then how do you explain this?' I asked, touching my puffy lip. My fingers went to the bruise that still throbbed, and I remembered the lash of Francis's hand. 'And this?'

Drew's hesitation was answer enough.

'You think I did it to myself, don't you?'

'You don't think that's a more likely explanation than you slipping between the centuries?'

Of course it was. But how could I make him understand? 'Look, I know how it sounds,' I said with a touch of desperation. 'I've been through all the arguments myself, but it's so *real*, Drew. The smells, the tastes, the textures of things – it's not like a dream.'

'Imagination is a very powerful thing.'

'It's not that powerful,' I said shortly. 'I don't care what you say about recovered memory. There's no way I could know so many details about the period just from reading some mythical book that I've now forgotten.'

I sat forward, cradling the glass in my hands. 'There must be some way to check whether or not Hawise really existed.'

Drew looked tired. 'Grace, we've been through this. It's not possible. From what you've told me, I doubt very much you would find any trace of Hawise' – I could practically hear him putting inverted commas around her name – 'even if I believed that she existed.'

'So you think she's just in my mind?'

Drew hesitated, choosing his words carefully. 'It's obvious you've had a very strange and frightening experience,' he began. 'I'm not denying that for a moment, but—'

'It's not just me,' I broke in, remembering the notes I had found just before I had slipped back to the orchard. 'I think Lucy went through exactly the same thing. How can Hawise be in my head, if she was in Lucy's too?'

'Come on, Grace . . . '

'It's true. I can prove it.' Excited, I leapt to my feet. 'Lucy wrote notes, all about Hawise.'

'Grace—'

'No, I want to show you.' I ran back next door and up to Lucy's study. Drew followed reluctantly. My laptop still sat on the desk, its screen blank and sullen. I scrabbled around the papers scattered around it for the page that I had seen. 'It was here! I read it. It must be somewhere. *There*!' I pounced on one of the pages that the wind had blown onto the floor. Even face-down, I recognized Lucy's emphatic handwriting. 'Look at that.' I shoved it into Drew's hand. 'How do you explain that?'

He looked down at the page for a moment, and then his eyes lifted to mine. 'Explain what?'

Snatching it back, I stared in disbelief. The rain through the window had splattered the page, making the ink run and turning the notes into a mass of grey blots. Where Lucy had written Hawise's name there was only a large smudge.

An unpleasant feeling uncoiled in the pit of my stomach. I looked at Drew, hating the concern in his expression. 'It was *here*! She *wrote* it. She *did*.'

Drew didn't say anything. He just took my arm and steered me back down into Lucy's sitting room. I dropped heavily onto the sofa.

'It was real,' I said, but I could hear the uncertainty in my own voice.

'You need some help, Grace.'

'I'm not crazy!'

'I'm not saying that you are.' His calmness was more frightening than impatience would have been. 'You're the one who said you were frightened,' he reminded me. 'Don't you think it would be a good idea to talk to someone qualified to deal with this kind of thing?'

'You mean a psychiatrist?'

'They might be able to help you.'

'There's nothing wrong with me,' I said in frustration. 'You've seen me. I'm a normal, functioning adult. This thing that's happening – Hawise – it's not in my mind. It isn't. I'm not going to go to a doctor. Next thing I'd know I'd have a "mentally ill" label slapped on me, and no one would ever again believe anything I said. I don't need help,' I told Drew.

He sighed. 'Why do I get the feeling that you say that a lot?'

'Because it's true,' I said. 'I'm thirty-two, I'm independent. I've dealt with worse things than this, and I can manage perfectly well by myself. I know how it must look, but I'm not making this up.'

'And those bruises on your face? That cut?' My eyes slid from his. 'You're hurting yourself, Grace. Wouldn't it be better to get help, and face up to whatever it is that's making you do that? I've got a friend,' he went on when I said nothing. 'A psychiatrist. I could ask her if she would talk to you, if you like. Keep it informal, without going down the GP route just yet.'

Yet. I fingered my sore lip. I was very tired, and battered by Drew's relentless rationality. His explanation did make sense, I could see that, but he hadn't been beaten and nearly raped under the old apple tree. I – Hawise – had been helpless then. I wasn't going to be helpless now. I didn't need Drew murmuring concern to his psychiatrist friend.

'I don't think so, thank you,' I said, getting to my feet. 'Look, I'm sorry about your kitchen. I'll have a look through Lucy's papers tomorrow, I promise, and see if I can find anything about insurance. If not, I'll talk to John Burnand. He said he would be able to advance some money from the estate, if I needed it.'

At the unmistakable signal that I wanted him to go, Drew got up, brushing the issue of the flood damage with a gesture.

'I'm more concerned about you than the kitchen,' he said. 'I don't think you should be alone. Why don't you sleep in Sophie's room tonight?'

I hesitated. Drew's house was warm and light and safe, but I couldn't run round there every time I felt wobbly. I'm independent, I had told him. I didn't like needing anybody else for anything.

'That's kind of you, but you've done enough for me tonight, I think,' I said. 'I've spoiled your evening as it is. I'll be fine.'

'You say that a lot too,' said Drew.

'What?'

'That you're fine.'

'I *am* fine.'

'Sarah – that's my psychiatrist friend – has a theory about the word "fine",' he said. 'She thinks it stands for fucked up, insecure, neurotic and emotional.'

I bared my teeth at him. 'Okay, I'll be "all right". Is that better?'

Oddly enough, I *was* all right. I slept dreamlessly and, when I woke up, the bruises on my face had subsided. A brisk wind had pushed the rain away overnight and left a bright, blowy day behind it. I was still getting used to the way the weather changed from one day to the next. Only the day before it had been hot and humid, but now I was glad of the jacket I'd bought for Lucy's funeral.

I had plenty to do, but I was too restless to settle to my lesson plans. I set off to walk along the river, but the closer I got to it, the more reluctant I felt to see where Lucy had died and where Hawise had drowned. In the end I turned away before I got there, and wandered around the ruins of St Mary's Abbey instead. The breeze blew my hair around my face, and I had to take my hands out of my pockets to pull away the strands that kept sticking to my mouth. There was a strange razor edge to the light. Every zingy green leaf, every brick, every person I passed jumped out at me in startling detail, while billowing clouds skated across the sky and sent deep blocks of shadow sweeping over me.

I sat for a while on a bench and watched some Australian tourists videoing a grey squirrel. I hadn't been to the Museum Gardens before, but they were obviously popular. Students lay sprawled on the grass, careless of the damp, while small children ran around chasing pigeons, and teenagers huddled in groups and texted on their mobiles. An elderly couple rested on the bench next to mine. Families wandered by eating ice creams, and tour guides hustled their groups around the ruins. Everyone looked so normal.

The elderly couple smiled at me as they got up to go, and I smiled back, pathetically grateful to realize that they thought I was normal too. I didn't look crazy. I just felt it.

I touched my lip where Francis's ring had struck, disturbed by the idea that I might have beaten myself. Before he left, Drew had again offered to put me in touch with his psychiatrist friend, but I loathed the thought of anyone rummaging around in my subconscious. I had coped with a tsunami, for God's sake. Surely I could cope with this? Maybe Hawise *was* just a figment of my imagination. That was the rational explanation, and as long as I understood that, I would be fine. Yes, *fine* – whatever Drew might think it meant.

I couldn't see that I needed to visit a psychiatrist. What would be the point? I didn't need help, I decided. I just needed to sell Lucy's house, leave York and get back to normality.

The first step in that was to finish clearing the house. Reassured, I headed briskly back. I was wondering about the cheapest way to redecorate when I found myself walking past a gate leading into a quiet churchyard tucked away behind Goodramgate, and my steps slowed.

And I knew that rationality hadn't won after all. There was a rushing around my heart, pulling me back, pulling me along the path towards the church. I couldn't have walked past if I had tried. This was Holy Trinity, Hawise's parish church. I knew it in my bones.

To my twenty-first-century eyes it was a humble, higgledy-piggledy building, a cottage of a church in comparison with the bulk of the Minster that soared behind it, but at the same time I saw it as sanctuary, as certainty. The churchyard was a tiny oasis in the centre of the city. There were three or four gravestones leaning in the grass, and a cherry tree bursting with blossom. Two Japanese tourists were sitting on a bench, heads bent over their digital camera, but they smiled and nodded as I walked up to the porch. Somehow I managed a smile back.

I didn't want to go in, and yet when I pushed open the door and stepped down into the nave, it felt like coming home after a long journey.

Inside, age had buckled the church out of shape. The flagstones, worn smooth by generations of feet, dipped and sagged, the stone arches were squashed and slightly askew. My pulse boomed as I walked down the central aisle towards the altar. Those high wooden box pews dominating the nave shouldn't be there, I thought, but when I laid my palm against one of the sturdy pillars, the stone seemed to thrum.

Hawise was right beside me now. I could feel her – part of me, and yet separate for once. I stood very still, watching the meagre sunlight that slanted through a window, briefly striping the flagstone beneath my feet.

Yes. Yes.

The words rang in my head, and approval settled like a hand on my shoulder. *Yes. At last. Now, remember how it was . . .*

After a week of rain, the sun has come out for my wedding day. It pours through the stained-glass windows and makes puddles of colour on the stone floor. They look so pretty that I try not to stand in them.

I am married. I stood with Ned Hilliard in the church porch and we exchanged the vows that made us man and wife, and then we came inside for the nuptial mass. Now Meg is pouring hippocras for all our guests, and Agnes is handing around the cakes with a martyred air. She said she was too tired to go out with Meg and the other girls to gather flowers this morning. She said it was just a tradition, and that there was no point in throwing flowers in the street. They would just get trampled into the mud.

I would have collected armfuls of flowers if this was Agnes's wedding. I know she thinks that I have been unfairly fortunate, and I dare say it is true, but I would be happy to change places with her if I could. Does she think I want to marry a widower, a stranger? But Agnes sees only that she has been unlucky again. I wish my sister could be happy, I wish it as much as I wish happiness for myself, but I am afraid that she doesn't know how to feel joy. I am afraid that if we could change places, so that she was the bride and I her maid, she would still be discontented and envious.

Perhaps the flowers *are* trampled now, but the street looked like a meadow when we set out in procession from my master's house. Dick, Mr Beckwith's apprentice, held the bride-cup aloft and the ribbons fluttered gaily in the breeze as we followed behind the waits. No expense had been spared. There were fiddlers and drummers and trumpeters and pipers, and we laughed and smiled and clapped our hands in time to the music and the passers-by all stopped to watch us, craning their necks to see me in my bridal finery. My maids walked with me, carrying the great wedding cakes that will be broken at the bridal feast later, each with a sprig of rosemary tied to their arm. Meg is going to put hers under her pillow tonight and dream of her future husband. I did the same when I was a bride's maid.

But I never dreamt of Ned Hilliard.

Now I slide a glance at him under my lashes. He is standing beside me, wearing a handsome silk-damask doublet and hose with a brown velvet jerkin, but he still manages to look austere. I try to remember what he looks like when he smiles. I know it is surprising, but it happens so rarely that I have forgotten. I wish I knew what he was thinking, but I know no more of him now than I did when I used to serve him wine as my master's guest. I still have no idea why he would wish to marry me.

He didn't have to woo me – we both knew that – but he did. He brought me gifts, tokens of his love, he said, and I accepted them, so that everyone knew we were betrothed. He brought me gloves embroidered with butterflies, and a gold ring. A pair of green silk garters, and a purse. A length of scarlet kersey. An orange that he peeled with deft fingers. Its sweetness stung my lips and trickled down my chin. Ned licked his thumb and dabbed it off. He didn't smile, but my eyes tangled with his like a deer in the briars, and all at once my heart began to pound.

And once he brought me a seashell and held it to my ear, and I heard the rush and roar of the ocean. He did smile then, watching my expression. I remember that now.

He has given me a beautiful new gown as a wedding gift. It is made of the finest, softest wool, dyed blue, and is trimmed with silver buttons that flash in the sunlight that is slanting through the windows. I smooth it down, still scarcely able to believe that it is real, that I am wed, that the man standing next to me is my husband, till death do us part.

'How does it feel?' Meg asked me last night. She was sitting up in the bed we share – the bed I used to share with Elizabeth – and hugging her knees as she watched me brush out my hair. 'Tomorrow you will be married.'

In truth, I wasn't sure how it felt. I'm still not sure, but I am resolved to make the best of things. I have learnt my lesson. I will not risk my reputation with a stranger again. I will accept Ned Hilliard as a husband and be glad.

Chapter Eight

I was afraid when I came back from Paynley's Crofts that day.
I told my mistress that I had fallen over a branch to explain
my cuts and bruises, but she knew. She sent Meg off on an
errand and climbed up to find me, lying curled in a tight ball
on the bed with Hap – Hap who had known Francis for what
he was right from the start.

'Hawise.' She sat heavily on the edge of the bed. Normally
she would have ordered Hap back to the kitchen, but that night
she pretended she didn't see him. 'Who did this to you?'

I shook my head. I was too ashamed to tell her the truth
and I was frightened of Francis, of what he might say to the
neighbours and how easily he could still hurt me. *You led me
on*, he had said. What if it was true? What if it was all my fault?
I clutched Hap to me, and he endured it without so much as a
squirm of protest.

'Are you still a maid?'

'Yes.' My voice was barely a thread, and Mistress Beckwith put a hand on my shoulder. I flinched at the feel of it.

'Do you swear?'

'I swear.'

'Very well.' She took her hand away. 'Stay in bed this evening. I will say you are unwell.'

The bed groaned as she pushed herself upright. I heard the squeak of floorboards underfoot, the rattle of the latch. I didn't lift my face from Hap's velvety ear, but I knew my mistress had paused at the door and was looking back at me.

'This marriage is a great chance for you, Hawise,' she said. 'You will not get another such. You must be more careful. Your reputation is all you have.' She hesitated, weighing her words. 'Ned Hilliard is a good man and he has a fondness for you, that much is clear, but you are not married yet. There will be those who call themselves his friends who will think he could find a more suitable wife. A man must listen to his friends. They will be urging him to break the betrothal, telling him that you will do him no honour. You must give them no reason to think that they were right all along. You understand?'

I still couldn't look at her, but I nodded into Hap's fur. I did understand.

The next day I went back to my duties, but for a week or so after that my belly knotted with fear every time I stepped out of the house, in case I came face-to-face with Francis.

I was anxious, too, when the banns were read here in Holy Trinity, Goodramgate and in St Martin's, Coney Street, which is Ned's parish church – and mine now, I suppose – but Francis didn't appear and speak up to say that I was promised to him, and after the last banns were read I began to relax. I didn't want to ask the neighbours about him, but only a few days ago I overheard Mistress Rogers telling Thomas Barker's wife that Francis has gone back to London with his master, and it feels as if a great weight has been lifted from my heart.

He has gone.

He has gone, and the relief has made me light-headed. Oh, yes, I have learnt my lesson. I know how lucky I am that things did not go a lot worse for me. From now on, I vow, I will be grateful for what I have. Perhaps I would have liked a younger bridegroom, or a smiling one, but I will try to be happy.

And, in truth, it's not hard to be happy when you are a bride and everyone makes a fuss of you. Agnes offers me one of the cakes that have been blessed. I thank her, and she manages a wan smile in return. Poor Agnes. To my sister it must seem as if I have everything, and I cannot tell her that it is not so – not when she has to go back to our father's house in Hungate, with little to look forward to other than for her head to stop aching.

The church is filled with the chatter and laughter of our guests. Everyone loves a wedding. Ned has no kin here in York, but he has invited his neighbours, and my father is here with Agnes, and the Beckwiths of course, and *their* friends and neighbours. Between them all, Ned and I haven't had a chance to exchange a word privately, but as I sneak another glance at my husband, he catches my eye and smiles one of his unexpected smiles.

Ah, yes, now I remember. He looks younger, less severe. Less daunting. Without thinking, I smile back at him, and something blazes in his eyes. I don't know what it is, but it makes me feel as if the butterflies on my gloves have taken flight and are fluttering frantically around inside me.

All at once I am filled with optimism. I will be mistress of my own home, a fine house in Coney Street. My husband is rich and sober and, when he smiles, he doesn't seem so old. I think about the shell he brought me. He knows what will please me, while I – I have my virtue to offer him, which I so nearly lost. I am luckier than I deserve. I have my family and friends around me, and all is well.

No sooner have I thought it than a quake runs through me. Ned looks down at me. 'Are you cold?'

'No.' I shake off the strange feeling of unease and put on a bright smile. 'Not at all.'

When the spiced wine is finished and the cakes have been eaten, we go out through the porch and my maids shower me with wheat, in token of fertility. Then the musicians strike up and the entire wedding party sets off again for Ned's house in Coney Street, where we are to have the bridal feast. This time I walk with Ned. We make a quiet centre to the party, which is already buoyed up by the hippocras, and his arm is solid beneath my hand. I notice that, in spite of his stiff manner, my husband walks like a man easy in his own skin. I find myself remembering the warmth of his mouth when we exchanged a kiss in the church porch to seal our vows.

I should have told him about Francis perhaps, but what could I have said? I don't want Ned to know that I am a fool.

I want to be a good wife to him, to forget Francis and put the past behind me.

And then, as if the thought has conjured him out of the air, I see him, and my smile freezes.

Francis is standing at the edge of the street, watching as the procession passes. He is smiling, but when his gaze meets mine, it is so full of malevolence that my heart thuds sickeningly. I stumble and would fall, were it not for Ned catching my arm.

A ripple of concern goes through the watching crowd, and some mutter superstitiously about it being a bad omen for the bride to trip.

Ned's hand is steady at my elbow. 'More like a sign that the Chamberlains still haven't mended the mid-part of the street,' he says, raising his voice so that others can hear, and there is some laughter and nods of agreement.

When I look again, Francis is gone.

My eyes flicker from side to side. Did anyone see? Could they tell that he was watching me, the way a cat watches a mouse? Did they sense the malice in his gaze?

I have to swallow hard before I can answer Ned when he asks if I am hurt.

'No, it was just a stone,' I say, but my fingers tighten on his arm.

Ned's house is huge, bigger even than Mr Beckwith's. The first time I saw it, my eyes widened like a little owl. The shop that fronts Coney Street is leased to Richard Lydon, apothecary. Inside, it is heady with the fragrances of the East. On the counter are sugar loaves and pitchers of wine, and glass jars filled with comfits and dried fruits, and wooden boxes of quince paste, while the back of the shop is lined with wooden drawers filled with the spices Ned buys in the great markets of the Low Countries: verdigris and wormwood, cinnamon and pepper and nutmeg, cloves and knobbly roots of ginger, precious saffron.

Behind the shop there is a fine hall, with its own entrance from the courtyard, and a parlour that Ned says I can make my own. There is a buttery and a closet, where Ned keeps his books. Further back, a great kitchen with larders and a bake-house, and stables across the yard. The main chamber is above the hall, but there is another over the shop, where the linen is kept, and two more, plus chambers for the servants over the kitchen and under the eaves.

And of all this I am now mistress. I try not to look too daunted by it all.

The hall is lined with wainscot, and on the wall hang fine painted cloths that Ned has bought in Antwerp and Bruges. Today the hall is set up for the bridal feast. The trestle tables are arranged on three sides of the room and covered in linen cloths. Great jugs of spiced wine are set out at regular inter-vals. I sit with Ned at the table on the raised dais and am served the way I have served so many others in the past.

I make an effort to push Francis from my mind. It was a shock to see him like that, but what can he do, after all? I am married before God. It cannot be undone.

Still, my head is whirling with the look in Francis's eyes and with the strangeness of finding myself suddenly a wife and mistress of this enormous house. Normally I have a hearty appetite, but I only pick at the feast before me. I nibble at a slice of roast swan. Its pungent taste clings to the top of my mouth. It makes me think of the Ouse when the tide is low, when its banks are sludgy and slimy, and all at once the thought of the river sends another ripple of unease through me. I put the slice down without finishing it.

There is a salad of herbs with cucumbers and hard eggs, which I like, and I take some of that instead, and some spiced custard. Ned urges me to try trout baked in a pie with eels, so I do. But the rest of the feast is a blur – a seemingly endless parade of roast meat, from rib of beef to pig, from goose to lark, and all manner of sauces. There are stuffed cabbages and fruit tarts, and fricassées and trifles, and almond custards and oyster chewets. The sugar deceits are very clever. They are made to look like dishes, and we break them and eat our plates at the end of the feast, although I am almost too tired by now to enjoy the sweetness.

I sound like Agnes.

The voices and laughter grow ever louder over the sound of the fiddles. Beside me, Ned is as unreadable as ever, and I am finding it hard to keep smiling. The ring that he put on my finger in the church porch keeps catching my eye, and I can't get used to the sight of it glinting on my hand. My life has changed now. I have stepped through a door. I am no longer Hawise Aske; I am Mistress Hilliard, and after tonight I will be a maid no more.

I have tried so hard not to think about Francis, but I can't help remembering how it was in the orchard, and I shudder. Is that how it will be with Ned? Will he push his tongue in my mouth like that? Will he heave and shove? Will he hurt me?

I bite my lip as I glance at him under my lashes. He is my husband now. He can do what he likes.

The feast seems to go on forever, and I am grateful when the wedding cakes are broken and shared at last and I can retire. Agnes left to lie down long ago, but the other women laugh and make suggestive comments as they help me take off my dress and brush my hair. I climb into the big bed in my shift, wishing they would all go away and leave me alone, but as soon as they do, I want to call them back, because the men are loud and boisterous outside and are pushing Ned into the room. They bang the door behind him, bellowing crude advice, until they grow tired (or thirsty, more like) and clatter back down the stairs to rejoin the feast.

Ned and I are left alone. He seems bigger than I had remembered, more male, and the pulse in my throat flutters like a trapped bird.

I don't know what I had expected – that he would throw himself on me and push into me perhaps, or lie down beside me and kiss me, but Ned does neither. He walks over to the chest and pours wine into a goblet, then sits on the side of the bed and offers it to me.

'Drink, Hawise,' he says. 'There is no hurry.'

My fingers are shaking as I take the cup. 'Thank you, sir.'

'Here, in our bedchamber, I hope you will call me Ned, as my friends do.'

I have never called him that to his face before. 'Ned.' I try it on my tongue and he almost smiles.

'Are you nervous?' he asks.

I moisten my lips. 'A little,' I confess.

'I will try not to hurt you.'

'I know my duty,' I say quickly. 'I am your wife now.'

'Perhaps,' he says, 'I do not want your duty.'

There is a note in his voice that I do not understand. I shift uneasily. The sheet has been scattered with rosemary and, as I move, the fragrance stirs the air, reminding me of the water the Widow Dent used to bathe my face and hands after Francis tried to force me. Today the rosemary is for faithfulness, but it is always for remembrance too.

I try to push the memory away. I don't want to remember Francis. I should be thinking about my husband now, but my tongue is cleaved to the top of my mouth. We have never talked like this before. We have never been this intimate before. He is very close, and shyness overwhelms me.

'I am yours now,' I manage to say after a moment, and he lets out a long breath as he reaches out to stroke my hair.

'Yes, you are mine,' he agrees. 'What more could I want?'

His hand drifts from my hair to brush along my jaw, very gently, and he traces the outline of my mouth with his thumb. My skin tingles beneath his touch. 'You are very beautiful, little wife.'

'I?' My mouth drops open and his eyes crinkle. It's as if he is smiling and not smiling at the same time.

'Yes, you.'

'But I am plain!' I am so surprised I almost spill my wine.

Ned shakes his head. 'Perhaps there are other maids who have golden hair and rosebud mouths, and who like to think they are pretty, but they look pale and colourless next to you. You are like a candle flame, Hawise,' he says, his voice deepening as he strokes his thumb very gently down my neck so that I shiver, but not with fear. 'You bring warmth and light with you wherever you go.'

I stare at him. Can this be Mr Hilliard, this man with the voice so deep it reverberates down my spine? I thought I had married a cool, calculating merchant, and instead I have a lover with a poet's tongue. I am amazed.

Ned can read my expression easily enough. 'Why do you think I married you, Hawise?'

'I don't know,' I say honestly. 'My mistress . . . ' I stop. I have no mistress now. I *am* the mistress. 'Mistress Beckwith says that your friends don't like this marriage.'

'Perhaps they do not,' says Ned, 'but I have not married my friends. It is true, when first I wed, I took the views of my family and friends into account. I thought more carefully about the advantages of the match, the connections it would bring. But I was younger then, and had more to prove.'

His touch is tugging at something inside me. It's as if there is a cord deep in my belly, tightening slowly with every stroke of his thumb, and I can feel myself begin to quiver with the tension of it.

'I was not unhappy,' he goes on, his eyes never leaving my face. 'We do what we must. But when my wife died, God rest her soul, and the child with her, I saw a chance to start anew. I came to York, I thought perhaps . . . perhaps I could please myself, and so I have. I've wanted you since I first saw you at William Beckwith's, Hawise. You were so bright, so curious, but you were so very young. And now I have what I want, is it greedy of me to wish to please you too?'

My mouth is dry. He is still sitting on the side of the bed, facing me, and he is very solid and very close – so close I feel hazy with it. His hands feel nice. They are warm and dry and capable, gentling down my arm, lifting my hand from the cover to press a kiss into my palm, and at the feel of his lips I hiss in a breath.

Ned raises his head to look at me, and the candlelight throws his face into relief, making the ordinary features seem stronger, more definite. He has a quiet mouth, with no angry spittle.

Our fingers entwine and on impulse I lean forward and press my lips to his before I lose my nerve and pull back. I am suddenly afraid that Ned will think me wanton, as Francis did.

I wish I hadn't thought about Francis.

Ned isn't angry, but he shifts closer. His nearness is suffocating, but he doesn't try to kiss my mouth. Instead he lets his lips travel down my throat to the neck of my shift, and I shiver again. My heart is stuttering, my pulse booming in my ears. I want him to stop. I want him to go on.

He nuzzles my shift aside to kiss his way along my clavicle, but pauses when he reaches the mark above my breast, and I remember how Francis had recoiled from it. *A harlot's mark*, he had called it.

'I was born with it,' I say.

Ned leans up on one elbow to that he can trace the outline of the mark with his finger. 'A little hand,' he says, smiling. 'Sweet, like my wife.' And he bends back to kiss it.

He doesn't mind. He thinks I am sweet. He thinks I am *beautiful*. The touch of his mouth is making me tremble.

'Ned,' I say shakily, and he looks up. He sees the cup, takes it from me and sets it aside. Then he pulls back the cover and I shift over in the bed so that he can lie down beside me.

I don't look as he slips off his robe and blows out the candle. The bed dips and creaks under his weight, and the fragrance of rosemary fills the air. In the darkness he turns to me, his fingers feeling for my face. Then he kisses my mouth, very gently at first. I am taut, but he murmurs low, as if he were soothing a skittish horse, and I feel his lips on my throat, his hand sliding under my shift, hot and hard on my skin. That cord inside me is twisting and tugging again and my blood shivers in my veins and I find myself arching beneath his touch.

'Does it feel good?' he whispers, his mouth at my breast.

'Yes,' I sigh. 'Yes.'

He is naked, solid, warm. I smooth my hands over his shoulders, feeling his muscles flex beneath my fingers, and he makes a sound that is almost a groan. Dragging himself up, he covers me, and through my fine linen shift I feel him hard and insistent and suddenly panic grips me. He is too heavy. I am suffocating beneath his weight, but I can't move now. My legs are spread wide and he is pushing into me.

And it hurts. It *hurts*. I want to struggle, to push him off me, out of me, but I can't breathe. The sprigs of rosemary are digging into my back and buttocks, their fragrance drowned out by the stench of rotting apples. I am back in the orchard, the blackness roaring in my mind, and this time there is no Sybil Dent to rescue me. There is no Ned any more, either. There is just a man, shoving into me, and I have to lie there and take it. I have forgotten that only moments ago I liked the feel of his mouth. Now I turn my head on the pillow. I concentrate on taking small breaths and I endure it, because there is nothing else I can do.

My face was tight, my jaw clenched, and when I raised a shaky hand to my mouth, I felt the trail of a slow tear. Ned's weight was no longer crushing me. I could breathe. I was sitting rigidly in one of the box pews in the church. God only knew how I had got in there, or how long I had been staring blankly ahead. Long enough for dark clouds to swallow the brightness of the morning, anyway. The puddles of sunlight on stone had vanished, and the light was gloomy and oppressive.

Shivering, still churning with Hawise's distress, I leant forward and put my head in my hands. I pressed my fingertips against my forehead and slowed my jerky breathing. I needed help. I couldn't deny it any longer, and I found myself thinking about Drew Dyer. Drew with his cool eyes and cool mouth. Not like Ned at all, and yet somehow just the same.

That was even more disturbing.

Stiffly I got to my feet, wincing at the raw, bruised feeling inside me, and walked back to Lucy's house. I didn't go in, but rang the doorbell next door instead. When Drew opened the door, I found I couldn't meet his eyes.

'I think I need to see your friend, the shrink,' I said.

I peered at the intercom. Sarah Wilson lived in the shadow of the Minster, in a flat hidden away behind a nondescript door off the street. When she buzzed to let me in, I followed a short alleyway and found myself in a courtyard of contemporary houses, their glass and wood and metal striking in contrast to the medieval cathedral looming behind them.

Sarah's apartment was cool and calm and uncluttered, a perfect metaphor for analysis. She laughed when I told her that. 'It's interesting that you should think of it that way.'

Immediately I was on the defensive. Why was that interesting? Didn't everyone think that? I'd never talked to a psychiatrist before, and I was nervous. Drew had persuaded me that I needed help, and I knew he was right, but I was frightened that I would end up shut in a mental ward, or at the very least labelled as mentally ill. I hugged my arms together as I prowled around Sarah's sitting room. It was intimidatingly tidy. Three perfectly aligned books on a shelf. A contemporary sculpture. Cream sofas. Not a speck of dust anywhere. How could anyone who lived in this kind of order understand what was happening to me?

Sarah made tea, chatting to put me at my ease, but I couldn't relax. I could feel Hawise lurking in my head. She didn't want me to be there, I could feel it. I wasn't sure *I* wanted to be there. But Sarah was gesturing me to a chair, pouring me a mug of tea.

I sat reluctantly. 'It's good of you to see me at home.'

'Drew's a good friend,' she said. 'I know he wouldn't have asked if it hadn't been important.'

How good a friend? I found myself wondering. Sarah was an attractive woman of about Drew's age, as coolly poised and carefully groomed as her house. I could see how they might be friends. They both gave the impression of being capable and in control of their lives. When I thought about my own – drifting around the world and now apparently between times, unable to control anything – I felt depression closing in on me.

'This isn't a clinical interview, we need to be clear about that,' said Sarah as she handed me the tea. 'But I'm very happy to have a chat. Do you want to tell me what's worrying you?'

'Well . . . ' I took a breath, opened my mouth and shut it again, overwhelmed by the impossibility of explaining to someone as calm and rational as Sarah. I cleared my throat. 'Well, I know it sounds strange, but ever since I arrived in York, I've been . . . I don't know how to explain it. Time-travelling, I suppose.'

'*Time*-travelling?'

Her brows shot up, and I flushed. Clearly Drew hadn't passed on what I'd told him. Sitting in that ordered room, my story sounded absurd.

Immediately I started to backtrack. 'Not literally, obviously,' I said, embarrassed. 'But it feels like there's this other person from the past in my head, and sometimes I . . . sometimes it's like I'm her . . . I'm sorry, I'm not explaining this very well.'

I stumbled to a halt. Sarah took a sip of tea and put her

mug down. 'Don't worry about it,' she said. 'Why don't you start by telling me a bit about yourself?'

So I told her about where I grew up and the fact that I was an only child, and of course it took her no time at all to find out about my mother dying. I was expecting that. I might choose not to dwell on it, but it didn't take a genius to figure out that her death had had an effect on me. Not as much as some ex-boyfriends had claimed, mind you. I was never the most sweet-natured of children and, for all I know, I might have been just as prickly if Mum had never had cancer.

'So what brought you to York?' Sarah asked when we'd been through all that.

I told her about Lucy, and how I had been working in Indonesia, but then she wanted to know what happened before that, and before that. Turning points, she called them.

She had a habit of stroking her chin and nodding thoughtfully. It began to irritate me. I didn't see what working overseas had to do with what was happening to me in York, either. Any minute now she was going to get to Khao Lak, and I didn't want to talk about what had happened there. I couldn't. I *wouldn't*. I could refuse, couldn't I?

But there was something implacable about Sarah's patience. She went back and back – why was I there? what was I doing? – until, sure enough, we ended up in Thailand.

I shifted in my chair, fiddled with the piping around the arms. This wasn't what I had expected. Shouldn't we be talking about Hawise, about now, not then? Thailand wasn't the problem. York was.

'You seem uncomfortable,' Sarah commented.

I snatched my hand back from the piping as if she had slapped me, which is probably what she felt like doing. 'It just feels all wrong to be sitting here talking about myself. It's not like a proper conversation. I feel as if I should be asking you questions. I don't know anything about you.' I knew I sounded sulky, but I couldn't help myself.

'What would you like to know?'

I really wanted to know how well she knew Drew, but I couldn't think of a way to ask that without sounding as if I was interested in him, which I wasn't. Not really. I was just . . . curious.

'I don't know,' I said. 'It feels awkward, that's all.'

'I get the feeling you don't want to talk about Thailand.'

She was right, I didn't, but if I admitted that, it would imply there was a problem.

'I'm fine about it.' I shrugged, wincing inwardly as I heard that 'fine'. 'I don't see what it's got to do with what's happening now, that's all.'

'You said you were teaching English in Bangkok. How did you end up there?'

I sighed. 'I went with my boyfriend. Matt was a teacher too.'

'You're not with Matt now?'

'No.' I looked back at the rain smearing the big window. 'We split up.'

'Whose decision was that?'

'Mine.'

Sarah nodded slowly, as if that was precisely what she had expected me to say. 'And why did you decide that?'

'I just felt the relationship had run its course.' I could hear myself sounding defensive and forced myself to sound relaxed. 'These things happen.'

'How long were you together?' Sarah asked, and I relaxed some more. I didn't mind talking about Matt.

'Five years or so. We met as students, and then we travelled together. I always had itchy feet, and when I got a job teaching English in Bangkok, Matt came with me and got a job at the same school. We had a great time,' I remembered a little wistfully.

'Sounds like you knew each other very well.'

'We did. Matt's lovely,' I told her. 'We're still friends, although we haven't seen each other for ages.'

'So if you got on well, what made you decide to end the relationship?'

'I told you, it was over.' I was a snail, horns shrinking back into my shell as Sarah trod closer. 'There doesn't have to be a reason, does there?'

'No,' she said, 'but when a couple really like each other and get on well, there usually is.'

'We wanted different things, that's all.' I knew I was sounding hostile, but I couldn't help myself. 'Matt's married now and lives in London. He's got a mortgage and a good job. I never wanted any of that,' I told her. 'The whole idea of settling down makes me twitchy. I think I'd suffocate.'

'So it was Matt who changed, not you?' said Sarah.

'Yes, he—' I stopped, seeing where this was going. I looked suspiciously at Sarah, who smiled faintly.

'It's not a test, Grace. I'm just wondering what happened, because clearly something did.'

I let out a long breath that sounded like defeat. 'Matt and I decided to go to the beach for Christmas,' I said. 'We went to a place called Khao Lak and were caught up in the Boxing Day tsunami. We were lucky,' I added quickly. 'We both survived, but I guess it made us realize that we wanted different things out of life. Matt was keen to come home and settle down to what he insisted on calling "real life", but to me that felt like jumping deliberately into a great big rut, so we agreed to go our separate ways.'

Memories were a dead weight, pressing me back into the chair. I could hear my voice thinning, tautening, under the pressure and I swallowed. 'It was no big deal.'

Sarah did more thoughtful chin-stroking. 'What do you remember about the tsunami?'

'Why?' I said rudely. Her calm voice and her calm manner and her calm, cool house were getting on my nerves. 'What does it matter?'

'You've just implied that the tsunami was a major turning point in your life.'

I banged down my mug and got to my feet. I half-expected Sarah to tell me to sit down again, but she didn't. 'I survived it,' I said, going over to the window. The Minster towers were blurred and watery through the rain. 'I wasn't even hurt.'

'Tell me about it anyway. What were you doing when it happened?'

I blew out a frustrated sigh. 'We were on our way to the beach. We'd felt the tremors earlier, when we were in bed, but we'd laughed about them. We used to laugh a lot,' I remembered, then squared my shoulders, hoping that Sarah hadn't noticed the embarrassingly wistful note in my voice. She would be bound to make too much of it.

But when I glanced at her over my shoulder she just nodded, and waited, and then I had to go on.

'Matt gave me a jade pendant for Christmas the night before, and I'd just realized I hadn't taken it off.' My hand went unthinkingly to where it nestled in the base of my throat. 'I loved it, and I didn't want to lose it, so I said I'd go back to the room and leave it there. We were quite near the beach,' I said. 'You could see it through the coconut palms. There was a little boy digging in the sand, in our place.' I made myself sound casual. 'You know what it's like when you go to the beach. You find a favourite spot, and that was ours. Anyway, we agreed that I would go back to the room and leave the pendant somewhere safe, while Matt bought some water, and then we'd meet under "our" tree.'

I turned back to the rain. 'Sometimes I think, if I hadn't been fretting about the necklace, we'd have been together,' I said slowly. 'They say that makes a difference, doesn't it? But then we might not have survived, if we had just kept on walking together. We'd have been in a different place when the wave hit. It would all have been different.'

Sarah let a beat or two go by. 'Then what happened?'

'Then it was just . . . chaos. It was so fast, so strong.' I hugged my arms together and kept my eyes on the Minster. 'One moment I was walking along this track in flip-flops. I could feel the sand under my toes. It was warm and very fine. I could feel the sun on the back of my neck. I'd tied up my hair, and the clasp on the chain was getting hot.

'I was happy, I remember that,' I told Sarah. 'I could smell coconuts. There were dried husks scattered under the trees, but I think it was probably from my suntan lotion. It might have been that.'

I'd forgotten I was in York by then. I'd even forgotten Hawise. I was looking at the Minster, but I wasn't seeing it. I was remembering the way the fringed leaves of the coconut palms threw a jagged pattern of shade across the track. I remembered how I had thought: I've never been this happy before.

'And then?' prompted Sarah after a while.

'Then there was shouting, screaming. Suddenly people were running.' I lifted my hands in a helpless gesture and let them fall again. My skin was shrinking from the memory. I had to brace myself against it. 'I turned and there was this wall of water coming towards me.'

I hadn't even recognized it as the sea. The day before it had been a perfect serene blue, but this water was brown and boiling and savage, gobbling up everything in its path like some ravenous monster.

'I couldn't comprehend what I was seeing,' I told Sarah, 'and I didn't have time to make sense of it anyway. I was staring at it, and then it just . . . ate me up. It was like being tossed around in some washing machine. I was tumbling round and round, and there were trees and poolside chairs and beach umbrellas and God knows what else . . . '

I trailed off. How could I describe the force of the water, the *power* of it? The noise and the horror of it? What it was like to choke and flail and drown?

'What happened next?' Sarah asked quietly after a moment.

'I don't want to talk about it,' I said.

Sarah said nothing. After a moment I went back to sit in the chair. I looked at my shoes. I looked at her three perfectly positioned books. I looked at the cold tea. I shifted the mug so that it was sitting on a mat.

'I was pushed into some railings and I grabbed onto them,' I said abruptly. 'I've never held onto anything as tightly as I held onto those railings. Then—'

'Then?' she prompted when I stopped, panic squeezing my lungs.

I couldn't talk about it. I wasn't ready.

'I . . . nothing. I mean, I didn't know what was happening,' I lied. 'It was like a nightmare, you know. Nothing makes sense.'

Sarah nodded. She probably understood the not-making-sense bit, anyway.

'I lost my grip on the railings,' I told her. 'There wasn't anything I could do. The water just grabbed me back, and the next thing I knew, I popped up in the middle of the sea.'

It had felt endless – nothing but noise and water and fear – and then suddenly I could breathe and all that mattered was being able to drag oxygen into my desperate lungs.

'There was debris floating all round me,' I said. 'I hung onto a branch, and eventually a boat came round. They were picking up bodies, and people who'd been badly hurt, but I was fine. Some cuts and bruises, but fine.' I attempted a smile. 'I was still wearing the pendant Matt gave me.' I pulled the chain out from my throat to show her. 'I haven't taken it off since.'

Letting the pendant fall back into place, I lifted my chin. 'Everyone told me how lucky I was, and they're right, I was. I am.'

Sarah was silent for a while. 'Grace, have you heard of post-traumatic stress disorder?' she said eventually.

'I'm fine,' I said instantly. 'Matt's fine. We weren't traumatized. I've told you. I wasn't even hurt.'

'Let me tell you a bit about it,' she said as if I hadn't spoken. 'People react to traumatic events in different ways. Some re-experience the trauma, and that can be triggered by a particular sound or a smell associated with the event. So, for instance, you mentioned the smell of coconuts. Someone else in your situation might find that smell would tip them back into all the feelings they had had at the time of the trauma.'

I folded my arms, looked away from Sarah. I think I was probably looking mutinous. I felt spiky, uneasy, but I was listening.

'Then there's avoidance,' she said. 'A refusal to think or talk about what happened. And others still have symptoms that we call "arousal": irritability, sleeplessness, and so on.'

'I don't have any problem sleeping.'

Sarah nodded. 'You seem to be functioning without any difficulty. I suspect you've been avoiding it, but nothing you've told me makes me think you're not a normal person having a normal reaction to an abnormal event,' she said. 'As I said earlier, this isn't a formal interview, but if it helps, I don't think you need clinical treatment.

'You say you're fine, and physically you are, but I wonder whether you've ever come to terms with the psychological impact of what must have been a terrifying experience,' Sarah went on. 'Sometimes when we go through a traumatic experience, the memory of it is so overwhelming that we choose to put it away,' she said. 'We put it in a little box in our heads, and we say that we're not going to look at it. We tell ourselves that if we can't see it, it's not there. But it *is* there, and the more we don't look at it, the more frightening it becomes. It gets bigger and bigger and more and more horrifying, so that we're afraid to think about it. We're afraid of feeling, because feelings make us vulnerable.'

'I feel,' I protested. 'I'm a very sensory person.'

'How many people have you been intimate with since Matt?'

'I've had boyfriends,' I said quickly. 'It's not as if I never got over him or anything.'

Sarah's expression didn't change, but I could tell that she was unconvinced. 'How many of those boyfriends did you let close to you, Grace?'

'It's not about being close,' I said irritably. 'It's about having a good time. I've never been good at all that touchy-feely, let's-talk-about-our-relationship stuff, and none of the guys I've been out with have wanted to do that, either.'

'Of course they haven't. I suspect you deliberately choose men you can easily keep at a distance,' said Sarah. 'Because if you let someone close, they might want you to start talking about your feelings, mightn't they? They might want to look right inside you and wonder what you kept hidden away in that box. Perhaps you learnt to do that when your mother died, so it was natural for you to close off even further when you experienced another, very different trauma.'

I chewed at my thumb. I didn't like what Sarah was saying, but I recognized myself.

'You said this post-traumatic stress disorder is a normal reaction,' I reminded her.

'It is.'

'So is there anything I can do about it?'

'Is there anyone you can talk to? Someone you trust?'

My mind flickered to Drew Dyer, and then away. I didn't know why I thought of him. 'My best friend,' I said. 'I trust her.'

'Does she know what happened to you?'

'Not in any detail.' I'd brushed aside Mel's concern and questions.

'Then why not tell her?' Sarah suggested. 'It's not a magical cure, but if you let yourself remember once – if you're brave enough to look in that box – you might find that it's not quite as horrifying as you remember. You might find that it can't hurt you the way you're afraid it will and, knowing that, you'll be able to look at it another time, and gradually you can learn to deal with the memories.'

I thought about what Sarah had said as I walked back to Lucy's house. I was so relieved that she had used the word 'normal' that I forgot I hadn't told her the whole truth about what had been happening to me.

Was it possible that Hawise was just a repressed part of my personality that had temporarily taken over my imagination? Perhaps instead of putting them into the box that Sarah had talked about, I was dealing with my memories by recasting them into a strange, but vivid story.

The more I thought about it, the more it did seem to make a kind of sense. It wasn't hard to see some parallels between Hawise and me. We were alike in personality and appearance – we even had the same birthmark – and we'd both lost our mothers early, but otherwise our experiences were completely different. I was independent, while Hawise was a servant and then a wife. She lived a circumscribed life in the city, while I'd travelled to places she could only dream of.

And the very first time I'd dreamt of her, she had been drowning.

It seemed odd that my mind should choose to work out its trauma in such a way, but weren't dreams supposed to be a way the mind processed experiences? Of course that didn't really explain how vivid my experiences as Hawise were, or where I had got such details from, but then, I reasoned, how was I to know whether or not they were authentic? Drew had more or less said that there was no way of checking whether Hawise had really existed or not. I might be making it all up.

So I let myself be reassured, because I wanted to be. After all, Sarah was a psychiatrist. She would have been able to tell if I were mentally ill, surely? Instead she had agreed that I was a functioning adult. A normal person having a normal reaction – that was what she had said. Perhaps now that I understood what was happening to me I would be able to cope with it better.

That was what I told myself, anyway.

Chapter Nine

By the end of that week I was feeling much more myself. I liked teaching a group of mixed nationalities, and my classes were going well. I clung to Sarah's theory that I was suffering from a bizarre form of post-traumatic stress disorder, and whenever I found myself wondering about Hawise and what had happened to her, I would remind myself firmly that she was just a figment of my imagination. For some reason that I couldn't fathom I was avoiding thinking about the tsunami, by inventing a parallel world where a girl like me was brutalized by one man and handed over in marriage to another.

Poor cow, I thought. Married or not, Hawise had effectively been raped that night after her wedding. I could still taste the rasp of the wine Ned had poured, still feel the soreness between my legs, and the suffocating panic at his weight on top of me . . .

And that's when I had to catch myself up. It hadn't happened. Still, I avoided the older buildings in York whenever I could. I skirted around churches that were uncannily familiar, and walked back to Lucy's house the long way so that I didn't have to walk under Monk Bar. Every time I headed down the street, I had to brace myself against the memory of the fields and garths; every time I let myself into the house, I braced myself against the smell of apples rotting in a neglected orchard.

It seemed to work. If I was careful, I could keep the memories at bay. I concentrated on my classes, and on clearing out Lucy's things. John Burnand had assured me that the house was 'eminently sellable', but I wasn't so sure. The dark paint and witchy decor felt oppressive to me, and I planned to redecorate before it went on the market. Nothing fancy – just neutral colours slapped on to brighten the place up. I had it all worked out: sell the house, finish the course I was teaching, get on a plane.

I emailed Mel to tell her to expect me before the end of the year. *Christmas in the Yucatan?* I wrote.

Fab, she replied. *Cant wait.*

She left out the apostrophe, just to annoy.

It felt better to be getting on and doing things. I even spoke to John Burnand about Drew's kitchen wall, which now had a large damp patch, thanks to the overflow pipe that had leaked while I was in the bath. He said he would sort out the insurance. I knocked on Drew's door to tell him, and on impulse invited him and Sophie to supper that Saturday. 'To thank you for putting me in touch with Sarah,' I said. 'She was really helpful.'

I was glad of the prospect of some company, I had to admit. The evenings were harder. Alone at night, I could feel Hawise, baffled, frustrated, nudging at the edges of my consciousness, calling still for Bess. No matter how insistently I reassured myself that it was all in my head, an icy feeling coiled itself around my spine every time I heard that desperate whisper that was not really a whisper at all. But as long as I fixed on the here and now, on the everydayness of teaching and cleaning and cooking, I was in control.

I was fine.

'I thought it might be a chance to get to know Sophie a bit better,' I said, even as I sneered at myself for feeling that I needed to find an excuse for talking to Drew. But it was true. I felt bad that I hadn't tried to talk to his daughter earlier. I saw Sophie occasionally, usually stomping along the street on her way to or from school, but the time never seemed right to propose a girly coffee. I wasn't convinced Drew was right about Sophie admiring me, either. I couldn't see any reason why she should, but once or twice – more than that, if I'm honest – I'd found myself remembering how my eyes had met Drew's. *You* are *exciting*, he had said.

Sophie, it turned out, would be with her mother that weekend, so I could hardly withdraw the invitation, and we agreed that Drew would come on his own.

'That'd be great,' he said after the tiniest of hesitations. 'Thanks.'

If I'm honest, I was a little miffed that he wasn't more enthusiastic. He was the one who had called me exciting, after all.

Not that I cared particularly. I would be leaving York as

soon as I could, I reminded myself. I just fancied some company, that was all.

I decided to make *opor ayam*, a basic chicken and coconut dish that was easy to prepare. It reminded me of Indonesia and the kind of person I had been before I came to York. I went shopping on the way back from my morning class that Friday lunchtime. There was a farmers' market in Parliament Street and the awnings were still dripping from the downpour earlier. Huddled into their coats, the stallholders grumbled about the weather, while a busker defied the dreariness and belted out opera to the accompaniment of a portable CD player. Nobody was in the mood to linger and listen, though. The rain was relentless. Every day you woke hoping for a glimpse of the sun, only to find the clouds lying sullen and heavy over the city again. It made people sour and scratchy.

I bought chicken, onions, fresh ginger and lemongrass in the market and went home to lay out my ingredients. I'm a methodical cook, and I like to prepare everything in little dishes, as if I'm a television chef. Mel gives me a hard time about it, but there's something about having each ingredient in its own little compartment that appeals to me.

The knife felt odd as I trimmed the excess fat from the chicken pieces. I kept hefting it in my hand, pursing my lips as I studied my array of ingredients. Garlic, ginger, lemongrass. Oil. Coconut milk. The can tugged at my eye as if there was something strange about it. I'd forgotten something vital, I was sure of it.

Exasperated with myself, I pulled the onions towards me

and started peeling them. The fumes stung my eyes and made them water. Squeezing them shut with a grimace, still holding the knife, I lifted my arm to cover them.

'You should have given them to Isobel to do.'

The hectoring note in Margery's voice is already familiar. She is a big-boned woman with a raw face and small, sour eyes. She was Ned's first wife's maid, and has been keeping house for him since her mistress died. She's been running it well too, I can see that. The floors are swept, the carpets beaten, the linens brushed. I have no reason to complain of her. But she doesn't like me. She has transferred her devotion to Ned and cannot understand how he has chosen me, a plain dab of a girl with no dowry and an uneasy reputation. She doesn't know that he thinks I am beautiful.

My face is still screwed up as I lower my arm and set to the onions once more. 'Isobel has enough to do,' I say.

As well as Margery, there are two maids, Alison and Isobel, who are often to be found giggling together, just the way Elizabeth and I used to do. I feel lonely when I see them, which is foolish of me, I know. I am their mistress, not their friend, but it is a big change. I am used to the Beckwiths' house, where we all sat at table together and talked. I miss that. I miss Mr Beckwith grumbling about the state of the paving, about blocked sewers and encroachments, about taxes and statutes and the untrustworthiness of southerners. I miss my mistress. I miss Meg. I even miss Dick, for all that he used to pinch and tease. Now I eat with Ned in the hall, and the maids wait on us, the way I used to wait on the Beckwiths when they had guests.

Isobel is only fourteen, a whey-faced girl who blinks, while Alison is as sturdy as a cob. I would like them to like me, but they are both taking their lead from Margery and, whenever they catch sight of me, they fall silent and watch me out of the edges of their eyes. That's why I'm chopping onions. I want them to see that I'm not too proud to do the jobs they would do.

Or perhaps I am hoping that if I don't make them do the hard tasks, they will like me for it.

They are more likely to despise me, I know.

At least the onions give me an excuse to sigh. My eyes are stinging so much that I can hardly see, but it seems to me there is something wrong about the table. Putting down the knife, I squint through my tears at the ingredients I have set out in front of me in neat piles, the way Mrs Beckwith taught me. Mutton, yes. Ale, yes. And onions, of course. And there are the herbs I need: rosemary, thyme, parsley. I have set the spices around a plate, ready to use. I touch them in order: cinnamon, ginger, cloves, nutmeg. I am frowning. What have I forgotten?

'What's wrong?' Margery pinches her lips together. She is making pastry for an apple pie, kneading the dough irritably at the other end of the table. She pushes it with the heel of her hand, lifts it, turns it and lets it drop once more. Slap, thud. Slap, thud.

The apples for the pie are piled in the middle of the table. They are perfectly good apples. Isobel has polished them on her apron, and their skin is smooth and shiny and not in the least wrinkled, but every time I look at them I am sure I can smell them rotting, and I think about Francis pushing into me in the orchard and my stomach heaves. I would rather chop a whole sack of onions than touch those apples.

Margery doesn't like me in the kitchen. *Her* kitchen, she thinks of it. She prides herself on the table she has kept for Ned. His wife, Anne, let Margery do everything while she sat in her chamber and prayed, I hear. She was a lady, Margery says, implying that I never will be. And she is right, if being a lady means closeting yourself with a Bible and a prayer stool. I would lose my wits with boredom. Besides, I am determined that this will be *my* kitchen. I will never be mistress of the house otherwise. Mistress Beckwith told me that.

'Nothing . . . ' I shake my head. I use the corners of my apron to dab the onion tears from my eyes. The puzzled sense that something is not quite right about my ingredients has gone. It is all there. Prunes and dates and currants to add with the spices, and the precious oranges and lemons that Ned imports.

I am making stewed mutton steaks. It is one of Ned's favourite dishes. I remember how he used to comment on it when he came to dinner at the Beckwiths', and I want him to know that I am trying to be a good wife. We have been married a month, and I am used now to the way he turns to me in the dark and pulls up my nightgown. I still don't know why Alice smiled the way she did, but it is all right. It doesn't hurt any more, anyway.

And Ned has let me keep Hap. This I have learnt about my husband: he is a man of rare understanding. He waits and he looks, and he sees things for what they are, and not for what other people tell him they should be. When he looks at Hap, he doesn't see Satan's pup; he sees a small dog whose paw has been broken, that is all.

He is a good man, and a kind one. He has filled his house with misfits. Margery has no family, and nowhere else to go. The maids Alison and Isobel are both poor orphans with no one to speak for them, either, while his servant, Rob, is a gowky lad whom the other apprentices make fun of. His agent, John, who looks after Ned's affairs in Hamburg, has a crooked shoulder, I hear.

And then there is me, of course.

It is odd of Ned. My husband is not just good and kind, I find, he is *interesting*. A merchant so rich should flaunt his wealth – what is the point in having it, otherwise? The neighbours puzzle over him, but they don't forget that for all his strange ways he is richer by far than they, and they respect that, if not his choice of a wife. No one would have been surprised if Ned had forbidden Hap the house, but he didn't. He let me keep my dog by my side, and that has been more comfort to me than I can say.

The servants are mistrustful of Hap, though, mainly because Margery dislikes him, and I keep him out of sight as much as I can. He sleeps by the door in our chamber, or sits with me in the parlour, but I don't take him to the market any more. I remember what Mistress Beckwith told me about my reputation, and Ned's.

Ned is at the wardmote today. All the men of the ward are

there, appointing an inquest jury and, as I know from Mr Beckwith, that can take some time. It's not easy to persuade men to take time away from their workshops to walk around the streets, to inspect blocked gutters and broken paving and listen to complaints about nuisance neighbours. It is a thankless task, too. No one likes to have their offences pointed out, and Mr Beckwith used to come home bristling after being shouted and sworn at. Bootham ward is more prosperous than Monk, but empanelling the jury still takes some time, and Ned will be ready for his dinner when he comes home.

He will invite some of his neighbours to come back with him, he said, and I must have a good dinner to set before them. The neighbours don't like Ned's marriage any more than his servants do, that is clear. I want to impress, for Ned's sake. A fine dinner and a modest wife. Will that be enough to show them that he has not made the mistake they think he has? I am hoping so, but I am nervous.

So when I hear the clunk of the door latch, the stamp of boots and male voices in the hall, I jump. 'Master is back,' says Margery unnecessarily. She heaves herself to her feet. 'I'll take some wine.'

'I'll take it.' It is not for Margery to greet Ned's guests. It is my place, as Ned's wife. I take off my apron. 'Will you check the pie?'

Without waiting for her reply, I ladle wine into a jug and take it into the hall, where Ned is making welcome some five or six other men. They stand with their legs braced, chests pigeon-puffed to show that they are not over-impressed, but their eyes dart around the hall, measuring the cost of the hangings, the wainscot, the carpets on the chest. Measuring Ned's profits. Wondering, perhaps, if they outweigh the mistake he has made in marrying me.

I recognize Mr Fawkes, and Christopher Milner, whom they call master of physick, although I suspect Mistress Beckwith or Sybil Dent knows far more about curing sickness than he does. The others are strangers to me. This is a new ward and a new parish, and it still feels odd to me. I knew everyone in Goodramgate. Here, in Coney Street, I find myself among strangers, and my neighbours eye me askance. I am mistress of a fine house, and I have a kind husband who thinks me beautiful, but still, it's hard not to feel homesick for my old life sometimes.

But I smile and offer spiced wine to my husband's guests, and I try not to notice how their eyes run assessingly over me, gauging my worth. Ned is at the door, greeting the last guest, so I don't see who it is at first. When I do, my grip loosens on the jug and I almost drop it. Steadying it with my other hand gives me an excuse to arrange my expression, but my bowels have twisted into a painful knot.

Francis Bewley is standing with my husband, smiling, at ease, looking around him. No, he's not smiling. He's *smirking*.

I want to throw the wine at him. I want to beat at him with my fists. I want to run back to the kitchen and hide. But I do none of those things. Ned has seen me, and is bringing Francis across the hall to where I am standing rigidly with the jug of wine between my two hands.

'We can feed an extra mouth, can we not?' Ned says easily. 'As you see, I have brought our new neighbour, Francis Bewley, to dine.'

'Mistress Hilliard.' Francis sketches a mocking bow and glances up at me, daring me to admit that we have met before.

'Mr Bewley.' I can't bring myself to curtsey to him. I incline my head instead. It is all I can do to unseal my lips. 'Will you take some wine?'

'Thank you.'

I hate the way my hand shakes as I fill the goblet and pass it to him. Ned doesn't notice, but Francis does. Oh, yes, he notices, and it pleases him.

'Francis is but newly come to Coney Street, but he has already made his presence felt in the wardmote.' Ned claps him on the shoulder, the way men do. 'Meet our new churchwarden, solemnly sworn this morning! It is not often we get a volunteer.'

'I am always ready to do my godly duty.' There is a complacent look to Francis now. It is only a month since the wedding, but already he seems fatter, sleeker, his red mouth redder.

I have just stopped dreading this moment. After seeing him on my wedding day, I was afraid to go out in case I came face-to-face with him again, but I couldn't stay in my chamber, like Ned's first wife. I had to show Margery and the other maids that I was no fool, to be fobbed off with musty corn or putrid fish. I can weigh a loaf of bread in my hand and tell if the baker is skimping on flour. I dig my hands into a sack of oats to check they are fresh below the surface, and watch the measures when the sugar loaf is weighed. In the Shambles I have a sharp eye to the look of the meat, a sharper nose to its smell, and I expect no less of the maids.

So I had to go out to market with them, but I held myself stiffly, as if braced for a blow. York is a city of walls and sly corners, of narrow alleys and sudden turns. There was no way of knowing when Francis might suddenly appear. I made excuses not to visit Mrs Beckwith in Goodramgate in case he still lodged there, but little by little I let myself think that I had imagined seeing him on my wedding day after all. And even if I hadn't, I knew I was safe in Coney Street. This is one of the most prosperous streets in the city. What would a penniless clerk do here?

And yet here he is, and his eyes are crawling over me, and my flesh shrinks away from him in disgust.

'Francis is a notary,' Ned is explaining. 'Always a useful man to know! He has come from London. Most men make the journey the other way.'

'Indeed?' I manage. 'And what brings you to York?' I nearly say 'back to York', but catch myself just in time.

'Everything I want is here,' Francis says, looking straight into my eyes, and I have to force myself not to look away. He smiles blandly. 'I was fortunate to inherit everything from my old master in London, and now I can please myself where I go.'

I know, without him telling me, that I am the reason he has come back, and I remember how callously he planned for his master's death. *I will see to it.* My blood runs cold at the thought that Francis has, in fact, seen to his master.

'I came to York with my late master,' Francis goes on. 'I had a fancy to come back. My house is small, just across the street in fact, but this is a respectable neighbourhood. I like that. I have set up my business here. I am here to stay.'

It is a warning. No, it is a threat, and there is nothing I can do about it. I cannot move away. I cannot complain. I cannot tell Ned that I don't want Francis Bewley in the house, because then he will want to know why, and I can't tell him. Ned has taken a risk in marrying me. If I lose my reputation, he will look a fool, and Francis can destroy my standing with a word or two. I know that, and Francis knows that I know.

All this whirls around my head as Ned and Francis talk about the shufflings and grumblings at the wardmote. I am just standing there with the jug of wine. I am trapped by this man, with his small, intense eyes and his red lips; this man who smiles at me as if he is remembering how he hurt me, as if the thought gives him pleasure still.

'Ned, what say you to this new tax on brewers?' It is Mr Fawkes, drawing Ned away, leaving me stranded with Francis.

He holds out his goblet for more wine. 'So, Mistress Hawise, where is that Hell-hound of yours? I hope your husband has got rid of him?'

'On the contrary. Hap is upstairs in my chamber. He doesn't care for the company.'

'You have your husband besotted, I see. Clever of you.' Francis sips his wine, and his eyes never leave my face. 'Does he know?'

'Know what?'

'About us, of course.'

My throat is so tight it hurts to swallow. 'There's nothing for him to know.'

'Oh, I think there is. If I were married, I would want to know if another man had had his hand on my wife's cunny.'

The worst thing is that he is smiling. To everyone else in the room, it must look as if we are having a pleasant conversation, but I can feel my gorge rise. I have to press my lips together to stop myself vomiting.

'Oh, don't look like that,' says Francis, tutting. 'I'm not going to tell him, and you won't either, will you?'

I can't bear to be near him any longer. 'I must see to the other guests,' I say and turn away.

I can't believe nobody has noticed that I am sick and shaking. The wainscot on the walls seems to be pressing in on me, and I only stop myself from fainting by concentrating very hard on the warmth of the jug on my palm, the smoothness of the handle in my grip. Autumn sunshine is slanting through the glass and striping the hall with bars of light. They make the room look like a prison.

My eyes rest on Ned. He is nodding, listening to Mr Fawkes, his head bent courteously towards the older man. I see him as if for the first time. My husband. He is not a very tall man, but he is compactly muscled, and I find myself remembering how solid his shoulders feel beneath my hands in the dark. I no longer see the pockmarks on his cheeks. He is not handsome, no, but I like the quiet angles of his face, and when I look at the line of his mouth I feel something warm uncoil inside me.

I wish I could go over to him and burrow my face in his chest. The longing to lean into him, just for a moment, to close my eyes and feel safe, is so strong that I am dizzy with it, but

I know Francis is watching me, his malign presence thickening the air. I know he would take it as a sign of weakness, of fear, and that would please him.

So I move on with the wine instead. I am a modest wife, and I am here to make sure Ned's guests are well wined and well dined, and nothing else.

It is a relief to go to the kitchen and order Alison and Isobel to start setting out the table. I wish I could stay there, but I have to go back and take my seat at the table. If I have to sit next to Francis, I will pretend I have been taken ill, I decide, but in the event he is beside Christopher Milner, who sits opposite me. This way it is worse, I realize. I can feel Francis's eyes on my face all through the meal.

The conversation turns to the new preacher in St Martin's, who is by all accounts a godly man. Myself, I find his sermons very long, and my mind tends to wander to what I will cook the next day, but I don't admit that. Besides, no one is interested in my opinion. I am only a woman.

Francis is giving a fine impression of pious devotion. He attends divine service in the Minster every day, he says, and now that he is appointed churchwarden, he intends to tackle sinfulness in the parish.

'I take my office seriously,' he says. 'I will root out abominations wherever I find them.'

'What abominations?' asks Christopher Milner, his mouth full of mutton.

Francis looks grave. 'There is witchcraft rife in the city, I hear,' he says and the men at the table look uneasy. They are hard-headed men, for the most part. They go to church, but their hearts are in their workshops and their warehouses. They don't like talk of witchcraft and abominations. Women's work, I can almost hear them thinking.

'I fear the signs are all too real,' Francis says, perhaps sensing their lack of encouragement. 'Wherever you look there is disaster. Poor crops, sickness, lewdness and unrest. Only last week they say a young woman in Selby gave birth to a cat.'

'I heard there was a two-headed calf born up Haxby way,' offers Charles Batchelor.

Francis's eyes are alight with fervour as he leans across the table. 'And who is to blame for all these monstrous abominations?' he demands. 'Persons of lewd and ungodly life, blasphemers, and sorcerers!'

'It is not the job of the wardmote to enquire into witchcraft,' Ned puts in mildly from the other end of the table. 'Our business is the everyday. We must worry about paving and ditches and market offences, not sorcery and bewitchment.'

'I worry about that cursed Anne Ampleforth,' Christopher Milner grumbles, and there are some nods around the table. 'What a scold that woman is! No one can live quietly beside her.'

'Indeed, but there is no suggestion that she is a witch, I think,' says Ned, who has his own quiet authority.

'Nothing that a spell in the thew wouldn't sort.' Christopher grunts his agreement. 'And the sooner, the better, in my opinion.'

Francis, I can see, is growing impatient. 'I know nothing of the Ampleforth woman, but there are others, I assure you. Two witches were arrested last week, and I trust will suffer the punishment they deserve at the Assizes, but there are others still practising unhindered. The Widow Dent, for instance – why is she not taken in for questioning? Everyone knows she is a witch.'

'She is not a witch,' I say clearly. I am the only one who knows how much he fears and hates Sybil. And why. 'She is a cunning woman, who makes salves for cuts and bruises – that's all. You are new to the city. You do not know folk as we do.'

'I make it my business to know about evil-doers.' Francis's response is smooth, unfazed by my tartness. 'It is God's work.'

'Most so-called witches are but poor witless women,' Ned says. 'They are scapegoats for every misfortune and every grudge.'

'You are too tolerant,' says Francis thinly. He is unimpressed by Ned's lack of fervour, that is clear. 'It is not enough to be ardent in religion ourselves. We must seek out those who have renounced Christ and entered into a bargain with the Devil, or we will none of us be safe.'

'We should look to our own souls before we meddle in others',' Ned says and changes the subject.

Francis subsides then, and I realize that my husband, quiet as he is, has a presence that Francis can never match. I can see that the other men respect Ned, and it is not just for his wealth. There is a steadiness about him, an unobtrusive strength, which means that he does not need to raise his voice or flaunt his prosperity for men to listen to what he has to say.

My husband is a good man. I haven't realized this until now. I have been too taken up with my own feelings of strangeness and loneliness to think about his, but now I watch him and marvel that I haven't seen him properly before. I have never noticed the creases at the edges of his eyes, or the line of his jaw and throat. His linen is always very clean. So are his hands. I *have* noticed that.

I don't realize that I am studying him until Ned looks down the table and our eyes meet. He doesn't do anything as obvious as smile at me, but *something* happens. A shortening of the air, a crisping of the senses. Something that leaves me feeling startled and hot. Flustered, I look away, and as I do, I catch Francis's glance. His is dark with malice, but suddenly I don't care. Tonight I will lie with my husband, and my pulse jumps at the thought.

'Alison.' I beckon to the maid. 'Bring Mr Bewley more wine. His cup is quite empty.'

I was holding the knife, and my eyes were stinging still from the onions that lay half-chopped on the board. My lips were curved in a smile, but it faded as I saw what was sitting beside the onions.

An apple, brown and loathsome, and putrid with mould.

My pulse roared in my ears at the return to reality. Very carefully I set the knife down and groped my way to a chair in the dining room, where I dropped my head between my knees. The faintness passed after a minute or so, but the fear remained, and I sat with the back of my hand pressed against my mouth, trying to summon up the courage to go back into the kitchen.

When I did, the apple was still there. I made myself touch it. It was real. And it hadn't been there when I started chopping the onions – I was certain of it.

Hawise had put it there.

She was real.

This was not post-traumatic stress disorder. I faced it for the first time, hacking my way through every rational instinct that told me it was impossible. Hawise was a ghost, trapped somehow between the past and the present, and she was using me. But what did she want? And why me? I thought wildly. What had I ever done to be possessed by a girl four centuries dead? And what was I supposed to do about it?

Fear fluttered frantically in my throat, but I swallowed it down. I was *not* going to panic. I was not going to fall apart. I was not going to let Hawise use me any more.

I hadn't tried hard enough to resist her, I could see that now. Part of me had been frightened, but I had been fascinated too. But now I felt as if I had stepped onto a train that was going in quite the wrong direction; I was unable to open the doors or jump out, and there was no one to see me waving frantically for attention. No one to help me.

I *wasn't* imagining things. That apple had been real; Hawise was real. There was no point in going back to Sarah or trying to persuade Drew about what was happening to me. I didn't know what Hawise wanted from me, but I was determined not to give it. I didn't like not being the one in control. Somehow I was going to have to wrest control back from Hawise, and I was going to have to do it by myself.

I put on rubber gloves and picked up the apple, gagging at the feel of it, saggy and squelchy, between my fingers. Opening the kitchen door, I threw the apple out, disgust propelling it in a high arch out into the garden. And as it sailed through the air I saw the orchard, with its gnarled apple trees and unkempt grass – a snapshot – and then the apple plopped behind the laurel bush and the picture was gone.

This was where it had happened, I realized. This was the neglected orchard where Francis Bewley had forced himself on Hawise. Was that why she was here now, and not in the fine house in Coney Street?

I remembered that scrap of paper I'd found on the desk upstairs. Lucy had lived here. She had known about Hawise too.

And Lucy was dead.

My face was grim as I stripped off the gloves.

Oddly, I was less frightened now that I accepted the reality of what was happening than I had been before. My greatest fear had been that I was losing my mind, that I would be diagnosed insane and shut up somewhere and pumped full of drugs. I would rather believe in ghosts than that.

By the time Drew arrived I had myself under control, but it wasn't a successful evening. My fault. I was distracted. I tried to shut Hawise out of my mind, but I kept thinking about Ned and how I had looked at him and suddenly *seen* him for the first time. Now I couldn't take my eyes off Drew, couldn't stop noticing how solid his body was, how firm the line of his jaw, how competent his hands. Couldn't stop wishing he would smile at me.

I didn't like it. That was Hawise's fault, I knew. If it wasn't for Ned, I would never have *dreamt* of looking at Drew like that. It left me feeling edgy and uneasy and unable to concentrate. The *opor ayam* was pretty good, but the conversation kept sticking uncomfortably. Drew didn't seem bothered. He was better at silence than me.

'Am I allowed to ask how you got on with Sarah?' he asked. And by that point I was so grateful for a neutral topic of conversation that I told him about post-traumatic stress disorder, which meant telling him something about the tsunami too, but it wasn't so hard once I started. I told him about Matt. I told him about being swept out to sea. I told him I was scared.

But I didn't tell him about Lucas. I did think about it, but the words jammed in my throat. I would have had to vomit them out, and I couldn't face Drew's disgust. I wanted him to think of me as calm and capable, rational – the way I *was*. I couldn't talk calmly about Lucas. At one level I knew that Sarah was right. The longer I locked that away, the more I feared it, but knowing that I should talk about it and actually letting the words out were two very different things. I wanted to, but I *couldn't*. I was afraid of what Drew would think of me, afraid of what I would have to face about myself.

I wanted to be normal, and for Drew to think of me as normal too. Was that so much to ask?

So I didn't tell him about Lucas, and I didn't tell him about Hawise, either. I would have to deal with her myself.

'So, there you go,' I finished lightly. 'You'll be glad to know that they're not going to cart me off to the funny farm after all.'

I thought Drew would appreciate a rational explanation, but

he frowned. 'That doesn't explain your bruises,' he said. 'Why would you hurt yourself?'

I got up to clear away the plates. There was no way I was going to tell him what I really believed. 'It made sense, the way Sarah explained it,' I said. I pinned on a smile. 'Now, would you like some pudding?'

Chapter Ten

'Hey, Sophie!' I spotted her trudging off to school the following Tuesday and on an impulse trotted to catch her up.

She turned at the sound of her name. 'Oh, hello,' she said as I joined her, but not with any great enthusiasm, and I wondered if Drew could possibly be right about her admiring me.

'Where are you off to?'

She gave me a *duh* look. 'School.'

'Mind if I walk with you?'

'It's the wrong way for you, isn't it?'

No, Drew was definitely mistaken, I decided, but I wasn't going to let her put me off. I remembered what it was like to be a teenager, to be surly and graceless, to be terrified that someone was going to pay attention to you and even more terrified that they weren't.

'I'm not teaching till this afternoon,' I said breezily. 'I fancy a walk. Besides, I wanted to ask you something.'

'Oh?' Sophie looked wary as we began walking.

'Do you remember Vivien, who came to Lucy's funeral?'

'Of course. They don't call her the leader, but she's the one in charge of Lucy's coven.'

And the one who had decided that Sophie herself was too young to join, I remembered.

'You don't happen to know how to get in touch with her, do you?'

Lucy had left instructions for her funeral with John Burnand, and he had made all the arrangements. I had never contacted Vivien directly, but now I wanted to talk to her. Ever since coming round in the kitchen with the knife in my hand and that smile of anticipation on my lips, I had been grappling with how to deal with Hawise. A sense of unease nagged at the back of my mind. Oh, I was worried about what was happening to me, of course I was, but beyond that I couldn't shake off the feeling that I needed to do something about what was happening to Hawise too.

But how could I? I couldn't change the past, I knew that, but still the feeling persisted all weekend. I didn't want to go back to Sarah. She was a scientist. She had offered an explanation that made sense as long as Hawise wasn't there in my head, but now she was back, tugging insistently at my mind, impossible to ignore, impossible to deny.

Several times I had considered confiding in Drew again, but he was like Sarah. He was a historian – *an* historian, he would have said, I was sure – and while I thought he would want to help, I didn't see how he could. He would need to believe in Hawise, and I didn't think he could do that.

Then I had remembered Vivien – Vivien who had sensed what had happened in the orchard. *There is violence here*, she had said. *Violence and hate and fear*. Vivien would believe in Hawise.

I could have gone to John Burnand, I supposed, but I didn't want to tell him why I wanted to speak to Vivien, and Sophie seemed a better bet.

'I don't have a phone number or anything, but I know where she lives,' said Sophie. 'I went there once with Lucy. It's not that far from here. I could show you, if you like.'

'I don't want to make you late for school.'

She shrugged. 'It's okay.'

'I haven't seen you for a while,' I said, uncomfortably aware of my relentless cheeriness as she led me down a side street. But it was hard not to sound cheery in comparison. 'What have you been up to?'

'Nothing.'

'Your dad says you go out quite a bit,' I persisted.

For the first time a trace of animation warmed her face. 'I go to the Temple of the Waters. I'm training to be an initiate.'

'What does that involve?'

Sophie cast me a sidelong glance, obviously wondering why I was being so nosy, but just as obviously she couldn't think of a reason not to answer.

'I go to gatherings. We meditate.' Enthusiasm warmed her voice in spite of herself. 'Ash – that's our leader – is so charismatic. He's taught me how to see Gaia in everything.'

Forgetting her reluctance to confide, Sophie plunged into an involved description of what the Temple of the Waters believed in. I nodded along. It sounded to me like a rehash of any other pagan mythology – not that I knew much about it. Sophie talked about worshipping Mother Earth, and acknowledging the power of the elements and our place in nature, and while it all sounded rather silly and self-important, I could sort of see why it appealed to her. I wasn't entirely sure where the waters came into it, but it all seemed fairly harmless. I wondered if Drew was worrying unnecessarily. I could think of worse things for Sophie to get into.

I couldn't see that having coffee with me was going to hold much appeal for her, but I had promised to offer, and I was wondering how to introduce it into the conversation when we rounded a corner and ran slap into a couple of goths coming in the opposite direction. I was in the middle of the whole side-stepping and apologizing thing when I realized that Sophie had stopped dead and the colour had rushed into her face.

My first impression, it was clear, had been based on little more than the fact that both were wearing black leather jackets. On closer inspection they had a gloss that I had never seen on any goth I'd met before. He was tall, with beautiful cheekbones and a wide, sensuous mouth, and had long, silky ringlets that should have looked girly, but which somehow emphasized the dark masculine beauty of his face instead. The girl with him was two or three years older than Sophie, with piercings in her brow and nose and a sexy, sullen expression.

Sophie was looking bedazzled. 'Ash, hi,' she stammered. 'Hi, Mara.'

So this was the allegedly charismatic leader of her temple. I could see that there was a certain glamour about both of them, but they were very young. I was amused more than impressed as I glanced back at Ash, only to find myself caught by the intense, shiny green of his eyes.

Francis Bewley's eyes.

My heart stuttered in shock, every instinct in me recoiling from him as from a slap. I wanted to grab Sophie's hand and run, but I just stood there, churning with revulsion and confusion while Sophie gazed worshipfully at him.

'Little Moon,' he said to Sophie, and he glanced at me and he smiled.

He knew the effect he had on me, I was sure he knew. Struggling to mask my expression, I was certain I could see amusement in those horrible light eyes.

My mind scrabbled uselessly. What was Francis doing here? It felt like longer, but it was probably no more than a few seconds of panic before reason reasserted itself. Francis couldn't be here. Francis was dead.

This wasn't Francis. He was just an ex-student of Drew's, who didn't even look like Francis. I inhaled slowly, made myself calm. Francis hadn't pursued me across the centuries. What a ridiculous idea! This boy, Ash, just had light eyes. It wasn't a crime.

Still, I understood now just why Drew mistrusted him.

I pulled myself together. 'Little Moon?' I asked, looking between Sophie and Ash.

'It's our special name for her.' Ash's voice was low, caressing and, in spite of reason, loathing crawled between my shoulder blades. 'Isn't it, Moon?'

Sophie nodded, the hectic flush still running under her skin. 'It's my spirit name.'

'What's wrong with Sophie?' I knew I sounded taut, but I couldn't help myself.

'Moon does honour to the elements,' said Ash gravely, and I could see Sophie lapping up his intensity. 'The moon is a symbol of woman, the female. It is the moon that rules the tides as she waxes and wanes. Little Moon here has a power she does not yet know.'

I only just stopped myself rolling my eyes. No wonder Drew was anxious! Sophie was drinking it all in, in thrall, and now I remembered something else Vivien had said: *Watch out for Sophie.*

'Yes, I heard your group was something to do with water,' I said, wanting Ash to know that I was unimpressed, and he smiled faintly, condescendingly.

'That's like saying light is something to do with the sun,' he said, and beside him Mara closed her eyes. It was difficult to tell whether she was praying or plain bored. Either way, I had the distinct impression that she had heard it all before. 'Water is the source of all life, of all love,' Ash went on fervently. 'Open your mind, and all the power you need is at your disposal.'

His mirror eyes rested on me for a moment and, looking into them, I felt a chill. Ash wasn't Francis – he wasn't anything like him really – but all I could think about was Francis and the mad gleam in his gaze.

My mouth was dry. 'I get all the power I need from clicking on a switch,' I said.

Sophie looked shocked by my flippancy, Mara openly contemptuous, while Ash only shook his head gently.

'Get Little Moon to bring you along to one of our gatherings,' he said. 'I think we can teach you a better way.'

'No, thanks,' I said rudely. 'I don't like water.' Then I caught sight of Sophie's disappointed expression and wished I hadn't been quite so abrupt. Ash might give me the creeps, but I didn't want to hurt her. 'I'm afraid of it,' I found myself explaining.

'Afraid of *water*?' Mara's expression was incredulous.

'Yes,' I said evenly.

'A tragedy for you,' said Ash, but I had seen the glint of satisfaction in his eyes. He might not be Francis, but there was something wrong about him all the same. 'Come, Mara, we must go.' He reached out and flicked Sophie's nose lightly. 'We will see you tomorrow, Little Moon?'

She nodded eagerly, blushing with pleasure at a gesture that to me had reeked of contempt. 'I'll be there,' she promised.

Ash lifted his hand and gestured a graceful circle. 'Blessings,' he said to us both, and sauntered off with Mara.

Sophie gazed after them with such naked longing in her face that I averted my eyes. I would have to be very careful.

'Wow!' I commented lightly as we started walking again. 'So that's Ash.'

'I know.' Sophie was still lit up by the encounter. 'Isn't he wonderful?' Fortunately she didn't wait for me to answer. 'He's so . . . so powerful and so *spiritual*,' she sighed.

And so cold and so calculating, I wanted to add, but didn't. There was no point in alienating Sophie. Criticism would only push her further under Ash's influence. I needed to find a way of puncturing the image she had of him, very carefully, so that all that so-called charisma leaked out of him and she saw the emptiness left behind.

So I just made a non-committal sound.

'When Ash talks to you, it's like he's really *seeing* you,' Sophie went on.

'Funny,' I said lightly, 'I remember thinking the same thing about your father when I first met him.'

'About *Dad*?' She stared at me. 'Dad's nothing like Ash!'

Thank God, I thought, but I just shrugged and shifted my battered bag to my other shoulder.

'Drew mentioned that Ash was one of his students.'

'*Ex*-students,' Sophie corrected quickly. 'Ash dropped out when the spirits called him.'

'Did they call before or after his exams?'

'Ash can't be limited by oppressive conventions,' she told me. 'What's the point of a piece of paper proving that you can recite a few facts?'

'Well, it usually means you have a better chance of earning some money to live on,' I said.

'Money!' Sophie's voice held all the contempt of one who had never had to earn any. 'Money is only good for buying things. I'd rather have wisdom, and Ash says you can't buy that.'

'Can't argue with that,' I agreed.

'I have to stay at school until I'm sixteen,' Sophie confided with a hint of defiance, 'but then, if I'm ready, Ash says I can become his pupil.'

I didn't waste my breath pointing out the downside of that idea. Sophie was too dazzled by Ash to listen. I tried another tack.

'Was that his girlfriend?' I asked instead, and was pleased to see her face cloud a little.

'Mara, yes.'

'She didn't seem very friendly.'

'She's ascended to the seventh level,' said Sophie enviously, as if that explained everything.

'What – they can't do smiling and saying hello on the seventh level?'

But that was a mistake. I had gone too far. Sophie bristled at my implicit criticism. 'She's really cool when you get to know her.'

I cursed myself as sullenness shuttered her face once more.

We walked in silence for a while, until Sophie broke it abruptly. 'Did you mean what you said back there? About being afraid of water?'

'Yes.' I wished I hadn't admitted it, but I couldn't lie now. 'I was caught up in a tsunami a few years ago,' I told her. 'I nearly drowned.'

'A real tsunami?' she gasped, fascinated – as so many people were – by catastrophe. I didn't blame her. I had been the same until it had happened to me. '*Really*?'

I nodded. 'The wave swept me out to sea.' At least the thought of it had taken her mind off Ash.

'Wow, that must have been so scary!'

'It was.'

'What happened . . . I mean—' She blundered to an awkward halt, blushing furiously at the realization that she had sounded crass. 'I'm sorry,' she said. 'Do you mind talking about it?'

'It's okay,' I said, though it wasn't, not really. But I had talked about the tsunami with Sarah and with Drew and, beneath her gauche exterior, Sophie was a nice girl. I would rather she was interested in the tsunami than in Ash, with his creepy eyes and his stupid Temple of the Waters.

I told her about going to Khao Lak with Matt, and about parting at the beach, and I admitted to myself that it was getting a little easier in the telling. Sophie listened, absorbed.

'Did Matt . . . ?'

'No, he didn't die,' I said. 'We were both okay.'

'Did you know anyone who died?'

'We didn't really know anyone else there. There was a little boy on the beach the day before,' I found myself saying. 'He was called Lucas.' I stopped, shifted my bag back. 'I don't know what happened to him,' I said.

But that wasn't true, was it? I did know. Or I was afraid that I did.

I had forgotten my plan to talk to Vivien Price until Sophie stopped. 'I'm going straight on here,' she said. 'Vivien lives in Meadow Street . . . Meadow Road . . . something like that anyway.' She pointed down a road on the right. 'You just go down here, follow the road round, then it's on the left. I'm sorry, I can't remember if it's the second or third turning, and I don't

know the number, either, but there's a pentangle in the window
– I remember that.'

I thanked her, and headed in the direction she had pointed.
Preoccupied by Ash, by his eerie resemblance to Francis and his
influence over Sophie, I didn't even notice how confidently I
was walking until I stopped at the end of Vivien's road. Then
I realized that my scalp was shrinking and tingling with recognition.

I had been there before, but not when there was tarmac
beneath my feet. There had been no buses with squealing
hydraulic brakes, no rumble of trucks, no lines of terraced houses
squaring off against each other. Through a shimmer of petrol
fumes, I saw scrubland as it petered into woodland. A scraggy
cow regarded me incuriously before lowering its head to graze
once more. I followed the narrow path as it wound behind a
stand of willow, startling some sheep, which blundered away
across clumps of rough grass.

And there, at last, huddled into the shelter of the wood was
Sybil Dent's cottage, mossy and skewed.

I blinked, and the image was gone. I was standing outside
a perfectly ordinary terraced house, with my hand on the front
gate, jarred back to the present, with adrenaline pumping through
my veins.

The door opened before I was able to move. 'Welcome,' said
Vivien.

'You knew I was coming,' I said. I didn't even sound surprised.
'You knew where to come.'

I opened my mouth to deny it, but then I remembered how

unthinkingly I had made my way there and shut it again. Of course I had known where to come.

'I need help,' I said.

Inside, Vivien's house was very calm and simply decorated, with none of the weird images that had cluttered Lucy's walls. The kitchen at the back opened out onto a small yard, as Lucy's did, and I caught my breath with pleasure at the sight of it. Every spare inch was crammed with plants, and already the air was heady with the scent of flowers. Fat bumble bees lumbered among the stocks. I had forgotten how beautiful an English garden could be on a sunny June morning.

'Sit down.' Vivien indicated a wooden bench charmingly set beneath a tumble of roses. 'I'll make some tea.'

I felt myself relax in the sunshine. It was a lovely place, a secret haven from the hard streets and the ceaseless traffic. A cabbage white fluttered past, and I followed it idly with my eyes. I found myself looking at an old ash tree. It was a big tree for such a tiny yard, I thought. It was funny I hadn't noticed it when I'd first stepped into the garden. Absently, I reached down to tug Hap's ears.

When Hap sees me pulling on my gown and my sturdy clogs, he scrambles up and stands watching me, his small black body quivering with anticipation from nose to tail. He knows they mean that I am going out. His head is cocked, his eyes alert as he waits for a word from me.

I hesitate. The neighbours like Hap no more than the servants do. They eye him with suspicion, and call their children away from him. Mindful of Ned's reputation, I don't take him out with me the way I used to, but I don't like leaving him here with Margery and the maids, either. I can't be sure they won't be unkind to him when I am not by. Today, though, I am going out to Paynley's Crofts. Why should I not take Hap with me? Have I become so scared of what others think since I married?

I am worried about Sybil Dent. Francis has been whipping up suspicions against her in the street. Alison came back yesterday, full of it. I overheard her telling Margery and Isobel. 'They say she has a familiar, a cat with a swine's face and a man's beard.' She paused while they squealed and shuddered. 'And she has christened it Satan.'

'Nonsense,' I said briskly, coming into the kitchen behind her. 'Who told you such a thing?'

Alison was vague on that point. She had it from Mistress Fawcett's servant, who had it from Anne Dobson, who had it from Elizabeth Lamb, but I know it is Francis who started it all. Suddenly everyone is muttering about witches.

'Sybil has a fine tabby and she calls it Mog,' I told them, but I am not sure it has done much good. Now they are just wondering how I know so much about her. Already they shrink from Hap. Perhaps I have made things worse.

Still, I cannot rest until I have warned Sybil to be careful.

Hap's withered paw is trembling. His eyes, fixed on my face, are dark and shining with anticipation.

'Come on then,' I relent, and I laugh as he leaps forward with a yip of exultation and starts to chase his tail. It takes so little to please him. All he wants is to be with me. 'We'll go together.'

Hap scampers lopsidedly down the stairs in front of me, claws clicking on the boards. Margery is waiting at the bottom, and her lips thin at the sight of him.

'Where are you going?' she asks, as if she is the mistress and I the maid.

'Out,' I say coldly, fastening my gown. Ned has business in Hull and will be away for a fortnight at least. In the meantime Margery seems to have appointed herself gatekeeper, but I do not need to account to her. I pick up my basket and click my fingers as I open the door. 'Come, Hap.'

Outside a weak sun has dispersed the pall of fog that has been hanging over the city all morning. In Paynley's Crofts the air smells of wet leaves and wet earth, and the last wreaths of mist are still straggling over the hedgerows like rags.

I draw in a long breath. It's only now I can feel my shoulders easing that I realize how rigid they have been. I've avoided the crofts ever since that last desperate encounter with Francis, and I've forgotten how much better I always feel outside the city walls, away from the press of buildings, where there is always someone to watch you or listen under your windows. The mood in the streets is often combative. Folk are quick to take offence, quick to argue, quick to fight, but they are better than the ones who whisper and point, and spin scandal out of suggestion or slander out of spite.

Out here in the crofts it is very quiet. There is just the sound of Hap snuffling joyously along the path, and the squelch of my clogs in the mud. In the hedgerows the teasels are bare and brown now, the willowherb bent and bedraggled. The brambles look tired too, and they spill across the path, catching at my skirts. Hap pounces on unseen creatures in the long, wet grass, and sends a pheasant bursting out of the hedge with a whirr of wings.

I am taking Sybil a cheese, and I swing the basket as I walk. I realize that I am smiling. I am thinking about Ned, and how in the privacy of our bed things have changed between us. I still flush with heat when I remember how it was for us that night after Francis came to dinner. I stopped remembering the orchard, and thought instead about the hardness of Ned's body, about the sureness of his hands and the touch of his lips. About flesh against flesh, skin on skin. And something unlocked inside me. It was like blowing on sullen coals and seeing the embers glow, seeing dullness and greyness crackle into flames, into fire. My husband is a quiet man, a still man, but when the curtains are pulled around the bed, he explores me as if the marvels of the East are inscribed on my body, and the words pour from him, lover's words that draw me into a web of desire and make my blood sing.

My husband, my lover. I think about the way he smiles against my skin, about the hard possession of his hands, and pleasure shivers down my spine.

Now I know why Alice smiled in the market that day.

I am so busy thinking about Ned that I don't at first notice that Hap has gone. 'Hap!' I stop and turn to see if he is behind me. My first thought is that the mist has rolled in, but then I realize that the path itself is blurred and receding, and there is no sign of Hap. Frightened, I whistle for him, but no sound comes from my lips.

I lurched into the present, my lips still pursed in a whistle. Disorientated, I looked around the garden, and my heart raced with terror. Why were the flowers blooming? It was autumn.

No. Not autumn. It was summer. I pressed my hands onto the slats of the bench. It was summer and I was Grace Trewe.

'Here we are.' Vivien handed me a mug. 'Nettle tea. Don't knock it till you've tried it—' She stopped, catching sight of my face. 'What is it?'

I clutched my hands around the mug. 'I'm frightened,' I said.

'Hap! Hap!' I am calling frantically, and suddenly he is there, wagging his tail, clearly puzzled by the note of fear in my voice.

I am puzzled too. My heart is beating fast, but I can't remember now why I was in a panic. The mist has gone, the path is as it should be, Hap is at my feet. What could be wrong?

I bend to fondle Hap's ears. 'I don't like it when I can't see you,' I tell him. 'Stay close.'

He does until we reach the widow's cottage, but he won't come inside. He lurks at the edge of her garden, which is very neat, for all that her cottage is so poor.

Sybil accepts the cheese, but shrugs aside my warning about the rumours that are rife in the city. 'We do what we must' is all she will say.

I whistle up a skulking Hap and head home. He is relieved

to be away from Sybil, and dashes in circles around me. I laugh at his antics, relieved, too, to be out of the strange cottage. I am thankful to Sybil for saving me from Francis, but the truth is that she makes me uneasy. But I have done what I can, and now I can go home with a clear conscience.

I am thinking how lucky I am, and deciding to make more effort to like Margery, when Hap stops suddenly and lowers himself to the ground. The hackles on his shoulders are rising, and his growl is so low it is little more than a vibration.

There is no one on the path ahead.

'Hap! Stop that!' I don't want to admit how unnerved I am by his strange behaviour, but I can hear the telltale shrillness in my voice. I walk past him purposefully, swinging my basket to show that I am not afraid. 'Come on now.'

He will follow eventually, I reason.

When I look over my shoulder, Hap is still there, still quivering with tension. I turn, exasperated now. 'Hap!' I call again. 'Hap, come!'

He doesn't move, and I shake my head irritably and swing back to go on, only to suck back a scream at the sight of a black-gowned figure blocking the path ahead of me. He seems to have appeared out of nowhere, and I take a faltering step backwards, my hand at my throat, where my heart hammers. It is Francis Bewley.

Now I know why Hap was growling. Why didn't I trust him and turn back to go another way? It is too late now.

'What are you doing here?' I ask, and I am furious to find that my voice is quavering.

'I was about to ask you the very same question,' says Francis, 'although I have a good idea of the answer. You have been to see your witch friend, have you not? You should have a care to your reputation, Mistress.'

I swallow the tremor of fright that his sudden appearance has given me. 'There is nothing wrong with my reputation.'

'Now *there* you are mistaken, Hawise. Do you really think that now you are married no one will notice that you dream your way through divine service? The women who frequent the alehouses are more devout than you!'

'And how is it that you notice what I am doing during divine service, Francis Bewley?' I am angry now, not afraid. 'Should you not be wrapped up in prayer yourself, not eyeing the wives of the parish?'

His voice rises as he talks over me. 'You flout your familiar in front of the neighbours. You consort with witches!'

'Oh, sweet Jesù!' I throw up my hands. 'Hap is a *dog*. Sybil is an *old woman*!' I stare at him and shake my head. 'Truly, I think you must be mad.'

Something shifts behind the blank eyes. I have made a mistake. I take another step back.

'You should rein in that tongue of yours, Mistress Hawise,' he advises softly. 'I am not a man to make a fool of.'

'Why won't you leave me alone? What have I ever done to you, Francis?'

'You led me on,' he answers instantly. It as if this has been rankling with him all this time, and now he spits the words at me. 'You let me believe you were like family to the Beckwiths.

You let me believe you wanted me, looking at me with those big eyes, asking all those questions . . . '

'I wouldn't have needed to, if you had shown any interest in anyone but yourself,' I snap back. 'I never lied to you, Francis. It is not my fault if you judged me wrong. If you had once thought to ask *me* a question, you would have learnt that I had no expectations.'

'No, and yet here you are, married to one of the richest men in the city! Quite a prize for a maidservant with no expectations.' Francis leans forward, his face alight with malice. 'I am not the only one wondering how you managed that, Hawise.'

Only pride stops me backing further away from him. I am not going to tell Francis Bewley that Ned thinks me beautiful. I don't want him to guess that my husband is a poet who seduces me with his words. I shrug instead. 'He saw me, he wanted me, and wealthy men usually get what they want. It's as simple as that.'

'No little potions from your friend Sybil? No magic spells?' He's crowding me against the hedge, his breath sour on my cheek as I turn my face away. My flesh is prickling with disgust. I am sure I can smell apples, and my gorge rises. I can't believe that once I hurried to meet this man. How our desires warp our understanding!

'Let me past!' I push at him with the flat of my hand, swinging my basket at him.

'Oh-ho! So high and mighty now,' Francis jeers as he bats the basket aside.

The next instant there is a blur of black, a snarl and a snap, and Francis yells as Hap sinks his teeth into his leg. Hap is only a small dog, but he has sharp teeth, and he isn't letting go, no matter how Francis tries to shake him off.

'You whoreson cur!'

It happens so quickly. There is a scraping sound, a flash. I see the brutal sweep of Francis's arm.

Too late I think: *knife.*

'Stop! Stop it!' I scream, but it is too late for that too.

Francis is breathing hard, his hand clapped to his leg, and Hap lies boneless and still in the mud. He isn't whimpering, he isn't crying. He's just lying there while a terrible silence closes around us.

I fall to my knees beside him. 'Hap! Hap!' I gather him up, but the little body is limp. I stare up at Francis. 'You've killed him,' I say, blank with disbelief.

He wipes his knife on the grass. 'No loss,' he sneers. 'It was but a runt, and a misbegotten fiend at that.'

I surge to my feet, Hap in my arms, my rage and my grief so great I can hardly speak.

'*You* are the fiend, Francis Bewley! You talk of God, but you are the Devil. I wish Widow Dent *were* a witch. I would ask her to curse you for what you have done today.'

'I would advise you not to talk about curses, Mistress,' he snarls. 'You already walk too close to the dark side. Bewitching a rich merchant, consorting with witches, grieving for a deformed cur that everyone can see is the spawn of Satan?'

'I will tell my husband what you have done,' I say, but my voice shakes and Francis pounces on my weakness.

'But you will not, because what if he were to ask me if it were true? Then I would have to tell him that we were lovers long before he had you.'

'It is not true! He knows that I was a maid when I wed him.'

'There are plenty of tricks to fool a doting husband, and if Mr Hilliard should ask for proof – well, what if I were to tell him about that mark you have on your shoulder, hmm? Will he recognize that? How would I have seen that, if we had not been lovers?'

'You tried to defile me,' I say stonily.

He purses his lips. 'And yet there are plenty who would swear they had seen you come into the Groves to meet me. I can find witnesses if need be. You came willingly, Hawise.' He smiles, and the breath curdles in my throat at the look in his eyes. 'It does not need to be force now.'

'It would always be force,' I say, Hap limp in my arms. 'I would never lie with you willingly. Never. And do you know why?' I push my face into his, mine contorted with hate. 'You disgust me. I would rather couple with a toad! Do you never lay a finger on me again, Francis Bewley, or I swear I will curse you to Hell and back.'

Then I push past him with Hap in my arms, and I run back the way I had come. I cannot go home. Ned is away, and even if he were not, how can I explain what has happened to Hap? Francis is right, I cannot tell him. I think Ned would believe me, but I cannot be sure. I would have to admit what a fool I was, how careless of my reputation. I *did* smile at Francis. I *did* meet him in the crofts. I cannot deny that. That was my mistake, and I am paying for it now. I want to be a good wife to Ned, but how will he believe that if he knows how foolish, how reckless I was? I don't want him to think less of me. I remember how his eyes warmed, how he compared me to a flame. My husband, a poet. I can't bear the thought of his expression cooling with disgust and disappointment.

My mistress warned me to be careful of my reputation. 'Now, more than ever, you must take care,' she told me. 'Ned Hilliard is pleased with you, but others will deplore his choice. You must give them no reason to suggest that they are right and he was wrong.' If I claim now that Francis defiled me, there will be a scandal and doubts. The neighbours will shake their heads and say: No smoke without fire. My reputation, and Ned's, will never be the same.

So I go back to the Widow Dent. She is waiting outside her cottage as if she knows I am coming. I can't talk, but Sybil knows what has happened.

'Come,' she says. 'We'll find him a place to lie in the sun.'

Old as she is, the widow digs him a grave in a clearing, at the edge of the shade of an old ash, where the sun will warm the ground and sift through the leaves in summer. I hold Hap in my lap, stroking his wiry head, his velvety ears, feeling him grow stiff and cold. My throat is so tight I can hardly swallow. I wish I could rewind time, decide to leave him behind. I think, if I close my eyes tight enough, I will feel him breathing once more, feel his warm snuffle in my palm, the wriggle of his stumpy tail.

Sybil comes for him. She holds out her hands. 'Let him go now,' she says. 'It is time.'

'No,' I say. 'No.'

But she shakes her head. 'Yes,' she says. 'Let me take him.'

'I will do it.'

It is the last thing I can do for him. I get stiffly to my feet and carry Hap over to the hole in the ground. I kiss his nose one last time. 'Goodbye, dear friend,' I say and lay him tenderly down. And then, before I can change my mind, I push the earth over him with my hands, scrabbling frantically to cover him, as if I could cover the memories of him pressing by my side, greeting me with a squirm of his body, his lip lifted in that silly dog grin of his. He was only a dog, but I loved him as I loved Elizabeth, and now both are gone.

Chapter Eleven

I drew a shuddering gasp, but the tears wouldn't stop. I rocked forward over the earth, my body clenched with misery.

'Grace . . . ' Vivien laid a hand on my back. 'Grace, can you hear me?'

'He was just a *dog*,' I sobbed. 'Why did he have to kill him?'

'It's over, Grace,' she said, but I wasn't listening. I was still crouched over the grave of my little dog.

'I can't bear it. *Hap* . . . '

'Grace.' Vivien's voice firmed as mine rose. 'Get up now.'

Groggy with grief, I lifted my head, to find myself looking at an utterly strange woman, but even as I wondered, the past was fading and I remembered where I was. Who I was.

I was kneeling half-in, half-out of one of Vivien's pretty flowerbeds, and my hands were filthy from scrabbling in the earth. I'd ripped up a whole clump of pinks in my frenzy to bury Hap.

I felt sick.

'Vivien . . . I'm so sorry,' I stumbled through the words, appalled. 'I'm really sorry.'

'Come.' She helped me up. 'Come and wash your hands – we'll have that tea, and then we'll talk.'

Shakily I knuckled the tears from my cheeks. 'Sorry,' I said again, but she shushed me and led me inside to a sink. I scrubbed the earth from my hands and splashed cold water over my face, and began to feel a bit better.

'Your poor garden,' I said guiltily as I sat back beside Vivien on the bench.

'The garden will grow again,' she said. 'Here, I made some fresh tea. Drink it.'

I sipped obediently, although I would have sold my soul right then for something stronger. It was tasteless, but after a few moments, calmness stole over me.

'Is this just nettles?'

'Among other things,' said Vivien.

'Drugs?' I paused with the mug halfway to my lips.

She smiled and shook her head. 'Just a little kitchen magic.'

What was a little magic, in the strangeness of my life right then? I took another sip and put the mug down on the arm of the bench.

'How long was I . . . like that?'

'Not long. I saw you fade out, so I took the mug away in case you burnt yourself. You just sat and stared ahead. I could tell you weren't here. I sat beside you until you started to cry and began scrabbling at the ground over there.'

'That's where I buried Hap.' I ached with the memory. I

looked at Vivien's calm profile. Anyone else would have been running for a doctor, but she just sat there, and she *knew*. Was she Sybil? 'Do you remember?'

'No,' she said. 'That doesn't mean it didn't happen or that I wasn't there.'

'Do you believe you've lived before?'

'Many times,' she said simply.

I could hardly believe I was having this conversation on a bright Monday morning. 'I don't know what's happening to me,' I said. 'I was just sitting here, looking at that tree . . . ' My voice trailed off as I realized the tree had gone. In its place was a lilac bush, covered in butterflies.

'Tell me,' said Vivien.

I told her everything, and in that charming little garden with the drone of bees loud in the air, it didn't sound as bizarre as it had done when I told Drew.

'What do you think?' I asked when I had stopped.

Vivien eyed me thoughtfully. 'I think you're fortunate to have been given the chance to re-experience the past so vividly.'

'I don't feel fortunate,' I grumbled. There was earth under my fingernails and, kitchen magic or no kitchen magic, I was still churning with reaction. 'I feel . . . I feel as if I'm being used.'

'I think you're right,' said Vivien composedly. 'Hawise seems to be using you to tell her story.'

'But *why*? And why me? There's nothing special about me.'

'Isn't that what Hawise thinks too?'

'Yes.' I nodded slowly as I thought about it. 'I mean, she's a bit different, but she tries to fit in. It's not like she's trying to be unconventional. That's more about the way other people think of her than about anything she does.'

'Isn't that true of all unconventional people?' Vivien's smile was wry, and I shifted on the bench, remembering how easily I had always dismissed Lucy's unconventional ideas. 'From what you've told me, Hawise doesn't understand that befriending a deformed dog or a woman suspected of being a witch makes her not only different, but dangerous in the eyes of her neighbours.'

'It's so stupid the way they think,' I said angrily. 'Why can't they see that Hap was just a dog?' My heart clenched like a fist at the memory of him, of that terrible squeal as Francis's knife slashed through the light.

'You think the way Hawise does,' said Vivien, and then she paused. 'Or perhaps it's the other way round. Have you considered that *you* might be possessing Hawise?'

The strangeness of the idea had me gawping at her. 'Me? I'm not the one who's dead!'

Unperturbed, Vivien sipped her tea. 'Time doesn't always work the way we think it does. We like to think that if something has happened in the past, it's finished, but how do we draw a line and say "Now this is over" or "This started *then*"?'

Drew Dyer had said something similar, I remembered.

'I've often thought that time is a circle, not a straight line,' Vivien went on, watching a butterfly dip and dart around the lilac. 'And if that's the case, who came first: you or Hawise?'

'I've got no reason to haunt anyone,' I said, hardly able to believe I was actually having this conversation.

'Haven't you?'

'No! The whole idea is ridiculous!'

Vivien just shrugged. 'Perhaps,' she said.

'Besides, no one is obsessed with me the way Francis is obsessed with Hawise,' I argued as if she had insisted that she was right. 'I feel so sorry for Hawise,' I said. 'She has so few options. She can't leave York. She can't run away and start a new life. She can't take out a restraining order. And Francis . . . he's so creepy.' I shuddered, remembering the redness of his mouth and the blankness of his eyes. Those eyes that were so like Ash's eyes. I thought about Sophie's expression as she gazed after him, and disquiet trembled at the edges of my mind. I'd been so taken up with my grief over Hap that I'd forgotten about Sophie.

But what could I do? I couldn't do anything about the darkness that I sensed in Ash, any more than Hawise could do anything about Francis.

'There's a slipperiness about him,' I tried to explain to Vivien, and I wasn't sure myself whether I was talking about Ash or Francis at that point. 'It's like trying to pick up wet soap. He just slides through your fingers. You can't catch him out. And he's shiny. He reflects back what people want to see, I think, and no one looks past that to what he's really like. No one sees him except me.'

I stopped, realizing that I was rattling on, sounding more than a little obsessive myself. And why was I talking in the present tense? I hardly knew Ash. I was thinking about Francis, and he was Hawise's problem.

'Why won't he leave her alone?' I said. 'It's almost as if he loves her and hates her at the same time.'

Vivien nodded. 'He's obsessed with her. It's a form of delusion. Modern medicine would call it de Clérambault's syndrome, I suspect.'

'What would *you* call it?'

'It sounds to me as if Francis is possessed, just as you are.'

'Unless I've got a syndrome too,' I said, thinking about Sarah and what she had told me about post-traumatic stress disorder.

'Which would you rather have?'

'Neither.' Edgily I got to my feet. 'I don't like this,' I said, hugging my arms together. 'I'm not mad!'

'I didn't say you were.'

'Some of it fits with post-traumatic stress disorder,' I said. 'There's a smell or a sound – something that tips me back – but I'm not re-experiencing the tsunami, I'm reliving Hawise's life. She's too real for me to make her up.'

'And the idea of being possessed scares you,' said Vivien.

'Of course it does!' I snapped. 'I mean, I'm drawn to Hawise in lots of ways,' I said more calmly. 'Part of me wants to know what happens to her, part of me *wants* to go back, but I don't like the way she seems to be able to control me.'

'So it's the idea of losing control that scares you, more than the idea that another spirit is sharing your mind?'

'Yes . . . no . . . ' I dropped back onto the bench, defeated. 'I don't know.'

Vivien sat quietly beside me as I stared unseeingly at the garden, at the mess of earth where I had scrabbled to bury Hap.

Where *Hawise* had buried Hap. I had to keep her separate from me, but it was hard when her memories seemed to be my own.

'What can I do?' I asked Vivien at last. 'The obvious thing is to leave York, but that feels like running away. Besides, I can't go yet. I've got students who need to finish their course, quite apart from the fact that I won't be able to buy a ticket to Mexico until I've sold the house. I have to stay for a while longer, but I can't keep on like this, never knowing if I'm going to suddenly find myself back in Elizabethan York. What if I'd been walking along a road just now, instead of sitting in your garden? I might just have walked into the traffic!'

'Yes, there are dangers,' said Vivien. 'You must be careful. Hawise is clearly very strong.'

Stronger than me. I didn't like that. I was used to being the strong one.

'Can you make her go away?'

'Is that what you really want?'

I didn't answer immediately. 'I'm not sure,' I admitted. 'I've got this feeling that I need to know what happened to Hawise. Something must have happened, mustn't it? Or why would she be so determined to make me relive her life?'

Vivien nodded. 'Yes, clearly she is not at peace.'

'So I think I'd feel as if I were letting her down somehow, if I shut her out completely,' I said. 'I know it sounds stupid, but yes, it feels as if she's part of me, and I'd be closing off something in myself. Oh, I can't explain what it's like.' I shook my head in frustration. 'I just hate this feeling that Hawise is controlling me.'

'Then you must learn to control her,' Vivien said. 'You must find out what she needs in order to rest, but first you must be able to contain her. Can you summon her at will?'

'I've never tried.'

'Try now. You'll be safe if I'm here.'

I hesitated. 'How?'

'Close your eyes,' said Vivien. 'Empty your mind. I think Hawise will come.'

I felt a bit silly, but I did as she said. I tried not to think about anything, but my mind wouldn't stay still. It bounced around between Francis and Vivien and Hap and Sybil Dent, only to veer off inexplicably to Lucas, then Drew Dyer, and the look on Sophie's face as she gazed up at Ash.

My eyes snapped open. 'It's not working.'

'You're trying too hard. Close your eyes again and tell me what you can hear.'

Biting my lip, I squeezed my eyes shut once more and strained to listen. 'I can hear a flutter of wings,' I said slowly. 'It's a bird, a pigeon perhaps, or a blackbird, settling on a branch. And I can hear a bee . . . that's odd.' I frowned. 'There shouldn't be a bee around in the middle of winter.'

A tiny pause. 'What else can you hear?'

My clogs on the cobbles. I'm trying to keep up with Ned's easy stride. His legs are much longer than mine, and I'm puffing out breaths that hang in the cold air.

Henry Judd's apprentices are working late, unloading casks of wax from a cart and rolling them up planks into his workshop. I can hear the crunch of the casks as the apprentices dump them on the gravel, the chink of the iron bands against stone when they tip them over, and then the rumble of the casks on the wooden slope.

Thomas West and his wife are arguing as usual in the chamber above their shop. You can hear their quarrel halfway down the street, but no one is taking much notice. Robert Wharfe's dog is barking, but no one takes much notice of that, either. The sound of barking reminds me of Hap, and my heart twists as it always does when I think of him.

There is laughter spilling out of the alehouse, the jingle of harness as a stable boy leads a horse into the courtyard of the Bull Inn, and now the Minster bell is bonging in the chill air. It is six of the clock on a dank November evening, and the street is still full of noise.

We are on our way to my father's house in Hungate. I am not looking forward to it. I am ashamed of myself for being ashamed of my family, but my father is raucous when he is in his cups, and Agnes is pale and trembling, and Jennet is a terrible cook. It will not be a comfortable evening for Ned or for me.

We must go, of course. I cannot naysay my family. I have chosen my dress carefully. It has to be fine enough to do them honour, but not so fine it makes Agnes look shabby. In the end I chose a blue damask gown with puffed sleeves and a pleated skirt. I have to hold it up to step over the gutters as I walk with Ned, who is looking not handsome, no, but steady and solid.

Every now and then I peep a glance at him under my lashes and remember the night before, when he pulled the curtains around the bed and drew me to him with a smile.

'I have missed you, little wife,' he said.

I laughed. 'You were only gone half a day!'

'Still, I missed you.'

I think of his hands, of his mouth on my skin, and I shiver with remembered pleasure. No one looking at my husband would guess the passion that burns in him when we are alone in the dark.

Ned had noticed straight away that Hap was missing. 'He was caught under a wagon's wheel,' I said. I did not tell him the truth. I am not going to speak of Francis. It will not bring Hap back and, besides, what if Francis is right? What if Ned doesn't believe me?

For Francis is quite the gentleman now. The neighbours speak admiringly of him. Everyone has noticed how devout he is, how seriously he takes his duties as churchwarden. His house is modest enough, as befits an unmarried man, but he is careful to be generous without being ostentatious. His clothes are good, but not so rich that he makes his fellow notaries suspicious.

Oh, yes, he is clever. He has judged the neighbourhood to a nicety. They see a young man who is sober and devout. They do not know that he has hastened his master to his death, for so I am certain that he did. They don't see the ugliness in his eyes, the brutal violence that simmers just below that smooth, smooth surface.

I do. Before Hap, I was afraid of Francis and what he might

do to me, but now hatred has settled low and hard inside me, ready for a long ride. I am not weeping and wild-eyed. My loathing is cold, dark, unmoving, like the Foss when it freezes. I can feel it in my gullet, in my belly.

I do not have to see him often – that is something. He is at church, always, but I keep my eyes lowered. I know he watches me, though. I can feel his gaze burning through my gown. Once I looked up and found him staring at me with an expression that made my stomach churn. He smiled when he saw me looking, and ran his tongue around his lips in a way that made the hatred clog in my throat, and I wrenched my eyes away before I beat at him with my fists. I haven't made that mistake again.

Now, as we walk through the streets, I look at my husband and marvel that I could ever have thought him homely. Ned's mouth is firm, his eyes steady, and beneath my hand his arm is very solid.

He brings me a gift whenever he comes home. A ring, a pair of gloves, a girdle. Yesterday he brought me a book – and oh, what a book! My eyes stung with tears when I opened it very carefully.

It is a book of travellers' tales, and I am entranced by it. When I turn the pages and run my fingers over the pictures, I even forget my hatred of Francis Bewley. There are pictures of the men with only one foot, of the tribe who have only one eye in the middle of their foreheads and – my favourite – the Great Khan, with his costly robes.

Strange to think that outside York's walls, far, far away, they are living such different lives. When I read my book I wish that

I could be there, to see for myself, to be away from York and the fear that, whenever I step outside my door, Francis Bewley will be there with his red mouth and his black heart and his strange, shiny eyes. What would it be like, I wondered last night, turning the pages of the book for the first time, to go to the Spice Islands? To be free?

And as I wondered, there was a rushing in my ears, and a feeling as if I were being sucked out of my body so that I could look at myself with another girl's eyes. A girl for whom it was *my* life that was different. My head was bent over the book, but I could see myself, the strangeness of me.

Then the feeling was gone, and my heart jumped into my throat as I slammed back into my body. There was no one else, just me and my book.

And my husband, watching me. My good, kind husband who sees me for who I am.

'Do you like it?' he asked.

I shook the strange feeling aside and smiled at him. 'It is a book of wonders,' I said. I laid it down and got to my feet so that I could go over to him and rest my palms on his chest. 'Thank you, Husband,' I said, and I stood up on tiptoe to press my mouth to his. 'Thank you.'

I hoped my kiss would tell him everything I didn't know how to say: that I was glad to be his wife, that it didn't matter to me now that he is older, that I craved his touch and the feel of his body.

That I would like him to take me up to our bed, right then. His arms did tighten around me, his mouth opened over mine and I melted into him, but then the latch was lifting and Isobel was bringing wine into the parlour and the moment was broken.

I wish we were alone again now, instead of rapping on the door of my father's house.

Jennet lets us in with a grunt. Everything feels mean and faintly grubby here, and I am ashamed to compare it with Ned's house. But I fix a smile on my face when we step into the parlour. I don't want to hurt Agnes's feelings.

The smile freezes on my face when I realize that there is one other guest.

It is Francis Bewley.

His lips are glistening as he licks them slowly at the sight of me.

My heart lurches sickeningly and I take an instinctive step backwards, but Ned is behind me on the threshold and urging me forward, and there is nothing for it but to go on.

Somehow I greet my father, sketch a nod in Francis's direction and turn to my sister – my poor sister who has no defences against a man like Francis. What is my father thinking of, inviting him here?

'Agnes,' I say, kissing her cheek, hoping to convey my sympathy, but her face is bright as she draws back, and she looks flushed and happy. Happier than I have ever seen her before.

A sense of foreboding grips me around my gullet. 'You look well,' I say. It is true.

'Thank you, Sister.'

My father rubs his hands together and shouts to Jennet to bring wine. 'Come, we are to celebrate! I have good news. Your sister has found herself a husband too,' he says, and even though I have feared this is what he is going to say from the moment I saw Francis standing there, my heart leaps in shock.

'No,' I protest without thinking. 'No, that cannot be!'

There is an appalled silence while my words ring around the room. *No, no, no.*

'Hawise . . . ' Ned's voice is troubled. Too late, I look at Agnes. She stares at me as if I have struck her, and her face crumples.

'Come, come, Daughter.' Even my father, usually oblivious, is uncomfortable. 'You have a fine husband. You cannot begrudge your sister one too.'

'It's not that,' I say, stumbling over my words. 'It's just . . . ' But what *is* it? I cannot say, without explaining what Francis did to me, to Hap, and I have left it too late for that. I wanted to spare Ned and myself the humiliation, and instead I have left my sister exposed.

Agnes stifles a sob, and Francis puts a hand on her shoulder. His eyes meet mine, and I want to scream at the others, *Look! Look at him gloating!*

'I'm sure your sister didn't mean to be unkind, my dear,' he says.

'I thought you would be *happy* for me,' she wails.

'I am, Agnes, I . . . '

I feel as if I have waded into a river, the mud and water

weighing down my skirts, clutching at my feet. What can I say? What can I do?

For now, there is nothing. I wish I could believe that Francis really wants Agnes, but I only have to look into his eyes to know that it is me he wants. He loves me and hates me in equal measure. He cannot let me go, and he will do anything to be near me. I know this without being told.

My tongue feels stiff and unwieldy in my mouth. 'I *am* happy for you, Agnes,' I say because I cannot say anything else. 'I'm sorry. I spoke without thinking. Of course this is good news.'

I go over to kiss her, but she jerks her cheek away.

It is the worst meal of my life. My father drinks too much, Ned and Francis carry on the conversation, and Agnes sits and casts me wounded looks.

None of them can see Francis as I do – not even Ned. He can't see the malice in Francis's eyes, or hear the slyness in his voice. He doesn't understand that every time Francis looks at me, I feel as if I am covered in slime.

They talk as men do, about trade and taxes, about the Spanish and the Lowlanders and the keelmen who ply the river between here and Hull, as if those things matter. Surely what happens in our houses, in our streets, matters more than that? Isn't it more important that our families are safe, that a man like Francis cannot walk in and foul everything he touches?

This is all my fault. Francis is using Agnes, I know this. How can she possibly be happy with him? And yet, she is happy now – or she was, until I spoke without thinking. She believes that

Francis cares for her, that is clear. She won't want to hear the truth.

I pick fretfully at my food, very aware that Agnes never takes her eyes off Francis, while Francis makes a point of watching me. His gaze rests on my mouth, on my breasts. Can't Ned *see* what he is doing? Can't Agnes see? I want to squirm, but won't give Francis the satisfaction.

At last we can go.

'You are very quiet,' Ned says as we walk home. 'Why aren't you happy for your sister?'

'I don't trust Francis Bewley,' I say flatly.

'He is pleasant enough,' says my husband, 'and he will make your sister a good husband. She needs a home of her own.'

'I know, it's just . . . I'm not sure Francis is the right man for her,' I try.

'He is willing, and that is enough.' Sometimes Ned surprises me with his practicality. 'Agnes is not well favoured. She has been lucky to find a husband at all. She is not like you,' he adds, his voice dropping to a caress. 'There is no warmth or sweetness to her.'

'She is sickly.' I make excuses for her, the way I always do. 'It is not her fault.'

'All the more reason not to oppose this marriage. Agnes has little enough. Do not deny her that as well.'

I sigh. He is right. 'I will apologize to her,' I promise. 'I will go and see her tomorrow.'

And perhaps then, I think, I will be able to talk to her alone and make her understand what kind of man Francis is.

But Agnes doesn't want to understand.

'Francis explained how it would be,' she says when I go back the next day.

'What do you mean?'

'We have no secrets from each other.' There is a triumphant look in her eyes as she spreads her skirts and sits at the window. She is very pleased with herself today.

She hasn't invited me to sit, but I am too restless to settle anyway and am wandering around the chamber, touching things, wondering how to extricate my sister from Francis's clutches.

'He told me how you used to meet,' says Agnes. 'I know how in love you were with him.'

'In love with *Francis*?' I swing round in shock. 'Never!'

'You told me so yourself.'

'What? When?'

She points at the bed. 'You sat there and told me that you were in love.'

I stare at the bed, remembering that day, remembering how excited and full of hope I was then. How foolish I was. I *did* say that.

'Agnes, I hadn't even met him properly then,' I try to explain. 'I didn't know what I was saying.'

She doesn't listen. 'It must have been a terrible shock when you saw him last night. I should have warned you, but I was so excited. That was wrong of me.' She folds her hands in her lap with a little sigh. 'I hoped – I *hoped* – that you would care enough for me not to make a scene, but I understand why you were upset, Sister. I know what it is to love him.'

'Agnes . . . ' Helplessly I drop onto a stool and press my fingers to my temples.

'You don't need to explain,' she says. 'Francis told me how it was with you.'

Ah, yes, he would have done. I should have anticipated that Francis would put his own twist on the tale first.

I lift my head to look at my sister. 'How was it?' I ask dully, knowing I am not going to like the answer.

'He was very wrong to meet you before,' says Agnes with a suitably sombre expression, but I get the feeling she is enjoying this. 'He knows he was weak and led astray, and afterwards he was sorry, but he was unprepared for how forward you were. I understand your desire for him.' Here my sister lowers her eyes, and a knowing smile trembles on her lips. 'But Francis is very devout. It pains me to say this to you, Hawise, but he was shocked. He was sorry that you were forced to marry Ned, of course, but I think it was a relief to him, and then when he met me . . . '

She trails off with a contented sigh. 'He didn't know it was possible to feel like this. That's why he was determined to woo *me* properly.'

The look that accompanies this is needle-sharp. I haven't missed the emphasis on that 'me'. I am the trollop, it says, and she is the pure virgin, worthy to be courted with respect.

Agnes can't leave it there, though. '*I* am not to be romped in the grass,' she says sweetly.

I whiten with fury. 'I *never*—' I begin, leaping from my stool, but she lifts a hand.

'We don't need to speak of it.' She is all understanding. 'It is over.'

Francis has played his hand well. Whatever I say, she will not believe me now.

Swallowing my rage, I pace the chamber, as if looking for a door that will let me out of this situation. 'Tell me something,' I say, swinging round. 'Did Francis know you were my sister when you met?'

'Not at first, but then when he heard your name mentioned, he guessed, and he told me everything.' Her smile is smug. 'He didn't want there to be any secrets between us.'

'Agnes . . . ' I shake my head in frustration. 'You don't understand. Francis is not who you think he is!'

With a sigh, Agnes gets to her feet and smooths down her gown. 'Francis warned me you might be like this,' she says, letting disappointment creep into her voice, 'and I see he was right. Can't you just accept that he loves me, Hawise? I do think you might at least *try* to be happy for me. You have had everything – everything! – and I have had to stay and look after our father.'

I want to say that she hasn't looked after him, Jennet has, but I don't. There is truth in what she says. I have been luckier than my sister.

'Is it so hard for you to believe that a man might be interested in me?' Agnes sweeps on. 'That he might actually *prefer* me to you?'

'No, of course not.'

'Or is it that you think I'm not pretty enough for Francis?'

I sigh. 'It's not that, Agnes. You know that.'

'You can't bear not being the centre of attention, can you? Every man has to look at you, you, you!'

'What?' I reel back as if she has punched me. Where has all this come from? 'No! What do you mean? No one has ever looked at me!'

'Oh, yes,' Agnes laughs wildly. 'Act the innocent! It is what you do best, after all!' And she throws herself face-down onto the bed.

I stare at her in consternation. This is Francis's doing. Already he has driven a wedge between me and my sister, already she thinks differently of me.

'Do you want to know what I think?' she says, her voice muffled in the coverlet. 'I think you are jealous just because I will have a young husband and yours is old!'

'Ned isn't old,' I protest, stung.

'And Francis is handsome and kind.' Agnes pulls herself up and flings herself back against the pillows. There is a hectic flush in her cheeks, a feverish glitter in her eyes. 'I cannot believe how lucky I am. This is the first time anything has gone right for me, and you want to spoil it!'

In dismay I watch tears fill her eyes. What can I say? If I persist, if I convince her that Francis tried to defile me and killed Hap, I will destroy her fragile happiness. If I say nothing, I abandon her to Francis Bewley, a man who would kill a dog without hesitation. He will push himself into her, the way he tried to do with me. I am terribly afraid that he will hurt her and use her to punish me.

This is the first time anything has gone right for me. Her words echo around the chamber. I think of my sister, of the years she has spent here in this dreary house, lying abed with the shutters closed. Now, at last, she has someone paying her attention, someone offering her an escape from this.

I will never be able to convince her that it is a mistake. And I do not want to be the one who makes her unhappy. I will have to accept this, as Ned said, and make the best of it.

'I won't spoil it, Agnes,' I promise her. I sit on the edge of the bed and smooth a strand of hair back under her cap. 'I just want you to be happy.'

She turns her face away, her lip trembling. 'How can I be happy when everyone is so unkind? Father says he has no money to pay for a proper wedding feast. We will be lucky if we can offer our guests a boiled turnip!'

I recognize my cue. 'My husband and I will give you a feast to remember for your wedding,' I say, and instantly Agnes is all smiles again.

'Truly? And you'll speak to Father about a new gown? I cannot be married in this!'

'It will be my gift to you,' I say, and I wonder what else I will have to do to make it up to her.

Chapter Twelve

All week the servants have been busy preparing a lavish wedding feast for Agnes and Francis. Margery is torn. She doesn't want to be helpful, but her pride is at stake, and in the end she enjoys showing off her skills as a cook, while Isobel and Alison have swept and polished and scrubbed. There are fresh rushes on the floor of the hall and the waits are tuning up in the corner, ready to play after the meal. No one will be able to say that I did not honour my sister with the best of everything.

It is late January, and the markets are thin, but I have set a feast fit for a queen before my sister. There are boiled capons and stewed mutton steaks, a roast calf and baked fish. There are tarts and pies, jellies and custards, sugar comfits and the best manchet bread. And, best of all, a grand centrepiece: a goose stuffed with a pheasant, stuffed with a chicken, stuffed in its turn with a pigeon, which I have made myself to make up for my ungraciousness when I first heard of her betrothal.

It is the least I can do for my sister, I think guiltily. I am terribly afraid for her, but Agnes herself is ecstatic. She is besotted with Francis and watches him hungrily. I watch him too, waiting for him to show himself, but he is unctuous in his dealings with her and never less than courteous, I have to admit. So I try to tell myself that I am wrong about the way he looks at me. I tell myself that I am imagining it and that his obsession with me is over.

I want to believe that it will be all right.

Agnes and Francis sit together in triumph on high table, presiding over the feast. Afterwards there is dancing. I supervise the clearing away of the tables, while Ned moves among the guests, making sure everyone has had enough to eat, clapping one on the shoulder, beckoning for more wine for another.

I watch him under my lashes. He is so solid, so steady, the calm centre around which the rest of the room swings giddily, and I feel the heat spilling along my veins and pooling in the pit of my belly. I want to go to him, to my cool, contained husband, wrap my arms around his waist and press my face into his throat. I am not the enchantress, whatever the neighbours think. It is Ned who has enchanted *me*, with the touch of his hands and the feel of his mouth.

Across the hall Ned glances up and sees me watching him. My hunger must show in my face, because he smiles slightly. I smile back. A promise. Later, his eyes say, and I smile again and nod, suddenly giddy with happiness. *Later*. Later we will lie together between the curtains, and I will forget Agnes and Francis and the distrustful servants and the neighbours who take Ned for a fool. There will just be the two of us, and the heat and the rush and the certainty that nothing and nobody else matters.

I am in love with my own husband. Agnes is right: I have everything.

I am glowing as I turn away.

'Dance with me, Sister.'

Francis's voice is a snail trailing stickily over a perfect rose. All day, in spite of my attempts to convince myself that it will be all right, I have avoided him, and now he is there, standing too close, and my happiness leaks out of me.

I have been fooling myself. I have been dancing in the dark. Francis has not forgotten me. It is not over.

It will not be all right.

I force a smile while every piece of me screams to step away from him. But it is his wedding, and Agnes's wedding, and people will be watching.

I glance at Agnes, who is watching us from the table. Beside her, Mistress Beckwith is trying to make conversation with her, but Agnes has no eyes for anyone but Francis.

'You should dance with your wife,' I say coldly.

'I want to dance with you.'

'But Agnes—'

'Agnes wants what I want. You cannot refuse me,' he says.

The waits are all set to play and dancers are taking to the floor. I can make a scene at my sister's wedding, or I can take Francis's hand and dance with him. What can he do to me in front of everyone, after all?

Swallowing my revulsion, I nod tightly and let him take my

hand and lead me into the middle of the floor, but my flesh shrinks from his touch. We join a circle and I marvel that the others cannot see the sickliness of my smile.

The music starts. We hold hands, dance to one side and then the other. We turn to our partners, press our palms together. Francis leans towards me and murmurs close to my ear.

'I'll think of you every time I fuck her.'

It is as if he has slapped me. I jerk my head back, unable to believe that he actually said that. I want to believe that I made it up, but I know I didn't. Francis is smiling. His red mouth is shiny between his beard and his hands are hot and moist, and I am sick with loathing.

And with fear. Because there is a wrongness in Francis's eyes that curdles my stomach, a heat and a hunger that raise the tiny hairs on the back of my neck.

'How dare you say such a thing to me in my husband's house,' I whisper fiercely. 'You are vile!'

Francis continues to smile. He is enjoying my fear and my loathing. 'I can say what I like to you, Hawise. You won't tell.'

'Do not push me!'

The dance sends us out and around in a circle, back again.

'No,' he carries on musingly, 'you won't say anything. You're too afraid of upsetting your little sister. Strange how you crave her approval,' he muses. 'Why is that? Why do you try and make her like you? You feel you must pay for being beautiful while she is plain, don't you? For being clever while she is stupid, for being rich while she is poor.'

'Agnes is your *wife*,' I say tautly. 'How can you speak of her like that?'

'I can speak of her however I like,' says Francis. 'She is my wife, as you say.'

Nobody else can hear our conversation over the music. They are all laughing and talking, as if they are in a different world.

'Don't hurt Agnes,' I say, my voice shaking with hatred. 'You will regret it if you do. I promise you that.'

'That is up to you,' says Francis. 'If you are kind to me, I will be kind to your sister. That is fair exchange, is it not?'

I stare at him with such disgust that he clicks his tongue. 'Come, come, Hawise,' he chides me gently. 'Smile. You don't want to spoil Agnes's wedding day, do you? Everyone will see you quarrelling with your new brother and wonder what is between us. You know how little it will take for the gossips to cry Ned a cuckold, and Agnes is already suspicious of your love for me.'

'Love!' I am revolted by him, but I do smile. I know it will hurt Agnes if I expose Francis for what he is, and Ned has risked enough by taking me as a wife. 'You know nothing of love,' I say. 'You are hateful.'

His smile flickers and something shifts in the shiny eyes as he spins me round in the dance and our hands clap together, but the next moment that insolent smile is back in place.

'Is that any way to talk to your brother, hmm? You will never be rid of me, Hawise,' he says and, when he runs his tongue over his lips, I close my eyes at the glee in his face. 'I am family now.'

*

When I opened my eyes, my stomach tilted in shock to find myself sitting in a garden instead of dancing. The relief of not seeing Francis's face was countered by a vicious headache that skewered my brain, and the jarring effect of being jolted through time had the breath whistling in my throat.

'It's all right,' said Vivien's calm voice. 'You're safe.'

How could I be safe when Francis was always there, stalking me like a cat with its prey?

'God, I hate him!' I buried my face in my hands, rage and revulsion still surging through me. 'I *hate* him! Why can't he leave me alone?'

'Tell me what happened this time,' said Vivien, and listened, fascinated, while I told her of my horror at the way Francis was using my sister.

'Hawise's sister, not mine,' I corrected myself hastily. I didn't have a sister. I was getting increasingly confused between Hawise's life and my own. 'It's horrible,' I said. 'Francis isn't doing anything – he's just looking – but if you could see how he wets his lips and smiles at me . . . at *her*—' I broke off with a shudder.

Vivien studied my face with concern. 'Perhaps it was a mistake to deliberately try and regress yourself. You don't need to go on with this if you don't want to, Grace.'

I thought of how easily Hawise could take over my mind. She had been there, just waiting for the slightest opportunity to slip in. 'I'm not sure I'm going to have a choice.'

'There's always a choice,' said Vivien.

We were silent for a while. Absently I fingered my pendant, thinking about Hawise, and the desperation I felt to relive her story. About her frustration, her love for Ned and her loathing for Francis. There was still so much I didn't understand.

'I can't help feeling that there's something I should be *doing*,' I said at last. 'Something in the here and now.'

'Like what?'

'I don't know.' I lifted my hands helplessly and let them fall. 'Like finding something in the records, perhaps. Sometimes, in Lucy's house, I can hear Hawise calling for Bess.'

'That's her daughter?'

'I know that from the nightmare,' I told Vivien. 'I dreamt that I was Hawise drowning, and she was desperate because she'd abandoned Bess. That's what is driving her, I can feel it, but I don't know what to do about it. I did ask Drew Dyer,' I went on, annoyed to feel my face heat at the sound of his name. 'He's a historian, and he said it would be almost impossible to find someone like Hawise, let alone track down her daughter. But maybe Hawise wants me to try harder.'

To hide my ridiculous blush I got up and began brushing the earth back into the hole that I – Hawise – had dug for Hap. 'I just feel that I have to do *something*,' I said. 'I can't sit and wait for Hawise to take me over again, can I? It's so passive, for a start, and what about my own life? I can't get on with that when I've got no idea when I might find myself in the sixteenth century. One way or another, I need to see this through,' I decided.

'In that case, you need protection.' Vivien got to her feet, matter-of-fact. 'I will cast a spell for you.' My scepticism must have shown in my face. 'You don't believe in magic, do you?'

'Well . . . '

'Like you didn't believe in ghosts?'

I didn't answer. I just brushed the dirt from my hands and looked back at her, and she smiled and went inside to fetch a knife.

'What's that for?' I asked a little nervously when she came back.

'I'm going to cast a circle.' She swept the knife over the patio bricks. 'Step inside,' she said to me.

Feeling self-conscious, I stepped over the imaginary line. Vivien turned me briskly until she was happy with the way I was facing, and then she tapped the ground with the knife.

'Guardians of the watchtowers of the west, I invoke thee,' she chanted. 'Protect your servant Grace from harm. Guide her through the darkness that threatens her, and keep her safc. As I ask, so mote it be.'

In one fluid movement she moved round the imaginary circle. 'Guardians of the watchtowers of the north, I invoke thee,' she began again, and went through the same chant.

I stood in the circle, holding onto my jade pendant as she moved to the east and then the south. Perhaps I should have felt foolish, standing in the middle of a suburban garden in broad daylight while a witch chanted around me, but something about the place held me still and silent. There was a power in Vivien's voice that made the air thrum and the blood beat in my veins. My headache was gone.

'As I ask, so mote it be.' Vivien made a final gesture in the air with her knife and fell silent.

'That's it?' I said uncertainly, and she smiled slightly.

'That's it. Except ' – she pulled a pendant from her throat and lifted it over her head – 'wear this,' she said.

It was very simple, just a clear stone on a cord. The stone was still warm from her skin. 'But this is yours,' I stammered.

'I made it for you.'

'But . . . you didn't know I was coming,' I said, lifting my eyes from the pendant.

'Didn't I?' Vivien took the pendant back and slipped it over my head. 'This will protect you. Don't take it off. And make sure it lies against your skin, over your heart.' She adjusted the length so that the pendant fell between my breasts. 'There, like that.'

I couldn't settle. Vivien's pendant felt heavy, almost hot, on my skin as I tried to concentrate on my lesson plans, and in the end I gave up and went downstairs to make myself some lunch. I wasn't teaching until three that afternoon, so I fiddled around in the kitchen, making myself a Spanish omelette while I churned with Hawise's sense of frustration, and my own. She was trapped by him; and I, it seemed, was trapped by her.

Usually I find cooking soothing, but chopping and slicing didn't help that day. I didn't like the feeling of helplessness. All I had wanted was to do right by my godmother and then move on, I remembered. I could have left everything to John Burnand, but instead there I was in York, ricocheting between the past and the present, trying to coax a surly adolescent into conversation and having spells cast over me.

And feeling resentful and sorry for myself, to boot. I caught myself up guiltily. I had to stop that.

I had meant what I said about trying harder to track down Hawise and Bess, but in the meantime, was it so bad to want to be normal for a while? I wished I could talk to Mel. I wanted a gossip. I wanted to have a conversation with someone who didn't know anything about York or the sixteenth century, and who didn't care; someone who didn't believe in ghosts or spells, and who would laugh at the idea that the stone lying against my heart could be pulsing with heat.

But Mel was in Mexico, and it was too early to Skype her. I sent her an email instead and checked out her page on Facebook. She'd put up new photos, of her and some friends in a bar. They were mugging for the camera, tipping their beer bottles, sucking in their cheekbones. Mel on some guy's lap, laughing. Having a great time. Living for the moment, not obsessed with the past.

The way I should be.

That was my life – not this strange half-and-half existence between past and present, protected by a crystal. I touched the stone where it nestled next to the jade pendant. I had thought about taking Matt's necklace off, but somehow that felt like a betrayal. I didn't know why, but I'd worn it ever since the tsunami, and taking it off felt like a big thing. There was no reason I shouldn't wear two pendants, I reasoned. Neither of them was obtrusive.

I was thinking about Matt and the pendant he had given me just as my eye caught his name and photo on Facebook, and I clicked without thinking onto his page to see what he was up to. We had stayed vaguely in touch since splitting up, but I hadn't heard from him for ages. Or perhaps it was me who hadn't been in touch. Matt was married, and I'd always thought that his wife, Emily, sounded unbearably twee. Still, Matt obviously adored her, and I was glad he was happy.

And then there were three . . . He had posted next to a photo of the two of them beaming at the camera. *We're thrilled to announce that we're expecting a baby in December. Emily is doing fine and only throwing up every other morning!*

So, Matt was going to be a father. I shook my head with a wry smile, trying to imagine it. Babies had been the last thing on his mind when we had been together. That had been something we'd had in common.

Would Matt have wanted the whole marriage-and-family thing if it hadn't been for the tsunami? I wondered. We had had a lot of fun together. Had he changed, or had I? Or had the tsunami just stripped us both back to the people we had been all along? If it hadn't happened, we might still have been racketing around the world having a good time. Did Matt ever think about that?

Still, he clearly had what he wanted now, and I was pleased for him. It wasn't for me, but that was fine. As long as I didn't have to change any nappies. I left a message congratulating them both, then shut down my computer and went out to teach.

It was after seven by the time I finished my classes and had packed up, and I was still restless. When I was teaching I didn't have time to think about Hawise or Francis, or anything other than what was happening in the classroom, but now that was over, I realized I didn't want to go back to Lucy's house, where the stench of the rank orchard still seeped through the rooms, no matter how carefully I cleaned them.

Deliberately I made myself walk along Coney Street, testing myself against Hawise. I longed to be normal again, to see only chain stores and mobile-phone shops, but while there was nothing of the Tudor street left, recognition clamoured at the edges of my mind. There was an odd feeling in the soles of my feet, and my steps slowed until I stopped outside a lingerie shop.

If I looked hard enough, I knew I would see the apothecary shop fronting the street, shutters open to show the blocks of sugar and the glass jars filled with comfits. Above was the jettied window where I sat turning the pages of my book, and behind it the chamber with its great bed, hung with curtains. The bed where I slept with Ned, where I leant over him and kissed his throat, his jaw. Where I slid my body down his, and made him smile. Made the heat pulse in us, between us.

Wriggling my shoulders at the shudder of memory, I turned abruptly away and ran slap into Drew Dyer, and every cell in my body leapt at the sight of him.

'What are you doing here?'

Drew lifted his brows at my tone. 'Getting tickets for a film tomorrow night. What about you?'

'Oh . . . ' I let out a breath. I was scratchy, frustrated, and my blood was pumping with the thought of Ned and the wicked pleasure we had shared. 'I'm just . . . oh, nothing.'

'You sound like Sophie. How about a drink to make you

feel better?' he added when I smiled reluctantly. 'The cinema has a decent bar overlooking the river.'

'Not the river,' I said quickly. Without being aware of it, I'd managed to avoid the Ouse since I'd arrived. It reminded me too much of Lucy, and of that dark, desperate dream of Hawise drowning. I smiled at Drew, in case he had picked up on my instinctive flare of alarm at the mention of the river. 'But, yes, a drink would be nice.'

We found a pub tucked away off Stonegate, right next to where John Harper put out his stall a whole foot further than anyone else. That was typical of him, of course. There was an insolence to everything he did. He wasn't a handsome man, but something about the way he would watch me as I passed made my cheeks prickle with heat and feel as if I had walked out in my shift.

Desperately I pushed the thought away. That was Hawise's memory, not mine. I didn't want her in my mind just then. What good was Vivien's protective amulet if Hawise could still slide into my head without me knowing?

The pub was quiet, with no frills. A bit like Drew Dyer in fact. He was real, present, and I concentrated on him so that there was no room for Hawise, but that turned out to be a mistake. I was excruciatingly aware of him as he sat next to me. I'd forgotten what a solid body he had, and his thigh was long and lean beside mine. I'd just need to shift an inch or two and I would be touching him.

I swallowed and eased myself further away. 'I saw Sophie today,' I said, to distract myself.

I told Drew about Ash and Mara, and he pulled his mouth down at the corners. 'I didn't like Ash,' I said. 'It wasn't anything he said or did. I just felt that he was . . . dangerous.'

Drew sighed and rubbed a hand over his face in a gesture that was already unsettlingly familiar. 'I know what you mean. I never trusted him. Ash was the sort of student who would cheat, but get away with it. Nasty things happen around them, but somehow it's never their fault. I wouldn't be surprised myself if he was a sociopath,' he said as he took a sip of his beer. 'But you can't go around making allegations like that against students without proof.'

Realizing that I was watching the muscles work in his throat, I tore my gaze away. 'What does that mean exactly, a sociopath?'

'Sociopaths can be superficially charming, but in fact they're manipulative and cold,' said Drew. 'They've got no empathy and are often pathological liars.'

'Did Sarah tell you that?' I moved my glass around the table, making patterns with the wet rings that it left on the wood. I felt crabby in a way I couldn't quite analyse.

'Yes, as a matter of fact. I talked to her about Ash when Sophie first met him. She thinks he fits the profile perfectly.'

Oh, well, if *Sarah* thought it, it must be right. I was beginning to irritate myself with the wet glass. I pushed it away with a scowl.

'Apparently sociopaths have a grandiose sense of self, and a disproportionate belief in their own abilities,' Drew went on. 'Sarah said they're often driven by a deep-seated anger, which means they see other people as tools to be used for their own ends. They feel no remorse for their actions, she said. The only thing that matters to a sociopath is getting his or her own way. They don't care what anyone else thinks or feels.'

It sounded a perfect description of Francis.

'But unless they commit a crime, there's nothing you can do,' Drew said. 'You can't arrest someone for being selfish and manipulative, more's the pity.'

'I can see why you're so worried about Sophie,' I said.

'I'm just hoping she'll get bored, or see through all the hocus-pocus eventually. She's a bright kid – but then my mother was clever too,' he said, and although he spoke lightly I could hear the bitterness running as deep as a tide. 'Not that it did her much good. All those brains and she still couldn't see what was right in front of her. She didn't like the real, my mother. Where was the fun, where was the *magic*, in caring for your family? In washing socks and cooking meals and talking to teachers?'

He stopped, clearly afraid that he had revealed too much. I watched him pick up his beer and drink, and although I tried not to look, I couldn't help noticing the strength of his hand around the glass. I could see the creases in his finger joints, the bumpiness of his knuckles, the broad wrists and the flat hairs beneath his watch, and I found myself remembering Ned again, and the warmth of his hands on my skin.

Swallowing, I looked away.

'Do you think that's why you became a historian? So that you could fix on the real – things you could prove and back up with evidence?'

'Perhaps,' he said slowly. 'I hadn't thought of it like that before, but . . . yes, perhaps.'

I picked up my beer mat and began refining the patterns I'd made with the bottom of my glass. I drew the edge of the mat through the wet rings, pulling out the circles and pushing the droplets in different directions. I was thinking about evidence, and how I might find out whatever it was that Hawise was so anxious to know. Perhaps if I did that, I could go back to my ordinary life.

Whatever that was – it was hard to remember when life had been ordinary.

'You know those records you're using? The ones about ordinary people mending streets and stuff?'

I could tell by Drew's pained expression that he was unimpressed by my grasp of his research. 'The wardmote-court returns?'

'Yes.' I wasn't going to tell him that I knew all about the wardmotes. I remembered the jurors setting off to inspect the wards, the grumbles in the street, the abuse (not all of it good-natured) as they noted blocked gutters and potholes or heard complaints about noisy neighbours. 'I wondered if I could look at them sometime,' I said, super-casual, but Drew's brows drew together.

'Is this still about the servant you wanted to track down? What did you call her?'

'Hawise.'

I wished I'd never said anything to Drew about what I was experiencing. If I hadn't been so shaken by Francis's attempted rape, I wouldn't have told him what had happened, but it was too late to take it back now.

'I thought Sarah had explained all that as post-traumatic stress disorder?'

'She did.' It was easier to let him believe that was all it was. He would never accept the idea of possession, I knew. 'I'm just interested. I wanted to put some names into your database and see if any of them come up.'

I've never been very good at flirting, but I wanted to distract Drew from asking too many questions. I looked him straight in the eyes and gave him my most winning smile. 'Would you mind?'

There was a tiny pause. Drew's eyes dropped briefly to my mouth and then he was looking back at me, and even though his expression was unreadable, I felt the colour swoosh up into my face.

'No, I wouldn't mind,' he said.

'Great!' I was mortified at the strangled sound of my own voice. I cleared my throat. 'When would suit you?'

'Tonight?'

'Sure. Why not?' My heart was pounding ridiculously.

Drew drained his beer and set his glass back on the table. 'Drink up then,' he said.

I had to hug my arms together when we left the pub, frightened that if I didn't, my hands would take on a life of their own. I was flustered by how badly I wanted to touch Drew. It was a long time since I felt that jab of lust, that twitchy craving to press skin against skin, to feel that aching slide of bone and muscle.

It was just because I'd been thinking of Ned earlier, I tried to excuse myself. With Hawise's memories running through my head like a private erotic show, it wasn't surprising that I was muddling the two men up. Drew and Ned didn't look alike, but they had the same contained air, the same cool mouths, the same capable hands.

Drew was talking as we headed back to Monk Bar, but I hardly heard him. I couldn't think clearly. I was dizzy with lust, fizzy with it. I was like a balloon tethered by a single strand, billowing up, ready to float out of control. I kept telling myself that it was wrong – that *he* was wrong – but it didn't do any good. I couldn't drag my eyes from his mouth, his hands. I couldn't stop thinking about what it would be like to spread my hands over his shoulders, to press my lips to the pulse that beat in his throat and breathe in the scent of his skin.

Who are you going to see the film with? The words hovered on my tongue, but I swallowed them. I didn't want to know the answer. I didn't want him to wonder why I cared.

It was just the mood I was in, I told myself, with an edge of desperation. I'd been like this all day, ever since Vivien had given me the amulet that pressed hot against my skin. I just wanted to anchor myself in the present – that was all it was.

I tried thinking about Drew as a small boy instead, hoping that it would sober me up. I'd hardly drunk anything, but I was reeling with lust and needed to give myself a mental slap in the face. What had it been like for him to realize that his mother didn't care about him? I made myself wonder, while we waited for the pedestrian-crossing lights outside the bar. How could she have left him like that?

I was just trying to distract myself, but at that thought a wave of desolation barrelled out of nowhere and smashed through me, pushing the air from my lungs and making me suck in a breath at the misery of it. I knew straight away what was happening, but I didn't want to slip back to Hawise in front of Drew. Desperately I dug my fingers into my arms, hoping the pain would keep me fixed in the present. My knuckles were white, I remember that, and I remember thinking that if I were lucky enough to conceive, I would never abandon my child. *Never*.

'Hello?' The Widow Dent's cottage looks just as it did a year ago. I am drawn to it and repelled at the same time. It stands in the clearing, misshapen and leaning, as old and bent as the widow herself. It is barely a hovel, and yet it seems to me that this place resonates with a power greater than the Common Hall, greater even than the Lord President's place where they do the Queen's business. The air is shiftier here, the silence deeper. There is a thudding in my ears.

The door is ajar, but I do not dare push it open and step inside. My knuckles are white against the handle of my basket, and I make myself relax my grip. Shifting the basket to my other arm, I call again.

'No need to shout.'

Sybil's voice behind me makes my heart lurch, and I spin round, clutching my throat. I have been straining for a sound in the silence. How could she have come up right behind me without me hearing her? Unless she appeared by magic. My mouth dries.

What am I doing here? This is no place for a young wife. But I want a child, and I can't think of anywhere else to go.

I didn't think it would be as hard as this. I conceived not long after Francis and Agnes's wedding, and for a while I was so happy I didn't even mind about Francis any more. Even Agnes seemed pleased when I told her of my conviction that I was with child. We grew closer, and for a while it was how I always imagined it would be: two sisters, both wed, talking about women's business. I told Agnes even before I told Ned. I wanted to be sure, before I got his hopes up. And Agnes was kinder than she has ever been. She made me rest and brewed special possets to make the baby strong, which she made me drink, scolding me when I made a face at the taste.

And then one day, just after I whispered the truth to Ned, I started to bleed. I was with Agnes when the cramps hit me, wrenching and racking and jerking at my belly, turning my body inside out until I hollered like a beast.

Ned was in London, and Agnes was all I had. She let me hang onto her hand, and she prayed for me, and she stayed with me until the desolate end. I was grateful to her for that.

Dear God, the pain was terrible, but I fought it all the way. I *wanted* that baby. But the screaming didn't help, and the prayers didn't help, and the yearning and the hoping didn't help, either. A last desperate convulsion and through a red haze I felt my child slip out of me and away, leaving me with only loss and loneliness.

I turned my face into the pillow while Agnes dealt with everything. She sent the maids for rags and hot water, and she cleared up the mess which was all that was left of my baby. 'It is God's will, Sister,' she said, smoothing the sheet down around me. 'There will be other chances.'

My eyelids were leaden with grief. I didn't want other chances, I wished I could shout. I wanted *that* baby. But I couldn't say that to Agnes, who had stayed by my side. All I could do was thank her. My head was so heavy on the pillow that it was a huge effort to move it, but I made myself turn, only to surprise an expression in her eyes – a gleam of something I couldn't read, something elusively familiar.

A blink later and the look was gone. I might have imagined it. I probably did. My mind was clouded with pain and grief. But sometimes the memory is like a sliver of ice in my head, and I puzzle over what it was and what it meant. Then the other day I watched John Acclam's mastiff chase a tomcat across the street. Swarming up a wall, the tom stopped to wash its paws, and the look it gave the raging dog below was replete with insolence and something that reminded me of the way Agnes looked that day: satisfaction.

I must be wrong.

There has not been another baby. 'Give it time,' says Ned, even though I know he longs for a child as much as I do. Agnes hasn't conceived, either. When I asked her if she yearns for a baby in the same way, a strange look crossed her face.

'I have Francis,' she said, as if that is an answer.

'Yes, but—'

'You should not talk of such things, Hawise,' she said curtly. 'It is not seemly. Whether we conceive or no is God's will.'

Perhaps she is right. Margery and the maids didn't know that I was with child, although I dare say they guessed. They will have heard my groans, will have seen the bloody rags, but no one ever says anything. It makes me feel as if have done something shameful, but how can it be shame to grieve for a babe lost?

So I keep it balled up inside me, the sadness and the longing, like a knot of brambles, and I hold myself very carefully. I don't cry and weep and wail. That would mean letting go, and even breathing too deep catches me on the thorns of my pain, tearing at me and making me flinch. I breathe shallowly and I don't look inside or try to untangle it; and then the sadness recedes to a constant dull ache of emptiness and loss and I can live with that.

Chapter Thirteen

My breath hangs in the iron-grey air as I stare at the cottage. The ground beneath my clogs is rigid and bumpy with ice, and my hands are very cold. It has been more than a year since Ned and I were wed. The neighbours, I know, suck in their teeth when they talk about me, and shake their heads at Ned's fool-ishness in marrying me. I should have given Ned a son by now. There are mutterings about curses, about how they always knew that I was no fit wife for him.

Agnes says I should ignore them. She is being very solici-tous, and brings me her special spiced mead every day, which I drink obediently. I don't really like it – it has a sour aftertaste – but she is eager to help and I don't want to hurt her feelings by refusing, not now that we have grown closer.

She and Francis live just around the corner now. My father, God rest his soul, died suddenly just after Lammas. He left everything he had to Agnes. What need had I of anything, with my rich husband? Francis argued. It is true that I lack for nothing, but I would have liked a keepsake.

Francis sold the house in Hungate and bought one in Jubbergate. It grates with him, I can tell, that he cannot afford a house like Ned's, but he has not done badly all the same. In a little over a year he has gone from a notary's assistant to a man of property with connections to one of the wealthiest men of the city. Sometimes I remember how coldly he spoke of his master – *I will see to him* – and I think of how unexpectedly my father died, but there is no one I can share my fears with. To the rest of the world Francis is a godly man with a respectable wife, welcome in the neighbourhood.

Unlike me.

But it doesn't matter what the neighbours say. Agnes is right. I can ignore them, but I cannot ignore the ache inside me. It will never go away until I hold my own baby in my arms.

I have been patient, I have prayed, to no avail. Now I will see if Sybil can help.

I didn't tell Agnes I was coming. I don't know why. I opened my mouth to ask if she wanted to come with me, but then I shut it again. Agnes will tell Francis, and I don't want him to know. I have accepted that I cannot change the fact that he and Agnes are married, but I avoid him as much as I can. Agnes seems happy enough. Sometimes I wonder if I imagined what he said to me at their wedding. He has said nothing since, but still, I do not want to meet him out here again. I may have accepted his marriage, but I have not forgotten what he did to me, and what he did to Hap.

'Come in then, as you're here,' says Sybil and pushes past me into the cottage. Inside it is as clean as I remembered.

'This is for you.' I hand over the basket of food I have made up: a pie, some cheese, a loaf of bread.

The widow pulls back the cloth and inspects my offering before grunting in acknowledgement. She puts the food on the table and jerks her head at a stool.

I sit obediently. The cat, Mog, appears and rubs her head against my skirts. Now that I am inside, I wonder why I was afraid. It is strangely restful in the dim light, just sitting and stroking the cat while the widow moves purposefully around, pulling dried herbs from the bunches that hang from the ceiling and whose scent mingles with the woody smell of leaves and earth.

'What are you doing?' I ask at last.

'Making you what you came for.'

My hand stills on Mog's fur. 'How do you know what it is that I want?' I say, and she snorts.

'You want a child.' Her strange eyes gleam at me. 'What woman doesn't?'

It cannot be so hard to guess, after all. I moisten my lips. 'Can you help me?'

'Can't promise,' she says, 'but this will make it easier for the baby to take hold.'

'What is that?' I'm not sure whether I really want to know the answer or not.

'Nothing you couldn't find yourself if you knew where to look.'

Intrigued, I get up from the stool and go over to where she is picking over the herbs.

'Nettles.' I recognize one plant at least. 'And this one?' I ask, pointing.

'Blossom of red clover,' Sybil grunts.

I lift a third bunch to my nose and sniff. The smell is familiar, but I can't place it. 'What's this?'

'Raspberry leaves.'

'Of course.' I should have known that one. Mistress Beckwith made many of her own simple remedies, as I do in my kitchen, and raspberries have many uses.

Sybil shakes the herbs into a square of old paper, mutters an incantation over it and twists it up with surprisingly deft fingers, for one so gnarled.

'Make an infusion of this, and drink every day, but you must do it yourself. Drink nothing prepared by anyone else.'

'My sister has been making me a drink that she says will help.'

'And has it?'

'No,' I say slowly, 'not yet.'

'Drink hers or drink mine.' The widow shrugs indifferently.

I rise slowly to my feet, the twist in my hands. The thought of Agnes's drink niggles in my brain. It hasn't helped. But I cannot let myself believe that it has done more than that.

I find a coin in my purse and give it to Sybil, who examines it carefully and nods. 'Thank you,' I say and then hesitate. 'Will you be all right? There is much muttering in the city about witchcraft. Janet Walker was taken for trial the other day, and Mary Thomas too. They say that the city is rife with witches.'

'And you think I am a witch?' The widow seems amused.

I don't answer directly. The truth is that I am not sure. 'I fear for you. There are folk who think any cunning woman is a witch.'

'I don't bother them.'

'I know, it's just . . . ' I don't know how to explain to Sybil the fever that has caught hold in the streets. Suddenly every old woman is suspect, every tiny problem blamed on witchcraft. How can she know about that, out here? 'I don't think you should go into the town at the moment. There is something . . . not right . . . in the air.'

'Don't you worry about me,' says Sybil. 'Look to yourself, that's all you can do.'

'Grace? Where are you going?'

'Home,' I said. 'I must go home.'

'Home's this way.' There was a shifting, a sliding in the air, and Drew's face slipped into focus. He was watching me with a slight frown. Beside us, people were crossing the road as the light turned green, but I had turned and was facing back to Monk Bar.

Back to Coney Street, back to the past.

I was getting better at adjusting. The shift from past to present had been so subtle that I had barely more than a moment's disorientation. It was enough for the green man to turn red.

'Sorry,' I said to Drew. 'I thought I'd forgotten something. It doesn't matter, though.'

I'd forgotten quite how acute his eyes could be. Had he noticed the blankness in my face? I wondered. Had he sensed that, for a few moments, I had been somewhere else? Sometime else? Someone else?

I hoped not. I didn't want to answer any questions. I didn't want to lie to him, and I didn't want to tell the truth, either. He wouldn't understand – wouldn't *want* to understand – how I could be aching still with the loss of the baby that Hawise had longed for.

Drew was still studying my face. He had a way of looking at you, as if he could see right inside you. It was very disconcerting.

Sliding my gaze from his, I made a big deal of shifting my bag from one shoulder to another and tried to think of a way to distract him.

'What are you seeing tomorrow?' It was the best I could do, but at least I had the satisfaction of catching him unawares for once.

'Tomorrow?'

'You said you were going to the cinema.'

'Oh . . . yes.' He told me the title, but I didn't recognize it. Something Italian, with subtitles. Not my kind of thing at all.

'Are you going with Sophie?'

All right, I was fishing, but it worked. 'No, actually I'm going with Sarah.'

His voice was a shade too casual, and in spite of myself my lips tightened, sure that it meant he and Sarah were seeing each other. I felt a fool, remembering the lust that had gripped me, until Hawise had dragged me back to the past.

'Oh.'

'We're just friends,' said Drew.

Our eyes collided and veered away, and I stared at the red man, mortified to find that I was blushing.

'Oh,' I said again, but I was glad.

'Are you sure you want to do this?' Drew wiggled the mouse to bring the desktop's screen back to life. 'A lot of the material is very repetitive. I'm not sure it'll mean anything to you.'

'Yes,' I said, although the truth was that I *wasn't* sure. Did I want proof or not? If none of the people I knew as Hawise had ever existed, then I would be forced to conclude that it was all in my mind, and I didn't like the idea of having such a vivid fantasy life. It smacked of mental illness to me, and that felt as bad as the idea of being possessed. Either way, it meant I had lost control of myself.

But now I was doing something to take back control, I reminded myself. 'I'd like to try anyway,' I told Drew.

'Okay.' Standing, he clicked around the screen until a database appeared, and motioned me to the chair. 'Sit down,' he said. 'You might as well make yourself comfortable.'

The screen was divided into columns. 'This is the manuscript reference,' said Drew, pointing. 'Date, ward, first name, surname, occupation, and so on. I've included the category of offence and the fine, as well as the location, if known, and there's a final field for a transcription of any particularly interesting entries.'

'Right,' I said, peering at the screen. The type was so small it was hard to make out any details. There were clearly pages and pages of entries. 'How do we find an individual?' I was eager to get started by then. 'I presume you can search the database somehow?'

'Of course, but the more information you can provide, the better. If you just have a first name like Thomas, John or William, you're going to get thousands of matches. Bear in mind, too, that there was no standardized spelling at this period, least of all when it came to surnames, so you need to do a search that will bring up all possible variations. If you know an occupation, or where the individual lived – even if it's only a ward – you can narrow down your search.'

'Okay.' I drew a breath. 'Let's try.'

But Drew wasn't finished yet. 'The database includes all individuals who appear in the wardmote-court records between 1575 and 1586, so it's a narrow window, but even then, it doesn't really prove anything one way or another,' he warned. 'All the men in the ward were invited to the court, but only those chosen to be jurors had their name recorded; or if they were officials of some kind – a churchwarden, say, or a constable, or an alderman presiding over the court, of course. Or they might appear if they were presented for some offence, but they could just as easily slip through and not appear in any of the records at all.'

'I understand.' I was finding it hard to contain my impatience. 'We could have a go, couldn't we?'

Resigned, Drew pulled up another chair and sat down next to me. 'What name did you have in mind?'

I drew a breath, let it out carefully. 'Ned Hilliard,' I said, and his name felt plump and sweet and *right* in my mouth.

'Ned as in Edward?'

'Yes.'

Drew filled out some complicated filter, typing in Hilliard, Hilyard, Hillyard, Hiliarde.

'Any idea where this "Edward Hilliard" lived?'

'Bootham ward,' I said without thinking, and then, when Drew looked at me, 'Coney Street.'

'As it happens, Coney Street *was* in Bootham ward in the late sixteenth century,' he said.

I said nothing.

'Occupation?'

'Merchant.'

I was very aware of Drew's jean-clad thigh close to mine, of his fingers on the keyboard, and I wondered how they would feel against my skin. The thought made me shift uncomfortably in my chair. I felt guilty, as if I had been caught ogling another man in front of my husband.

But of course Ned wasn't my husband. He was dead. He'd been dead for more than four hundred years, if he had ever lived at all.

'Okay.' Drew clicked on 'apply filter', and the answer popped up in a fraction of a second.

No match found.

I stared at the screen, shaken by the bitterness of my disappointment. Only then did I realize how much I had wanted Ned to be real.

I gnawed at my thumb. 'Try . . . try Francis Bewley.' Just saying his name sent a wave of loathing through me.

A William Bewley popped up, but no Francis.

Drew was carefully not saying 'I told you so'.

'Do you mind trying one more?' I asked him. I could feel Hawise in my head, urging me on. Look harder, look further.

Drew opened his mouth and I was sure he was going to point out that I was wasting my time, but in the end he just put his fingers to the keyboard. 'Name?'

I thought of my master, and how he had grumbled about the streets. Surely there would be some record of him? I remembered him so vividly: a brash, bluff man who rarely realized how cleverly his much more interesting wife managed him. He had to have been real.

'William Beckwith,' I said, leaning forward, tense. 'He lives in Goodramgate. *Lived*,' I amended quickly at Drew's look. 'Maybe.'

'Monk ward then.' He pulled up another database and filled out the filter fields: name, surname, location.

And there he was on the screen: William Beckwith, mercer, Goodramgate.

I hissed in a breath that was part-shock, part-satisfaction.

'It's not an uncommon name,' said Drew, watching my face. 'It doesn't prove anything.'

'I know,' I said, but it did for me. I *knew* that William Beckwith, and no amount of psychoanalysis by his friend Sarah would tell me otherwise.

'Is this all you have?' I asked Drew. 'Just this database?'

'No, the records are transcribed. I'm not sure they'd mean much to you. They're very repetitive.'

'Can I look at them anyway?'

With an air of resignation, Drew got out a folder of closely typed pages and handed them over to me. I sat at his kitchen table. The entries were laid out in a strange way, and I didn't understand all the symbols. Although they were mostly in English, the spelling made it hard to read, but if I said it out loud I could make sense of it, and the phrasing rang like a bell inside me.

I turned the pages, and my back prickled with the uncanny sensation of Hawise leaning over my shoulder. I recognized so many of the names. John Standeven, Robert Cook, Mr Frankland . . . I – she – knew them all. John Harper. I could picture him exactly, with his carnal mouth and the lazily insolent way that he undressed with his eyes every woman who passed. And my eye snagged on an Andrew Trewe, although I didn't think Hawise could have known him well, for the name felt only vaguely familiar. It was strange to look down at my own surname, written so casually and so long ago, and to wonder if he might have been some distant ancestor.

Nicholas Ellis. The name jumped out at me and I grew very still as I reread the entry, until only my eyes were moving, flicking backwards and forwards over the lines. *We present Myles Fell mylner for kepinge a mastis bytche unmossyllid whiche dyd bytt Nicholas Ellis legge.*

My mouth was dry as I showed the entry to Drew. 'What's this *mastis bytche unmoss*-whatever?'

'Miles Fell was a miller,' he said, and I didn't tell him I knew that already. 'He's presented here for not muzzling his dog, a mastiff bitch, which obviously bit this Nicholas Ellis on the leg. All the bigger dogs were supposed to be muzzled in the street. It seems to have been quite a problem.'

I wasn't listening. I was remembering the miller and his brutish dog, the fury on Nick Ellis's face. If it hadn't been for that commotion, Hawise might never have met Francis Bewley.

'You okay?'

Drew was watching me. I tried to keep my expression neutral, but I was certain now. Ned might not be there; Hawise wasn't there; but their neighbours were. There was no point in trying to convince Drew of that, though.

Moistening my lips, I closed the file at last. 'You're right, it must just be coincidence,' I said.

'It's not proof, Grace.' I didn't like the way he seemed to be able to read my mind. I just hoped he hadn't been able to read it earlier.

'I know.'

In a way, Drew's insistence on a rational explanation for everything was comforting. When everything I had ever believed to be true was shifting and crumbling, his steadiness was something I could hold onto. 'I know, I do,' I said and, without thinking, I reached out and laid my hand over his.

Perhaps I meant it as reassurance. Or perhaps I just wanted to touch him.

Drew looked at my hand and then he looked at me, and when his fingers curled around mine, I wondered if he could feel the pulse running erratically beneath my skin, twitching and jumping and shivering in anticipation.

Yes – touch, I thought, as I turned my palm up to meet his. I needed the here and now, not the there and then. I needed to forget about Hawise and Francis Bewley, and lose myself in the present, in touch and in taste, in the slow build-up of sensation and the urgent glittery rush.

'Do you want to search for another name?' Drew asked me, and I shook my head slowly, letting out a long breath.

'No.'

He smiled then, a smile that blew the smouldering embers inside me into a flame. 'Then why don't you come here instead?' he said, and my final thought for a very long while was: Thank God, thank God, *at last*.

Pain. Wave after wave of it, wrenching and twisting and tearing me apart. My knuckles are white, my throat arches tautly back as I scream. The straight back of the birthing chair presses into me.

'No,' I said when they brought it in. 'I'm not ready. I've changed my mind. I don't want a baby after all.'

But Eliza Skelton, the midwife, only laughed – not unkindly – and bustled around closing the shutters and directing Alison to stoke up the fire while, trapped by my unwieldy body, I lay on the bed, my eyes swivelling in fear like a skittish horse.

The air is suffocatingly sweet with the smell of the almond oil they have rubbed into my swollen belly. The linens are all clean. The midwife has laid out her knife and her binders. Below, in his study, Ned is praying. Everything is ready.

Everything except me. I am not ready for this pain that devours me, and I scream for it to end.

Sweat pours off the women who have gathered. Agnes is here and Margery, who the moment she knew that I was carrying Ned's child became brusquely protective. She might not approve of me, but she will do anything for the child, and I am glad she is here. Or I was. Now I can't think of anyone or anything but the agony that consumes me. I hurl abuse at Eliza, who doesn't seem to understand that I am dying from it.

'Sweet Jesus, sweet Jesus . . . ' I howl. 'Help me, *help* me, you lardy sow!'

'Hush now.' A familiar firm voice cuts through my moans. They have called for Mistress Beckwith to quiet me, and when she lays a hand on my forehead I feel the pain's terrible grip on me ease just a little.

'Mistress,' I choke out pitifully, clutching the chair until I think my fingers will dig into the wood. 'Make it stop.'

'You must be patient, Hawise,' she chides me. 'You must endure, as we all do. It is our lot.'

'But why does it hurt so much?' I am whimpering with it, my breath so jerky I can hardly speak.

'We suffer for our grandmother Eve's sin,' says Mistress Beckwith. 'She did eat the apple.'

Pain fastens its teeth into me and shakes me like a dog with a rat. 'I wish it had choked her!' I cry, and Mistress Beckwith tucks in the corners of her mouth so that she doesn't laugh. 'It's not funny!' I accuse her, and she does laugh then.

'Come, it is not so bad. Not long now, and you will have a fine babe.'

I don't want a baby any more. All I want is to lie quietly and feel that my body is my own, and not a plaything for pain to punch and pummel. But there is an irresistible force building in me, stretching, stretching, stretching me until there is nothing but the dreadful ripping and tearing inside me.

'One more push.'

It might be Eliza's voice, but it is faint and seems to come from miles away, from another world where there is no pain, no darkness.

'I can't . . . I can't . . . '

Why did I ever think I wanted a child? It is killing me. The pain is worse than I could ever have imagined.

'Nearly there, lovey.'

Dimly I am aware of hands, of encouraging voices and purposeful movement, but my body is lifted up on a tide that bears me on and on, until there is a huge cry – a shout that rings in my ears – and I realize that it is mine, and suddenly everything has changed. The women are drawing the pain out of me and I slump in the chair, exhausted.

'Just one more push . . . Ahhh, that's it.'

There is a murmuring, a slap and a thin wail. I open my eyes. 'My baby. Is the baby all right?'

'A girl, but she seems healthy enough.'

'Can I see her?'

'In a minute.' The baby's cries rise as Eliza cuts the cord and they wash her briskly and swaddle her in clean linen.

And then, at last, they put her in my arms, close to my heart.

Her face is red and scrunched up, and her mouth is open in a yell of fury at being wrenched from the comfort of my womb, and all I can do is stare at the miracle of her. She was inside me and now she is here at my breast, and the world has changed completely. The pain forgotten, swept away by a giddying rush of love so fierce it takes my breath away.

I am beaming with joy as I lift my head to thank Eliza for her care of me. 'I'm sorry I was rude to you,' I say and she nods. She has seen it all before. With one finger I stroke my baby's cheek. 'Isn't she the most beautiful baby you've ever seen?'

'Aye, she's a bonny one.' Margery leans over to admire my daughter as the midwife is too busy clearing up. Perhaps every mother thinks her baby is beautiful? None can be as beautiful as mine, though.

I exchange a smile with Margery, her past rudenesses all forgotten now that we share the utter belief in the wonder of my child. As Margery coos, her slab-face softened, I glance over her shoulder and surprise a strange expression on my sister's face. I can't put a name to it, but it sends a sliver of unease into my happiness.

'What are you going to call her?' Margery asks, following my gaze. She expects me to say Agnes. Margery approves of Agnes, who is very devout.

I should say Agnes. She will be godmother, with Eliza, the midwife. The baby should be named for one of them, and it would do honour to my sister. But there is no joy in Agnes and, holding my daughter in my arms, I want so much for her to know only happiness. It is a foolish hope, I know, for what life can be purely happy? Still, it is what I want, and all at once I have a picture of Elizabeth, my friend, and the times we laughed together.

'Elizabeth,' I say, and I look down into my daughter's face. Agnes doesn't need to know that I have not named her for the midwife. 'Her name is Elizabeth.'

She has stopped screaming. She is perfect, with a tiny nose, a tiny bud of a mouth and eyes that stare unblinkingly back into mine. 'My Bess.' I will do anything to keep her safe, I vow silently, to keep her happy.

Anything.

The stench of rotting fruit clogged my nose, making me gasp and gag – and I woke up, still retching. For a while I just lay there, drawing shuddering breaths as I adjusted to the fact that my arms were empty. I was empty and sore and close to tears, and I ached for Bess.

She wasn't there. She would never be there for me.

Wretched, I rolled over to clutch the pillow next to me for comfort, and my fingers closed over a soggy, sagging apple.

I didn't stop to think. Jackknifing out of the bed, I stumbled away from it in horror and leant back against the chest of drawers, my pulse thundering and my stomach heaving. It was several minutes before I could bring myself to pick up the apple and throw it out of the window.

It left a repulsive stain on the pillow. I stripped off the pillow-case and tossed it into the laundry basket with a shudder. Only then could I flop back into bed, turn my face into the mattress and weep for the baby I had never had.

Much later, when the misery had subsided to lethargy and I was listlessly watching the shadows shift over the ceiling, I remembered Drew.

My hand went instinctively to my neck. The jade pendant was still there, nestled in the hollow of my throat, but the amulet Vivien had given me was gone. I had taken it off the night before, I remembered. It was lumpy and awkward and it kept getting in the way, bumping between Drew and me, frustrating our frantic attempts to press skin against skin. I had been too giddy with lust to remember what Vivien had said about not taking it off. I had taken *everything* off, except the pendant, which was so unobtrusive I barely noticed it any more.

In spite of myself, my mouth curved at the memory. It had been so good to give in to desire, to let my mind spin away and my body take over. Drew might be dry and precise in the way he thought, but his hands were sure and his mouth was wickedly warm. It had been a long time since I had felt that heat, that rush, that breathless excitement, and afterwards I had sprawled languid and sated beside him, my body cheering.

But it had been a mistake.

Drew fell asleep, and I dozed for a while, but couldn't settle. His arm was hot and heavy over me, and the familiar sense of suffocation began to steal over me. What was I doing, getting involved with a man like Drew? I knew instinctively that he wasn't a guy who would be interested in a casual relationship, and I couldn't offer him more than that.

Disentangling myself from him, I slid out of bed and dressed without waking him. Quietly I let myself out and into Lucy's house next door, to dream not of loving, but of giving birth.

Now I lay in bed and churned with confusion, memories tumbling over each other, blurring and fragmenting until I couldn't tell one from the other. The warmth of the hand sliding over my skin: had that been Drew's hand, or Ned's? Had those been my sighs and soft gasps, or Hawise's? Who had I shared the night's shattering pleasure with?

The memories beat at me, intercut with the intense emotions of giving birth. My breasts ached, my heart ached. Was this what it was like to lose a child? I wondered. To go through the pain and the overwhelming joy, only to wake to emptiness and loss? Grief rose up, overwhelming me, and I wept again: for Bess, for Hawise, for myself.

I hated crying – it smacked too much of losing control – and I struggled to pull myself together, scrubbing the tears furiously from my face. Bess was gone.

My body felt battered and I had to move very carefully, but I showered, washed my hair and put on a summer dress, hoping to lift my mood. I had left Vivien's amulet at Drew's; I would have to go and get it, and apologize to him while I was at it.

But when I knocked on his door there was no answer.

Somehow I got through the day. I had two classes that afternoon and, as I walked into the school, I couldn't believe how many babies I passed. I'd peer into prams, racked with longing, or watch yearningly as a mother held a baby strapped to her front. And all the time the need to hold Bess again beat at me. I didn't need that chilling whisper to remind me any more.

On the edge of King's Square I paused to watch a young mother bending over a pram. Her baby was crying, the thin, high wail of a newborn, and when I felt wetness at my breasts I started to tremble. I had to pad my bra with tissues when I got to the school. I went into the Ladies and shut myself in a stall, pressing the heels of my hands against my eyes. I was producing milk for a baby that I knew didn't exist, but I ached and ached for her anyway.

I have to stay in the room for three days. Usually I would rail at the confinement, but I am sleepy and sluggish and happy just to watch my daughter. Ned is allowed into the room to see me and Bess. He looks drawn, and I remember that he has already had a wife and child who died. My confinement hasn't been easy on him, either.

Ned picks Bess up and smiles first at her and then at me, and I wonder how I could ever have thought of him as homely.

'She is a beauty,' he says. 'Like her mother.' And when he kisses me, my heart soars at my good fortune.

'We should give some thought to her godparents,' he said. 'Your sister, as she is a girl, and the midwife, but what about your sister's husband too?'

'No!' I say instinctively, pulling myself up against the pillows in a panic. I don't want Francis anywhere near my daughter. 'No, Ned. Please. You haven't asked him yet, have you?'

He looks puzzled. 'Not yet, no. Why, what is it that distresses you so, Hawise?'

'Nothing.' There is no point in trying to explain. He won't understand. 'It's just . . . Francis will be no benefit to her,' I argue in a rush. 'Can we not ask Mr Beckwith if he would stand as godfather to her, Ned? He is a man of good repute.'

'As is your sister's husband,' Ned points out.

'Mr Beckwith has better connections,' I say with an edge of desperation. 'And Agnes is already godmother. We do not need Francis too.'

'Very well,' says Ned, obviously prepared to indulge me. 'It shall be as you wish.'

I let out a long breath that I haven't realized I have been holding until then, and smile brilliantly at him. Francis is Agnes's husband and I cannot keep him from seeing Bess, but at least now he will have no claim on her. He should have little interest in a girl child, but still, I will keep her out of his way as much as I can. I do not trust him.

The neighbours come to see Bess and to keep me company. Having a child has made me one of them. I am not different any more. I am a mother who suffers in childbirth, just like they do; who feeds her baby at her breast as they do. It is as if I have passed an unwritten test and stepped from one world into another. There was my life before Bess, and now there is this life, with Bess at its heart. It feels strange to me sometimes. All my life I have been the odd one, the one folk eye askance.

I have never felt as if I belong. But now, suddenly, I have a place. I can be just like everyone else. I am bound into the neighbourhood by the miracle of childbirth.

Little Bess is a source of wonder to me. She is so tiny, so perfect, I cannot believe that she is mine. I lay my hand on her to check that she is breathing, and the feel of her small chest rising and falling is like a fist around my heart. And although I am pleased that the women have taken me as one of their own, I long to be alone with my baby too, just to marvel at her.

I am tired as well, and at last the women do leave, shooed out by Margery, who has decreed that I need my sleep. Bess lies in a cradle near the bed. I lie on my side so that I can watch it. I am scared to sleep, because if I sleep, who will watch Bess? How can I guard her from harm if I am asleep? I am determined to stay awake, but my eyelids close anyway.

I'm not sure what makes me stir, but I open my eyes to see Agnes bending over the cradle. I can't see her expression, but there is a tension about her shoulders, a stiffness to her arms, that makes me think something is wrong.

Instantly I am wide awake. 'Agnes?' I haul myself up onto the pillows as she spins round, her face shocked. 'What is it?' I say sharply. 'Why do you look so? What's wrong?'

'Nothing's wrong.' The startled look is smoothed from her face and now it is blank and unreadable.

'Are you sure? Is it the baby?' Fear sharpens my voice.

'The baby is well.'

I am throwing back the coverlet, trying to struggle up.

Something about Agnes's lack of expression makes me afraid. 'I want to see her!'

'Be calm, Sister.' Irritation feathers her voice and she lifts Bess from the cradle and hands her to me. 'You see?'

Frantically I check Bess, whose face is screwed up in sleep. She is breathing! She seems fine. I hold her tight, wondering how long I am going to have to live with this terror that something might happen to her. Childhood is a dangerous time, we all know that.

'I'm sorry,' I say to Agnes. I can sense that she is exasperated by my fancies. 'I was just . . . it was the way you looked.'

'I was just admiring my goddaughter,' she says, but she doesn't sound as if she admires Bess. She has kept her distance from the baby until now. I think this must be the first time Agnes has touched her in fact, and she handed her over to me as if she were a bolt of cloth, as if she didn't like touching her.

But it must be hard for Agnes, I realize, ready to feel sorry for anyone who isn't me and who doesn't have my beautiful Bess as their daughter. There is no sign that Agnes has conceived. She cannot feel my happiness. My poor sister, married to Francis Bewley and without the joy of a child of her own.

'A new mother's fancies,' I apologize.

Agnes and Eliza Skelton take Bess to be baptized, and I fret all the time they are at the church. I haven't been churched yet, and must stay at home. Ned and Margery will be there, I reason, and Mistress Beckwith, who has had children of her own. She knows how to hold a baby. Agnes just needs to stand there and make her promises. There is no need to feel unease.

But I don't like the fact that Francis has announced that he will attend the baptism. I have seen little of him for the past few weeks. It was one of the best things about my confinement, and now I am to stay in my chamber until I am churched. This will be the first time Francis sees Bess. I don't want him to touch her.

He cannot do anything to Bess in church, surely? I wish Agnes hadn't told me that he was going. I don't relax until Bess is back in my arms. I have to keep Francis away from her. As soon as I am churched I will be able to watch her all the time, but until then, I want my baby safely with me, where he cannot even look at her.

Chapter Fourteen

'You look terrible,' said Drew when he opened the door.

'Silver-tongued devil, aren't you?' My hand went to my pendant and I drew a breath. 'Have you got a minute?'

'Sure.' He stood back and held open the door. 'Want a cup of tea? Or something stronger?' His voice was pleasant, but cool.

I probably didn't deserve even that.

'Tea would be good. Thanks.'

I followed him into the kitchen and was glad to sit down when he gestured me to a stool at the tiny breakfast bar. Drew filled the kettle, clicked it on and then leant back against the worktop while he waited for it to boil, studying me with a crease between his brows. I was drawn and pasty-skinned, and the hair tucked behind my ears was lank, I knew. I'd seen myself in the mirror and been appalled by the lines of strain bracketing my mouth, and the anguish in my eyes. Drew wouldn't think I was exciting now, that was for sure.

'You really do look rough,' he said. 'Aren't you well?'

'I'm—'

'Fine, I know,' he interrupted me, exasperated.

'I *am* fine. I just didn't sleep very well, that's all.'

Then I wished I hadn't said that. The memory of the night before twanged in the air between us. I looked away. Better to get it out of the way. It was why I was there, after all.

'Drew, about last night . . . '

But he stopped me again, holding up a hand. 'You don't need to say anything, Grace. I got the point when you left without saying goodbye.' His voice was even, but I flinched as if it had been a whip.

'I'm sorry,' I said, shame-faced. 'I really am. I just . . . I'm not very good at intimacy,' I stumbled on when he raised his brows. 'I mean, the sex was great – really it was. It's nothing to do with you.'

'Oh, wait. Is this the whole "It's not you" speech?' he said. 'I love that one.'

At the kettle's frantic whistle he turned to pour boiling water over the teabags and I looked helplessly at his back.

'It *isn't* you,' I said. 'It's me.'

There was a silence. 'Is there someone else?' Drew asked without turning round.

'No. At least . . . ' I thought of Ned, of how easy it was to confuse my feelings for the two men. 'No, not really. It's not that.'

I wanted what Hawise had with Ned, I realized, but I couldn't imagine ever getting close enough to anyone to get married. I would have to let down my guard and make myself vulnerable, and that felt too dangerous.

Hawise hadn't had a choice. If she'd had one, would she have married Ned? I didn't think so, and that meant she would never have known what it was like to love him.

I had a choice, but the responsibility felt huge, stifling. How could you possibly know that you were making the right decision? How could you know what it would be like to live with someone, day in, day out, knowing that you couldn't – or shouldn't – walk away whenever you wanted?

Drew turned at last. Handing me a mug, he pushed the milk across the breakfast bar. 'If it's not someone else, what is it?'

'It's just that I've got a lot on my mind at the moment,' I said weakly. 'Everything's so complicated right now.'

That at least was true. I was living Hawise's life as well as my own – I had just had a baby, for God's sake! – while teaching and trying to sort out Lucy's affairs. I couldn't be expected to embark on a relationship too.

'Last night was a mistake,' I said.

Drew wasn't going to let me off the hook that easily. He was leaning against the kitchen units, ankles crossed, watching me with that unnervingly level gaze. 'In what way?'

I turned the mug round and round between my hands, wondering how to explain. I could hardly tell Drew that I was possessed, that I feared that I had been aroused by memories of another man, of a man who had died hundreds of years earlier.

And I couldn't blame it all on Hawise. I had known what

I was doing. The memory of Drew's mouth on me speared through my misery, quick and clean and hot. I hadn't been making love with Ned. Drew smelt different, felt different. It had been him.

'Look, the truth is, I'm not into a committed relationship,' I said, knowing that I sounded bolshie, and Drew raised his brows.

'I wasn't planning on asking you to marry me,' he said coolly. 'Don't you think you're taking things a bit too seriously? It was just one night, but you're right: it *was* good. It doesn't have to be complicated.'

'I'm just no good at the whole holding-each-other-afterwards and sleeping-together stuff.' I stirred my tea, not looking at him. 'That's why I left last night. I should have said goodbye, I know, but I get all panicky . . . To be honest, I thought you might regret it this morning too.'

'Why?'

'Well, we're so different, aren't we? We want completely different things.'

Drew set his mug carefully on the worktop and gave me a level look. 'How do you know what I want?' he asked.

'I know you're a settled kind of guy,' I said. 'You've got your job, your house, your daughter, and I know they're all important to you. I don't want any of those things.'

'Have you ever tried them?'

'The closest I got to it was with Matt, but it would have been a disaster for both of us,' I said. 'I can see that now. He's happily married, and his wife is about as different from me as you could imagine. If we'd stayed together, one or other of us would have been fooling ourselves that we wanted something that we really didn't. At least the tsunami made that clear.'

'So what do you want, Grace?'

I didn't look at him. Until the night before I would have been able to answer without hesitation. Now, I had given birth. I knew what it was like to hold my daughter in my arms. My breasts were still tender, my body churning with hormones, my mind swerving between the past and the present.

'I want to know that I can pack up my case and move on whenever I feel like it,' I said in the end. That had always been true, and there was no reason to change now. 'I don't want to need anybody or anything.'

Drew took off his glasses and began to polish them with the bottom of his shirt. 'Are you afraid I'm going to trap you somehow?'

'No . . . I don't know . . . ' I was horrified to find myself close to tears as I twisted the chain of my pendant round and round. 'I just don't want you to get the wrong idea.'

'So what's the right idea?'

I lifted my eyes at last and looked at Drew. His head was bent over his glasses, and he was solid, real, rock-steady in the middle of a world that seemed to be spinning ever more wildly out of my control. As I looked, the swirling seemed to still for a moment of extraordinary clarity and I saw him as if for the first time, in startling detail. The dent on the bridge of his nose, where his glasses pressed. The faint prickle of stubble along his jaw. The furrows of concern on his forehead. The firm angles of his face, the formidable line of his mouth. I knew what that mouth felt like, what it tasted like, and I stamped down on the heat that threatened to uncoil within me.

Only now did I realize how familiar he had become to me. How important.

I wished I could go over and lean against him, but I couldn't afford to depend on him. Drew couldn't sort out Hawise for me. I had to deal with that myself and, when I had, I would be leaving York. I didn't want to feel that I needed him. I didn't want to miss him when I had gone.

'I'd like to be friends,' I said. I looked at him doubtfully. 'If you want to, of course.'

Drew put his glasses back on. He looked at me for a moment, then blew out a long breath of frustration. 'Of course,' he said, resigned. 'Of course we can be friends.'

There was an awkward pause. I cleared my throat. 'I think I left my other necklace here last night. I don't suppose you found it?'

'It's by my bed. I'll get it for you.'

He came back into the kitchen, the pendant that Vivien had given me dangling from his hand. 'I haven't seen you wearing this before. Is it new?'

'It was a present.'

I got up from the stool and held out my hand for the necklace, but Drew spread the cord between his hands and slipped it round my neck, lifting my hair and smoothing it back into place. We were standing very close. I could feel the rough cord scratching at the nape of my neck, and the stone pulsing between my breasts. Drew's hands lingered on my hair, and when he bent his head to touch my lips with his, I closed my eyes.

His palms slid round to cup my face, and for a moment I let myself lean into the solid security of his chest, let myself feel safe. Let myself remember the breathless slide of skin on skin, the heat and the hunger and the wild, wicked pleasure. Why not? I remember thinking.

Bess. The whisper was gurgled through a lungful of river water. Drew didn't hear it, but I did. My eyes snapped open and I stepped back without thinking. Bess was why not. How could I have forgotten her?

Drew's hands dropped. There was a questioning look in his eyes, and I felt my colour rise.

'Friends?' I asked. I couldn't explain, not now.

An infinitesimal pause, then he nodded slowly. 'Friends,' he agreed. 'If that's what you want.'

The house felt very empty when I let myself back in. I wasn't hungry, but I made myself some noodles for something to do, then pushed them listlessly around my plate. I wished I'd said yes when Drew asked if I wanted to stay, but the thought of Bess was clamouring at the back of my mind and I knew I wouldn't be able to settle.

I thought about Skyping Mel, but I couldn't get an Internet connection, and anyway, I knew that the moment she heard my voice, she would demand to know what was wrong. And what would I say? *I miss my baby?* Mel was like me. She had no interest in motherhood. She wouldn't understand that I was aching for Bess, for a baby I had never had. For the baby I never would have. Mel would be horrified, I knew. She would tell me to get a grip and get help. And if I told her I was desperate to get back to the past, she would tell me not to be a fool.

But I wanted to see Bess again. I *needed* to see her, to hold her in my arms again.

Maybe I could. I thought about the time I had slipped back to Hawise's life in Vivien's garden. 'Try to control her,' Vivien had said. Maybe I didn't need to wait for Hawise to come for me. Maybe I could go back by myself again. Take control.

The cool, clear-headed part of my brain protested that it was madness, but the longing for Bess was ballooning inside me, blotting out all rational thought. Just once, I told myself. Just to see that she was all right.

I felt calm and strangely detached as I drew the curtains in the bedroom and lit one of Lucy's candles. Watching a candle flame had worked once before, I remembered. I would try and regress myself.

Deliberately I took off Vivien's pendant and sat cross-legged on the floor while I tried to focus on the flame, but the harder I tried to reach the past, the more aware I became of the present. My legs were uncomfortable, a stray hair was tickling my nose, and from next door I could hear that Drew was working to music. All at once I was remembering the night before and the pleasure that had shivered through me when he smiled against my skin.

I began to feel a little foolish. Exasperated with myself, I climbed stiffly to my feet, blew out the candle and pulled the curtains back. What had I been thinking?

Outside, the golden evening light was slanting across the street. A posse of students passed below, talking and laughing, elated by the prospect of a warm summer night. I should be out enjoying it myself, not stuck in a stuffy bedroom with the curtains drawn. I opened the window and leant out to breathe in the fresh air.

'Come away from there!' Margery pulls me back from the window and slams it closed, turning on me with a ferocious scowl. 'What do you think you're doing?'

The last few weeks have turned her tyrant. While I have been confined to childbed, she has been running the household again and has let everyone know it, in no uncertain terms. But her brusqueness doesn't fool me now. I have seen her tenderness as she lifts Bess from the cradle. I know that she has made the delicacies that she plonks ungraciously on the bed especially to tempt my appetite.

It is Margery who has laboured in the kitchen to produce endless dainties to serve the gossips who have come, as is the custom, to keep me company and give me good cheer. She has grumbled mightily about it, of course, but I know she has been determined to impress the women so that they will go home and tell their husbands that Ned Hilliard has the finest house in the city.

'Don't you be giving them that best wine,' she scolds Ned.

'That parcel of busybodies'll guzzle the barrel dry, if you let them. Why do you think they keep atrooping in?'

But she makes sure the cups are gleaming, and poor Isobel and Alison have been kept busy, running up and down the stairs with jugs of wine and plates piled high with pastries and seed-cake.

For a time I was content to lie there and watch my baby while the gossips chattered over me, exchanging gruesome childbed stories, grumbling about their servants and complaining about their husbands. I was shocked and delighted to discover that these women, so modest and demure if you meet them in the street, have an earthy frankness that would startle their menfolk if they could hear how they talk of them.

When the gossips grow bawdy, Agnes gets up. 'I am going to pray, Sister,' she says, or 'I have the headache, I will go and lie quietly'. There is always an uncomfortable little silence after she has gone before the cackling starts again.

I don't mind the bawdiness. I love to listen to them laughing, but I don't join in. I have no complaint to make of Ned. I miss him. Our chamber has been taken over by women, and there is no place for him here.

But now the gossips are gone. Today I will be purified, and tonight Ned and I will be husband and wife again.

'It's such a beautiful day,' I tell Margery, who is grimly stripping the sheets from my bed. I am practically dancing around the chamber, giddy with relief that the day of my churching has come at last. 'I can't wait to go outside again! It's so stuffy in here.'

'That's as may be, but that baby needs warmth,' she says, yanking the coverlet aside. Margery doesn't believe in fresh air. She thinks it's dangerous.

'I can't believe a bit of sunshine will harm her!'

'Oh, and you'd know, having had so many babies, I suppose?' Margery snaps.

It is on the tip of my tongue to retort that I have had more than her, but I don't want to hurt her feelings. I go over to help her instead, but she swats me away. 'You sit down. I've got enough to do without you getting gripes.'

'I haven't had any pains,' I protest, forgetting those long hours of giving birth to Bess. 'I've been lying down long enough. I'm sick of it! I want to go out and be able to *breathe* again.'

Margery only sniffs. 'Why can't you be like your sister and sit still for a change? You should be at your prayers, not capering around the chamber.'

I should be more like Agnes, I know. She is so good, so devout, and if she doesn't seem to care overmuch for Bess, well, I can understand that. I know how much it hurts to hold a babe when you long for one of your own. I have been lucky again. Every time I see my sister, I feel that familiar mixture of pity and guilt. No wonder she prays.

Margery is right. I should pray too, in thanks for my good fortune.

It is not far to the church, but I savour every step when the time comes for me to be churched. The smells and sounds of the street beat at me as if I am in a strange country, as if I have never heard the signs creaking in the breeze; and the cries of hawkers that I have heard all my life might almost be a different language, so odd do they sound.

As we leave the courtyard I pause by the door of the apothecary shop and sniff. I can smell cloves and cinnamon and sacks of peppers. It should be familiar to me, but all at once it is as if I am standing outside myself again, marvelling at the strangeness of it all. Coney Street is athrong in the sunshine. The women sit in their doorways, minding their husbands' stalls, while from the workshops comes banging and snipping and clattering to mingle with the sound of banter and barter. I have only been abed one month, but I stand agog. The street is colour and noise and smell. My skirts are redder than red, my gloves silkier than silk. I brush my hand over the velvet trimming of my gown, and the nap is so plush that I am certain I can feel it in every tiny loop in the pile. It is extraordinary.

The feeling fades when I go into the church. It is dim and cool, and the new pews smell of fresh wood still. Eliza Skelton is there, and Margery and Mrs Beckwith. And Agnes is there, with Francis. My joyfulness falters at the sight of him.

He shouldn't be here. This is women's work. But Francis is always in church nowadays, making a great show of his piety. I don't know how he ever has time for his business, he is so busy at his devotions.

'I have come to pray for you, Sister,' he says, and I can tell from the approving glances of the other women that I am supposed to fall down with gratitude for the honour he does me. It is a great thing, his smile seems to suggest, for so godly a man to offer up thanks on my behalf.

'I thank you.' For Agnes's sake I keep up the pretence of civility, but every time I see him, I feel Hap's weight in my arms, I remember his tongue pushing wetly into my mouth and I shudder.

Francis has not forgotten, either. I know this as surely as I know that the cream in my dairy will curdle in the heat.

I do my best to ignore him, and move with Eliza to the front of the nave.

Head bent, I kneel and listen to the psalm. The minister's sonorous voice rolls around the church. Sir John is a stout man, fond of good living, but he suits the church. He has the voice for it.

Together we say the Lord's Prayer, and again it feels like the first time for me, the first time since Bess. Everything, it seems, is fresh and new because of her. The words have a meaning I never understood before.

'Save this woman thy servant,' says Sir John. 'Be thou to her a strong tower.'

'From the face of her enemy,' we answer, and I can feel Francis's eyes on me.

I am here to thank God for delivering me from the pain and great peril of childbirth. I am well and Bess is thriving. I *am* thankful. I pray fervently, asking Him to keep my daughter safe. I can bear anything as long as she is well and happy, I think.

Francis cannot touch her, I comfort myself. He cannot touch me any more. I have my husband and my daughter, and the gossips in the street have sat around my bed and treated me as one of their own. I don't like the sly heat in his eyes, but it cannot hurt me. *He* cannot hurt me.

Purified by God's grace, I rise to my feet at the end of the service. My breasts are heavy with milk, and my heart leaps at the thought of my sweet Bess. I will cradle her as she suckles, and stroke her downy head. I will kiss the tiny fist that lies against my breast and give thanks again for what I have.

I am lucky, I remind myself as I walk back down the aisle with Eliza, but barely have I thought it than I step into a pocket of cold air, and a premonition of such horror overwhelms me that I stumble. It is like a scuttle of foul water splashed over my face, like a bat's wing wrapped tight around me. My scalp shrinks and my lungs shrivel in dread, and for a moment I cannot breathe with the terror of it.

'Mistress Hilliard?' Eliza's homely face is puckered with concern. 'What ails you? Are you sick?'

At her touch, the blackness unfurls and flaps away. I draw an unsteady breath, then another. I touch my nose, my mouth. I can breathe. The feeling has gone.

'No, I am well,' I manage. Over Eliza's shoulder, my eyes meet Francis's. Slowly he runs his tongue over his lips and he smiles. I could almost swear he knows what I felt just now, and rejoices in it. I lift my chin.

'I am as well as I could be,' I say, and when I give Sir John a fat purse as my offering, I know that it is true.

When I came to that day, I was still leaning out of the window. Time in the past – in Hawise's past – seemed to be accelerated, so that when I returned to the present, it was almost always with that jarring sense of dislocation. I remember once being on a train, stopped on the track while we waited for a signal. An express blurred past so quickly that it felt as if we were moving too. Perhaps it was something to do with the eyes, or the brain, but when the last carriage passed my window and I realized that we were still stationary, I felt a great jolt, as if I had run into a wall at high speed.

That's how it felt when I came back to the present, not slipping so much as plummeting. I ended up gasping with shock, my heart galloping in my chest. I drew my head back inside, my hands unsteady as I pulled down the sash window and let it rattle into place.

There on the narrow sill an apple balanced, decomposing into slush.

I opened the window again, took off my shoe and used it to flick the apple outside. I didn't look where it landed. I knew it wouldn't be there if I went outside.

The sense that time was out of joint did fade eventually. That evening it became an uncharacteristic wistfulness. Hawise was lucky, I found myself thinking. She had Bess, and she had Ned. No doubt, for Hawise; no wondering if Ned would go or stay. He was hers, and she was his, and there was nothing more to think about.

Nothing could be that certain in the present.

Anyway I didn't want that, I reminded myself fiercely. I didn't want to be tied down. I would suffocate if I couldn't walk away whenever I liked, but that didn't mean I couldn't see the appeal. Sometimes. My mind flickered to Drew, and then away. Being physically compatible was one thing, but it was nonsense to think that we could have anything in common beyond that. I liked to keep my boundaries clear. There was work, there were friends, there was sex, and they worked perfectly well in their separate compartments.

But what about a baby? Could I fit one of those into a compartment?

I padded restlessly about the house all that night. I'd never wanted a baby before. Mel and I used to talk about it. No way, we'd decided. I'd heard horror stories about the body clock, of course, but I never thought it would happen to me.

Now my body was screaming at me that it was ready to conceive.

Of course, I rationalized it. It was just because of Bess. The feeling would pass, as this whole strange episode would pass, as soon as I left York. I just had to endure it and not do anything silly – like knocking on Drew's door and asking him if he wanted to make love to me again. Then it would all be about a relationship, about commitment, about being sensible for the baby. I didn't want a baby that much.

Did I?

All at once, there were babies everywhere. I went out of my door and a young girl was pushing a pram past the door. On the way into work I walked past a school and saw all the young mothers delivering their children. One of the other teachers announced her pregnancy. There were adverts for nappies on the television.

I took to wearing Vivien's amulet again, and gradually the longing began to subside. I was relieved. I even began to think that I had gone through some kind of breakdown, I had been acting so out of character. But as the days passed, and summer slipped away, I stayed firmly in the present. I stopped looking for apples, stopped listening for that gurgly whisper.

I was glad to feel myself again, but there were times when I missed Hawise, if I'm honest. Only once did I dream about her. It was a stuffy night and I had kicked off the duvet. I thrashed restlessly from side to side, turning to punch the pillow into shape, throwing myself onto my back with a sigh, then tossing the pillow aside altogether. I was hot, I was itchy. I was thinking about Drew, asleep on the other side of the wall. I was remembering his hands on me, his weight and his warmth, and the extraordinary, unexpected heat that had flared between us. And somewhere along the way I must have slept.

It is too hot in the bed. Usually I like it when Ned pulls the curtains around us, making a cosy island where there are just the two of us, and no one else to see what we do to each other, no one to think that I am immodest, that together we are lascivious and shameless about it. I like the way Ned turns and smiles at me when I slide down the pillows and hold out my arms to him. I like how he settles over me, how his hands and his lips leave me boneless with desire.

Usually, yes, but tonight we were both slick with sweat when we fell apart, and now the hangings trap the claggy air and the darkness slumps heavy on me.

I did sleep at first, but uneasily. I dreamt I was walking along a shore beside the sea I have never seen. I remember it very clearly. Ned tells me the sea is grey and turbulent; he says I wouldn't like it, not really, but in my dream the sea was green as an emerald, and a hot wind blew my unbound hair back from my face and stirred the leaves of the strange, spiky trees. Beneath my bare feet the sand was warm and soft and white, like no sand I have ever seen before. There was a necklace around my neck, hot and heavy, and I wore curious undergarments. My shift was no more than a thin sheet wrapped around my breasts, but as is the way of dreams, my nakedness seemed natural. I was smiling, I remember that.

And then I turned and the dream became a nightmare. The sea rose up and engulfed me, and I was tumbling around and around and around in the water. I was choking, I was drowning.

I woke gasping for breath. Thanks be to God, it was just a dream. 'Drew,' I murmured and reached for him as he lay beside me, but just before I touched him, I jerked my hand back.

It wasn't Drew, I thought in horror. I was in bed with the wrong man.

Then I came fully awake and realized I had been trapped in the nightmare still. There was nothing wrong. I was lying next to Ned, my beloved husband. Deliberately I laid my hand against him, recognizing the texture of his skin, the familiar smell of him. Of course it was Ned. Who else had I expected it to be?

The dream is fading, but the sense of panic and confusion lingers. *Drew*. Andrew is an uncommon name in these parts. Why would I wake with it on my lips?

The air is suffocating, as hot as it was in my dream, but

without the warm wind. The nightmare has left me with a sense of foreboding and now I cannot get to sleep again.

Beside me, Ned is sprawled across the bed, oblivious to my discomfort, his breathing a slow, steady rasp. A quill from the feather mattress is sticking through the sheet, and every time I turn over it pricks me. We might as well be lying on straw, I think crossly.

Somewhere outside a dog is barking, barking, barking incessantly, but at least it can breathe. The heat is smothering. Cautiously, so as not to wake Ned, I pull back the curtain by my pillow. Now I can hear Bess snuffling on her truckle bed, and Margery's whistling snores from the chamber overhead. Everyone is asleep, it seems, except for me.

And the dog.

Puffing out a sigh, I shift my legs into a more comfortable position, then I try turning onto my side. I normally like to lie against Ned's back, but it is too hot to press my flesh to his tonight. Not that he would care. I am irritable with him for being able to sleep when I cannot, and I stare broodingly up at the canopy, determined to dwell on all the difficulties of my life.

Which in truth are not many. I am happier than I have ever been before. Margery dotes on Bess, and I am included in her fussing. Alison and Isobel, taking their lead from her, are less sullen too, and make no fuss when Ned finds me a new maid, Joan, who is supposed to help me with Bess; but with Margery and me, there is little enough for her to do. But she is a good lass and fetches and carries and is willing. All in all, we are a happy household.

Strange my dream should take me to the East, if so it did. No longer do I yearn to fly. Perhaps sometimes I think about the world outside the city walls, and remember my childish dreams of travelling across the seas, but on the whole, I am content. Yes, when Ned goes to the Synxon market in Antwerp, I wish I could go with him, but it is really only tonight that it seems unfair that I cannot. I would not leave Bess in any case.

My daughter grows bonny and bright. She is a sturdy child, with huge eyes the same colour as Ned's, but hers have none of his quietness and calm. Instead they are full of mischief. She laughs easily, and why should she not? She has poor Margery twisted around her small finger, and her father is no better, although he conceals his doting better than Margery.

And as for me . . . I cannot measure the love I feel for my little girl. I marvel at the miracle of her every day: at the skin that blooms like the petal of a rose in May, at the impish smile and the eyes that widen with wonder at the world. I discover beauty again through my daughter's eyes. Together we spend long hours watching a butterfly or grasping at the motes of dust that dance like specks of gold in a sunbeam. When we walk in the garden, Bess picks up a pebble and examines it with the delighted attention a woman might give a priceless jewel. I read her stories from the book Ned gave me. She is too young to understand them, but she likes the pictures and she smacks the page, her baby hand fat and dimpled.

She accepts the adoration of the world as her due, and gives it back tenfold.

Except to my sister and Francis Bewley.

Bess doesn't like Francis. When he lifts her onto his lap, she squirms and squeals to get away, and I snatch her back. I don't like his hands on her.

I am sorry for the fact that she doesn't like Agnes, either, but there is nothing I can do about it. I pity my sister. I am the only one who loves her, and deep down I know my love is a sad, dutiful thing. There is no dizzying rush of feeling when I look at her, the way there is when I look at Ned or Bess.

Nobody looks at poor Agnes that way. She has no child to love her, and her husband barely seems to notice her. Not that Agnes appears unhappy with him. Far from it. She watches him hungrily whenever he is in the room, and she talks proudly about how godly he is, and how everyone respects him.

I cannot imagine what they say to each other when they are alone. It makes me shudder just to think of it. Their house in Jubbergate is cheerless and cold, and I avoid it as much as I can, but I have to be careful not to slight Agnes. I try to visit when I know Francis will be at his business. Agnes is right. He has a reputation in the street for devotion, and he flourishes as a notary, but his showy piety doesn't fool me. I haven't forgotten the way Francis promised to see to his old master.

So I steer clear of him as much as I can, and he hasn't touched me again. But every now and then he glances at me when no one else is looking, and runs his tongue slowly around his lips, the way he did at my churching. It is his message to me. It tells me that he hasn't forgotten me, that he is biding his time, but for what, I don't know.

Chapter Fifteen

The day after I dreamt about Hawise dreaming about me, Drew came to help me paint Lucy's sitting room.

I was restive after the broken night, and unsettled by my dream, just as Hawise had been by hers. It was very strange to see myself in someone else's dream, and to experience my nightmare at second hand, as it were. Oddly I hadn't dreamt about the tsunami since I arrived in York. I wondered what that meant.

My face burnt every time I remembered her reaching out and murmuring for Drew. I didn't want to think about what *that* meant. It's an uncomfortable feeling to see your subconscious at work. There had been moments when Hawise had been aware of me before, but never so explicitly, and I didn't like it. I felt as if some secret camera had recorded me in the bathroom and posted on YouTube. There were some things you didn't want to share, even with a ghost.

It made me scratchy and out of sorts, and I snapped at Drew

when he insisted on pulling all the furniture to the centre of the room and covering it with a sheet.

'All we need to do is splash on a coat of paint,' I grumbled. 'All I want to do is make the place look fresher. Anyone buying the house is going to redecorate anyway. There's no need to wash everything as well.'

'Why do it at all, if you're not going to do it properly?' Drew handed me a roll of masking tape. 'You do the skirting boards, and I'll prepare the walls.'

So I had to crouch down and stick tape along the top of the skirting boards and around the door, and then he made me run in and out with buckets of hot water, muttering ungratefully.

Drew ignored my bad mood and worked steadily and sensibly, rubbing down the walls and carefully taking out picture pins.

'You know, there's really no need to fill in every little crack,' I said as he squeezed Polyfilla onto a trowel. For someone so intellectual, he had a disconcertingly practical streak.

'You've heard of the expression "painting over the cracks", haven't you?' said Drew. 'It means there's no point in prettying up the surface unless you deal with the problems beneath – although I can see why that would be your preferred approach,' he added.

'What, so now you're a psychologist as well as a historian and a painter and decorator?' I said snippily, tearing off a piece of masking tape with my teeth, and perhaps with rather more force than was strictly necessary. 'Quite the Renaissance man, aren't you?'

'Isn't that what you do?' said Drew, unperturbed. 'Skate along over the surface and make sure nobody ever gets close enough to find out what you're really like? Slap on another layer of paint, move to another place – anything rather than deal with your issues.'

'I don't have any *issues*, thank you!'

'Oh yes, I forgot, you're fine.'

Irritably I slapped the length of tape against the window frame. 'I'm just saying, it's not worth spending a lot of time on decorating. Chances are, the first thing anyone who buys this house will do is to repaint this room.'

'But if everybody just does a slap-happy job, the house gets in a worse and worse state,' he pointed out disapprovingly. 'Left to people like you over the years, this whole room would collapse under the weight of endless botched paint jobs.'

I sighed. I couldn't myself see what was wrong with letting the next owners worry about that, but I knew that was the wrong attitude. It wasn't an argument I was ever going to win, anyway. Drew would go ahead and do whatever he had decided to do, regardless of anything I said.

And he had the nerve to call *me* stubborn.

We had spent quite a lot of time together by then, and we knew each other in a way that was hard to explain. I didn't really understand why we got on so well. We had almost nothing in common. His habit of precision drove me wild at times, while I know my tendency to impatience and restlessness was equally irritating to him, but somehow it was easy being together. We laughed at the same things. That helped a lot.

I often had supper with him, and with Sophie when she was there. Sophie liked it when I did the cooking, and I was happy to potter around Drew's kitchen, which was so much brighter and more welcoming than Lucy's, where the scent of rotting apples persisted in spite of the fact that Hawise had thankfully receded from my mind.

Sometimes Sophie and I trawled the charity shops together or just sat and drank coffee. She could be very good company and had a real talent for mimicry when she forgot to be serious and spiritual. I was just sorry that the Temple of the Waters was off-limits, as I would have loved to have seen her take off Mara. But the slightest hint of flippancy in connection with the Temple put her prickles up, so I learnt not to tease.

Drew never mentioned the fact that we had slept together, so of course I didn't either, but I didn't like how clearly I could remember it. It annoyed me, too, that Drew didn't seem to have any difficulty in just being friends, while I found myself thinking about the night we had spent together at the most inappropriate times. I didn't even know why. He *wasn't* attractive. Not really. He was very ordinary-looking in fact. He was just . . . Drew.

And it wasn't that I wanted to sleep with him again, I reassured myself. Nothing had changed. I would still be leaving, and the last thing I needed was to get involved in that way. Falling back into bed with him would be a big mistake.

But whenever I was with him my mind would drift alarmingly, like it did that day in Lucy's sitting room, with the masking tape in my hand and only half my attention on what I was doing. Out of the corner of my eye I watched Drew paint, his arm stretching rhythmically up and down the wall, and lust jittered under my skin. Every time he pushed the roller up, his faded T-shirt rose too, giving me a glimpse of his taut belly, until my mouth was dry and my blood pounding with frustration.

'You okay?' he asked at last, squelching the roller through the paint in the tray.

'Fine.' I cursed inwardly as that word slipped out, and Drew cocked an eyebrow at me. My voice was thin and high too, and my instinctive reaction was to go on the offensive. 'Why?'

'You're very quiet.'

'I'm thinking.'

'What about?'

About what it would be like to nip his throat, to push up the paint-spattered T-shirt and kiss my way down his long, lean body. My mouth dried. For a dizzying moment my mind was blank and I was terrified the words would fall out of my mouth of their own accord.

'About Sophie,' I said in a rush, clutching onto the first idea that came into my head. 'Did I tell you that we saw Ash yesterday?'

We'd been in a charity shop in Goodramgate. I'd just found a sleeveless dress in a wonderful shade of yellow that I thought would work with a belt and vintage cardigan that I'd found in the Save the Children shop a couple of weeks earlier. It was a beautiful fabric too, silky and slithery, and I couldn't wait to try it on.

'I was showing her a dress I wanted to buy, and she was

rolling her eyes and giving me a hard time about it, but that was fine,' I told Drew. 'She was being normal.'

One minute Sophie was relaxed and laughing, and the next her face had coloured up as she saw someone behind me. Even before I turned I knew who it would be.

'Ash Vaughan was outside, looking at us through the window.'

I twitched my shoulders, remembering the shiny malice that reminded me so much of Francis Bewley.

'He looked at me and then he looked at Sophie, and I could *tell* he didn't like the fact that she had been enjoying herself with me. He summoned her like a dog,' I said tightly. 'He didn't move his lips or anything; he just *looked*, and she turned without a word and trotted out to join him. And then he looked back at me and he smiled.' I pulled a face. 'He gives me the creeps. I can't prove anything of course, but I think he did that just to show me he could control her. It was a challenge.'

Drew's face had darkened at the first mention of Ash's name. 'That sounds like him. Arrogant little tosser.'

'I slung the dress back and hared out after her, but there wasn't much point. Ash already had her just where he wanted her.'

When I went back into the shop someone else had snapped up that yellow dress. I was still cross about it.

Drew loaded more paint onto his roller. 'I can't suggest it to Sophie, but I've got a nasty feeling that he's deliberately targeting her because she's my daughter. Ash isn't the type to forgive or forget, and I know he blames me for not giving him better marks – conveniently forgetting the fact that he didn't do any bloody work.'

'I thought he'd decided university wasn't spiritual enough for him?' I said, and Drew snorted.

'He says that now, but at the time he was furious. Ash likes to think of himself as king of all he surveys, and that's hard to pull off when you're a university dropout. Much better to recast it as being victimized by the system – that's me – that is too stupid or corrupt to understand his unique talents. I wasn't at all surprised he'd set up his own cult. I just wish he'd done it somewhere else, where Sophie wouldn't have crossed his path.'

'I'm guessing he's someone who prefers to be a big fish in a little pond,' I said.

'I just wish I knew why Sophie is so impressed by him,' Drew sighed as he attacked the wall with the roller.

My masking-tape duties finished, I perched on the windowsill. 'She's looking for somewhere to belong,' I said, spinning the roll around my forefingers. 'From what she's told me, she's lonely, and torn between you and her mother, and she doesn't find it easy to make friends at school. Whatever they do at these "gatherings" that she talks about, they're giving her something she needs. You may not like it, but she loves all that spirituality stuff.'

'Then why doesn't she go to church?' asked Drew. 'I wouldn't mind that so much.'

'I don't think the Church has quite the glamour that Ash offers. We might think it's all mumbo-jumbo, but for Sophie it's mystical and powerful and it's different from conventional forms of spirituality. It's a heady mix.'

Drew sighed. 'So what should I do? Just accept that Ash can manipulate my daughter at will?'

'I wonder if it's more about accepting *her*,' I said slowly. 'She knows how much you hate what she believes in. Maybe that makes her feel that she doesn't belong with you, either.' I hesitated. 'Does Sophie know about your mother?'

He shook his head. 'I never wanted to encourage her.'

'She didn't need any encouragement,' I pointed out. 'She's looking for someone to feel a connection to, and neither you nor her mother share her beliefs. Maybe she needs to know that she's not the first in her family to feel the way she does.'

I saw Drew thinking about that. 'Do you think I should tell her how her grandmother died?' he asked after a while. 'Show her how dangerous these cults can be?'

'Not yet,' I said. 'She'll just think that you're getting at Ash. First, let her feel that you're not completely hostile to everything she believes in. You could give her something of her grandmother's, maybe. Or why don't you ask Vivien Price to invite her back to their coven, or whatever it's called? I know you haven't got much time for Wicca either, but it's harmless compared to Ash.'

I thought about Vivien's garden, and her calm, powerful presence. I didn't think 'harmless' was really the right word, but she had none of the malevolence I sensed in Ash.

Drew was frowning at the wall, the roller moving more and more slowly as he thought. 'That might be worth a try. Sophie was right into witchcraft before Lucy died. She might be tempted back – although, God knows, I never thought I'd be encouraging my daughter to join a coven!'

'Sophie's too young to join their coven, but I'm sure Vivien would find a way to include her,' I said. 'She's quite an impressive person really.'

'Hmm.' Drew looked unconvinced, but when I offered to have a word with Vivien, he didn't say no. And when I was round for supper a few days later he produced a small box decorated with moons and stars.

'What's this?' said Sophie when he pushed it across the table towards her.

'It was your grandmother's. Look inside.'

She pulled out a pentagram hanging on a fine leather cord, and her mouth dropped open. 'My grandmother was a *witch*?'

'Among other things,' said Drew.

'Wow, that is so cool!' Sophie's smile was brilliant as she slipped the pendant over her head. 'Is it really for me?'

'I think she'd have liked you to have it,' he said gruffly.

'Thanks, Dad.' She patted the pendant as if to reassure herself that she wasn't imagining it. 'It's like a real *connection*.' Her eyes lifted to her father's. 'Why didn't you tell me about her before?'

Drew opted for honesty. 'I was hoping it was a phase you'd grow out of.'

He told me later that Sophie bombarded him with questions about his mother all evening after I'd gone, which I think must have been quite difficult for him, but Sophie certainly seemed a lot happier for a while. I'd given her Lucy's jewellery, but this was special. It was a link to her own family, and she was delighted with it.

I kept my word and went to see Vivien about Sophie, too. She noticed straight away that I wasn't wearing the amulet.

'I'm fine,' I said. 'It's over. I'm chalking it up as an amazing experience.'

Vivien studied me, a frown touching her eyes. 'Over? Are you sure?'

'I'm sure,' I said. 'Nothing's happened for weeks now.'

'I don't think you should let down your guard,' she said. 'Your aura is still very cloudy. Hawise is with you still.'

'Well, if she is, I've got her under control,' I said lightly.

'That's what Lucy said. And Lucy died.'

Something – a lift of breeze? a breath? – touched the back of my neck. I felt it all the way down my spine, but I shook the sudden chill aside.

'I'm not Lucy,' I said. 'Besides, I'll be leaving soon.'

In the meantime there was no hurry. The house still needed a bit of work before I could put it on the market. I liked my job, and with new courses running all the time, it was flexible enough for me to stay, but leave whenever I needed. As summer slid into September and I stayed resolutely in the present, I let myself relax and enjoy myself. Sometimes, it's true, I missed Hawise and wondered about her story, but I never again tried to regress deliberately. It had to be the right moment, I'd realized. Somehow on each occasion there had been a sharing of some sensation or feeling, and there was no way I could know what might trigger a slip into the past.

Besides, I didn't want to. I'd had enough of being dragged backwards and forwards through time. Vivien could say what she wanted about it being a privilege, but I'd hated that feeling that Hawise was controlling me, that she could take over at any point and make me wild with lust, or long for a baby. I wanted to be my own person again.

So I did exactly what Drew said I always did. I papered over the cracks and told myself that life was back to normal. Once when Drew and I were out we bumped into Sarah with, I was glad to see, her boyfriend, and we all went out for a drink together, but it was awkward. I wished I hadn't had to tell her about the tsunami. I didn't like her knowing what had happened, and when she asked me how I was, I brushed her concern aside.

'I'm absolutely fine now,' I said.

And for a while I was.

It was early September before I put the house on the market, and I had the first offer barely two weeks later. I don't know what I had been expecting, but I hadn't thought it would come so soon. Didn't it take months to sell a house?

'Congratulations,' said Drew when I knocked on his door to tell him the news. 'So you'll be leaving soon?'

'I . . . well, yes . . . ' I said, brought up short. 'Yes, I suppose I will.'

Leaving. Leaving would mean never seeing Drew again, which would be fine, of course, but I'd sort of got used to his dry voice and the way everything felt steadier and safer when he was near.

But what was the alternative? To stay in York? Stay with Drew? And if I did, how long would we be happy to stay just friends? And if we weren't friends, we'd be lovers, and he would expect me to talk about how I felt and everything else that went along with having a 'relationship'. The thought of all that emotional intimacy opened up a yawning chasm in front of me and instinctively I backed away from it.

'I was thinking it was time that I was moving on anyway,' I said. 'Mel's having a great time in Mexico, and she says there are plenty of jobs there. I'll probably go and join her.'

And that's when I heard it, for the first time in weeks.

Bess. It sounded feebler than before, a last desperate gurgle before Hawise's lungs filled with water.

'What?' said Drew as I froze.

'Nothing.'

The familiar dread was uncoiling in the pit of my belly. 'It's over,' I had told Vivien, and it *was* over. I was selling the house and leaving York. I wasn't going to get sucked into the past again.

'In fact I'm going to see if Mel can fix me up with a job right now,' I said to Drew, but the defiance in my voice was meant for Hawise.

'Sounds like a plan,' he said.

Not: *Don't go.* Not: *Please stay.* Not: *I'll miss you.*

Which was exactly why I had been sensible not to get involved with him.

'Want to have a drink tonight to celebrate the sale?' I said, determinedly cheerful, but he shook his head.

'Can't, I'm afraid. I'm going to a conference in London tomorrow and I still haven't finished my paper. Can we celebrate when I get back?'

'Sure,' I said. 'Let's do that.'

I knew that when I went back into Lucy's house there would be an apple waiting for me – and there was, right next to the kettle where I couldn't miss it.

My lips tightened and I set my jaw in what Drew called my pig-headed look. 'I'm going,' I insisted out loud.

My laptop had been working fine over the summer, but now when I logged on to the Internet the screen kept going blank.

Bess. Bess.

The whisper curdled the air, and I felt Hawise's anguish settle on my skin like a fine web. I scrubbed my hands over my face as if I could brush it away.

'I'm sorry,' I said into the empty air. 'I'm sorry you drowned, but I can't do anything about it. I don't know how it all went wrong. I can't help you. I'm sorry.'

Bess. It was faint, but implacable. Hawise was as stubborn as I.

I gritted my teeth. 'I'm leaving,' I said and closed the laptop with a snap. 'You can't stop me.'

Outside, a dreary mizzle was falling as I marched into the library near the Minster. I was all riled up, and ready for a fight. Drew hadn't begged me to stay, which was just as well, as I wasn't going to; and now Hawise was trying to get into my head again. I wasn't having it.

I found a computer and logged on to email.

Mel, I typed, making the keyboard rattle. *Have sold house, which means will be buying my ticket any day now. Can you suss out job situation? Am thinking*

The screen went dead before I could finish.

'That's odd,' said the assistant when I asked for help. 'I've never seen that before. Try one of the other computers.'

I did, but that crashed too, and the one after that. The assistant was looking at me strangely, as if it was all my fault. 'Weird,' he said.

'Must be a problem with the server,' I said.

'All the other computers are working.'

'Oh, well, maybe it's me.' I rolled my eyes to show that I was joking. 'Don't worry, I'll try somewhere else.'

I found an Internet cafe and bought myself a coffee. I had a wild idea that the coffee would somehow fool Hawise into thinking I wasn't trying to contact Mel at all. It didn't work, anyway. I could google to my heart's content, but the moment I logged onto email and tried to send a message, the screen went blank again.

In the end, I gave up. Which wasn't the same as giving in. The thought was aimed at Hawise. I was very conscious of her lurking in my mind. It felt as if it had become a battle of wills between the two of us. This time I wasn't frightened at the idea of her. I was cross, and it was all bound up with feeling edgy about Drew and the house sale, and with myself for not being as delighted at the prospect of moving on as I ought to be. I'd been perfectly happy all summer, and now everything was changing.

It was partly my own fault, I knew. I had let my guard down, just as Vivien had warned. I had let myself relax and Hawise had snuck back, but this time I wouldn't let her take over. I would put on my amulet as soon as I got home.

It was raining properly when I walked home. I'd forgotten my umbrella and the wind-tunnel effect on the south side of the Minster blew the rain right into my eyes. Preoccupied by my thoughts, I turned up my collar and screwed up my face, glad when the wind dropped away as I reached Goodramgate. I paused there, wiping the worst of the wet from my face with the back of my hand.

I was careless. I'd grown used to not needing that guard on my mind, and I didn't stop to wonder why, instead of turning left to Monk Bar, I looked right, down to where the Beckwiths' house once stood. The street shimmered through the rain and a sense of foreboding crept over me, so strong that I caught my breath and my hand went to my mouth. Frantically I blinked to fix myself in the present, but it was too late.

'They say there's sickness in Selby.' Isobel is back from the market and is unloading vegetables from her basket onto the table while Margery checks them, lips pursed.

We are in the kitchen. I am showing Joan how to make an infusion to calm the stomach, and trying to ignore the sweatiness that is making my ruff itch and my hair stick to my scalp beneath my cap. Alison is plucking a chicken and Bess is on the floor, grasping at the tiny feathers as they drift in the sunlight through the open door. It is July, and the days are long and remorselessly hot. It hasn't rained for weeks. The streets are baked hard and the flies are thick around the middens. The gutters are dry, the Ouse shrunken and sluggish, and the smell of the privies hangs heavy in the air.

'There's always sickness in Selby,' Margery snaps. She holds up a cucumber so limp that it bends at one end, and waves it at Isobel. 'What do you call this?'

There is a pause while we all look at the cucumber, then as one we break into helpless giggles. Even Bess joins in, not understanding how lewd the cucumber looks, just laughing delightedly because we are laughing, and for a moment I forget the heat and the stickiness and the discomfort. There is just a kitchen full of sunlight and laughter. I should reprove the maids for their silliness, but I don't want to. I want to hold onto this moment forever, I think.

'It's a . . . c-cucumber,' Isobel manages, wiping her eyes, as the rest of us try to stifle our giggles.

'Oh, you girls!' Margery tsks and shakes her head, and it pleases me that I am obviously included with the maids. I can see that she is only pretending to disapprove anyway. A smile is tugging at the corner of her mouth in spite of herself.

'Could do with a codpiece, couldn't it?' she says, and we all burst into laughter again, until Joan gets hiccups and throws her apron over her head, which just makes us laugh even more.

At last we subside, apart from a few hiccups from Joan, and Margery goes back to grumbling about the state of the vegetables.

'It was the best they had,' Isobel protests. 'There's nowt decent in the market right now.'

'They're closing the bars,' she adds, when Margery simply sniffs and starts to pick over the strawberries that she has bought. 'No one from Selby way is allowed into the city. Lucky the master got back in time, in't it?'

It is. Ned only returned from Hull yesterday. Rob is still there, overseeing the unloading of the ships from the Baltic and negotiating with the keelmen who will bring the goods up the river to York. Ned didn't come back on the Selby road, it is true, but when rumours of sickness start, the Lord Mayor is quick to shut the city gates to strangers. It happens most summers and it interferes with business, but we don't fret overmuch. It is a long time since the plague hit York hard – since before I was born anyway. A few people die every summer, but it is never as bad as the older people tell.

So when Margery reports a couple of days later that the baker Stephen Robson is dead, we cross ourselves, but are not afraid. In life we are in death. The next day there is news of another death in the parish – Elizabeth Lamb, the innkeeper's wife – and the next day there are two more: the widow Catherine Bowman, and William Young's servant, Ralf.

It starts slowly and then, without warning, it is out of control. One day we are at the market, waving the flies from our faces and complaining about the heat. The next the streets are empty and the air is sour with fear. I wake up one morning expecting it to be a normal day. I am thinking about the tasks I will set Isobel and Alison and Joan, about whether it is too hot to clear out the larder. It is so hot that we have been sleeping with the windows wide open, and still we cannot sleep.

The bells are tolling. Ned goes out and comes home, his face grave. The sickness is spreading. Already two of the aldermen are dead, who yesterday were going about their business.

'What should we do?'

'Stay home. Take care of our own. Do we have food?'

'Enough,' I say. It is hard to believe that it will affect us. Others perhaps, but not us. We are lucky.

The news of the sickness is spreading as fast as the plague. Alison and Joan have heard it from Isobel, who had it from Mistress Richardson across the street. It is not the sweating sickness, it is the dreaded pestilence – the one Mistress Beckwith told us about, and which ravaged London some twelve years ago. I was just a child then, but I remember the hushed way folk spoke of what was happening to the southerners. The maids are whispering of boils and black skin, of buboes that split and ooze blood and pus, and a stench like no other. It sounds horrible, but it cannot really happen, not to us.

And for a day or two it seems that it is so. The streets are quiet, the country people stay away from the markets, and the workshops fall silent one by one. It is as if we are all waiting, holding our breaths and keeping very still, so that the sickness won't see us crouching in our houses as it prowls the city like a fox around the henhouse. If we do not move, perhaps it will pass us by, the way it always has before.

It takes a long time before we realize that it will not go away, that it has settled in like a dog with a bone. The maids are frightened, and even Margery looks grim, so I try and keep up a semblance of normality. I am worried about the Beckwiths, though.

Ned doesn't like the idea of me going to see them. 'Better everyone stays close to home at the moment,' he says.

But I was part of the Beckwiths' family for many years. 'I will go straight there,' I promise. 'I just want to see they're all right.'

'What about your sister?'

As always with Agnes, I feel guilty. I should have thought of her first. But going to her house means I might meet Francis.

'Could you go?' I ask Ned. 'Tell her I'm thinking of her. Promise her anything that she needs.'

The streets are eerily quiet as I walk through Thursday Market and up Goodramgate. A lot of the shops have their windows shut up, and the workshops are silent. There are no women sitting at the doors, no children playing in the street. A dog slinks along the gutter, skittering away at my approach. The few people who are out scurry along, hunched as if the pestilence is stalking behind them, waiting to tap them on the shoulder. Ordinarily I would linger outside, but not today. I feel as if I have walked into a different world.

The Beckwiths' shop is shuttered, and the door is closed. My gut tightens with fear at the sight of it and I pound frantically at the door. It seems a long time before it is opened. My mistress stands there, and her face is so ravaged that I take a step back.

'No,' I say before she has said anything. 'No.'

'You shouldn't be here, Hawise.'

My mouth trembles. This was my home, my refuge. The Beckwiths have been constants in my life. They are good, decent people who saved me from my father. 'Who?' is all I can manage.

'Your master. Dick. And now Meg has the headache.' Her voice is leached of all emotion. She looks exhausted.

I can't take it in. My master, with his beefy face and his bluster, cannot be dead. And Dick, who teased Elizabeth and me, had almost finished his apprenticeship. He should be making his masterpiece, joining the tailors' guild, not lying in a grave.

'The carters came last night,' my mistress says. 'They have taken them away.'

There are already too many dead for proper burials. There is just a pit. My master will not lie in the fine tomb he had planned. He will be tossed into a pit next to his apprentice, who never had the chance to plan his own tomb.

'What can I do?' I ask, my throat so tight I can hardly speak.

'Go home,' says my mistress. 'Keep safe.'

I can't just leave her here with poor, sick Meg. I take a step forward without thinking. 'You need help. Let me come in.'

'No.' She bars the door. 'You have a child to think of.'

The thought of Bess makes me hesitate. 'But—'

'No, Hawise, it is too dangerous,' she says as firmly as her exhaustion allows. 'I'm surprised your husband let you come at all.' Seeing my expression, she guesses the truth and shakes her head. 'You always were wilful, but you're a good girl. You look after that daughter of yours.'

She makes to close the door and I can't bear the thought that this may be the last I see of her. 'I'll come tomorrow,' I insist. 'I'll bring you food at least.'

But when I go back, there is no answer. The door stays shut. I knock and knock and no one comes.

This time there was no jarring, no dislocation. The edges of time were blurred, and all I did was blink to slip between one world and the other, a sideways step rather than the precipitous fall it had been before.

My face was wet as I stared at where the house had been. The facade was changed now beyond all recognition, but the memories of the place resonated beneath the tarmac and the concrete, layer upon layer of events and actions and feelings that had settled into a thick crust. It seemed solid and stable, but it could shift with no warning, just as the Earth's crust had slipped beneath the Indian Ocean.

Leaden with grief, I turned and walked back out through the bar to Lucy's house – the house I kept forgetting not to call home. Mistress Beckwith had been a fine person, much cleverer than her husband and sensible enough not to let him know it. She was the closest Hawise had to a mother, and I knew what it was like to lose a mother.

I remembered when mine had died. I hadn't cried, all the time she was ill. Not that I was brave or sweetly supportive. I was furious. I was angry with her for being sick, for wasting away before my eyes, for the tubes and the bags and the stink and the pain. I was angry with my father for not being able to stop it happening, and with myself for not being kind or heroic, the way I knew I should have been. I was fifteen and cruel and selfish, and part of me knew it at the time. That made me angry too.

So I was thinking about my mother as I walked home in the rain, and I forgot to think about Hawise or how easily she had overcome my resistance. The rain plastered my hair to my head and ran down my face, and I knuckled it away from my cheeks. I wasn't crying, I was just wet.

A stone had settled cold and hard in my chest. I let myself into the house. I dropped my bag onto the table in the little dining room, right next to the apple I had known would be there. For once, I barely noticed it. I was too sad to care.

I set the basket wearily on the table in the hall. Ned is there and he looks a question at me. I shake my head in reply, my lips pressed fiercely together to stop them from trembling.

'Oh, little wife,' he says and puts his arms around me.

I lean against him. He is strong and solid and safe. 'I'm frightened,' I say quietly.

'I know,' he says. 'It is God's will, Hawise. We must accept it.'

I nod – what else can we do? – and pull myself away from him. Only then do I see Francis Bewley standing in the shadows.

'What are you doing here?' I demand, too heartsick for courtesy.

Too late I realize that Agnes is behind him, hanging onto Francis's arm. 'I knew she wouldn't want us here,' she says in a trembling voice.

'I asked them to stay,' says Ned.

'We agreed that it would be easier if the family were together,' Francis puts in, and even in this time of trial his hot eyes seem to leave a slimy trail as he looks over my body. 'Agnes cannot manage on her own. Our servant has gone home to her mother, who is sick. We do not have others, as you do.'

Ned can see my face. 'It is sensible, Hawise,' he says. 'We must look out for each other.'

I am too tired and sad to argue. 'As you wish, Husband.'

Chapter Sixteen

Margery is the first to die. The next morning she is creasing her eyes as if the light is too bright. I send her to bed, my gut churning with anxiety, and ask Agnes to keep Bess well away.

Margery's eyes glitter with fear. Her body is racked with fever and she retches into the basin that I hold helplessly. I wipe her face with a wet cloth, but she is burning up. It is only now that I realize how much I have come to rely on her to keep the household running.

'Please get better,' I beg her. 'I need you.'

She doesn't get better. The fever gets worse and she tosses and turns, crying out at the pain in her limbs. And then I see the swellings on her neck and have to bite back my own cry of fear.

Margery turns black and rotten under my eyes. The lumps swell and burst, they ooze pus and blood, and black boils erupt all over her body, no matter how quickly I try to cool her. The blood is everywhere, the pain consumes her. I struggle to change the sheets and clear away the bloody stools, and the stench makes me gag.

In the end I pray only for her to die soon, and when she does, I do not feel guilty. I feel only relief for her.

My face like stone, I wash my hands and press the cold cloth over my face. 'Call the carter,' is all I say when I go out, and Isobel gets up silently.

I sit down at the table and press the heels of my hands against my eyes. 'How is Bess?'

'She is with your sister.'

I need to see my daughter, but I cannot go to her with the stench of Margery's death on me still. Stiffly I get up and go to the hall to find Ned. He isn't there. I find him at last in our bed. He opens his eyes at my approach.

'I am sorry, Hawise.'

'Ned!' I lay a shaking hand on his forehead. He is burning up. 'No! This cannot be. Not you. I cannot bear it.'

'Perhaps it is just a chill.' The words are obviously an effort.

I thought I was afraid when I saw that Margery was ill, but that was nothing to the terror that grips me now. I am paralysed with it.

'Ned! Please, please . . . ' I rest my forehead on the bed beside him and weep. He lifts a hand and strokes my hair.

'Take care, dear heart.'

I scramble up, dashing the tears from my eyes. I will not accept this. I cannot. I *will* not.

'I'm going to find the Widow Dent. She has many potions. She can cast me a spell,' I say wildly. 'She will help me.'

'Hawise, no.' Ned's voice is weak already. 'It is too dangerous. You know what they say about her. You mustn't seek her out. Bess needs you here.'

'I have to do *something*.'

Ned tries to dissuade me, but the sickness is eating up his will already. Desperately I run down to the kitchen.

'Give me some bread,' I snap to poor, scared Joan. 'And some of that cheese.' Frantically I throw it into a basket. 'The master is ill. I'm going to get him some help. Please, please, don't leave him alone.'

Their faces are frightened, poor girls. Then Alison gets to her feet. 'I'll go to him.'

'Thank you,' I say on a sigh. 'Thank you, Alison.'

My clogs jar on the ruts in the street. The poor folk outside Monk Bar are gone, and there is just one wretch crouched by the barbican, his face turned into the stone. I toss a coin by him, but he doesn't even try to catch it. What good is money now?

It is only days since life was normal, but already the crofts look overgrown, neglected. There is no one out here bending over the crops, pulling up onions or weeding their patches of vegetables.

I hurry along the path where Francis killed Hap, past my father's orchard where he tried to rape me, too desperate to remember that now. I cannot think of anything but Ned.

The widow's hovel is smaller than I remembered. It has shrunk back into the trees, and the moss grows thick over the roof as the wood reclaims it, little by little.

It is a long time since I have been here. I brought Sybil a gift when I conceived, and another after Bess was born, but since then I have been preoccupied, with a house to run and a child to care for. Every now and then I have thought about the widow, with a mixture of gratitude and fear, but I could have come more often, I know.

Sybil is at her door. Mog lies in a patch of sunlight, utterly relaxed on her back, her paws curled. She knows nothing of the sickness rampaging through the city and cares less.

'I've got nowt for the pestilence,' the widow says when I offer her the basket and beg her breathlessly for a remedy for Ned. 'Bathe him with lavender and rue, and keep him cool.'

I am dismayed. I had hoped for something stronger, something more certain. I don't care if it is witchcraft. I only want to save Ned.

Even now he may be sickening. 'Please,' I beg. 'Please – anything. I'll do anything.'

Her strange eyes pin me. 'Most young wives would be glad to see off an old husband.'

It doesn't occur to me to wonder how she knows that Ned is older than I. 'He is the beat of my heart,' I say simply, my voice cracking. 'I cannot bear to lose him.'

'Aye, well,' she says indifferently, 'we must all bear what we must.'

'Please,' I say again. 'I thought . . . I thought you could cast me a spell,' I finish in a rush.

Sybil's face empties of all expression. 'A spell?'

'To keep my husband safe from the sickness, that is all.'

'You should be more careful, Mistress,' she says tonelessly. 'Folk will think you're meddling in things you shouldn't.'

'I don't care what they think! I only want to save Ned.' My voice runs up and down the scale. 'If a spell will cure him, I will have a spell. I would cast it myself if I knew how!' I stop and steady myself. 'I have money,' I say, looking the widow straight in the eye. 'I will tell no one that I had it from you. Please, please, just give me *something*.'

She looks at me for a moment, judging the desperation in my face, then beckons me closer, with a hand twisted like an old tree root.

'Help me up,' she says.

I lift her to her feet and she turns and hobbles back into the cottage. After a few minutes she comes out and hands me a jar. 'Rub this on his chest,' she says, then passes over a little bag done up with string. 'And hang this around his neck.'

'Thank you, thank you. Yes. I will.' The words tumble gratefully out of me. I don't ask what is inside the bag. I don't care. I just want it to work. I dig in the purse hanging from my girdle and find some coins. Too many, perhaps, for a token, but what price can we put on hope?

'I'm making no promises, mind,' she adds fiercely, watching me turn the little bag in my hands. 'It will do what it will do. No more, no less.'

'I understand.' I take a breath. The bag seems to pulse with the widow's power. Surely, surely, this will save Ned.

'Is there anything else I can do?' I ask as I turn to go.

'Aye,' says the widow. 'Hope.'

Picking up my skirts, I run back along the path. With a strange, detached part of my mind I realize that I once ran laughing along here with Elizabeth, but I remember it as if it happened to someone else. Laughter belongs in another world to mine. Panic is scrabbling in my gut, but I force it down. I must stay calm, for Ned.

There is a painful stitch in my side by the time I reach the house, and in spite of my haste to see how Ned does, I rest for a moment in the hall, my hand on the chest, bent over and breathing heavily.

'Where have you been?'

Francis's voice slices through the torpor of the afternoon and makes me jerk upright. He is watching me from the shadows by the staircase and, in spite of the heat, I am suddenly cold.

'What matters it to you?'

'Your husband is sick, and you are not at his side. Why is that, I wonder?'

I bite my lip. 'I went to get some remedy for him.'

'You've been out to that witch, haven't you?' Francis strolls forward and, before I can sweep it out of his reach, swings up the basket I have dropped on the top of the chest. He picks up the jar, unstopping it and sniffing it. 'I thought so. Some foul concoction. And as for this . . . ' He dangles the bag distastefully from his fingers and clicks his tongue. 'Tsk, tsk, Sister . . . the minister will not approve of this.'

I have no time for his games. Ned may be dying in our bed. I care nothing for what Francis may do now. Nothing he can do will be worse than losing Ned.

'The minister is not here,' I point out, my hand under my ribs where it still aches. 'I will do whatever I can to save Ned.'

'Even witchcraft?'

'Anything,' I say again, snatching the bag from his hand. I make to pass him, but he steps into my way, his eyes blazing.

'You must make repentance.'

'Get out of my way, Francis.'

'You are an evil woman. You put Ned's soul at risk.'

'I am trying to save him! Do you think I care for you or your tricks now, Francis? Ned is a good man – far better than you will ever be. Now get out of the way and let me tend to my husband!'

I push past him, picking up my skirts in one hand so that I run up the stairs, the jar and the bag clutched against my breast, the sound of my clogs urgent in the hot silence.

Praying under my breath, I rub the ointment on Ned's chest. I loop the bag around his neck. I bathe him with lavender and rue. I hope and I hope and I hope. But still the boils come, suppurating all over his body, until he is as black and bloody as Margery was.

'No, no, no.' It is all I can say. I whisper it brokenly over and over again. My dearest's body is racked with pain, twisted and wasted. No longer is he the solid centre of my world. I cannot bury my face in his throat and hold onto him and make everything else go away.

He lies naked on the bed, while the sickness consumes him. It is a loathsome thing, a monster writhing under his skin. I can see it pulsing and swelling, pushing out the dreaded buboes, making them bigger and bigger until they burst agonizingly. I sponge him clean as best I can, but I can do nothing for the torment.

'I'm here, Ned,' I tell him, not knowing if he can hear me or not. He is not Ned any longer. He is a creature tortured in the fires of Hell itself, bleeding from every orifice. I used to love the clean smell of Ned's skin. Now it reeks of death. I know it is coming, but I fight it all the way. I cannot lose Ned, I cannot.

'Please get better,' I say to him. 'Please. I cannot do without you. Don't let me down, Ned. Don't die.'

But he does die. I don't even realize when it happens. I am desperately sponging him, desperately praying, words tumbling incoherently from my lips as if I can keep death from the room with sheer force of will.

My hand slows as I sense the emptiness in the room, the knowledge that I am alone. There is no more laboured breathing, no tortured gasps from Ned. His chest is still.

I freeze. 'Ned?' But he is gone.

Despair engulfs me. It has happened too quickly. I am not prepared for this. Last night we lay together in this bed, and now he is dead. It cannot be right.

I want to stamp my foot and wail like a child. Ned is not supposed to leave me alone. He is supposed to be there for me always – solid, quiet, smiling that smile that warms his eyes and only just reaches the edges of his mouth. I think of the nights when his mouth was hot on my skin, when his hands were urgent. It is impossible to think that I will never feel him again.

I think of the way he threw Bess in the air and caught her

in his hands, the strength of his body, the quiet authority that made men listen to him. The pleasure that he taught me. The way he made me feel beautiful. He cannot be gone. He cannot have left me.

I rest my forehead against his cold hand and weep, and the sobs rack my body as the plague racked his.

'Mistress?' Isobel's voice trembles behind me. Dully I raise my head. 'Alison has the fever.'

Alison dies, then Isobel. My world shrinks to blood and pain and despair. Agnes has shut herself away with Bess. With what little thought I have to spare, I am glad that at least Bess is safe. She is away from the sickness. Agnes keeps to the room, and will only accept a tray of food if it is left outside the door. I have to believe that she is keeping my daughter safe.

Francis lurks, prowling the rooms uselessly, standing at the windows and watching the empty street for news. I am too tired and too heartsick to care by now.

When little Joan falls ill in her turn, only the thought of Bess keeps me going. She is very frightened, poor lass, and we both know by now what lies in store for her. When she is dead, I cannot pray any more. I cannot even cry. I am numb with loss. Ned. Margery. All three bonny maids. Now there is only Bess. And Agnes and Francis.

I drag myself to my feet. My limbs feel heavy and stiff with disuse. I try to think about what needs to be done, but every time I make myself contemplate life without Ned my mind swerves away in panic. All I can do now is hold my daughter to me.

The door to the room is firmly closed. 'Agnes?' I barely have the strength to rap on the door. 'Let me in.'

'I dare not.'

'You must. I need to see Bess.'

'She's sleeping. You should not come in. You may be infected.'

I lean my forehead against the door. 'If I was going to get sick, don't you think it would have happened by now? Let me in, Agnes.'

'Find Francis first.'

I would not have thought it possible for my heart to sink further, but so it does. 'Francis? Where is he?'

'I don't know.' Her voice trembles on the edge of hysteria. 'He was coming to check on us, but I haven't seen him since yesterday. I am afraid for him.'

She refuses to unbar the door until I bring Francis to her.

I find him in Ned's study, slumped in a chair at Ned's desk, his eyes rolling in his head. 'Hawise! Help me! I have the sickness too.' He clutches at me with damp hands, and I cannot prevent a shudder of disgust.

'You must get to bed, Francis,' I say wearily, too tired even to think that I may be rid of him at last.

I have to support him up the stairs, and the damp, rank weight of him is revolting. He is whimpering with pain and fear as I help him onto the bed. 'Don't leave me!'

'I'm going to fetch Agnes,' I say as calmly as I can. 'She should be with you.'

'No! You, Hawise.' He is panting, struggling up on the

pillows. 'I want you. I've always wanted you. I love you. You know that.'

'You're hallucinating.' I back out of the room, but his howls follow me along the passage.

'Hawise! I love you! Don't leave me.'

Sick to my stomach, I force myself to wait until he subsides into gibbering before I knock on Agnes's door. I don't want her to hear him like that.

'Agnes? Francis needs you. You must come.'

'Is he sick?'

'I fear so.'

Agnes breaks into a storm of weeping. 'What will I do without him?' she keens and I have to force patience into my voice.

'Come, Agnes, you should be with him.'

'I'm afraid. I don't want to die!'

Ned didn't want to die. Nor did Joan or Isobel or Alison or Margery.

'Francis is your husband. It is your place to nurse him.'

'I can't. I am too sickly – you know I am. You do it,' she says. 'You are strong and the sickness doesn't touch you, you said that yourself. Please, Hawise.'

'Agnes, I need to be with Bess. Open the door.'

'No! Not until you promise to look after Francis.'

I hadn't thought it possible to be any more afraid, but now I am. Agnes sounds irrational, and she is behind a barred door with Bess. I take a deep breath. I must go very carefully and let her calm down.

'All right,' I say. 'All right. I'll nurse him. I promise.'

Francis is arching on the bed when I go back to him. A few minutes and the fever has taken a firmer hold of him. In truth, I wouldn't leave a dog in this state, so I collect my cloths and my bowl of lavender and sage. I go through the motions of rubbing Sybil's ointment on his chest, hating the feel of him. I even put the little magic bag around his neck, although much good it has done any of the others.

I wait for him to die and wonder how I am going to persuade Agnes to open the door. Once I leave Francis to find some food in the kitchen. It is crowded with the ghosts of my little maids, and my chest is so tight I can hardly breathe, but I fix my thoughts on Bess. As long as she is alive, I can endure.

'Leave the food,' Agnes orders through the door. 'I cannot risk the sickness getting into the room.'

I can hear Bess talking in her own special language behind Agnes. She sounds cross, but not distressed, so I leave the tray on the floor outside the door and go back to Francis, who lies naked and writhing under the sheet.

I have lost track of time by now. How long is it since we could go outside to the market without thinking about it? Since we could laugh and talk and not imagine that, at the end of the day, half of us will be dead? Sometimes I think about the life I had – about waking with Ned, my face pressed against the warm skin of his shoulder, about laughing in the kitchen with Margery and the maids, and Bess on my hip – and it seems like an impossibly distant dream, another world entirely, not something that happened to me.

My life now is just sponging and cleaning up mess. Francis

is pathetic. His sly swagger is all gone, and he grasps at my hand and cries out for me in his delirium. Occasionally I think it is just as well that Agnes is not here to hear him. My flesh would creep, if I had the energy to be horrified. For now I close my mind to it.

I breathe through my mouth as that makes the stench easier to bear, and the sound of my breath is all that breaks the silence that has been thrown over the household like a coverlet on a table.

In one way at least, nursing Francis is easier than the others. At least this time I don't care. I treat him as I would any living creature, but when I see him suffering I don't feel as if my heart is being ripped out of my body.

And perhaps because I don't care, Francis lives.

When I realize that the fever has broken and he is going to survive, bitterness against God swells up inside me and clogs my throat, so that I can hardly breathe with it. Why him? Why Francis and not Ned? All those good folk who have died, and Francis – sly and malevolent Francis – lives. It is bitter as worm-wood on my tongue.

'Thirsty,' Francis croaks.

Burning with resentment, I help him lift his head and sip some ale. I don't like touching him.

'I'm so hot,' he says as he lies down, and I want to wipe my hands on my skirts to get rid of the feel of him.

Wearily I fetch more water and wring out my cloth once more, but when I begin to sponge the sweat from his naked body, his thing stirs and stiffens. Snatching my cloth away in disgust, I find Francis watching me between slitted lids, and his expression makes me shudder.

'I will fetch your wife to you,' I say coldly.

'But I like it when you touch me,' he says.

I make to step away, but he grabs my hand and pulls me down into his rankness and tries to kiss me. He takes me by surprise, so that I almost fall on top of him. I struggle frantically, retching with disgust, and finally manage to disentangle myself from him, thanking God that he is still so weak.

'Don't touch me again,' I warn him, wiping the back of my hand shakily across my mouth. 'I will pretend that you are delirious still, so this stays between us, but if you touch me again, I will go to Agnes, I swear it.'

'Ned is dead.' His eyes are feverish – or are they mad? 'We'll get married.'

I back away from him. 'Agnes is not dead,' I say clearly.

'If she were,' says Francis, and I remember what he said about his master. *I will see to it.* Will he see to my sister, too?

I had not thought it possible to feel any greater horror, but I feel cold as I look at him. He is a madman, and my sister is bound to him. I need to keep her safe. I have lost too many of those I care for already.

'You are brain-sick,' I tell him, shaking. 'Even if my sister were a hundred times dead, I would never marry you, Francis Bewley! Never! I would rather rut with a pig. Now, I will go and get your wife for you.'

Agnes, persuaded that Francis has survived, throws herself on him, thanking God and praising Him, and I can't help thinking that she should rather be thanking me. Poor Agnes, married to a man with a warped mind.

All I can do is pretend that he was delirious. I bury the knowledge of his lust and his madness and close the door on it, because I cannot face it, not now that I am alone. I hold my daughter close, rocking her in my arms and breathing in her sweet smell, and her warmth is all that keeps me from the blackness of utter despair.

I was in the sitting room, clutching a cushion to my chest, crooning softly as I rocked backwards and forwards. As in the street, it wasn't a jarring return to the present this time, but a gradual awareness that I couldn't smell Bess's hair any more, that my cheek was pressed against the tufty fringe of the cushion instead of the top of her head.

And that an apple lay rotting on the coffee table in front of me.

Very slowly I let the cushion fall onto my lap and sat staring ahead, my bones aching with an old, old grief. I felt empty and very lonely, and I wanted Drew.

But when I called him, I could hear the phone next door ringing on and on unanswered. The more it rang, the sadder I felt and the more I wanted to talk to Drew. I knew he hated talking on his mobile in public, but I tried it anyway, and to my relief he answered.

'Where are you?'

'I'm on a train,' he said, lowering his voice so furtively that I couldn't help smiling. It always amused me how shifty he sounded on his mobile. Sophie did a wonderful imitation of him.

'Where are you going?'

'That conference I told you about.'

'Oh . . . yes. I forgot about that.'

There was a pause. I could hear the train guard in the background, making some announcement about the buffet bar.

'Did you want something?' Drew asked after a moment.

I thought about telling him that I'd just wanted to hear his voice, but decided against it. It would just make me seem needy. 'I just wondered if you were around for a drink, that's all.'

'I won't be back until Sunday night, I'm afraid.'

'Oh. Oh, okay.' The bitterness of my disappointment caught me unawares.

'Is everything all right, Grace?'

'Fine.' I forced brightness into my voice. I could hardly tell him I was distressed by the scenes of sickness and death I had just endured. Drew had never accepted that Hawisc was real, I knew, and he certainly wouldn't want to talk me out of my depression about the plague that had hit York four hundred years earlier, while he was sitting on a train.

'Why do I even bother asking?' he sighed. 'It's always fine with you.'

'Well, it is.' My eye fell on the apple that was still sitting on the table, and I looked away.

'What are you going to be doing this weekend, since you're feeling so fine?'

I hadn't thought about it. The truth was that I was used to

him being around, and I'd fallen into the habit of seeing him most evenings. I didn't like the idea of spending it on my own, especially not now that Hawise was creeping back into my mind and there would be no Drew to keep my attention firmly fixed on the present. There was no fascination in the past this time, just a wrenching grief. I didn't want to know any more. I already knew too much.

'I might go away,' I said slowly, the idea forming in my mind along with the words. As soon as I said it, I knew that was just what I needed. Why hadn't I thought about it before? I might not be in a position to go travelling just yet, but there was no reason I shouldn't spend a weekend away. It would be good for me.

'Good idea,' said Drew. 'Where are you thinking of going?'

'The school's running a weekend trip to Edinburgh. I'll tag along with them. I'm sure they'd be glad of another teacher.'

Sure enough, Jan, who organized the trips, was delighted when I told her that I'd like to go. 'We're meeting at the station at nine-thirty on Saturday morning. I've made a block booking, so don't be late.'

Overnight rain had been blown away to leave a bright morning when I set off for Edinburgh that Saturday. A brisk wind chivvied billowy, bruised-looking clouds across the sky. Every now and then the sun would burst valiantly out, and I had to screw up my eyes against the brightness, but the moment I pulled out my sunglasses, it would be blotted out once more.

I was relieved to have got through the night without dreaming of Hawise's anguish, and the thought of getting away lightened my steps. I couldn't understand why I hadn't thought of it before.

Because you didn't want to leave Drew? I scowled, embarrassed by the very idea. It was high time I moved on.

It was always so windy around the Minster that I didn't take much notice at first when my walking became laboured, as if I was heading into a gale. I was thinking about the station and hoping I had left enough time to get there, and it was a while before I realized that something was wrong.

The wind was too strong and the light, once I started to notice it, was crystalline with menace. I paused for breath outside the south transept, and when I glanced uneasily up, the gargoyles seemed to jump out at me, leering and jeering. I could have sworn they had turned their heads to watch me as I passed.

There was a dragging feeling in my head too, like fingers digging into my brain, pulling me back, back, back. I set my teeth when I realized what was happening. I wasn't going to give in to Hawise on this one. I was going to Edinburgh.

Doggedly I leant forward, pushing my way through the air, which had grown gluey and padded with resistance. Every step was a huge effort. I started to feel dizzy with it.

I made it past the Red House and across at the lights. My legs were trembling by the time I passed the library, and when I got to the entrance to Museum Gardens I had to lean against the wall to rest, my breath coming in jerky puffs. The station seemed impossibly distant on the other side of the river.

The river where Lucy had drowned. Where Hawise had

drowned. Where I would drown too, if I couldn't shake her hold on me, I realized with a burst of horror.

I had to get away, but the recent rain had left the Ouse swollen and sullen under the bridge, and the thought of crossing it filled me with terror. I made myself leave the safety of the wall and face the river while my mind screamed: *No! No!*

I took a hesitant step forward, then another, but the conviction that I was stepping out over the edge of a cliff was so strong that I stopped again in the middle of the pavement, my skin clammy with dread. This was all wrong. There was no bridge. I should be going down to the ferry, not walking out high into the air as if I had wings.

That was Hawise thinking. I struggled to push her from my mind. There was no ferry any more. Instead there was a perfectly good bridge. I hadn't crossed the river once since I had arrived in York, I realized. Subconsciously I had been avoiding it, but there was no other way to get to the station.

It was ridiculous to think that I couldn't cross the river, I reminded myself fiercely. Of course I could. The bridge was real. It was concrete and tarmac and stone. All I had to do was put one foot in front of the other and not look at the water.

Tourists and day-trippers were flooding up from the station, walking three and sometimes four abreast across the bridge with its narrow pavement. They weren't tumbling through the air, down into the cold, brown clutch of the river. The bridge was real enough.

I took a deep breath and made myself walk on, but the morning had taken on a nightmarish quality. I couldn't shake the conviction that I was walking along a tightrope, suspended high over the water. I didn't know what was real any more.

There were too many people. They pushed towards me like cattle, their faces terrifyingly blank, bearing me back towards the Minster. I couldn't get past, and icy panic gripped my guts. It was as if the world had turned against me, and I was alone amongst aliens. If I fell, I was sure they would simply have marched over me.

As it was, the crowds broke around me as I faltered in the middle of the pavement, but there were always more people behind. An army of tourists, marching on up to Betty's and the Shambles and the Minster. They just kept on coming, many of them wearing little more than their shifts. They were grotesque: their heads were uncovered, the women's often polled short, their legs bare or encased in strange hose – a great, intimidating troop of shameless vagrants flaunting their nakedness, jostling past each other without courtesy.

I blinked, and they were once more just ordinary people, but Hawise's horrified reaction at the amount of flesh on display lingered and I averted my eyes in disgust. My heart was banging against my ribs, my blood rushing in my ears. There were so *many* of them that I couldn't get past.

Go back! Go back! You can't do this!

Ignoring Hawise, I gathered the last of my courage and tried to dodge out off the kerb to get past the advancing hordes, but a bicycle almost ran me down. The cyclist swore at me as he swerved and shot past, and then I looked up in terror to see a monstrous, roaring wagon bearing down on me, but there were no horses and the sound of it filled my head so that I could only gape at it, paralysed by fear.

'Watch it!' Just in time, someone grabbed my arm and yanked me back onto the pavement as the bus swept past with a blare of its horn.

'Th-thank you,' I stammered, but my saviour had already moved on.

I fought my way across the pavement to the wall and leant against it, pushing my palms against the stone to reassure myself that it was real. It felt real, but I was no longer sure any more. My head was ringing with resistance and I was sweating.

My phone bleeped. A text from Jan. *R u coming???*

Shaking, I pressed back into the wall. *Sorry, sick*, I texted back. *Can't make it.*

As soon as I turned back, that horrific drag in my head lessened. I pretended that I was waiting for the Park-and-Ride bus so that I could lean against the railings and rest my shaky legs. My heart was galloping frantically around in my chest. People were looking human again. I listened to snatches of conversation from passers-by and it all seemed so normal that I began to wonder if I had imagined that terrifying press of inhumanity blocking the bridge. When my knees felt steadier I decided to test it once more. I had missed the train, but surely I couldn't be trapped here?

The moment I stood up and turned to the bridge, the sick feeling was back, rolling over me in waves. I couldn't even make it as far as the bridge this time. The tightness in my head was unendurable. I thought my brain was going to explode. Sick and giddy, I stumbled back in the direction of the Minster, and instantly the feeling subsided.

So much for my imagination. I was frightened by the intensity of Hawise's hold on me, and resentful of her power. I hadn't realized until then that I was trapped. I've always hated that feeling.

At the junction I could see passengers queuing to get on a local bus. I might not get to the station, but what was to stop me getting on a bus and leaving the city that way? Defiantly I joined the queue, but the closer I got to the door, the deeper the pain dug into my head. By the time I got there I couldn't even lift my foot to put it on the step, and I had to hang onto the bus for support.

'You getting on or not, love?'

I looked up at the bus driver's face. He looked mildly concerned and impatient, obviously keen to stick to his schedule, but unwilling to encourage me on if I was going to be sick all over his bus, which was probably what I looked like.

Slowly, I shook my pounding head. 'I've changed my mind. I'm staying here.'

Chapter Seventeen

I didn't even bother trying a taxi. I knew getting in a car would drive the pain in my head past endurance.

Always in the past I had simply packed my bags and moved on when things got difficult, but now I couldn't even do that. I wondered what would happen if I asked Drew to put me in a car and drive me to an airport. Just thinking about it had those fingers digging agonizingly into my mind. I had a nasty feeling I'd be in such a state they'd never let me on a plane, even if I could get as far as a check-in desk.

I watched the bus drive away, and then I turned and walked back the way I had come.

Without quite knowing what I was doing, I found myself at the west front of the Minster, looking up at the soaring stone. I'd been inside before, wandering incuriously around, more out of a sense of obligation than anything else, but now something in the great building beckoned. I was exhausted and shaky, close to tears, and I wanted nothing more than to sit quietly somewhere peaceful and have my head to myself again. It was awful, that feeling as if I had a succubus in my brain, but as I made my way round to the south-transept entrance, Hawise unlatched herself from my mind and faded, leaving me shakier than ever.

I had forgotten there was an entrance charge. 'I just want to sit,' I said, as I fumbled in my purse, even the small act of finding money suddenly too much for me. My desperation must have shown in my face, because the volunteer on the admissions desk told me not to worry about the money.

'The Zouche Chapel is reserved for prayer,' she said, pointing. 'It'll be quiet in there.'

The nave and choir were full of tour groups. It wasn't exactly noisy, but even the muted buzz of reverence jangled in my ears, and when I unlatched the old oak door and stepped down the worn steps into the chapel, I was grateful to find that I was alone.

I'd never been a churchgoer. Weddings and Christmas, my mother's funeral . . . I didn't know what to do with myself in a church. I eyed the altar and fought the impulse to kneel in front of it. I didn't believe in God and, anyway, I didn't know how to pray. I wandered fretfully around the chapel instead, peering at the fragments of old stained glass in one of the windows. A fierce wren pecking at a spider. Monkeys carrying banners. A windmill. Some fish. These would have been old images, long before Hawise was born.

It was very quiet in the chapel. I sat heavily in one of the pews and stared unseeingly at the window above the altar, admitting to myself that I was scared. My heart was lurching unevenly along like an old Labrador and the breath seemed to be stuck in my throat.

My worst fear, being trapped, unable to outrun whatever was coming for me. I hadn't been able to outrun the tsunami, and I couldn't run away from this.

Hawise was stronger than I was, I had to accept that, too. I was stuck here in York until she chose to let me go. *If* she chose to let me go. Too late, I remembered Lucy. Had she been sucked into Hawise's story as I had been, only to find that she couldn't get out? Was that why she had been down by the Ouse that night? A coldness stole over me at the thought. Had she re-died Hawise's death, just as she had relived her life? Would I end up in the river, drowning again? I covered my face with my hands.

I am in church, my hands over my face. I am supposed to be thanking God for our deliverance from the pestilence, but I am not praying. God has taken Ned. He has taken my friends and my little maids, and He has spared Francis Bewley. I cannot thank Him for that.

Where my heart used to be, there is a stone: hard, cold, heavy. The sickness has swooped and now, sated, it has moved on, leaving me stranded in a wasteland. Only now do I truly realize what I have lost, and how safe Ned made me feel. The thought of never holding him again is like a great hand reaching inside me, twisting, wrenching, until I want to double over in pain. Sometimes I put my hand under my breast and flinch at the crack of my heart breaking again and again.

Gradually we crept out of our houses and looked around, dazed at the suddenness and savagery with which the sickness attacked. Incredibly, it is still summer. The birds are still singing, the trees are still green. The houses still stand, the dogs still scuffle in the gutters, but in the street are terrible gaps in the air where people used to be.

But I have Bess. I can thank God for that, at least. So I murmur along with the prayers and hold onto the knowledge that she is safe.

For Bess, I straighten my back and go on. She is too small to understand what has happened, but she knows enough to insist on staying with me now. She won't be left with Agnes any more, and I wonder what went on in that room when I was nursing Francis. So I take her with me when I go to market, balancing her on my hip as I go through the motions of inspecting grain or smelling fish. I have no heart for it, but we must eat.

Bess struggles to get down, and I set her on unsteady feet. Oblivious to the fact that we are all reeling still at finding ourselves in a strange, empty new world, she clings onto my skirts for balance and peeps a smile at the countrywomen, whose grim faces soften at the sight of her.

Bess staggers away as I buy butter. I am watching her out of the corner of my eye, but I am digging in my purse for a coin and wondering what I will do for money when the purse is empty, when there is rumbling and shouting behind me. The countrywoman's eyes widen in horror, and I swing round to see a cart bearing down on Bess, who is hunkered in its way, absorbed in picking up a pebble with precise fingers and examining it with wonder.

'No!' the word bursts from me. I am too far from her. Everything is happening in slow motion. The open mouth of the carter, the wild eyes of the horse, the creak of the wheels, Bess looking up.

And then at the last moment before the cart would have been upon her, she is snatched up out of the way. She screams in fright and protest, arching back furiously from the grip of a small, dirty girl.

'Bess!' I reach them seconds later and grab my daughter, holding her to me and patting her all over to reassure myself that she is safe. My heart is pounding with shock and fear, and my expression must be wild, because when I turn to her saviour, the girl flinches away.

That stops me in my tracks and I force myself to be calm. 'I'm not going to hurt you,' I say. 'I want only to thank you.'

Thank you. The words are pitifully inadequate for what I feel.

'Didn't do nothing,' she mutters.

She is not a well-favoured child, and one foot is twisted and crooked, but her eyes are bright with a mixture of wariness and intelligence. She reminds me of Hap. She is painfully thin and she smells disgusting.

'What is your name?'

'Jane.'

I see the way her eyes fix on the food in my basket. 'How long is it since you have eaten, Jane?'

Jane, it turns out, is fifteen, although she is so thin and small that she seems much younger. She is the only survivor of a tanner's family, which explains the smell. Their street is a poor one, and it has suffered even more than most. There are no neighbours left to take Jane in, and she has no kin that she knows of. They had little enough to begin with, and since the sickness she has been scavenging as best she can.

'I can take care of meself,' she says defiantly when I ask who is looking after her.

'Come,' I say, 'let us find you a pie.' The cookshops are open again, and when Bess sees Jane devouring her pie, she clamours for one too. I'm about to buy her one when, starving as she is, Jane breaks off a crust and gives it to my daughter, whose crying instantly subsides.

'Jane,' I say, 'Bess needs a nursemaid. Would you like to come and live with us?'

So now I have two children to care for, and where there are children there can never be utter despair. Francis and Agnes shrink back in disgust when I lead Jane into the house.

'What are you thinking of, Hawise? She is filthy!' Agnes's voice rises shrilly. 'What if she brings the sickness back?'

'She will not be dirty when she has had a chance to clean herself,' I say, holding firmly to Jane's hand. 'She has survived the sickness, just as we have. Besides, this is my house now, and if I choose to offer her charity, that is my choice, is it not? I do not ask you to take Jane into your own house.'

'We have been discussing that,' says Francis smoothly. 'You are a widow now, and Agnes and I are all you have. I am head of the family, and I think we should all stay together, Sister, and support each other. It is only right.'

I stare at them. I had not thought anything else would have the power to horrify me after the pestilence, but so it is. I have been too leaden with grief to think about getting through more than one day at a time, but I should have been on my guard. Francis has always coveted Ned's wealth, I know. He yearns for the fine hangings, the wine and the plate. He covets *me*.

He will not have me. I swear it to myself.

'I am not well,' Agnes said. 'You know I am not strong. We cannot go home. Our servants have fled or are dead!'

'My servants have died too, Agnes.'

'But you can afford to replace them.'

I look at my sister in disbelief. Margery and little Joan. Alison and Isobel. They were not things to be replaced. I cannot go to the market and get some more Joan, a new Margery.

'And if we are under one roof, I can offer you protection and a godly example,' says Francis. Francis who slobbered his mouth across mine while his wife cowered in another room, frantic for his safety. Francis whose thing rose as I bathed him.

'I need no example from you,' I say stonily, 'nor do I need protection.'

'Are you sure about that, Sister? I think you would be wise to reconsider.'

'What do you mean?'

'Already there are rumours. They're saying you are a witch.'

'What!' I glance down at Jane, still by my side, expecting

to see her recoil, but she is watching Francis with a narrowed expression. 'That is nonsense, and you know it,' I tell him.

'Is it? I know you went out to that old witch in the crofts, and came back with a magic "remedy".' He hooks his fingers in the air to add sarcastic emphasis to the word. 'The next thing, your husband is dead and you are a wealthy widow. You cannot deny it is convenient, hmm?'

Convenient? My heart cracks at the thought of Ned, my dearest dear. It is only now that I realize he really is dead. He has not gone to Antwerp or London. He will not be back in a few weeks. He is dead and I will never see him again.

'Get out,' I say to Francis through numb lips.

'Hawise!' Agnes protests.

I round on her. 'You know how much I loved Ned, Agnes. How can you stand there and listen to him tell me that my husband's death was *convenient*?' I practically spit out the word and she bridles.

'Francis is only warning you what people are saying. It's for your own good.'

'I don't need warning. I can look out for myself.' My cold gaze swings back to Francis. 'I think you should leave now.'

He hesitates, calculates. I am only a woman, with a girl and a babe, and I cannot force him out physically, but my will is stronger than his. I face him down, and in the end they do go.

'On your own head be it,' says Francis, and he moistens his mouth with his tongue very deliberately as he passes me.

The moment they have gone I start to shake. I miss Ned. I ache for him, and I cover my face with my hands.

'Mistress?' Jane tugs at my skirt.

'I cannot bear it, Jane. I cannot do it on my own.'

'You en't on your own,' she says stoutly. 'You've got Bess. And me.'

I lower my hands and muster a smile. 'Yes.'

'Who was that man?'

My face darkens at the thought of Francis. 'My sister's husband.'

'He's a wrong 'un, I reckon,' says Jane, and I nod slowly.

'Yes,' I say again. 'Yes, he is.'

'Can I help you?' The touch on my arm was very gentle.

I lowered my hands to see a chaplain sitting beside me. Above her dog collar, her expression was compassionate. A woman priest? I recoiled in shock at the strangeness of it before I remembered who I was, *when* I was.

'I'm frightened.' The words blurted out of me.

'Then you've come to the right place,' she said calmly. 'You don't need to fear when you're with God.' She hesitated. 'Do you want to tell me your name?'

'Grace. I'm Grace.' I said it with emphasis, as if to prove to myself that it was true. I was Grace, not Hawise. 'Grace Trewe.'

'I'm Penny. What are you afraid of, Grace?'

How much could I tell her? How much would she believe? 'Do you believe in reincarnation?' I asked, and she smiled.

'I believe in life after death,' she said. 'Of course I do.'

'I don't. I don't believe in God,' I said defiantly.

'And yet you've come here when you are afraid,' she

observed. 'You may just have a grain of faith, but a grain is all you need. God's love is infinite, Grace. If you believe in that, you will find peace.'

'It's not me that needs peace,' I said, and when she raised her brows, I opened my mouth and the whole story came tumbling out. I didn't mean to tell her everything, and I'm still not sure why I did. Perhaps it was something to do with the quietness of the chapel, and her calm certainty that both reassured and irritated me.

'I thought Hawise had gone,' I finished at last. 'I thought I'd beaten her, but she's taking over my mind again. I can't go on like this.' I'd been staring ahead at the altar, twisting my hands together, but at that I turned to look directly at Penny. I'd like to think I didn't look pathetically pleading, but I probably did. It felt like a betrayal of Hawise, but I didn't see any alternative, if I was to leave York and get on with my life. 'Can you exorcize her?'

Penny looked at me thoughtfully. 'It's not quite as simple as that, Grace. I think you should talk to Richard Makepeace. He's the Archbishop's advisor for the Ministry of Deliverance.'

Deliverance? I immediately thought of twanging banjos. She must have seen my look because she smiled. 'We don't talk about exorcism any more. He will listen to what you have to say, and you can talk together. And then, if needs be, he can perform a service of deliverance and help Hawise to find rest. And in the meantime, we can pray.'

I left the Minster feeling much calmer, but I was still walking tentatively, still caught between two worlds. The air was shifty, treacherous. One moment the tourists gawping up at the tower roof or clustered on the steps of the south transept looked blessedly normal, the next they were grotesque creatures from another world, horrifying in their casual demeanour and their obscene display of flesh.

Averting my eyes, I tested each step. The ground felt fragile, as if it might shimmer and dissolve at any moment, and I was concentrating so fiercely on placing one foot in front of another that I walked right into Ash.

'I'm so sorry – oh.' I broke off as I realized who it was.

'It's Grace, isn't it?' He studied me with the intense, shiny gaze that reminded me so horribly of Francis. 'Sophie's neighbour.'

'Sophie's *friend*,' I said.

He acknowledged the point with a faint courteous dip of his head, but there was something else there too, something condescending, as if he had taken my insistence on Sophie's friendship as a pathetic challenge.

'Are you unwell? You look pale.' Oh, he sounded solicitous enough, but I sensed the malice rippling beneath the surface, like the buboes under Ned's skin. I slammed a mental door on the image.

'I'm fine,' I said shortly.

'I saw you come out of the Minster,' said Ash.

'I was looking at the carvings in the chapter house,' I lied. 'Not that it's any of your business.'

'I sense a lot of hostility in you, Grace,' he said, shaking his head. 'Why is that?'

'I don't like what you're doing to Sophie.'

Ash spread his hands in a gesture of innocence as phoney as the rest of him. '*Doing* to her?' he echoed. 'I'm not doing anything. Sophie comes to our gatherings of her own free will. We do not force her.'

'She's only fifteen,' I said angrily. 'You're brainwashing her with all that mumbo-jumbo.'

'"Mumbo-jumbo"?' Ash repeated. 'Ah, yes, I can just hear Dr Dyer saying that.' His voice was light, but I saw the flare of dislike in his eyes. 'He's the type who dismisses as nonsense anything he can't understand. Luckily Sophie has a more open mind than her father.'

I was beginning to wish I hadn't got involved in this conversation. 'Is that what this is about? Drew?'

'*Drew*?' he mocked. 'Yes, I gathered that you're more than just a neighbour to the great Dr Dyer, too.'

My fingers were clenched around the strap of my bag. 'If you've got a problem with him, deal with him. Don't take it out on his daughter.'

'I am a mere servant of the gods,' said Ash, something vicious clinging to the edges of his smile. 'Sophie has opened herself to the power of the universe, and I cannot stand in her way.'

'She'll grow out of it,' I said, shaking with loathing. I couldn't disentangle him from Francis in my mind. 'And you,' I added.

'You think so?'

'Sophie's an intelligent girl. Sooner or later she's going to see through you, the way the rest of us do,' I said, probably unwisely, but I couldn't stand being with him any longer. I saw a flash of something unpleasant in his eyes as I pushed past him and I knew that I had made an enemy, but I dismissed Ash from my mind. I had other things to worry about.

'I didn't go,' I told Drew when he asked me how Edinburgh had been. 'I didn't feel well.'

I didn't tell him that I hadn't been able to cross Lendal Bridge. I didn't tell him why. Drew was uncomfortable with anything other than the rational. He would have come up with any number of scientific explanations rather than accept the fact that I had been possessed by the ghost of a desperate woman four hundred years dead. At the very least, he would have said that I had been imagining things.

When I found myself sitting in an airy house in the Minster Close the following Monday, I began to wonder, too, if I had imagined it all. In that tranquil room with the light pouring through the Georgian windows it was hard to explain the sense of horror I had felt. My story sounded more and more absurd, even to my own ears: I couldn't walk across a bridge, I couldn't get on a bus. I kept stumbling in embarrassment, sure it must look as if I was making it all up for the sake of getting attention.

Richard Makepeace listened carefully, not saying much at first, but I noticed his questions were designed to find out what else might be at work. In some ways his questions were not unlike Sarah's. I answered half-impatiently. I had *been* there. I *wasn't* mentally ill or unstable or screwed up. I was possessed.

There, I had said it.

'I need help,' I said, as I had to Sarah, and to Vivien.

'And God will help you,' he said. 'Come, let us pray together.'

I felt foolish, mouthing 'Amen'. How had I come to this, sitting with a bowed head and *praying*? I didn't do God. But I had tried science and I had tried magic, and the Church was all that was left. Besides, I was impressed by Richard Makepeace's quiet belief.

'We can help this lost soul to find peace,' he said with certainty.

I hoped he was right, but I wasn't sure that mouthing a prayer would be enough, so I was relieved when he said that he would come to the house and hold a service of deliverance.

I chewed my thumb. 'What if it doesn't work?' I asked.

'It will work,' said Richard Makepeace simply.

'Do I need to prepare, or anything?' I had visions of spinning heads and projectile vomiting. At the very least I could have a bucket and some cloths ready to clear up the mess.

He smiled as if he knew exactly what I was thinking. 'Just be ready to pray,' he said.

The stench of rotting apples was very strong when I opened the door to him the next day. He had brought the vicar from the parish church of St Maurice with him. James Sanders was young and fit-looking, and wore trendy glasses that sat oddly with his dog collar, but when I asked him if he could smell the apples, he nodded.

'There is a very unhappy spirit here.'

'I think this is where she was almost raped,' I said, whispering as if Hawise might overhear. 'I think this is where it all began.'

'Then this is where we will pray.'

I was half-embarrassed, half-apprehensive. All I knew about exorcism came from horror films, and however much I told myself that we weren't dealing with evil here, I couldn't help imagining myself gibbering at a crucifix, or howling in the corner of the room with Richard Makepeace and James Sanders standing sternly over me. What if Drew heard and came to find out what was going on? I thought I'd seen him go out earlier, but what if he came back and saw me bulging-eyed and foaming at the mouth?

My mind swooped nervously as I followed Richard and James around the house. They were extraordinarily matter-of-fact, sprinkling holy water in the four corners of every room, as well as the garden and even the dilapidated shed at the back. Richard sprinkled the holy water in the four corners.

'In the name of our Lord Jesus Christ, I command any spirit not at rest to depart from this place to your appointed place of rest, in God's care and keeping, never to return,' he said in each place. He had a marvellously sonorous voice, filled with such conviction that I was awed in spite of myself.

'You must pray too,' he said to me. 'However small your faith, you must pray.'

'I don't know how,' I said. 'I only know the Lord's Prayer.'

'Then say that.'

So I stumbled through 'Our Father, who art in heaven' in every room, and each time I felt Hawise's influence shrinking. It was like having a thorn pulled slowly out of my brain. My embarrassment and agitation faded. No gibbering, no howling.

Maybe it was just psychological, but Richard's calmness settled around me until I was still and steady.

When we had been round the whole house, it was my turn.

'We now pray for you,' he said, making the sign of the cross over my bent head, 'that you may be graciously set free from any disturbing influences in this place, and that you and your whole being may be filled with the peace of Christ.'

I was astounded to find tears stinging my eyes, and when I got to my feet I did feel peaceful in a way I had never felt before.

And the smell of apples had gone.

'Why didn't you tell me?' Drew was furious when he found out about the exorcism. He was letting himself into his house just as Richard Makepeace and James Sanders were leaving. I saw him register the dog collars and frown, and I wasn't surprised when he came round later to find out what was going on.

'I didn't think you were into the Church,' he said, half-accusingly.

'I'm not.' I told him then what had happened the previous Saturday, and about my visit to Richard Makepeace. I lifted my hands and let them fall. 'I didn't know what else to do.'

'You could have told me.'

'You weren't here.'

'There are such things as phones! I would have come back if you'd told me you needed me, but of course you'd never do that, would you? You'd never admit that you needed anybody!'

It wasn't like Drew to lash out like that. He was usually so measured, so steady. Now he was pacing around Lucy's sitting room, while I sat curled up in a chair. He was dragging his hands through his hair – what there was of it – and it was all standing up in different directions. It should have been funny, but I didn't feel like laughing. I didn't like it that he was upset. I didn't like the fact that I'd hurt him.

'I know how you feel about past lives,' I said, feeling defensive. 'Be honest, if I'd dragged you out of that conference to tell you that a ghost wouldn't let me across the bridge to the station, you wouldn't have believed me, would you?'

'I would have believed you were frightened,' said Drew. He stopped and rubbed his eyes behind his glasses in frustration. Taking a breath, he dropped his hands and looked at me. 'Look, I don't know what happened on Saturday,' he said. 'I don't know how to explain it. All I know is that I love you, and you won't let me close enough to help you.'

There it was, out at last. I stared at him, frozen in my chair, blindsided by how casually he had said it. *I love you.* The words were huge, crowding in on me, suffocating me.

'Drew, I . . . '

He let out a long sigh. 'Don't look like that, Grace,' he said. 'You don't need to say anything. I know you don't love me.'

'It's not that I don't . . . ' I stumbled into incoherent speech, only to lose my way as soon as I'd started. 'I *can't*,' I said at last.

'Can't what?' he said with a level look, and I pushed myself out of the chair.

'Oh, I *knew* this would happen!' I hugged my arms together

furiously. 'I meet someone and we get on well, but then it's all about getting close and needing each other and talking about your feelings, and I don't want to do it!'

Too late I heard the shrill tension in my voice and I stopped, horrified to find myself on the verge of tears.

'I'm sorry,' I said miserably.

Drew swore, came over and pulled me to him, holding me tight. I resisted at first, rigid as a board, but he didn't let me go, and after a moment I let myself relax against him. He felt wonderful.

'I'm the one who's sorry,' he said into my hair. 'I shouldn't have pushed you. I'm just worried about you – and don't bother telling me you're fine, because I know you're not.'

'I wish I could let you in,' I muttered, wrapping my arms around his waist, hanging onto him as if he were the only safe, certain thing in my world. 'But I can't. I just can't.'

'Just for the sake of argument, what's the worst thing that could happen if you did tell me how you feel?'

'I'm afraid I might hurt you,' I said, muffled against him. 'I'm afraid I might not be the person you think I am.'

It was out before I could stop it. Hearing my own words, I tensed and made to draw back, but Drew held me firmly in place.

'Okay, so now we're getting somewhere. What kind of person do you think I think you are?'

'I don't know. Snippy? Stubborn?'

'You're that,' he agreed, 'but you're also quirky and funny, and you're bright and you're brave.'

'I'm *not* brave!' I wrenched myself out of his hold at that. 'I'm *not*, Drew. That's exactly what I mean. You think I'm one thing, but if you really got to know me, you'd find out that I'm not that at all. I'd let you down,' I said wretchedly. 'I can't bear to do that.'

Drew's eyes narrowed. 'Who have you ever let down?'

'I don't want to talk about it.'

'Come on, Grace, we're not leaving this here.' He pulled me over to the sofa and made me sit down beside him. 'Tell me.'

I yanked my hands from his, all my bristles erect. 'Look, Drew, I've had a busy day being exorcized and all. Could we leave this for now?'

'No. No, we can't.' He didn't try to take my hands back, but sat at the other end of the sofa, not touching me. 'I want to know why you're so afraid of being needed. So come on, tell me who you've failed.'

I turned my face away, defeated. All these years I had kept the great, black, wriggling mass locked away inside me, and now it was bumping at the lid, poking tendrils out, writhing its way free. Sarah had been right about that. I was afraid of it. I didn't want to look at it. Just thinking about thinking about it had guilt setting its fingers around my throat and squeezing, so that my voice came out all thin.

'Lucas. His name was Lucas.'

The name rolled right out of my mouth and lay in the middle of the room, taunting me.

'Tell me about him,' said Drew quietly.

'He was just a little boy. I didn't know him at all. I only

know his name because his parents used to call him, and he'd ignore them. They were Swedish, I think. They used to sit on the beach near us.'

'The beach?'

'At Khao Lak.' Drew didn't even know that I was talking about Thailand, I realized. 'Matt and I went there for Christmas when we were working in Bangkok. I told you about that.'

'You told me about the tsunami. You didn't tell me about Lucas.'

I picked up a cushion, hugged it to me. 'I think he may have had Asperger's, something like that. He didn't like to make eye contact, and he didn't interact with other children. He was obsessed with this irrigation system that he was digging on the beach. It was really complex, and he liked his channels straight. He was a funny little kid,' I remembered. 'So determined and focused. I felt sorry for him, but I sort of liked him too. On Christmas Day he wanted to dig where Matt and I were sitting so that he could keep his channels all neat. I made Matt move his lardy arse, and we both got out of the way.'

A faint smile touched the corners of Drew's mouth. 'What did Matt think about that?'

'Oh, he grumbled a bit, but he didn't really mind. Matt's easy-going, that way. Anyway,' I told Drew, 'Lucas let me help him dig his channels. It's funny, but I was really flattered.' I smiled, remembering. 'We hardly said a word to each other, but I really enjoyed that afternoon.'

There was a pause. 'What happened when you finished digging?'

'Nothing. His parents took him away, and Matt and I went back to our room.'

'So you didn't let him down that day?'

'No.'

I stopped. I really didn't want to do this. My heart was slamming against my ribs. My fingers twisted in the chain of my pendant.

'What happened the next day, Grace?'

'I . . . well, I told you about the tsunami,' I said with difficulty.

Drew nodded. 'You said it seemed to come out of nowhere and swept you up.'

'Because that's what happened!' I said, as if he had accused me of lying. 'One minute I was walking along in the sunshine, and the next I was swallowed up by the water. It was just . . . roaring . . . and power . . . '

'You said you managed to grab onto some railings,' Drew prompted when I trailed off.

'Yes.'

'What happened then?'

'Something bumped into me.'

I stopped again. I could feel the words rising up from my stomach, jamming together into a knot that stuck in my throat like dread. I'd never spoken them to anyone, not even Matt. I willed Drew to break the silence, to ask something that would help me swallow them once more, but he didn't, and in the end I couldn't hold them back any more.

'It was Lucas,' I said. I couldn't meet Drew's eyes. I stared at the carpet. 'It was a child. About his age. I don't know for sure, but I think it was him. All I saw was a face. He was terrified, I could see that. He was screaming. It all happened so fast, but I'm sure it was him.'

I took a breath, tried to slow down, but the words were tumbling out now. 'I managed to grab his hand. The wave was so loud and so strong, but I did catch hold. I had the railings in one hand and Lucas in the other. I know I did. I thought I was holding him tightly. I thought if I could just pull him closer we'd be okay – and then he was gone. I must have let him go. I don't remember. He was there, and then he wasn't. I let him go.'

I brought my hands up to cover my face.

'God, I let him go. I should have felt his fingers slipping from mine. I should have held on tighter. He was so scared, and I let him go. I tried.' Lowering my hands, I made myself look at Drew at last. 'I did try. I *did*. I'm sure I did, but I just . . . I couldn't save him.'

There was a long silence. Or it felt long. I imagined the truth hanging in the air like gobbets of phlegm. I waited for Drew to wipe them from his face with disgust.

'You couldn't have done anything about it,' he said gently at last. 'You know that, don't you?'

'I should have held him tighter,' I said, my face averted. 'I should have done something.'

'You did what you could.' Drew moved across the sofa and took my hand. His grasp was warm, firm. 'It was a tsunami, Grace. A force of nature. You can't fight against that.'

'But I was the only one!' I burst out. 'He looked in my eyes and he knew me. I should have saved him, and I didn't.' My voice rose and I pressed my hands over my face to shut it out. 'I didn't! I looked for him afterwards, I looked everywhere, but I couldn't find him.'

'Grace.' Drew gathered me against him, ignoring my resistance and the hands I still had clamped over my face. 'You didn't cause the earthquake. You didn't make the tsunami happen. You're not responsible.' His voice reverberated through me. 'It was a terrible tragedy, and I'm so sorry about Lucas, but it wasn't your fault.'

I shook my head against his shoulder. It wasn't that I didn't understand what he was saying, but I couldn't accept that I wasn't somehow responsible. My palms against my cheeks were damp with memory. I could feel Lucas's fingers – if it had been Lucas – as if imprinted against my skin, there and then gone.

'You didn't let Lucas down,' said Drew. 'There's no reason to think you'll let anyone else down.'

Pulling myself away from him, I drew a shuddering breath and let my hands fall from my face as I got to my feet. I felt shaky and hollow, but Sarah had been right about one thing. I had told Drew everything and he hadn't recoiled in disgust. He hadn't demanded to know how I could have let a child die and yet lived myself. The world hadn't fallen apart.

I bundled the guilt and the horror back in the box and squeezed the lid shut. I didn't want to look at them again, but I'd done it, so I knew that I could. Maybe that was something.

'Are you okay?' Drew had got up too and was watching me in concern.

I made myself smile at him. 'You know what I'm going to say, don't you?'

'You're fine?'

'That's the one.' But actually I *was* fine, and when he came over and folded his arms around me, I let myself lean against him and breathe in the familiar smell of his skin. 'I've never talked about what happened before,' I said. 'I'm glad I did, and I'm glad it was with you, but it doesn't change anything.'

'Doesn't it?'

'I'm still leaving,' I told him, my face hidden in his throat. 'Now that there's been a service of deliverance, I hope that'll be the end of Hawise. There's no reason for me not to go as soon as I've exchanged contracts on the house.' I took a breath. 'I'm going to hand in my notice, Drew. I'll be in Mexico by Christmas. There's no point in loving me.'

'It's too late to tell me that *now*,' he said, and the grouchiness in his voice made me smile in spite of myself.

My mouth curved against his throat. 'Then why don't we make the most of the time we've got left?' I suggested. 'Why don't we be lovers as well as friends?'

Drew let out a long sigh, but he didn't let go of me. 'You know it will just make it harder to say goodbye when you go, if we do?'

'It will make the next two months harder if we don't.' I kissed the pulse beneath his ear the way I had thought about doing for so long.

The way Hawise used to kiss Ned.

I shoved the thought away.

'There's that.' Drew slid his hands up my arms, over my shoulders, to tip my face up to his. 'All right,' he said, and maybe it was against his better judgement, but his touch was warm and sure and not at all reluctant. 'Let's worry about saying goodbye when the time comes.'

Chapter Eighteen

I refused to think about what saying goodbye would be like. I braced myself for Hawise to slip back into my head after the service of deliverance, but my mind stayed clear and, after a while, I let myself believe that Richard Makepeace had succeeded in putting her to rest.

I felt lighter, although whether that was due to the service or to telling Drew about Lucas, it was hard to tell. I refused to think about the future and I refused to think about the past. I just thought about the ordinary day-to-dayness of going to work, of coming home to Drew and of the bone-melting pleasure of the nights we spent together.

I never stayed the whole night. I waited until Drew was asleep and then I slipped back to Lucy's house. Drew grumbled, but he accepted it, and I told myself I was being sensible, as if not getting used to those last few hours together would really make it easier to go.

September drifted into October and I drifted with it, until

one morning I woke up and it was autumn. I'd forgotten how suddenly the seasons could change. The air smelt different, of dark nights and dampness and winter lurking behind the north wind, and the light was fainter, fuzzier. It wasn't really that much colder than it had been, but all at once people were wearing boots and jackets, and drawing their curtains against the night. The trees turned, and the gutters swirled with fallen leaves.

Still Hawise stayed away. I tried not to think about her, but every now and then I would catch a fragment of memory. Bess, hauling herself up against Hawise's skirts, her triumphant expression as she managed a wobbly stand. Ned, turning his head, smiling his quiet smile. Sometimes Francis, slowly, lasciviously, running his tongue over his lips. I hated that, but it was like remembering a dream. I was there, and then I wasn't, the way dreams are.

It hadn't been a dream, I knew that, but it was all over. Sometimes, it's true, I felt guilty for the service of deliverance. Richard Makepeace had assured me that Hawise was at rest, but how could she rest if she was still agonizing about her daughter? Then I would think about Hawise drowning in the Ouse, about Lucy drowning in the same place, and I would be glad that I had called in Richard when I had.

The sale of Lucy's house was going through without any problems. John Burnand dealt with most of it, thank goodness, and all I had to do was go in and sign papers occasionally. Gradually the house emptied as I gave away as many of Lucy's things as I could. Her friends took some of the smaller pictures and pieces, and the rest went to charity shops. I didn't need any of it. I liked to travel light.

In any case I was spending more and more time at Drew's. Only late at night did I slip back into the house and climb into Lucy's bed. I kept my suitcase open on the floor, to remind myself that I was really going.

The weather was vile, a dark, lowering sky that meant you had to put the lights on in the morning, and sheets of rain, day after day after day. That made it easier to think about leaving. I dreamt about a clear sky and sunlight on the sea and warmth on my shoulders.

I bought a ticket to Mexico City. One-way.

I booked it online, and the computer didn't cut out on me halfway through. My server didn't crash when I emailed Mel to tell her when I would be arriving. I watched almost in disbelief as the message saying that it had been sent popped up on the screen.

Only then did I let myself believe that Hawise was really going to let me go.

'This time it really *is* over,' I told Vivien when I bumped into her in the street. It was the end of October and the air smelt of wet leaves. 'Hawise has gone.'

Vivien eyed me narrowly. 'You certainly look better than you did.' She lifted the hessian bag she was carrying with a faint smile. 'Can you face apples yet?'

A tiny muscle jumped at the back of my throat, but I made myself smile. It was a test to see if I was better, and I was.

'Sure.' I said. 'Why not?'

'Then have some of these. They're from my allotment, and

I can't give them away at the moment.' She held out the bag. 'Help yourself.'

'Well . . . thank you . . . ' I swallowed. I was braced for maggots and rotting flesh, but when I drew the apples out of the bag, they were firm and rosy.

I let out a breath that I hadn't realized I'd been holding until then. 'I'll make Sophie an apple pie,' I said as I took a few and put them in the plastic bag I was carrying. 'She likes her puddings.'

'How is Sophie?'

'She's spending more time with us – with Drew,' I corrected myself, flushing with vexation at the natural way that 'us' slipped out. 'She's getting on better with her father, and I think she likes my cooking.'

Worried about Drew being alone when I left, I was doing what I could to encourage Sophie to stay home, but I didn't tell Vivien that.

The fact that I was worrying stuck like a pip between my teeth, a constant, low-grade irritation that I could never quite dislodge.

'So she's not going to the Temple of the Waters any more?' Vivien sounded surprised.

'She is, I'm afraid, but Drew's hoping it's a good sign that she's not quite as obsessive as she was before.'

I was sure that Ash was working hard to keep Sophie close, and I wished I hadn't let him rile me that day I met him outside the Minster. I couldn't shake the certainty that he'd taken my hostility as a challenge. Drew said that was just me looking for

something to feel guilty about, but he hadn't seen the viciousness flash across Ash's face.

'Sophie may not be going to as many of their "gatherings"
as she did, but sadly there's no sign of her seeing Ash Vaughan
for what he is,' I told Vivien. 'She's still completely in thrall to
him. I don't suppose you'd like to cast a spell to bring her to
her senses, would you?'

I wasn't being serious, but Vivien looked thoughtful. 'Sophie
will have to make her own choices,' she said. 'But *you* could
cast a protective spell for her, if it would help you feel better.'

'Me? I'm not a witch!'

'You care about Sophie, though, don't you?'

'Of course I'm fond of her.' Vivien's eyes were very clear
and very blue, and again I had the uncomfortable feeling
that she could see right inside me. 'And I'm sorry for her,' I said,
my gaze sliding away from hers. 'Sophie's very insecure. She's
latched onto Ash, and she won't let herself see him clearly,
because that would mean admitting that she was being naive
and credulous.'

'None of us like to look at ourselves clearly, do we?'

I looked at her sharply. The words were innocent enough,
but I sensed they were meant for me. 'I remember what it's like
to be fifteen and lonely,' I said. 'I just want to help her if I can.'

'The strongest spell is the power of your love,' said Vivien.
'As long as you are not afraid to give it,' she added, leaving the
question unspoken.

'I'm not *afraid*,' I said, irritated. 'I'm *leaving*.'

'So you've decided to go?'

I was sure I could detect disappointment in her voice, and I put my chin up. 'I'm flying out at the end of November.'

Vivien nodded slowly. 'I see. Well, good luck if I don't see you before then.'

'Thank you for all your help, Vivien,' I said awkwardly. Something about her made me uneasy, but I owed her, I knew. 'And for the apples, of course!'

'You're welcome,' said Vivien. 'Blessed be. Oh, and Grace?' she added as I walked on, and I turned.

'Yes?'

'Tomorrow is Samhain.'

'Samhain?'

'Halloween,' she said. 'All Hallows' Eve. It's not just about pumpkins and trick-or-treating. It's a time when the worlds of the living and the dead become as one. You should take great care.'

I tackled the apples straight away. I knew that if I put them aside, I would worry about them rotting. I took them out of the bag and put them on the worktop in Drew's kitchen. There were seven of them. They were red and fresh and satisfyingly uneven, nothing like the tasteless, uniformly round apples I saw in the supermarkets. Apples that had come from a tree, not a container shipped from the other side of the world.

I made myself pick them up and sniff them. They were fine. They didn't smell of rage and despair.

I got out a bowl and started sifting flour for pastry. If I was going to make apple pie, I was going to do it properly.

I was feeling ruffled after my encounter with Vivien, and cooking usually calmed me down, but that day it took longer to shift my bad mood. The mention of Halloween had lodged a sliver of disquiet, needle-sharp, inside me.

Hawise had died on All Hallows' Eve.

I tried to shrug it off, to think about something else, but then I kept replaying Vivien's offhand remark about love. *As long as you are not afraid to give it.*

What did that mean, exactly? I wondered, crossly dicing butter and lard. The knife chinked against the plate, an edgy counterpoint to the grumble and whirr of the washing machine. I wasn't *afraid*. There was just no point in loving Sophie if I was going to leave her, the way I was going to leave her father. I couldn't pretend to love her. It would just hurt her even more when I left. I was being *kind*, I was being honest. I *wasn't* afraid.

Gradually the rhythm of pastry-making soothed me. I dipped my hands into the buttery flour and lifted them high, rubbed the mixture between my fingers then let it tumble back into the bowl. Dip, lift, rub. Dip, lift, rub. I stopped glancing at the apples out of the corner of my eye, stopped waiting for them to sag and moulder before me. They were just apples.

I did everything properly. I let my pastry rest in the fridge. I found an eggcup and turned it upside down to act as a pie-funnel once I'd lined the pie plate with the pastry. I peeled and cored the apples, and didn't flinch once from handling them. I piled the slices high in the pastry and sprinkled over a little sugar.

Admiring my efforts, I adjusted the eggcup slightly and found myself thinking about my mother. She had had a special pie-funnel shaped like a blackbird, and memories of Sunday mornings at the kitchen table crashed over me so suddenly that I caught my breath. It was almost a shock to remember my own mother instead of Hawise.

Mum always nestled three or four cloves into her apple pies. Subconsciously I had known something was missing. On an impulse I rootled through Drew's motley collection of herbs and spices.

Cloves – there they were! I pulled out the jar and shook a few into my cupped palm, breathing in the lovely, warm smell of them. They reminded me of Indonesia, and the men squatting in the *gangs*, the smoke from their *kreteks* curling through the heavy air.

I scoop up a handful of cloves from the sack and inhale. Next to rosemary, this is my favourite smell. To me, cloves are the scent of the East, of countries unseen and roads untravelled, proof of a strange, exotic world that exists alongside mine, yet is forever out of reach.

I pick one from my palm and hold it between my thumb and forefinger, studying it as if I have never seen one before. It is hard and stubby, like a tiny piece of wood, with a bulbous end – a peppercorn surrounded by four stiff little leaves. It is not quite a flower, not quite a nut. How does it grow? I wonder. On a tree? On a bush? Somebody far away in the Spice Islands has picked it and someone has collected it, and it has been bought and sold across the seas until it arrived in Hamburg, where Ned's agent, John Watson, bought two sacks and put them on a ship to Hull.

The keelman sent word this morning that he is tied up at King's Staith. Rob arranged for the carter to bring the sacks to our warehouse down by the river, and now we are checking that everything is as it should be. The cloves have come a long way, and so have I. I am not just a woman, not just a widow. I am a merchant adventurer now.

It is over a year since the pestilence. A year since Ned died. A year since I was able to turn into him at night and press my cheek against his chest. A year since I felt steady, and certain. And safe.

It is a year, too, since Jane saved Bess from the carter's horse. Bess is nearly four now, and she does not remember that dark time, and I am glad of it. When I look back, I wonder how we went from day to day, but we did. We all did.

Not long after they opened the city gates to strangers once more, the keelboats started to ply the river again between York and Hull, and one morning Ned's apprentice, Rob Haxby, appeared in the hall. He had done as Ned said and stayed in Hull to wait for the goods John had sent from Hamburg, stamped with Ned's mark. John was once Ned's apprentice, but now it is Rob's turn to learn how to merchant. He is a shy, gangly boy with huge hands and feet, and I saw something crumble in his face when I had to tell him that Ned was dead. I wanted to pull him to me and let him weep, but we had a shipload of goods to unload, and store, and sell.

I knew how to run a household, but merchandising was

men's work. But I had no man, only a boy to help me, so I went down to Trinity Hall and found Mr Appleyard, the governor of the company of merchant adventurers there, who had dined with Ned more than once. Mr Appleyard has pendulous cheeks and a red nose like my father's, but his eyes are quick and shrewd. It was my right to take over Ned's adventuring, as he well knew. He didn't like it, but he told me who I needed to see and what I needed to do, to keep the business going.

I remember standing in the warehouse with Rob by my side that first morning. We had a tun of wine, some pottery jugs packed into a barrel, three primers, beautifully painted, bales of ginger and nutmeg and peppercorns and, when we untied the cords and unwrapped the canvas, a quantity of luxurious furs. So many beautiful things, and all I could wonder was who was left to want them.

We sold the wine first. I heard later that Mr Bowes chortled that he had it so cheap he would have bought ten times as many tuns if he could, but I set my jaw and I learnt. I drive a harder bargain now, and my customers are more like to shake their heads and complain, but still they buy. This I have learnt. The world keeps turning and the money keeps going round and round. There will always be someone to sell and someone to buy.

Before we had sold the last jug, John wrote from Hamburg. He could sell wool and lead, he said, and buy more furs if we thought we could shift them. I wrote back, a hard letter to write, and told him that Ned was dead, but that if he stayed I would honour his contract and admit him to the merchants' company as his master would have done.

And so I became a merchant. John has a nose for a deal, but mine is the risk, and we work well together. I have a feel for it, I think. I know how to take a chance on a shipment, and how to make folk want just what it is that I have to sell.

Rob has stayed. Like Jane, he has nowhere else to go. We are a small household now, but we go on. What else is there to do? For a time we were numb with grief, but it fades. Alone in my great bed, I roll over at night and Ned isn't there, and his absence is a rusty knife twisting in my heart. Every morning, there is a moment between waking and opening my eyes when I tell myself that it was just a bad dream. I will open my eyes and there Ned will be, yawning and scratching his fingers through his hair. I *will* it to be just a dream. But it isn't, it is real, and Ned is gone.

But yes, we go on. We are even content. I thought I would never laugh again, but we do. Bess is a mischievous child and a loving one. When she has been naughty, she has a way of peeping a look at you that makes it hard indeed to keep a stern face. She loves Jane and Rob. We are a little family.

We are all outcasts of one kind or another, save Bess, of course, and Francis makes sure that everyone knows it. Francis's devotion is even more conspicuous since the sickness. He took his survival as a sign of God's favour, and prays loudly and long. The neighbours are impressed by him, and they know I turned him and Agnes from my house in their time of need – or so Francis tells it. In the battle for the good opinion of the street, Francis is the victor, and it makes a difference. I am a wealthy widow with a thriving business, a merchant in my own right, but no one has approached me about marriage.

Not that I care for marriage just yet. Jane says that I should look around for someone young and handsome, but she didn't know Ned. She doesn't know what we had. Bess needs a father, she points out when I tell her that, and it is true, but I can't bear to think of it.

'I will,' I promise whenever she mentions it. And I will. Just not yet. I am young still, and there is plenty of time.

Now I drop the cloves back into the sack and brush my fingers together with satisfaction. John has done well. They are dry and firm, and when I dig down, I find no dust, but more precious cloves. I will be able to sell them for a good price.

Taking a puckle in my hand for the kitchen, I leave Rob in the warehouse and walk back to the house. The streets are wet and slubbery with mud. The rain loosens the cobbles, and the horses' hooves dislodge them further, so that the potholes get bigger and bigger. They trap the rubbish that spills sluggishly from the gutters and cast a sour smell over the neighbourhood. It is not yet autumn, with its brisk winds and sharp air, but summer is long past. Everything is tired and dreary, and the mood in the street is sly, acrid with disappointment.

It is as if the losses of last year have finally caught up with us. We are weary and fretful instead of grateful to be alive. It is harder now. I can feel my sense of satisfaction fading as soon as I leave the warehouse. I pretend I don't notice the way folk have started crossing themselves again when I pass, or watching me from the corners of their eyes. I pretend I don't mind that my neighbours are no longer my friends. I don't care, I say, that they won't let their daughters come to me as maids to help Jane.

I have my daughter, I have my home. I have Jane and Rob, and my business flourishes. I tell myself that I have enough.

Jane has been to market, and Bess is helping her to unpack her basket when I go into the kitchen.

'What's the news today?' I ask, rescuing the cabbage that Bess is pulling off the table.

'They're all on about them witches that were arrested yesterday.' Jane doesn't hold with the hysteria that sweeps through the city every now and then.

'More arrests?' I frown as I stop Bess from tugging a whole pat of butter onto the floor. I sweep her up into my arms and tickle her nose to distract her and she shrieks with laughter, but for once my mind is not on her.

This witch-hunt is Francis's doing. After Sir John died of the pestilence, they sent a new priest, a diffident man who cares only for his books and lets Francis run the parish. Francis himself has taken to hectoring the neighbours in the street, calling down God's mercy on them. Their sins are not to blame for the sickness, he says, and makes them ask then: whose are? And it is not a long step for people to remember the witches who curdled their cream before, who made them stumble and drop their pie. If their cow sickens, if their corn rots, if their ale spills, they look around for someone to blame, and who better than the old women who have no one to speak up for them?

'Who is it now?' I ask Jane.

She pauses to search her memory. 'Bridget Dobson, I think they said, and Madge Carter . . . oh, and old Ma Dent.'

'Not Sybil Dent?' I say, my heart full of foreboding, but I know what Jane will say.

'Her as lives out on the common.' She nods. 'They've taken her in for questioning. Leastways, that's what I heard.'

Questioning? I think bitterly. More like they will torture her until she confesses to whatever they want. Sybil, who saved me from Francis, who gave me my Bess.

'Where is she?' I demand. 'Quick, tell me.'

Jane gapes at me in surprise. 'At t'castle, most like. Why, where are you going?' she asks, when I put Bess down and head for the door.

'I'm going to get her out,' I say.

But when I go to the castle, no one knows anything about Sybil. I spend a frustrating morning being passed around from official to official, every one of whom requires a coin to unfasten his mouth, even if it is only to suggest that I ask elsewhere. My purse is almost empty by the time I eventually find Sybil in the gaol on Ouse Bridge.

Surrounded by stone, she looks diminished. She is a creature of the woods, a hedge-pig of a woman, and I can feel that she craves the breeze in her face and the stars above her.

I crouch beside her. 'What can I do?'

'En't nothing you can do,' she says.

'This is Francis Bewley's doing,' I say in a low voice. 'He knows you are my friend.'

The widow laughs at that, a short wheezy bark of laughter. 'Bad choice of friends you have!'

'I don't think so.' I set my chin stubbornly. 'I do not forget what you have done for me.'

'Better for you if you do forget. There is mischief afoot.'

I lower my voice. 'Do you see the future?'

'Better not,' she says after a moment. 'Better not.'

'I will speak for you at your trial,' I promise, but she shakes her head.

'Won't do no good, and it'll be worse for you.'

I go anyway. The court is damp, and the widow's cough shakes her whole body. Francis is there, smirking and trium-phant. They lay out the accusations, one by one – that she cast a spell on Anne Harrison, that she made Percival Geldart's cow sicken, that she caused the corn to mildew – and they get progressively darker, as if the imagination of the city is peering into a dark hole. She communes with Satan, she has a familiar, she sucks innocents into her web of evil. And the proof, if proof were needed: she has a witch's mark. The women have stripped her and examined her, and the mark of the Devil is there on her leg.

Sybil just shakes her head, unable to speak for coughing, so I get to my feet. 'Good sirs, this is nonsense. Sybil is not evil. She is a cunning woman who makes remedies for folk who ask, that is all.'

'She is in league with the Devil himself,' cries Francis. 'Are you her accomplice to speak for her so?'

There is a hiss from the onlookers at his veiled accusation. I look steadily back at him and keep my voice level. 'I am her friend. Sybil Dent has helped me, as she has helped you.'

Francis's eyes bulge. 'I have never had any contact with that vile creature. How dare you suggest it?'

'Because it is true,' I say. 'During the sickness, I went to her for a remedy. I gave it to you when I nursed you, and you were cured.'

'It was God who saved me, Mistress, not you!' Francis is striding around, putting on a show of outrage. 'The witch's remedy didn't save your husband, did it? Or was that its purpose, hmm?'

I clench my fists in my skirts. My jaw is so tight that I can barely unlock it to speak. 'It was the pestilence killed my husband, not the Widow Dent,' I say, biting out the words, knowing I cannot give in to the rage and loathing that consumes me whenever I see him. 'She has only ever saved me from harm.'

I meet his eyes. There is no point in telling the court that Sybil saved me from him. They would not believe me, but Francis knows the truth, and I know it.

But no one listens to me. They have made up their minds about Sybil. She is to hang to make them all feel better.

I visit Sybil in the prison and pay the gaoler handsomely to treat her well, although whether he does or not I cannot tell. I take her a basket of food and an infusion to calm the spirits, for which she nods her thanks.

'You're a good girl,' she says as I crouch beside her. 'You look out for yourself now, though.' She reaches out and her frail hand closes around my wrist. 'There is danger for you, and it is close. You must be careful.'

'I'm always careful,' I say lightly, but she shakes her head.

'You rush like a fool into the unknown. You act without thinking of the consequences. You must stop and consider.'

I don't understand what she means. Yes, I did once rush to meet Francis before I knew what he was. That was a mistake, but I won't make it again.

I cover her hand with my own. 'I know Francis Bewley watches me,' I say. 'I know he would hurt me if he could, but I will not let him,' I promise. 'I have learnt my lesson.'

Sybil tries to speak, but her words are lost in the terrible coughing. 'The rope will put an end to this cough anyroad,' she wheezes at last.

'I'm sorry.' I wish I could help her, wish I could save her, the way she saved me.

'There's one thing you can do for me.' Even now she is able to read my mind, it seems. 'Look after Mog. She's a fine cat and I don't want them hurting her.'

They hang Sybil the next morning. The sky lours sullenly and weeps a fine drizzle that clings to my eyelashes. I am there as a witness. Stony-faced, I watch as they half-lift her onto the scaffold. She is so small and frail, she looks tiny standing under the noose. At the last moment she opens her eyes and looks straight at me.

'Remember,' she says. I don't hear her, but I know that is what she says.

'I will.' I will always remember, and in my heart I curse Francis Bewley and the jeering crowd around me, who think killing an old woman will make them feel less afraid.

When it is over I take my basket and I go out to Sybil's

cottage. Already it is lifeless and dank. I collect the herbs Sybil used, and I scatter them on the wind. 'I won't forget,' I say.

Mog appears and makes no protest when I pick her up and put her in the basket. Indeed, she appears to be expecting it, and curls up to make herself comfortable for the journey.

I open the basket in my kitchen and she gets out, stretches and sits down to wash her paws.

Bess is delighted with her. I expect Mog to hiss and spit when my daughter tries to pick her up, but no. She lets herself be clutched against Bess and seems happy to have Bess's face pressed into her soft fur.

'Where did you get that one from then?' asks Jane.

It's best for her not to know. 'I found her outside the walls,' I say.

'Found it?' Jane looks at me closely. 'Why'd you want to bring a cat home?'

'She can keep the mice down.'

Jane doesn't point out that there are plenty of cats in the city. 'The neighbours won't like it,' she tells me bluntly.

I know she's right, but I am angry and sad. I wanted to save Sybil, the way she saved me, and I couldn't. I failed her, but I won't fail her cat.

'I don't care what they think,' I say. 'The cat stays.'

I blinked down at the half-made pie. The pastry flopped pale and flaccid over the edge of the pie plate, and the slices of apple were turning brown in front of my eyes. My fist was clenched in front of me. When I uncurled my fingers, the smell of cloves made me queasy.

I dropped them into the apples and threw the whole pie away.

It wasn't over at all.

'You're very quiet.' Drew's eyes were narrowed as he studied me over the table that night.

'Am I? Sorry, I've got a bit of a headache.' I pushed the pasta to the side of my plate and put down my fork. I couldn't eat. I kept seeing Sybil's face as she hung from the gibbet, her face engorged, eyes bulging, tongue protruding obscenely. Foreboding was curdling in the pit of my belly. Something terrible was about to happen. I could feel it.

'Is there any pudding?' asked Sophie.

I swallowed the nausea that rose whenever I thought about that pie. I had so nearly served it up with the apples seething with mould inside. I imagined biting into the pastry and tasting rotting flesh, and I nearly gagged again. 'Not tonight,' I managed.

'Ohhh . . . Why not?' whined Sophie, slumping in her chair with an exaggerated grimace of disappointment.

Drew frowned at her. 'You're lucky Grace cooked at all tonight, young lady. Don't get used to her providing all these wonderful vegetarian meals for you. You won't be getting anything like it when she goes.'

His voice was quite even, the way it always was when he talked about me going. He'd never told me again that he loved me, but discussed my departure in a very matter-of-fact way. I was glad he wasn't going to make things difficult for me, of course, but sometimes I wondered if he wasn't secretly relieved that our relationship had a definite 'use by' date on it.

Sophie's bottom lip stuck out. 'I wish you'd stay,' she said to me. 'Dad's such a crap cook.'

'It's nice to be appreciated,' I said. I meant my voice to be dry, but I was still trying to shake the image of the rotting apple pie, which kept getting muddled up with Sybil's expression as they dropped the rope around her neck; my smile must have seemed forced, because Sophie's face clouded and she hunched a defensive shoulder as she bent her head.

'I didn't mean . . . ' She sucked a strand of hair and looked at me from under her brows. 'Why don't you stay?' she asked abruptly.

There was an awkward silence. 'It's complicated,' I said after a moment.

Bess . . . ess . . . ess

I stiffened as the whisper trickled slimily through the air.

'What is it?' Drew was watching more closely than I would have liked.

'Nothing.' With an effort I rearranged my face into a smile. 'I'm sorry there's no pudding tonight, Sophie. I'll make one tomorrow.'

'I'm not a *baby*, you know!' With a teenager's lightning change of mood she shoved back her chair.

'Sophie!'

'I hear you sneaking around at night.' Her voice rose over Drew's. 'Going home like a good girl! Do you really think I'll believe you're not sleeping together?'

'That's enough, Sophie,' said Drew at his most forbidding, but Sophie was beyond reasoning.

'You can't just make me a pudding, pat me on the head and pretend that everything will be all right! I'm sick of being treated like a child!'

'Then perhaps you should try not acting like one.'

Sophie shot her father a venomous look. 'I don't want her stupid pudding anyway. I'm going to be fasting tomorrow.'

'Fasting?' Her announcement, flung over the table, caught Drew unawares. 'What on earth for?'

'Because tomorrow is my initiation.'

'Initiation? What initiation?'

'To the Temple of the Waters. If I pass the test, and show myself worthy, I can ascend to the first level.'

'Oh, for God's sake!'

Sophie put up her chin and looked belligerently at her father. 'Ash says I'm ready. *He* doesn't treat me like a child. He says it's time.'

'I'll bet he does.' Drew visibly yanked on the reins of his temper. 'Sophie, can't you see that he's just using you to get at me?'

'He said you'd react like this,' she said, and I had a sudden, shocking memory of Agnes smoothing down her skirts and saying almost exactly the same thing to Hawise.

'Dad, Ash doesn't want to "get" at you,' she told Drew. 'The truth is that he's sorry for you. Your mind is so closed and warped by materialism.'

'*My* mind is warped? That little tosser is warped through

and through. He's a fraud and a charlatan!' I'd never seen Drew lose it before, and my mouth fell open at his roar. 'Why do you think he's taken such an interest in a fifteen-year-old girl? Ash Vaughan likes to manipulate people, plain and simple. He's motivated entirely by ego. If you think there's any goodness – any spirituality – in him, you're fooling yourself, and frankly I'd expected better of you.'

Sophie's mouth was wobbling, and she was blinking furiously, but Drew was too angry to see the defiant set of her jaw.

'If you think for one moment that I'm letting you undergo some kind of initiation rite with Ash Vaughan in charge, you've got another think coming,' he raged at her.

'You can't stop me!'

'I most certainly can. I'm your father and you're underage.'

He was losing her. I put a warning hand on his arm. 'Drew,' I murmured, but that was a mistake. It gave Sophie the perfect excuse to take out her distress on me.

'Don't interfere!' Her voice was shrill. 'What's any of this got to do with you, anyway? You're leaving.'

I couldn't argue with that. I took my hand from Drew's arm.

'Ash was right about you.' Sophie's voice was shaking with the black rage of adolescence. 'You're completely superficial.'

'Sophie, for God's sake!'

'No, it's okay,' I said to Drew, but I admit that my lips had thinned a bit. 'I had no idea Ash could analyse me so well, based on two short conversations! What else does he say?'

Sophie had gone too far to back down now. 'He says you

might seem super-cool, but you've got no spiritual connection to anywhere or anyone, so actually you're really *sad*!' She was on her feet now, her face red and blotchy with inarticulate distress. 'And he says you're using me and you're using Dad, but I don't care, so the sooner you go, the better!'

'Sophie!'

Sophie flinched at the lash of Drew's voice, but she couldn't stop. 'I hate you!' she shouted. 'I hate *both* of you! I'm going to be initiated into the Temple of the Waters tomorrow and then I can go and live with them, and you can't stop me!'

She slammed from the room and Drew put his head briefly in his hands.

'Well, that must have done your headache a power of good,' he said, looking up.

'She's frightened, poor kid,' I said. 'I remember feeling out of control like that, and lashing out at what I loved best. I was terrified by the strength of my own fury and frustration. Ash tells her what to do and think and feel, so she can channel all those churning emotions, and that makes her feel safe.'

'Safe's the last word I'd use in connection with Ash,' said Drew, grim-faced. 'I don't want her going through with this initiation thing, but how am I going to stop her?'

'Lock her in her room?'

'There's no lock on her door – and don't think I haven't been tempted to put one on!' He sighed. 'Besides, she's fifteen. I can't lock her up forever, however much I might want to, and I don't want to push her into running away altogether.' He rubbed a hand over his face in a gesture that was already shockingly familiar to me. 'Her mother has picked a fine time to go away on holiday!'

I didn't know what to suggest. I got up and began clearing the plates away. 'She seemed very insistent that the ritual – or whatever he's planning – had to be tomorrow,' I said at last. 'Maybe it's just a question of keeping an eye on her until Halloween is over.'

'So, what: I should just bar her from leaving the house?'

'Or follow her when she does go out, and make sure she knows you're going to stick with her, whatever happens.'

'I suppose I could . . . Shit, no, I can't.' Drew propped his elbows on the table and clutched at his hair. 'I've got to give a paper tomorrow. It's been organized for months. And my old mentor is coming over from the States. I'm supposed to be taking her out for supper. We were going to talk about my book—' He broke off. 'Well, she'll understand, if I tell her I can't make it.'

He swore. 'That bastard Ash! I'd call in the police, but what could they do? Sophie's going along of her own volition, and I'll bet you anything that little toerag has made sure everything is technically legal.' His hand swept wearily over his face again and he pushed his chair back from the table. 'I'd better email the organizers and tell them to cancel.'

'Is it important, this paper?' I asked, rinsing plates under the tap.

'It's not the paper so much, as the people who are coming to it. We're hoping to set up a new international research group that . . . Well, it's not brain surgery,' he caught himself up. 'It can wait, and Sophie is more important.'

'I can be here,' I said. 'I'm not teaching tomorrow night.'

Drew smoothed my hair behind my ear. 'I'm not asking you to do that, Grace. Especially not after Sophie was so rude to you.' He hesitated. 'You know that she's just upset because you're going? She's very fond of you.'

'I know that,' I said. 'And you're not asking me. I'm offering.'

'You'll be going soon. You can forget all about the Temple of the Waters and all the rubbish associated with it.'

Bess . . .

The whispery gurgle was so damp and so close that I had to resist the urge to wipe my face. It was hard to believe Drew couldn't hear it, but he was still talking.

'Sophie isn't your problem,' he said. 'She's mine. You don't need to get involved.'

He was right. Only a matter of weeks and I would be on that plane to Mexico.

Bess . . .

Sophie wasn't my responsibility. I didn't need to get involved. But I knew how important Drew's work was to him. I'd heard him talk about his mentor often enough to know that she was a big part of his life. I wouldn't be there, but I wanted him to have his research. I couldn't love him the way he wanted, but I could help him keep his daughter safe. I could do that for him.

'I'll be here,' I promised. 'You go and give your paper. I'll stay with Sophie. I'll look after her.'

Chapter Nineteen

'Dad's out.' Sophie was in the kitchen, drinking a glass of water when I let myself in the following evening.

'I know. But I'm not teaching tonight, and it's such a filthy night that I fancied some company.'

It had taken me some time to persuade Drew to go to his research group and let me stick close to Sophie, but he had agreed – reluctantly – in the end, on the condition that I rang him if there was any trouble at all.

'I'm going out,' said Sophie truculently. I had the feeling that she was regretting the argument the night before, but having insisted, she couldn't now see any way out of it. I felt sorry for her. 'I told you. It's my initiation tonight.'

The wind was wrestling at the windowpanes, throwing rain at the glass in short staccato bursts. I'd got soaked just running from door to door.

'You're going out in *this*?'

'It's Samhain,' she said, glancing uneasily at the angry night.

'It has to be tonight.' But she didn't look very happy about it, and I didn't blame her. The clocks had gone back the week before and it was already pitch-black out there.

'Well, do you mind if I hang around while you're waiting to go out?' I said. I knew there was no point in trying to dissuade her at this stage.

Sophie scowled as she turned the tap to refill her glass. 'Why can't you hang around in Lucy's house?'

'I prefer it here.' That was true. 'Now that it's almost empty, it feels . . . spooky over there.' With the furious wind screaming impotently in the dark outside, it wasn't hard to achieve a nervous laugh. 'I think there's a ghost in Lucy's house.'

'There is,' said Sophie.

I was taken aback. 'You know about it?'

'I only know what Lucy told me.' Sophie carried the glass to the table and sat down. 'She used to regress, and every time it was the same story. She told me once she preferred the past to living now. She said it felt more real. It must be amazing to travel through time,' she went on wistfully and her eyes rested on me with a trace of resentment. 'I didn't think it would happen to someone like you, though.'

'Because I'm not spiritual enough?' Ash's words had rankled, and she flushed a little.

'It just seems really unfair. I'd love to experience that, but it never works for me. I tried to do it with Lucy once, but nothing happened.'

'You should be glad,' I said, thinking of Sybil's death, of the sickness, of Francis's sweaty hands on me, and I shuddered. 'It's frightening.'

'Lucy wasn't frightened. She loved it.'

Had she loved it when Francis forced himself into her? When Ned died and her heart broke? When she watched Sybil Dent hanging from the gibbet? Lucy must have lived through everything I had done . . . and then she had died, I remembered with a shiver.

'Lucy's dead,' I reminded her, and Sophie's eyes filled with tears. I sighed and went over to put my arm around her shoulders. 'I'm sorry, Sophie. I didn't mean to snap. I'm just feeling edgy today.'

'Me too.' She managed a weak smile. 'Perhaps it's something to do with Halloween?' She looked out of the window, her expression distant. 'Did you know that this is the night when the boundaries between the real world and the spiritual world come down? Between the living and the dead?'

'Don't!' I said sharply. I was remembering what Vivien had said: *Be very careful.*

Sophie turned her head to look at me. 'Does Dad know you've seen a ghost?'

'Sort of,' I said. 'I've had some pretty bad experiences, Sophie. Don't wish for them.'

I'd spent a disturbed night after I'd left Drew. Part of me had longed to stay with him, but the old restless demon drove me out of the bed in the small hours, after Drew had fallen asleep. I'd lain in Lucy's bed, the image of Sybil's dreadful end circling endlessly around my brain, tense and afraid that Hawise would draw me back to the past again. I didn't want to go back any more. I'd had enough.

The awful sense of foreboding wouldn't go away. I told myself it was something to do with the relentless rain all day. There was something apocalyptic about the darkness of the air, the weight of the sky. It been like this for more than a week, and the Ouse was rising, swollen by the run-off from the moors and dales to the north. There were rumours of sandbags being stacked, and in the shops everyone was talking about the floods in 2000.

I had forgotten my delight in autumn. I was oppressed by the lack of light and the endless, dreary rain, and at the back of my mind something terrible simmered. If I tried to look at it, it evaporated like last night's dream, leaving only the sense of pooling dread of what was to come.

Sophie might be right about Halloween. Death felt very close. I wasn't bothered by the pumpkins and ghost masks, and minia-ture witch hats on sale in the supermarkets. They had nothing to do with the tug and swirl of darkness, or the way, ever since I arrived in York, time had spiralled round and round and up and down, billowing back and forth. That feeling had been inten-sifying ever since Sybil's death. I felt as if I was walking along a narrow path in the dark, expecting to slip any minute, but I couldn't think about that now. I had to concentrate on Sophie.

I forced brightness into my voice as I sat down opposite her. 'Are you nervous about the initiation?'

'Why should I be?' The edge in her voice told me that she was, and I shrugged, careful not to spook her.

'Initiation rites are always a big deal,' I said as casually as I could. 'Do you know yet what you have to do?'

'I have to purify myself.' Some of the truculence left Sophie's expression. 'I haven't eaten all day, and I've only drunk water.'

'So what's going to happen tonight?'

'I'm going to offer myself to the river goddess. If I prove I am worthy of her, and pure of heart, I'll ascend to the next level of oneness.'

I could just hear Ash intoning the words, see Sophie wide-eyed with awe as she drank in every word.

'How do you prove if you're worthy or not?'

Sophie's eyes slid from mine. 'I don't know yet. Ash is going to tell me tonight.'

As if woken by his name, her phone rang. The sound of it jangled through the quiet kitchen and we both jumped. I couldn't see the caller name, but I knew it would be Ash.

After an infinitesimal hesitation Sophie scraped her chair back and picked up the phone as she got to her feet. 'Hi,' she said as she turned away.

I watched her back, worried. Ash was doing all the talking while Sophie murmured agreement every now and then. Suddenly she stiffened.

'Millennium Bridge?' she said, clearly startled. I saw her look at the window where the wind was still hurling rain against the glass. 'But—' She broke off as Ash interrupted her. 'No, of course not,' she said humbly after a while. 'No . . . no . . . I'm sorry . . . Yes, I know where it is. Of course I'll be there.'

She ended the call and stood holding the phone, and looked

so much like someone looking for a way out and not finding one that I wished I could go and put my arm around her. When she turned at last, her eyes were miserable, but her chin lifted with grim determination.

'Don't try and make me change my mind,' she said.

'I won't,' I promised and nearly smiled at the struggle between relief and disappointment in her face.

'Well . . . good,' she said. 'Now I have to go and prepare myself.' She threw me a challenging look, as if daring me to argue with her, but I only nodded.

'Okay if I make myself something to eat?'

'If you must.'

She practically ran out of the room, and the next moment I heard her feet thumping up the stairs. The poor thing had to have been starving if she hadn't eaten all day. I made some cheese on toast, hoping that the smell would entice her down, but Sophie was stronger than I gave her credit for. I wondered exactly what Ash had said to her and when she would be summoned.

I was rinsing my plate under the tap when Sophie came back in. She was wearing a loose blue robe and sandals, of all things, and had cleaned her face of all traces of make-up. Her skin looked raw and naked, but although her eyes were frightened, her soft mouth was set. 'I'm going,' she said, pulling on a jacket that rather spoiled the homespun look, but was at least practical in view of the torrential rain outside. Which was more than could be said for the sandals.

Belatedly I realized I should have been prepared myself. I could at least have had an umbrella ready.

'I'm coming with you,' I said.

'No!' Sophie froze and stared at me, aghast.

'I won't interfere. I'll just make sure you're all right.'

'You can't come.' Her voice rose shrilly. 'It's secret!'

'Sophie, you're fifteen. You can't wander around on your own on a night like this.'

'I won't be on my own!' Sophie spat at me, on the verge of tears. 'Ash and Mara will be with me. Dad put you up to this, didn't he?'

'No, I—'

'He's determined to spoil it for me! This is the first thing I've ever done for myself. I've finally found people who'll accept me for what I am, but Dad hates that, doesn't he? He's just afraid of Ash because Ash lets me be myself and make my own decisions!'

'Sophie—'

Tears of fury stood in her eyes. 'Don't you *dare* follow me!' she shouted, and swirled for the door.

'Sophie, wait!'

Cursing myself for handling the situation so disastrously, I rushed after her, desperate to catch her before she left, but in my haste I skidded on the polished floorboards and bumped against the door frame. By the time I righted myself, clapping my hand to my arm where I had bruised it, the front door was slamming behind her.

My arm hurts. I rub it absently as I wait for Agnes. I must have bruised it, although I don't remember knocking against anything.

I am standing by the window in her chamber, looking out at the rain that has turned the street to a mire. It has been raining for what seems like months and months. The garths and gardens are sodden, the rivers swollen, the dykes and gutters running hard. September has turned into October and still it rains. The warmth has leached from the air and the wind blows bitter.

Agnes and Francis now live in a narrow house in Jubbergate. It is not far, but the street feels different here, meaner and more crowded. No wonder they preferred the space and quiet of Ned's house in Coney Street. They could have stayed in my father's house in Hungate, but no! They would come to the same parish, they would be close to me. That was Francis's decision, not Agnes's.

I'm trying to rehearse what I'm going to say to her in my head, but I keep getting distracted by the dirt on the glass panes and the frayed edge of the cushion on the seat. Agnes has ever been a poor housekeeper. She has a slatternly servant, Charity, who takes no more pride in her work than old Jennet did.

It was Charity who answered when I knocked. Her mistress was out, she said, and she would have closed the door on me if I had not overborne her.

'I will wait,' I said, pushing past her. I can be imperious enough when I try. The truth is that I don't want to have to come back. The women spinning at their doors fell silent as I walked along Coney Street and turned into Jubbergate.

The mood in the city is fractious and sour. Perhaps it is something to do with the rain that falls so remorselessly, but the streets are dark at the moment, and something dangerous runs unseen through them. You can feel the tautness in the air. Small disagreements flare up and blows are exchanged, where once an insult would have done. There is a vicious edge to the gossip, a sullenness to the way folk walk. Everyone wants someone to blame.

I felt the women's eyes on me as I passed, and heard the murmurings that followed me. These are the women who sat with me in childbed and offered me cheer. Have they forgotten how I screamed in pain? How I cried when I held my baby? How they clucked around me and cooed over Bess?

How can they listen to a whisper that I am a witch and not laugh it to scorn? But they are not laughing, and Jane reports that the rumours are growing more bitter by the day. Yesterday she came back, grim-faced, with the news that two goodwives in the parish have buried a witch's bottle beneath their doors to protect them against me.

And this morning it was worse.

I'd been to the warehouse and I was grumbling about the weather as I went into the kitchen. I stamped the mud from my clogs and shook the wet from my cloak, while Mog insinuated herself past my ankles and flicked her paws distastefully.

'It's like winter already. I can't remember the last time I saw the sun— Jane, what has happened?' I broke off as Jane turned half-defiantly to show a bruised face and a split lip.

'Got into a fight, didn't I?'

I tossed my cloak over the table and rolled up my sleeves. 'Let me see.'

'Other girl looks worse.'

I made her sit on the stool so that I could bathe her face and scold her gently. 'You are not supposed to be fighting, Jane.'

'Couldn't help it,' she said sullenly. 'She were saying such lies about you.'

I paused. 'About me?'

'Stupid lies,' she muttered.

I wrung out the cloth and laid it back against her puffy mouth. 'What are they saying, Jane?'

She twisted her thin fingers together. 'That you're a witch too. I said you wasn't, but she said everyone knew you was in league with Widow Dent. And now you've got that cat,' she said with a narrow glance at Mog, 'they think that proves it. I said it was just a cat, and then she said that before little Bess was born, you had another child. You didn't, did you?'

'I had a babe that was born before its time,' I said sadly. 'It happens.'

'It weren't a hare with two heads?'

I jerked back as if she had slapped me. 'Of course not!'

'That's what I said,' said Jane stoutly.

'Who says that?'

She shrugged. 'Dunno. Someone whispers it to someone else, and then *she* says what she's heard . . . all private, like.'

'And meanwhile what little is left of my reputation is gone,' I added grimly. 'Who could possibly know anything like that anyway?'

'The midwife?'

'The midwife came too late. Only Agnes was there.'

I would laugh at the rumours, but my business is beginning to suffer. Children are starting to point at Bess and whisper behind their hands. If it goes on like this, she will be an outcast, just as I was. And now Jane is hurt. I need to put a stop to it now, and for that I need my sister's help. So I will wait. I don't want to have to come back.

The sound of the door latch makes me spin round and my stomach plunges in dismay as I see Francis standing there, watching me with that glistening gaze that always makes me want to scrub myself clean.

'So, Sister, what can we do for you?' he says, turning to close the door. The sound of the latch dropping into place is very loud in the silence. 'You do not often grace us with your company.'

I put up my chin. 'I want to speak to Agnes.'

'She is not here, as you see.' Francis spreads his hands. 'Can you not speak to me?'

He is between me and the door. I don't want to be alone with him. For years I have avoided just such a situation, but it is Francis who has started these wicked rumours, I am certain, so perhaps it is as well that I have my say to him.

'They are saying in the street that I am a witch,' I tell him bluntly.

Francis strolls into the room, very much at his ease. 'Now why would they say something like that, hmm?'

'That is my question to you,' I say coldly.

'To me? I am not the one who flaunts her familiar as she walks around the city.'

Mog has not made it easy for me, it is true. She has attached herself to me and follows me around, the way Hap used to. She is so proud, so striking, that of course the neighbours have noticed. Cats are supposed to walk alone, but this one is like a dog, and they don't like it. They don't like it when she accompanies me to the market and looks at them with her great yellow eyes. Sometimes, I admit, it unnerves even me.

'It is a *cat*,' I say.

'A witch's cat,' Francis corrects me and puts his head on one side to study me. 'Is it true you suckle it like a babe?'

I flinch with disgust. If that is what they are saying, things are even worse than I thought.

'They are saying all sorts of nonsense,' I say, keeping my voice even with an effort. 'My servant heard a woman in the market telling her gossip that I had given birth to a monster before I had my daughter.' That one hurts the most. I have not forgotten the pain of losing that child before its time.

'Can you say it is not true?' asks Francis.

'Of course it is not true! Agnes knows the truth. She was there. She helped me.'

'She did not think you were strong enough to know the truth.' Francis shook his head sadly. 'Did she not say that she would deal with everything for you?'

'Yes, but I—' I stopped, making myself remember that terrible day. The pain and the tearing loss. My sister had stayed beside me. I had turned my face into the pillow and let her deal with it all. 'I would have known,' I say, but I can hear the uncertainty in my voice.

'You gave birth to an abomination and grieved as if it were a baby.'

Francis is enjoying himself. His face is bright with satisfaction, and all at once I find myself thinking about the look I surprised on Agnes's face that day – the sharp gleam of pleasure as I lay and wept for my lost child. The look I have pushed to the back of my mind.

Is it possible? Was the babe a monster? Surely I would have felt something?

'Better not,' Agnes said when I had roused myself to ask to see my child. She was wrapping it briskly in rags. 'I will dispose of it, and no one need know.'

And now it seems the entire neighbourhood knows. My throat is tight. I swallow hard. I mustn't let Francis glimpse that he has hurt me. Turning, I move back to the window, rubbing my arm without thinking.

'She said she wouldn't tell anyone.' I force the words through stiff lips. 'How do you know this?'

'Agnes is a dutiful wife. She has no secrets from her husband.'

The way I had kept my knowledge of Francis a secret from Ned. That was a mistake, I realize now. I should have told Ned and let him deal with Francis for me, but it was too late for that now. I had to deal with him by myself.

'She could tell everyone the rumours are mistaken,' I say after a moment. 'She could say that she saw the babe herself. Everyone would believe her.' They would. Agnes has a reputation for piety that has won her respect, if few friends.

'You want to ask your sister to *lie*?' Francis's voice is shocked, but when I turn to face him, his eyes are gleeful.

He wants me to beg, I realize. He wants me grovelling at his feet so that he can grind my pride beneath the heel of his boot.

I cannot do it.

'I don't believe you,' I say slowly. 'I think *you* suggested to Agnes that there might have been something wrong with the babe, just like you suggested that the remedy I had from Sybil Dent was witchcraft.'

'It was! I saw that token you hung around your husband's neck. It was the work of Satan.'

'It was harmless,' I say, exasperated. 'I hung it around your neck too.'

'You wanted me to die!' There are little flecks of spittle at the corner of Francis's mouth. 'You admit it!'

'I wish you *had* died,' I tell him. 'But you didn't. I nursed you and you survived. I saved you,' I say dully and he smiles.

'I was saved by God,' he says, and I clench my hands in my skirts.

'It was not God who nursed you!'

'Careful, Sister,' he warns, still smiling. 'You come too close to blasphemy. Are you really suggesting that it was you, rather than our Lord, who saved me? We are all in God's hands, you know that.'

'Tell them to stop the rumours,' I say, my face stony.

'Well, that is easily done,' he agrees. 'All you need to do is let us back into your house. Who would believe the rumours, when you have your sister and I to lend you countenance and guide you away from the darkness onto God's true path?'

'No,' I say flatly. The thought of sharing my house with him makes my skin creep with disgust.

Francis shrugs. 'Then I fear I cannot help you.'

'You're punishing me,' I say slowly. Why did I not realize it before? 'I am the only one who sees you for what you really are, Francis Bewley, and you cannot bear that. I'm the only one who knows that you are not pious, that you are no God-fearing man, but a brute who would defile a young girl.'

'You wanted it.' There is something wrong with his smile. It is too wide, too fixed, and when he comes closer I find myself backing away from him. 'Come, Hawise. Surely you remember what it was like? You know I want you. I have always wanted you, and you wanted me too.'

'No.' I have come up against a table and cannot go any further. I put my hands out to ward him off, but he brushes them aside and grabs my breasts, squeezing them painfully.

'Yes, you did. You know you did. You bewitched me, you led me on, you made me want you.' All at once he is panting, and his face is red and glazed.

'No, no.' I am squirming to get free of his grasp, beating at him with my hands, but he is bigger and more solid than I have remembered.

'Let me touch you, Hawise.' He is pushing his crotch against me, grunting and panting, while the back of my thighs are digging into the table. 'I've got to have you. You're mine, you've always been mine. I think of you every night when I lie with your sister.'

My mouth opens to scream for Charity, but even now, as I fight desperately to stave him off, I don't want my sister to know that Francis wants me like this, so I close it again and concentrate on shoving at his bulk. Besides, Charity is sly and deaf, and Francis is her master. She might choose not to hear.

Francis's tongue is thick and wet as it pushes against my mouth. He is dragging me away from the table, grappling with my skirts, and I am afraid now, while before I was just repulsed. He is stronger than me, and if he chooses he can take me here on the floor of his hall, where there will be no Sybil to rescue me.

Then, quite suddenly, he pushes me away. Gasping, I stagger back against the table. My sleeves are torn, my bodice gaping, my cap askew.

'What is this?'

'Agnes! Oh, thank God!' I start to stumble towards her, but her look of disgust freezes me on the spot.

'I see you are up to your old tricks again,' she says.

'Tricks? No! What tricks?'

Ostentatiously Francis straightens his doublet and comes to take Agnes's hand. 'I am sorry, my dear. I had hoped to reason with her, but she is beyond reason. It is moon-madness with her, I fear.'

'What are you saying? Agnes, no, please – it's not like that. I'm sorry, but Francis is obsessed with me.'

They exchange a significant look. 'Just as you told me,' Agnes said to him.

'You must not blame her too much. A woman like your sister has powerful needs that only a man can satisfy, and now that she has lost her husband . . . ' He trails off meaningfully.

'Well, she cannot have mine,' says Agnes tartly. She turns on me, her pale eyes as cold as a January dawn. 'Be off with you,' she says. 'You have caused nothing but trouble. You cannot come between my husband and me. We are too strong for you. How dare you come here and seduce my husband?'

'Seduce?' My laugh is too wild. I see them look at each other again. 'It is your husband who makes the trouble, Agnes. Ask him how my bodice is torn like this! Ask him why my sleeves are hanging from my shoulders.' I gesture wildly at myself. 'Do you think *I* did this?'

'You come here and throw yourself at him,' she says stonily. 'I saw him push you away. And you were not screaming for help, were you?'

'That's because—' I stop. What is the point of trying to explain that I was thinking of her? She will not believe me. She is so under Francis's influence that she will believe whatever he tells her to. 'You're not going to listen, are you?'

Agnes looks away. I think she knows the truth, but won't face it. Just as, deep down, I have known the truth that my sister dislikes me and haven't faced that.

'Agnes, you have to know this. Your husband lies.' My voice is thin and rising with frustration. 'Before I was wed, he tried to defile me. He tore at my clothes. He shoved his hand in my private parts. He tried to put his thing inside me!' I shout when she claps her hands over her ears. 'That is the truth, and I think you know it.'

'Get out of here!' she says, her voice shaking.

'Gladly,' I say. 'Just keep him away from me,' I go on, with a venomous look at Francis, and I push past them, reaching for the door before he can think of a reason to stop me.

My hand closed around the door handle, and it felt so wrong that I almost jerked it back – it was round, not a latch – but I didn't have time to think about it. I had to get out. Wrenching the door open, I ran through it, but the wooden stairs leading down to the hall had gone and I found myself outside, with the rain pelting into my face and the wind grabbing at my hair.

I gasped at the shock of it, and my hands went to my midriff as the jarring impact of my return to the present sent me doubling over. My mind reeled, but the certainty that something was terribly wrong shouted at the edges of my consciousness. I had to concentrate.

I pushed my wet hair back from my face and held it in my hands as I tried to focus on where I was. The wind snatched my breath and wrestled with the dark, tossing the rain around savagely. Terraced houses. Street lamps. I stared at them as if I had never seen such things before. A car drove slowly past, its windscreen wipers slapping furiously from side to side, and its tyres sent the puddles spraying outwards. It reminded me of the taxis in Jakarta, cruising through the downpours . . .

I was drifting. Fear hammered at the back of my mind and

I yanked myself into the present. I was in York. I was Grace and—

Sophie! I spun around as the memory hit me, and received a faceful of rain that made me gasp and splutter again. I had to find Sophie! Frantically I looked up and down the empty street, blinking through the rain, but there was no sign of her. I remembered her storming out of the house, but then I had been rubbing my arm as I waited for Agnes to come back. I had no idea how long I had been standing with my hand on the door knob.

Now Sophie might be anywhere. The thought of her out with Ash made my blood congeal with fear. She was in danger, and I had told Drew that I would stay with her. I had promised him that she would be safe with me.

Panic welled up inside me as I stood there in the rain, being buffeted by the wind, while the old guilt crawled around my lungs and squeezed the air from them. If only I hadn't slipped . . . I should have been more careful. I should have been *ready*. Instead I had wasted precious time in the past while Sophie ran headlong out to meet Ash. She was in danger, I knew it, and I had to find her.

'Think, think, *think* . . .' My teeth chattered as I swiped the rain from my face once more. I couldn't go tamely back inside and tell Drew that I had let Sophie go, without trying to find her. I had no idea where Ash held his gatherings. Vivien might know, I realized, but she had no phone. I would have to go there first.

That's when I remembered Sophie's muttered conversation with Ash on the phone. 'Millennium Bridge?' she had echoed.

Of course that's where she was. I ran into the house and scrabbled frantically around for my phone and Drew's key. I had never been to the bridge – it was too close to the river for me – but I knew where it was. It spanned the Ouse downstream of the city. There had been no bridge there in Hawise's day, just the fields where the laundresses set their tubs and washed and scrubbed the city's linen.

The fields that I had seen in my nightmare.

I was cold to the core at the thought of going there, but I couldn't stop to think. It would take too long to call a taxi. By the time it had arrived and negotiated York's one-way system, I could be halfway there.

I didn't bother with a coat – I was so wet, it wouldn't make any difference – but ran out of the house, banging the door shut behind me. I set off at a jog, fumbling with the phone with slippery hands. I squinted at it to check the time and was shocked to see that it was almost ten. Sophie had left before eight, which meant that I had been trapped uselessly in the past for more than two hours.

I had to slow down to dial Drew's mobile, but I picked up speed as soon as it started ringing, and cursed as it went straight through to voicemail. He must be at the conference dinner. I'd insisted that he went to that too. 'I'll look after Sophie,' I had said.

'It's me,' I gabbled into the phone. 'I'm sorry . . . so sorry . . . Sophie's gone.' I gulped some air and slowed down again so that I could speak more clearly through my heaving breaths. 'I don't trust Agnes, and I'm afraid of what Francis will do—'

I broke off. That wasn't right. I was getting confused. 'I mean, what *Ash* will do,' I said. There was no time to explain further. 'I think . . . I think Sophie's at the Millennium Bridge. I'm going there now. I don't know what else to do. Please come as soon as you get this, Drew. I think she'll need you.' I paused just as I was about to cut the connection. '*I'll* need you,' I added, still breathless, but more quietly. 'Please come.'

Shoving the phone into the pocket of my jeans, I began to run again. It was hard going against the wind, which was driving the rain in almost horizontal sheets. I'd never noticed that the car park was on a slope, either, and as I laboured up it I had an incongruous flash of memory, of running up this same path with Elizabeth, laughing in the sunlight, with the certainty that our whole lives lay ahead of us.

But that was Hawise's memory, not mine, I reminded myself fiercely. I was desperately unfit, and my chest was heaving, my side aching with a stitch that made me wince with every step. My jeans and top were sodden and clung, cold and clammy, to my skin while the rain streamed over my face and down my neck. My suede boots splashed through the puddles and pinched my toes.

The trick-and-treaters were long gone and the streets were virtually deserted. The pubs were open, and as I ran limping past I caught a fleeting glimpse of people laughing and talking, oblivious to the darkness and the danger of the night outside. I fought the conviction that I was running between two worlds, two times, and that if they looked out of the window they wouldn't even see me.

Certainly the few people I passed didn't seem to notice me.

They kept their heads bent beneath their umbrellas and didn't pause to ask why I was staggering wildly through the streets.

At the bottom of Goodramgate I had to stop. I put my hands on my thighs and bent over, dragging the air into my screaming lungs. I was terribly afraid for Sophie, so I couldn't let myself rest, but pushed on, not letting myself wonder how I knew the shortest way to the river. Not letting myself listen to the voice in my head that was shrieking at me to turn back, to run away from the river, not towards it.

I had to keep going. I couldn't leave Sophie there. I couldn't fail another child.

The gale redoubled its onslaught as I staggered along Jubbergate. All I had to do was get to the end of the street, turn left and then right, and I would be at the river. *No, no, no!* screamed the voice in my head, but I ignored it. I would follow the river along to the bridge and I would find Sophie and . . . I wasn't sure what I would do then, but I had to find her first.

Blinking the rain desperately from my eyes so that I could see where I was going, I paused at the end of Jubbergate.

I blink the rain from my eyes as I hesitate at the end of Jubbergate. Perhaps this is not a good idea. Agnes will always take Francis's side. What is the point of trying to persuade her of my innocence? But I have to try. We cannot continue as we are. I cannot bear the thought that she believes I desire her husband, that I would act on it. Why would I do such a thing to my own sister?

All I ask is to live quietly with my daughter, for my servants to go about their business unhindered. Jane's face is still bruised, and this morning Rob found a dead cat left at our door. Agnes could put a stop to all of this. I have to ask her one more time.

Francis is on some business with the Council of the North. I heard him say so, and the bad weather is no excuse not to wait on my Lord President, so I will find Agnes on her own and remind her that we are sisters.

'You sure?' Jane looked sceptical when I told her where I was going.

'I have to try,' I said. 'I have to try for Bess.'

Bess wanted to look at the book that Ned gave me when we were betrothed, and her small face was thunderous when I told her I was going out. I tucked my daughter's hair back under her cap and bent to kiss her as I buttoned my gown.

'I won't be long,' I promised. 'I'll read to you when I come back.'

Mog was meowing and rubbing herself against my skirts. 'As for you,' I said, pointing at her, 'you stay here.' And I slipped out and shut the door behind me before she could follow.

Chapter Twenty

It is All Hallows' Eve, and the sky is so dark with the storm that it might be night. The wind tugs at my cap and my gown is sodden. The shopkeepers have put up their shutters and retreated inside. The whole street seems to be sulking. Doors are left ajar to let in the meagre light, and candles flicker in the dim interiors.

Agnes's door is open too. A tallow candle burns on the chest and, in the guttering shadows, I don't see her at first. Then I realize that she is crouched over some kind of jar.

'Agnes?'

She gasps and the jar slips from her hands as she leaps to her feet. I hear the crack as it hits the stone floor, where Charity is too lazy to lay rushes.

'Hawise! What are you doing here?' Her voice is tight with shock.

'I didn't mean to give you a fright.'

I stoop to help pick up the pieces and the sour smell of piss hits me. 'What on earth did you have in here?' I sniff at a piece. It is unmistakable. I raise my brows. 'Agnes?'

'It is nothing to do with you!' She snatches the pottery from me, but my eye is caught by the metal glinting in the dull candle-light.

'Pins.' I pick one up between forefinger and thumb. Suddenly I know what she has been doing. 'You're making a witch's bottle.'

Agnes sucks in her breath. 'What if I am? It is All Hallows' Eve. We do what we must to keep the evil forces away.'

'And you think burying a bottle under your door will keep a witch away?' I laugh. 'That is just silly superstition, Agnes! And who are you trying to keep away? Your husband has had all the so-called witches hanged!' My amusement fades bitterly as I remember Sybil hanging from the gibbet, tongue bulging and tiny feet twitching.

'Not all,' says Agnes and looks at me.

There is a moment of stillness. The only sound is the rain drumming on the roof. I stare back at my sister and read the truth writ in her face.

'You think *I* am a witch? Agnes, you cannot believe so.'

'Can I not? Who else would flaunt their familiar so shamelessly?' She points a shaking finger beside me, and there is Mog, gazing unblinkingly at Agnes.

Mog, who I was so careful to shut in the kitchen.

I swallow. 'She is just a cat.'

'No ordinary cat would follow you around so. Get it out of here!' Agnes looks around wildly for a weapon and ends up throwing the broken pieces of pottery at Mog, who doesn't even bother to move.

I pick her up all the same. 'Agnes, what are you thinking?' I try to reason with her, but it is soon clear that she is beyond reason.

'Francis told me of your spells at the time of the sickness,' she says, panting. 'He told me how it is with you. He knows you for what you are.'

'And you believe him? We are sisters, Agnes!'

'Are we? What do we know of you, after all? My father was bewitched by your mother, just as you bewitched Ned Hilliard. Who knows where she was from, or what she was?'

'You never thought this before Francis suggested it to you,' I protest.

'Yes, I did. I never said it, because what was the point? You were always the favourite, always the one men looked at. I have spent my whole life in your shadow. No one ever looked at me while you were by.'

'What matters it now? You have a husband of your own.'

'Only because you did not want him!'

'I thought he told you that I pursued him?'

Confused, she puts a hand to her head. 'You did! And when he refused you, you put a spell on him so that he cannot think of anyone but you.' She shoves her face close to mine, careless of Mog's warning hiss. 'You unmanned him! In our bed he can do nothing for me unless I let him call me Hawise. A fine revenge you took on him!'

I take a step back, hugging Mog to me. 'Oh, Agnes . . . ' I

am sickened by the thought of it. I feel dirty knowing what Francis has put my sister through. 'How do you bear it?'

'What choice do I have? He is my husband, *mine*! He would love me if only you were gone,' she says wildly.

'Where can I go? I would if I could,' I say bitterly. 'We are both women, we have to stay where we are put.'

'You are always lucky. It is always easy for you.' Agnes hugs her arms to her and looks at me with hate-filled eyes. 'Oh, you loved to vaunt your fortune over me, didn't you? Your wealthy husband, your wealthy *adoring* husband. You couldn't be like everyone else and make do. No, you have to have everything: a fine house in Coney Street, a moonstruck husband, a child. I tried to make sure you would not have that, at least, but you went out to that witch Sybil Dent, didn't you?'

'What do you mean, you tried to make sure?'

'Those infusions I gave you.' She laughs. 'Dear sister, you don't really think I meant for you to have a child, when my own husband was incapable of giving me one, do you? And you were so pleased to be fond sisters! You drank them all up and then you conceived anyway. I couldn't have that.'

I have a horrible image of Agnes bending over me, pressing a goblet into my hand. *Drink this, Sister.*

'You killed my baby,' I realize slowly. I feel dull and stupid.

'What a mess you made,' she remembers with a shudder of disgust.

'This story of a hare with two heads – you started that, didn't you?'

'It could have been anything.' Agnes shrugs. 'It might easily have been a monster, with all the time you spent consorting with witches. She told you, didn't she?'

'Who?'

'The witch. You went to see her one day, and after that you wouldn't take anything I made. So you had a child after all, and all the gossips there to protect her. I couldn't get rid of them all, especially that old servant of yours, Margery. She was always watching me. She knew something.'

I am cold to my core at the knowledge that my Bess has had an enemy so close since she was born.

'You wouldn't have hurt Bess?'

'Babes die all the time. I nearly saw her off in her cradle, but you woke up, didn't you? Then Margery was pushing in, interfering, and the chance was lost.'

I look into my sister's pale eyes and realize at last that she is quite mad. My mouth is dry. All this time I thought Francis was the danger, and it turns out that my own sister was the greater.

I have to keep her talking. I will get away and take my daughter, take Jane and Rob and the cat and leave. I have been stuck like a fly in honey, when I should have been making plans to go. Without Ned, there was nothing to keep me here. Why have I stayed so long? We can take a keelboat to Hull, then a ship. We can go to London, to Hamburg – anywhere my Bess will be safe.

Agnes is between me and the door, and her empty eyes are fixed on mine. There is something awry in her. I thought it was just that she was sickly, but the wrongness in her goes deeper than that. How is it that I have never seen it before?

'Why did you not take your chance when you had Bess during the sickness?' I ask through stiff lips.

A sly look crosses her face. 'Francis wants her,' she says.

The horror of it freezes the breath in my lungs.

'Francis is a monster,' I say and my voice is shaking.

'You see?' Francis's voice behind me makes me swing round, but he is not talking to me. He is ushering in a triumvirate of goodwives. Barbara Cook, Anne Tyrry and Marion Carter. Bitter women, every one of them.

They look edgy and feverish. Has he kept them behind the door, waiting for the right moment to bring them in?

'See her with her familiar – mocking me, calling *me* a monster!' Francis points accusingly at me where I stand clutching Mog. 'Am I not at divine service every day? Do I not serve the Lord? I keep all His commandments, as you know. I am monstrous to the Devil she worships, no doubt.'

'*You* are the Devil. Only the Devil could desire a small child.' I turn to the women. 'Can you not see what he is? He is abominable! You are mothers. You know it is unnatural and loathsome to covet a child the way he does.'

'I desire only to bring up her as the Lord commands, away from her mother, the witch.' Francis's voice is sanctimonious.

'You will never take her from me! I am leaving this city,' I tell him. 'You can be rid of me, gladly, but you will not have my daughter.'

Francis shakes his head. 'You cannot leave now. Not now we know you for what you are.'

I laugh in exasperation. 'For the love of grace, how many times do I have to tell you? I am not a witch!'

'Your actions say otherwise.'

'I do not have to answer to you.' I make to push past them towards the door, but Francis moves in front of me to block my way.

'You cannot leave me, Hawise,' he says, his voice low so that only I can hear. 'I'm not letting you go.'

I draw in a breath and set my teeth. 'This has gone on long enough, Francis. Look to your wife. You cannot have me, and you cannot have my daughter. Ever. I'm going.'

He's not expecting my shove and he staggers back, letting me push past him to the door.

'Stop her!' cries Agnes. 'She is a witch! She will curse us all!'

Her words unleash something in the air, a wrongness that makes the tiny hairs at the nape of my neck prickle a warning. I know I have to get out, now. I have my hand on the door when Francis grabs my arm, swinging me round so that Mog is thrown from my grasp, spitting.

'Let me go!'

'No.' He has himself back under control, and his expression bodes ill for me. 'No, this is All Hallows' Eve. If we let her go, who knows what mischief she will wreak on us?'

Mog is growling now, her hair on end and her eyes fixed on Francis, who shifts back, but refuses to let me go.

'See her familiar? No ordinary cat would growl so.'

The women huddle together in fright. They can sense the evil too, but it comes from Francis and Agnes, not from Mog.

'Kill it,' says Agnes, quite quietly, but there is something so implacable in her voice that silence falls abruptly and the only sound is Mog, vibrating warningly.

Agnes reaches to the chest behind her and picks up a knife.

'No!' I scream, pulling frantically to get away from Francis. 'Mog! Go!'

'Close the window,' Agnes says calmly to one of the women, and she edges nervously towards the window without taking her eyes off the cat.

'Mog!' I scream again, and this time the cat reacts. She springs at Agnes, who has been advancing slowly on her. In spite of herself, Agnes jerks back, and the women screech in panic as, spitting and snarling, Mog leaps for the window and is gone.

I slump with relief, so glad at her escape that I forget the danger I am still in myself.

They have all taken Mog's behaviour as a sign. They will not listen to me now.

'We should call the constable,' says Marion.

'The minister,' says Barbara nervously.

'I say we deal with her ourselves,' says Agnes.

I stare at her. Can this be my meek, colourless sister? It is as if the venom she has suppressed for so long is surging through her, making her brighter, bigger, bolder. She is unfurling like a banner snapping in the wind. Hate has made her powerful. Her madness has transformed her. Even Francis suddenly looks diminished next to her.

'How much more proof do you need?' she demands of the women, who blunder together, sensing her power, catching something of her madness. Their eyes are growing sharp and frenzied. They have forgotten, these goodwives, that I am a woman no different from them, that I cook and I bargain and I raise my child just as they do. They are seeing me through Agnes's eyes, as warped and dangerous.

'If even I – her sister – know this about her, who can defend her?' Agnes demands. Francis keeps hold of me, but he has stepped back and is letting Agnes do the talking.

'We cannot go through the proper channels,' she says scornfully. 'You know what fools men make of themselves over a lascivious woman. All she has to do is turn those eyes of hers on them and they are bewitched. They will let her go, and she will be back in the parish. Do you feel safe with your children passing her house, knowing the black arts she practises in there?'

The women shudder as one.

'And your husbands?' Agnes goes on. 'One smile and they will be ensnared. They will be no good to you ever after.'

It doesn't seem to matter that I have never once flirted with their husbands, that I have been constant to Ned. The women believe her utterly and mutter amongst themselves.

'This is foolishness!' I cry. 'Think about what she is saying. There is no proof of any of it.'

'Then by all means let us prove it,' says Agnes. 'Husband, hold her still.' Obligingly Francis grips both my arms behind me, and Agnes thrusts her face against mine once more. She is still holding the knife. I brace myself for her to spit at me, but instead she slices through the ribbons of my bodice and wrenches down my sleeve. The women gasp and recoil.

'See!' Agnes points the tip of the knife triumphantly at the mark on my shoulder. The one Ned said looked like a little hand. *Sweet*, he called it. *Like my wife.* 'Is that not the mark of a witch?' she demands.

I can feel Francis's eyes hot on my skin, and I burn with the shame of my flesh being exposed. I think about the misgoverned women I have seen in the pillory, or whipped through the streets at the cart's arse, disgraced in their smocks, their heads uncovered, their hair polled. I am one of them now, but I am too proud to let Agnes and Francis see how utterly I am humiliated.

Lifting my chin, I look from Barbara to Anne and then to Marion. 'It is not so,' I say clearly. 'I am no witch. I am a mother, as you are.'

'Well, then, there is only one way left to prove it,' says Agnes before any of the women can react. 'We all know water will reject a witch,' she says and the room falls quiet. 'Let us see whether she floats or no.'

'Agnes, for God's sake!' I cry at that and she turns on me.

'How dare you call on God? You, who are in league with the Devil!'

'Oh, this is nonsense.' I actually laugh.

This is a mistake. The women gasp and shuffle back even further, and Agnes's smile is triumphant.

'So, this amuses you? Let us see if you laugh when we put you in the water! You can call on the Devil to save you then. Come.' She turns to the women, all business. 'Let us do it straight away. You are righteous women, and you know your duty to rid the streets of Satan and his accomplices. Will you help us?'

'Aye, aye.'

Infected by her madness, they surge forward suddenly, pushing and prodding me from Francis's grasp. 'Let's put her to the test!' They bundle me out of the door, bearing me out into the street before them. 'To the river!' they cry.

Desperately I try to hold up my sleeve, but the hands shoving at me throw me off-balance, and I stumble and fall heavily onto my hands and knees.

For a moment I couldn't move. I hung my head in despair, sobbing for breath, while the rain beat pitilessly around me. All I could do was wait for them to drag me back to my feet and prod me onwards to the river.

But no one did. Slowly I realized that the shouting had stopped too. All I could hear was the skirl of the wind and the rain drumming onto the ground. The women had gone.

Still I didn't move. I was afraid of some trick. My eyes flickered from side to side, calculating my options. It wasn't long since we had left Agnes's house, but I was exhausted, and my chest was heaving like a beaten horse. I couldn't outrun anyone in this state, but it wasn't far to the house. If I could make it back there, we could shut ourselves up until the women calmed down, as they would without Francis and Agnes whipping them into a frenzy. When the rain stopped and folk started about their business once more, everything would return to normal.

Except for me. I thought of the coins in the box in Ned's study. I would take what I could, and Rob could get us onto a boat. We would all go to Hull, to London, to the Baltic. Anywhere Francis and Agnes could not follow. The thought of them made my whole body clench with horror.

All I had to do was get back to the house and I would be safe.

Cautiously I got to my feet. I put my hand to my head instinctively to straighten my cap and was horrified to find my head uncovered. It was the final humiliation and my eyes pricked with tears of shame, before my mind cleared and I remembered.

The house in Coney Street was no longer there. There were no women. No Bess. There was no one to run from, and no one to run to. I slumped with relief. No one was going to force me to the river. I had woken from the nightmare just in time.

Only to find myself in a different one. The realization hit me like a slap. Sophie was still out there somewhere, by the river. And the rain was rank with the smell of rotting apples.

I turn and hands jab at me, but as I lift my head I can see Jane standing behind the crowd. Her eyes are wide with horror. Mog is by her side and I know without being told that the cat has fetched her, but what can Jane do? She is barely more than a child herself, and I need her to look after Bess.

I don't dare cry out to her, but our eyes meet. '*Take Bess*,' I will her. '*Go*.'

But she doesn't understand what I am trying to tell her. She just stands and watches, her hand to her mouth, her expression despairing.

Francis grips my arm. 'You think that urchin will save Bess?' he sneers, following my gaze. 'She can do nothing. Agnes and I will take Bess. We will make her our own. I will do what I like with her, Hawise.' He puts his face close to mine and his breath is foul. 'She will know that her mother was a witch, and she will shudder at the thought of you.'

'Why are you doing this?' I try and wrench my arm away, but he holds it fast behind my back. 'You cannot get away with it!'

'Can we not? Do you see anyone rushing to save you? Why should they? It's all your own fault,' he said, almost peevishly. 'All you had to do was love me, but you wouldn't.'

'I will love you now,' I say desperately – anything to get back to my daughter and Jane. 'I will, I promise.'

But Francis shakes his head. 'It's too late,' he says. 'I will take Bess instead. *She* will love me.'

'*No!*' My voice rises to a howl. 'A curse be on you, Francis Bewley!' I cry, and there is a gasp from the women. 'May you rot in Hell for what you have done to me and mine. May your arms droop and your pizzle wither. Your bones will ache and rattle in your skin, and your sinews crack. I call on the Devil himself to cast you into torment!'

There is one moment when the women waver at my curse, but Agnes moves quickly. 'You see?' she says. 'She cries out to her Master!'

I ignore her. 'You will never sleep easy again,' I tell Francis as he pushes me forward. 'And when you arrive in Hell, I will be waiting for you.'

I reeled from one side of the street to the other, so tired that I was weaving over the road as if I were drunk. I was lucky there was so little traffic around that night. The grazes on my palm stung and my knees throbbed as I stumbled on between the present and the past, hardly knowing or caring where I was going, until I turned down High Ousegate and saw the bridge ahead.

It looked bare and exposed without the buildings I was used to seeing, and I stopped. Everything in me told me to turn back, but I dragged the thought of Sophie to the front of my mind and forced myself on.

The nearness of the river repelled me. My chest was tight with terror, my breath wheezing thinly in and out of my lungs. I made it to the top of the steps leading down to King's Staith, where I had stood so often with Rob watching the loading and unloading of the keels from Hull, but the quay had gone, swallowed by the swollen Ouse. It surged high under the bridge, glistening malevolently in the lights from the buildings lining its banks, an obscene mass of black, swirling water bearing relentlessly onwards.

There was no way I could reach the Millennium Bridge that way. I should have thought about the river flooding. With a sob of frustration I stumbled blindly back the way I had come.

*

448

Still cursing Francis, I am bundled onwards, out of the postern where the officer is huddled over a brazier and doesn't even look our way, and down to St George's Field. When the sun shines the laundresses work here, but it is too dank and dirty today and there is no one around. The path is slick with mud, and I slip and slide as the mob hustles me further down the river. It is scrubland here, too close to the river to be tilled. The cattle stand against the hedgerows, their bellies encrusted with mud, resigned to the rain, watching us incuriously as we blunder past.

I don't now remember how I found my way to the bridge at last. No longer even aware of the rain, I stumbled along the streets that ran parallel to the river, my boots splashing through the puddles, my breath rasping in my ears. I was beyond thinking. I just knew I had to get to Sophie before the river carried her away. I kept making false turnings, only to be baulked by a river swelling grotesquely by the minute, and when I finally staggered into the field that Hawise had known as St George's Field, I could hardly believe it.

There ahead of me, just discernible through the gusting rain, was the arch of the suspension bridge. I bent over, retching.

'Sophie!' My thready voice was lost in the wind.

Dragging oxygen into my lungs, I forced myself upright. A mess of twigs, leaves and litter barrelled over the grass, while at the edge of the darkness the river heaved like a great, greedy snake. If I got too close, it would snatch me up. Every instinct ordered me to retreat, but I went closer.

'Sophie!' I called again.

The river was creeping high over the banks. I pushed my way along under the willows, splashing through the water, feeling it tug remorselessly at my knees.

'Sophie! Sophie!'

I almost missed her. Grabbing at the trailing branches of the willows to steady myself, I kept an eye on the water that sucked and swirled around my legs, until a glimpse of white made me turn my head, and there she was, huddled beneath a bush.

'Sophie!' I splashed frantically towards her, dropping to my knees beside her. Her eyes were blank with fear and shock, and she was completely naked.

'Oh, God . . . Oh, God . . . what have they done to you?' I crouched beside her. 'Sophie, we have to get away from here,' I shouted in her ear. 'The river's rising fast.'

For answer she latched her arms wordlessly around my neck and clung to me. My throat was so tight I couldn't speak. I just held her close and fought the horror of the river grabbing at me.

'It's okay,' I managed at last through clattering teeth. 'You're safe now.'

But she wasn't. I had no idea how to get her home and dry, and I could feel Hawise clamouring in my mind. The wind was screaming around us, tossing the willows about, and it was so wet and cold that every breath was a struggle.

'Come on.' I tried to urge Sophie to her feet, but her face crumpled.

'I have to stay.' I could barely make out what she was saying between the wind and the rattling of her teeth, or perhaps of mine. 'I have to be purified by the river goddess. Ash said I had to stay here until he came back for me.'

I didn't waste time trying to argue with her. 'He sent me to get you.' I had to shout over the sound of the gale.

'But he said I had to prove myself worthy of the next level.'

'You've done that,' I said.

'He t-told me I had to be n-naked. He t-took away my clothes.' She began to cry, curling in on herself.

The water was lapping at my ankles. 'Sophie . . . ' I dragged her bodily to her feet, but I could see her desperately trying to cover her nakedness. Why hadn't I thought to bring a jacket? I dragged off my hoodie and froze as the rain splattered against my bare back.

When they push me down to pull off my shoes and my stockings, I feel strangely detached. It is hard to believe this is actually happening, that they are tugging at my netherhose, exclaiming at the colour and fingering the quality enviously. The rain has lessened to a mean drizzle and I can feel it pattering on my bare shoulders. I make myself curse and yell at them, but I have become a thing, an animal, stripped of any feelings, and they do not even look in my face as they wrestle my arm down, so that they can tie my thumb to my toe with a lace pulled from my sleeves. I struggle, but there are too many of them. Francis isn't touching me, but he is watching, his face alight, and in a strange moment of utter clarity I glimpse him through the press of women, rubbing himself through his hose.

Nobody else notices. Intent on my utter humiliation, they don't even notice how quickly the river is rising. It is lapping around me as I lie twisted on the ground. It must be filling their shoes and saturating their skirts, but they pay it no mind.

I was lurching backwards and forwards between times, and my mind was spinning, but I struggled desperately to fix on Sophie. I had to get her out of the river.

'Sophie, we've got to go,' I shouted in her ear as I helped her pull the hoodie over herself. It was so wet it could hardly be a comfort, but at least it covered her breasts. Awkwardly, I kicked off my shoes and wriggled out of my sodden jeans. They would be better than nothing.

I pushed them at Sophie. 'Put them on when we get out of this,' I yelled as I took her arm.

By then I wore only a T-shirt and knickers, but I was too frantic to get Sophie out of the river to feel the cold. She clutched the jeans in front of her and we splashed through the water.

I could feel the river dragging at me, and with a mighty push I shoved Sophie forward, out onto the grass, so that I didn't pull her back with me.

'Stay there,' I shouted at her. 'Whatever you do, Sophie, stay there!'

I could see her standing on the grass, covering herself with my jeans, her hair flattened by the rain and her eyes stark with shock and fear. 'Grace, what's happening? *Grace!*'

I tried to call out to her, but she was fading, or I was

fading – I wasn't sure which. I saw her start to splash back and reach for me.

'No!' I cried, stumbling backwards into the river. If she touched me, she would be lost too. 'No! Don't touch me!'

'Enough.' Agnes takes one of my stockings and calmly ties it around my mouth. 'No more curses,' she says as my shouts are muffled and I intensify my struggle. 'You have done your worst. The Devil can save you,' she says, her eyes afire.

She directs the women to lift me by the shoulders and the ankles. The river is churning, tugging at their skirts as they wade into the flooded shallows.

'Deeper!' Agnes cries. 'Deeper!"

When they are up to their knees they swing me experimentally. I try and struggle, but I am twisted with my thumb tied to my toe, and my shoulder is on fire with pain. They cannot really mean to do this, I think. They have punished me enough, surely. They have made their point. I am beaten and humiliated. Now they will put me down.

But they do not put me down. One more swing, wider this time.

'Let her sink or swim, and may the Devil take her,' shouts Agnes and, with a mighty heave and a grunt of effort, the women send me up, up into the air and out over the water.

The river swirled around me, knocking me off my feet, and I fell into its cold, cruel grip. My mouth and nose were full of bitter brown water and I surfaced, choking and spluttering, as my feet scrabbled for purchase. The river wasn't deep – only up to my waist – but it was very strong and the current pushed me along.

On the grass Sophie was screaming. She was safe as long as she stayed there. I fixed my mind on that as the river wrenched me along and I lost my footing again and the water closed over my head.

The river closes over my head and I am tossed and tumbled around in it. The lace tying my thumb to my toe has snapped and I flail my arms around, but I don't know where the air is. My lungs are screaming for air. I must have air. Blackness pounds at me, but at the very last moment – just as I am about to give in to it – my head breaks out of the water.

I hauled in a choking breath, thrashing my arms in a desperate attempt to stop myself being swept away. A detached part of my mind was telling me that the situation was absurd. I couldn't drown in waist-deep water. I couldn't have survived the tsunami to drown in a shallow river.

But I was back in my nightmares, back in the tsunami, helpless against the relentless surge. My heels dragged along what was usually the top of the bank and I grabbed at a trailing willow branch, but the current shoved me on, so that it ripped through my hands. I staggered, slipped, sank under the water once more, and there was nothing but the roar of the river in my ears, its rank taste in my mouth, and the paralysing fear that hammered in my head. This time I really was going to die.

*

I am going to die. I realize it at last as my heavy skirts drag me down. I will never see Bess again. Never again will I rest my hand on her sleeping body to feel her breathing, never again trace the miraculous curve of her cheek with my knuckle.

I said I would go back and read from the book. I didn't know it would be the last time I saw her, the last time I tucked her hair back under her cap. I didn't know this morning that it would be the last time I ever woke up in the great bed with the red silk hangings that Ned had made for me. The last time I would push open the shutters and look up at the sky.

She will be waiting for me. Why did I go and see Agnes? What was I thinking of? Because of me, my daughter will be alone. Francis and Agnes will take her and defile her, and it is all my fault. The anguish of it hurts more than the screaming pain in my ears, the agony in my lungs. I will die knowing that I have failed her, and as the water fills my throat, all I can do is try and beg her forgiveness.

Bess . . .

I was swirling in the river, swirling in the pain and the grief, but when the current pushed me into a tree, I grabbed instinctively at the thrashing greenery, choking and gagging on the taste of the river and rotten apples. I was out of my depth and my strength was ebbing. I couldn't hold on for long. Already I could feel my fingers loosening, and I clamped them back around the fragile branch.

'Grace! Grace, take my hand!'

I could hardly see through the rain, but incredibly he was

there, one arm anchored around a sturdy branch, the other reaching out to me.

'Ned?'

'Let go, Grace. The current will bring you towards me and I'll catch you.'

Let go? I heard the words, but they didn't make sense. I couldn't let go. If I let go, the water would take me, the way it had taken Lucas, who had died because of me. I had let him down, the way I had let Bess down. I deserved to drown.

'Grace, look at me!' He inched closer, and I blinked the rain from my eyes.

'*Drew?*'

'I'm here,' he said calmly. 'All you have to do is take my hand.'

'I . . . can't.'

'You can,' he said.

'I *can't*!' I could barely speak. 'I can't. I'm afraid.'

'I know you are,' said Drew. 'But I'm here. I'll catch you. You have to let go first, though. I can't reach you.'

The river was grabbing at me. It wanted me to let go too, so that it could devour me. It would drag me off and I would drown, the way I should have drowned when the wave crashed through the palm trees that day.

I could see Drew edging closer. If he came any further he would have to let go of his branch and the river would take him too.

'No!' I cried desperately. 'Sophie . . . '

Sophie needs you, I meant to say, but Drew kept on coming.

'Sophie's safe,' he shouted back over the water. 'You found her. Now you can let go.'

'Don't come any closer!' I shrieked. My fingers were numb, the leaves sliding out of my grasp.

'I won't, but that means you have to come to me,' he said steadily. 'Trust me, Grace. Let go, and I'll catch you. It's only a few inches. You're almost there.'

The river swirled and surged around me. The thought of letting go of my fragile hold was terrifying, but Drew's voice was unwavering, and through the rain he beckoned, temptingly solid, on the other side of a chasm of water.

Only a few inches, he had said, but it might as well have been a mile.

'Trust me,' he said again. 'I won't let you go.'

The leaves slithered through my hand and I flailed towards him. It felt as if I were launching myself out over the edge of an abyss, but it was only a few heart-stopping seconds before his hand closed around my wrist and he was pulling me across the current, grabbing me with his other hand to yank me hard against him. I clung to him, spluttering, shivering, still babbling with terror, as he gathered me into him and buried his face in my wet hair.

'Grace . . . ' His voice was choked with fear. 'Jesus, Grace, I thought I was going to lose you.'

On the grass Sophie was wrapped in a blanket and was watching anxiously, a police officer by her side while two others waded through the water towards us. In the distance a cluster of blue lights revolved through the rain, throwing a surreal glow over the scene.

In spite of the blessed solidity of Drew's body, I could feel the river still sucking at me in frustration. I gulped a shuddering breath and groped for my pendant. The jade was my touchstone. It anchored me to reality, let me believe I was safe. But my fingers scraped uselessly against my skin.

'My pendant!' Wildly I looked over my shoulder at the black water surging past, as if I might somehow be able to find the jade in its bitter depths. But there was nothing there, unless –

I stiffened in the safety of Drew's arms. Far out in the middle of the river I thought I had seen something. I thought I saw Hawise's face, gleaming white and blue for a second as she surfaced, but the next moment she was swallowed up, swept on into the darkness, and she had gone.

'Sophie called the ambulance.' Drew held me against him and rubbed his hand comfortingly up and down my arm. I was bone-tired, but I couldn't sleep, and when he slipped back into bed after checking on his daughter, I'd demanded that he tell me again what had happened. I'd been too shocked and confused earlier on to take any of it in.

'How is she?'

'Sleeping. They gave her a sedative at the hospital, but I think worse than the cold was the realization that her idol, Ash, could really leave her there.'

'Did you talk to the police?'

He nodded. Lines of exhaustion were etched into his face. The evening had taken its toll on him too. 'They said they would have a word with him, but Sophie went there voluntarily, and there was nothing to keep her at the river. He'll say it was her choice to stay there, which it was.'

'He took her clothes away!'

'Sophie said she took them off willingly. Apparently Ash told her that the initiation rite involved her offering herself naked to the river goddess, but she thought they would come back for her after a few minutes. When they didn't, she didn't know what to do and hid under a bush. By the time you appeared, she was so cold and frightened she couldn't move. She said she thought she was imagining things at first, but you coaxed her out, and then she said a terrible look came over your face and you backed into the water. She said it looked as if someone was dragging you, but there was no one else there.'

I swallowed. 'That's what it felt like.'

'I'd heard your message by then and was already on my way. I'd been checking all evening, and of course the one time I switched my phone off for our discussions you'd called. I don't think I've ever run so fast,' said Drew. 'It wasn't just the thought of Sophie. You were rambling about Francis and Agnes in your message, and when you said you were heading for the river, I knew something was terribly wrong.

'Sophie was hysterical when I got there, but she'd found your phone in the jeans and had called an ambulance, and they turned up with the police just after I did. You were out in the current by then, and I saw you swept away—' He stopped, swallowed. 'I can't tell you how I felt then. If you hadn't been caught up in that willow . . . '

His arm tightened around me and I turned into him, pressing

my face against his throat. My hands were torn, my throat and stomach raw, and I was bruised and battered all over, but I was warm and I was dry and I was clean. And I was with Drew.

'I would have died,' I said. 'The way poor Lucy died. There was no one there for her.' I shivered. 'She had to go through that on her own.'

'We don't know that's what happened to her,' said Drew.

'*I* know,' I said. 'I just can't prove it. Hawise tried to live again through Lucy, just the way she did with me. It's as if she's driven to live her life again and again, and every time she hopes she won't make the same mistakes, but of course she always does.'

'We can't change the past,' said Drew. 'We can only accept it.'

I stroked the base of my throat. I was still getting used to the feel of it without my pendant. 'Sometimes you can't stop yourself wishing that you could go back and do things differently. You think "If only I hadn't", or "If only I *had*". You make a tiny choice – will I go on or will I go back? will I turn left or will I turn right? – and the rest of your life turns on it.'

'We can't afford to think about the implications of every little choice we make,' Drew said. 'We'd never get out of bed in the morning. The possibilities are too overwhelming. We'd be stuck, unable to move in any direction.'

'That's what I think has happened to Hawise,' I said. 'I think she's desperate to live it over again, to do it differently. She wants to walk through that market again and not smile at Francis. She wants to say no when he asks her to meet him. She wants to take Bess and Jane and Rob to London, instead of going to see Agnes. But she can't. It's always the same story, and it always will be.'

I shook my head.

'She's gone for now, but she won't rest. Maybe it won't be me next time, but she'll try and live her story again through someone else. I think Lucy's experiments gave Hawise a connection to the present, and now she won't stop until she can forgive herself for abandoning Bess.'

'She didn't abandon her. From what you've told me, there was nothing she could do.'

'But that's the whole point. She's tortured by the idea that she could have done something and, because she didn't, her daughter suffered. How do you come to terms with failing your own child?'

'When you're a parent you have to face that possibility all the time,' said Drew. 'Is it my fault that Sophie fell for the pseudo-religious nonsense Ash spouted?'

'No . . . At least, don't you feel a bit responsible?'

'Grace, I didn't force Sophie out there tonight. All we can do as adults is give our children the tools to make their own decisions. I can't control Sophie. She's not a little girl that I can pick up and hold safe any more. I wish she were!' he said. 'I've made lots of mistakes, and I'll go on making them, but all we can do is our best.'

I said nothing. Drew pulled me deliberately round to face him. 'None of us can do any more than try our best,' he said. 'It's not your fault Lucas died in the tsunami, Grace. It was a tragedy, but it wasn't your responsibility. You did your best. You tried to hold onto him, but you couldn't. You have to forgive yourself for that now.'

I couldn't meet his eyes. 'I can't,' I managed.

'That's what you said in the river,' he reminded me. 'But you *could*. You saved yourself, Grace. Let go,' he said, just as he had when the current dragged and pummelled me.

My chest constricted as the dread and the guilt surged back, suffocating me. I couldn't breathe, lying so close to Drew, and I rolled away from him to suck in some air.

Ignoring my protests, Drew pulled me firmly back against him. 'Let go,' he said again and, just like that, something inside me unlocked and it all came spewing out. I wept and I wept, howling out the grief and the guilt I had dreaded for so long, and it felt just as bad as I had thought it would.

Drew didn't say anything. He just held me, and when it was over, I tested my raw emotions. I felt empty and ravaged, but Drew was still there. The guilt and the grief were still there too, but I wasn't as afraid of them now as I had been before. I had come apart, but now I knew I could put myself back together again.

I put my arm over Drew and laid my cheek against his chest, listening to the slow, steady beat of his heart. He was almost asleep, I could tell. 'Thank you,' I murmured, and he stirred, rubbing a hand over his face as he yawned.

'Do you want to go back to your own bed now?' he asked, but I pressed closer into him.

'No,' I said. 'I'll stay here.'

*

Drew dropped his battered briefcase on the breakfast bar and kissed the side of my neck as I stood at the cooker.

'I found something interesting when I was looking at probate inventories yesterday,' he said.

His research leave was over, and he spent two nights every week in London, teaching and lecturing. When he had the time he worked on his book, poking around in the archives for evidence of neighbourliness. Quite how that had taken him to wills and probate inventories I wasn't sure, but he seemed to think it was useful. He was always coming home with little bits of information that he'd found interesting, so I didn't take much notice at first.

'Oh?' I blew on a spoonful of the sauce I was making and tested it. It needed more salt.

'I think I found Bess.'

The wooden spoon clattered into the pan. '*Bess?*'

Nearly a year had passed since that terrible night by the river.

I had had my ticket booked, so I went to Mexico as planned, and I had a good time with Mel, but I came back. I missed Drew. He sold his house in the Groves and we bought one together on the other side of the city. I got my old job back teaching English as a foreign language. It wasn't always easy, but I was learning to talk about what I felt, instead of booking myself on the first plane out of the country.

Sophie drifted in and out as it suited her. She never again mentioned Ash or the Temple of the Waters. Instead she put her hair in dreadlocks, became a vegan and joined an animal-rights group. It made mealtimes a bit of a challenge when she was staying, and Drew grumbled about the number of nut roasts that he had to eat, but otherwise he was just glad to have her there.

We didn't talk about that night much. As far as Sophie was concerned, it was something to be forgotten, and for Drew too, I thought, it was over. I pretended it was for me as well, but I knew that it wasn't, not completely. I never slipped back into Hawise's life again, but every now and then I would catch the smell of rotting apples, or Bess's name like a sigh in the air.

Now I wiped my hands on a tea towel. 'What about Bess?' I demanded. All at once my heart was pounding.

Drew rifled through his briefcase and pulled out a sheet of lined paper. 'I was looking through wills, to see how many friends and neighbours are mentioned, and I came across this.'

He handed me the paper. It was covered with pencilled notes made in his neat handwriting.

'St Botolph's parish,' I read. I skimmed the notes, but they all ran into each other. 'What am I looking for?'

'Here.' Drew pointed. 'The last will and testament of Jane Haxby, 1619.'

'Haxby . . . ' I said slowly. 'That was Rob's surname.'

'And Haxby is a York name. That's why it caught my eye.' Drew took the notes back. 'Jane left a valuable silver dish to one Elizabeth Turner, who, it seems, wasn't a relative.'

My mouth was dry, my pulse booming in my ears. I wanted so badly to believe that it was true. 'Elizabeth wasn't exactly an uncommon name at the time, and Turner doesn't tell us anything.'

'No.' Drew nodded as he rummaged in his briefcase for another piece of paper. 'Where is it now . . . ? Ah!' He pulled it out. 'Now, look at this. I looked up Elizabeth Turner to see if she had made a will of her own, and she did. She had three sons, and a daughter. Do you want to guess what she called her?'

I stared at him. 'Hawise?' I whispered, and he smiled.

'Hawise. And that *isn't* a common name at that time. It isn't conclusive proof,' he warned. 'At the most it's suggestive, but it's interesting, don't you think?'

'Yes. Interesting.' My heart was soaring. Drew could talk all he liked about evidence, but I knew straight away what had happened. Bess had made it to London. She had survived. And that meant Francis and Agnes hadn't found her.

'Jane and Rob must have taken her to London,' I said excitedly. 'They must have been on their way before Agnes and Francis got back from the river.'

'Perhaps,' said Drew. 'We'll never know.'

I imagined them bursting into the house and finding it empty. Jane was canny. As soon as she saw Hawise being prodded to the river, she must have known what would happen. She knew Hawise wanted her to save Bess, and she had. She would have found the coins, and Rob had a head for business. They had enough to start and make a success of their lives, and they had cared for Bess.

Perhaps Francis had been left with the house in Coney Street, but it would have been a hollow victory. Cheated of Bess, the object of his future obsession, he was left bereft. I didn't think it would have been long before he turned on Agnes and blamed her for Hawise's death. Or perhaps she turned on him, when she realized that getting rid of Hawise made little difference to his feelings for her. Either way, I thought with satisfaction, there could have been little happiness for either of them.

Drew was watching my face. 'And there's another thing you might like,' he said. 'Bess's daughter Hawise married in her turn. Do you want to know what her husband's name was?'

'What?' I was still fizzing with the certainty that Bess had got away. The fear that she had spent her life as the object of Francis's perverted obsession had haunted me nearly as much as it had Hawise.

'His name was Trewe,' said Drew. 'John Trewe.'

I stared at him. 'That's my name,' I said, as if he didn't know, and he nodded.

'Any idea where your family come from?'

I licked my dry lips. 'London, I think,' I said. 'I'm not sure. Do you think . . . ?'

Drew held up a hand. 'I'm an historian, remember. I like evidence. So I'm not thinking anything. I'll admit that it's a coincidence, that's all.'

A coincidence. I smiled at him. It was enough for me.

The next day I picked some rosemary from the bush I'd planted in the little courtyard garden and walked down to the Millennium Bridge. I still didn't like the Ouse much, but it was a crisp, clear day and the river was quiet. The merest ripples disturbed its surface and made the reflected sunlight glitter.

I stood on the bridge and waited until no one was round.

Then I lifted the rosemary to my nose and breathed in the smell of it, just as Hawise had done so often.

'Rosemary for remembrance,' I said, and I dropped it into the water, twig by twig. 'She was safe,' I promised Hawise. 'Your Bess was safe and she was happy, I think. She never forgot you, and she never blamed you. You can rest now.'

I put my hand on my belly and felt the first flutter of life there. I'd told Drew, but we hadn't broken the news to Sophie yet. 'If it's a girl, I'll call her Elizabeth,' I said out loud. 'I'll look after her, I promise.'

There was a flash in the water – it might have been a bird – and then a ripple in the air like a sigh of relief behind me. I turned quickly, but the sun was in my eyes and I couldn't see.

'Hawise?'

But there was no one there. Only the dazzling light and the sound of children playing in the field on the far side of the bridge, and after a moment I turned and walked away from the river.

Author's Note

The idea for this book grew out of my research on the wardmote-court returns of early modern York. In the late sixteenth century these courts dealt primarily with nuisances – petty offences that affected the quality of life for the neighbourhood as a whole: noisy neighbours, blocked sewers, potholed streets and broken fences. The entries are brief, repetitive and confusing in many places, but they offer an intriguing glimpse into everyday life in the Elizabethan city. The individuals who appear in these records were not powerful nobles or the destitute, nor were they criminals or sinners. They were just ordinary people living ordinary lives, and they were concerned with many of the issues that still concern us today.

Writing *Time's Echo*, I've been torn between my training as a historian and my instincts as a writer, for whom it is impossible not to wonder and speculate about the stories behind some of the unrevealing entries in the records. There really was a mercer called William Beckwith, although we don't know if he lived in Goodramgate or not. John Harper, a Scottish tailor of questionable reputation, had a stall in Stonegate, while Christopher Milner, Anne Ampleforth and other incidental characters did indeed live in York in the late sixteenth century. Miles Fell was a miller – clearly an unpopular one – whose dog really did bite Nicholas Ellis on the leg.

However, this is a work of fiction. Hawise (pronounced Ha-*wees*-e), Ned Hilliard, Francis Bewley and the other main characters exist only in the imagination. Like other historical novelists, I have aimed to create a world that is convincing and as authentic as I can make it, but Hawise's world is just that: hers, and hers alone. It does not pretend to be an accurate historical account of 'how it was', and so I have taken liberties with the evidence on occasions. There was no plague in York in the 1570s or '80s, for instance. The city suffered from outbreaks of plague, 'pestilence' and the sweating sickness in the first half of the century, but after 1558 York was free of major epidemics for nearly fifty years until a terrible outbreak of plague in 1604. Whether this was due to luck or to measures taken by the authorities is a matter for discussion, but the disease was certainly a very real threat at the time, and other cities and their inhabitants suffered in the way Hawise and her neighbours do in the novel. There will always be a tension between the storyteller and the historian, but in a novel the balance inevitably tips towards the needs of the story.

Acknowledgements

Writing is popularly supposed to be a solitary activity, but for me *Time's Echo* has been a shared enterprise from the start, and I am delighted now to be able to acknowledge and thank those who have made it possible. I could not have done it without the support and encouragement of many friends, most especially Diana Nelson, Julia Pokora, Stella Hobbs and Dr Isabel Davis, and John Harding, who (inadvertently!) set the whole process of writing this book in motion. Dr Ailsa Mainman and Barbara Hannay took the time to read drafts at various stages and offer perceptive comments. My greatest debt, however, is to Dr Richard Rowland, whose knowledge of writing in general, and the sixteenth century in particular, has been invaluable, and whose sofa and wine supplies saw me through many crises of confidence. I cannot thank any of them enough.

Stephanie Moon-Smith kindly shared her experience of the Boxing Day tsunami with me, and many others were generous with their time and expertise. I would like to take this opportunity to thank particularly the City of York Council, Dr Jeremy Goldberg, Professor Neil Greenberg, Dr Jane Grenville, Steve Hodgson, Claire Rugg, Dr Tony Rugg, Dr Sethina Watson and the Reverend Canon Glyn Webster. Needless to say, any mistakes, deliberate or otherwise, are entirely my own.

Finally, it is a pleasure to be able to thank my agent, Caroline Sheldon, for setting *Time's Echo* on its way; and, of course, Wayne Brookes and the team at Pan Macmillan, for the enthusiasm and expertise that have seen it through to the end.